Riley Pine is the combined forces of two contemporary romance writers as you've never seen them before. Expect delicious, dirty, and scandalous swoons. To stay up to date with all things Riley Pine head on over to rileypine.com for newsletters, book details, and more!

Jackie Ashenden writes dark, emotional stories with alpha heroes who've just got the world to their liking only to have it blown wide apart by their kick-ass heroines. She lives in Auckland, New Zealand, with her husband, the inimitable Dr Jax, two kids and two rats. When she's not torturing alpha males and their gutsy heroines she can be found drinking chocolate martinis, reading anything she can lay her hands on, wasting time on social media, or being forced to go mountain biking with her husband. To keep up to date with Jackie's new releases and other news sign up to her newsletter at jackieashenden.com.

If you liked *My Royal Temptation* and
Ruined, why not try

Sweet Thing by Nicola Marsh
Make Me Want by Katee Robert

Discover more at millsandboon.co.uk

MY ROYAL TEMPTATION

RILEY PINE

RUINED

JACKIE ASHENDEN

MILLS & BOON

First Published in Great Britain 2018
by Mills & Boon, an imprint of HarperCollins*Publishers*
1 London Bridge Street, London, SE1 9GF

My Royal Temptation © 2018 Riley Pine

Ruined © 2018 Jackie Ashenden

ISBN: 978-0-263-26640-5

MIX
Paper from
responsible sources
FSC® C007454

This book is produced from independently certified FSC™ paper
to ensure responsible forest management.
For more information visit www.harpercollins.co.uk/green.

Printed and bound in Spain
by CPI, Barcelona

MY ROYAL TEMPTATION

RILEY PINE

MILLS & BOON

CHAPTER ONE

Nikolai

IT'S NEVER IDEAL to wake up after a one-night stand to find a European boxing champion glaring at your bare ass. It's worse if the pissed-off guy in question happens to be a childhood best friend.

Scratch that…former best friend.

"Top of the morning." I wryly yank the hotel's satin sheet over my waist. A red thong is bunched on top of the unmade covers, right where I removed it with my teeth around midnight.

If looks could kill, Christian Wurtzer, Baron of Rosegate, would smite me faster than a lightning bolt hurled by an avenging god.

"You really are a first-rate bastard, aren't you, Nikolai?" He balled his hands into meaty fists, a useless gesture, because here in the Kingdom of Edenvale, it's illegal to strike a member of the royal family.

And as Prince Nikolai, third of his name, Duke of Westcraven, heir to the throne of Edenvale and our country's eminent blue-blooded bad boy, I fall square into the "no hitting allowed" category. Rules are often a nuisance in my world, but that particular clause has proved beneficial since reaching my maturity, especially in predicaments regarding the opposite sex.

"Bastard?" I scrub the morning scruff prickling my jaw with a yawn. "But I'm the mirror image of my dear sovereign father, and don't forget that my poor queen mother was forced to squeeze me out in front of an official court representative to ensure my legitimacy." There is a sharp localized pain in the vicinity of my heart; the twinge always accompanies a mention of my long-dead mother. She died bringing my youngest brother, Damien, into the world, the first life that banished asshole ever took.

"You've gone too far this time." Christian's warning growl yanks my attention back to the present moment. "This was my sister. You compromised her virtue."

Not the optimal moment to observe that he could give the ferocious bear stamped on his family crest a run for its money. Once our people were great hunters, the best swordsmen in Europe, as feared as the Vikings of old. Edenvale might be a small, landlocked kingdom, but we harbored a reputation as ruthless, lethal warriors. These days we're better known for luxury casinos, discreet banks and glamorous mountain hideaways. Edenvale is a high-altitude playground for the rich, the famous and those aspiring to the same.

"What will I tell my parents?" He rakes a hand through his blond hair, pacing the plush carpet. "Catriona is ruined. Her prospects for a marriage alliance are now nonexistent."

"Come, come. Ask any trust-fund baby in Ibiza. It's common knowledge that your precious little sister gave up her virtue well before I sunk my flag." If his family schemed to marry Cat off as a virgin, they lost that chance years ago. Typical Rosegate sentiment to attach significance to such an inconsequential thing as a hymen. But they are an old-fashioned people. The regional characteristic might be charming if their morals weren't so fucking medieval.

Catriona Wurtzer stirs, snoring lightly, her pink lips crooked into a satiated half smile. A hot pulse of lust spreads through my sac. That luscious mouth pouts from the cover of three different high-fashion magazines this month alone, and last night it worked over my cock with such deep-throated skill that the interlude nearly distracted me from this morning's royal duty.

I roll out of bed and slip on my tuxedo pants—commando—and shrug into my dress shirt, not bothering with the twenty-four-karat-gold cuff links on the nightstand. Catriona likes it rough, and the room was trashed during our sleepover. Those expensive baubles will serve as a more-than-adequate housekeeping tip. It's time for me to return to the castle.

My father, the king, and my hag of a stepmother, the current queen, have summoned me for a private audience this morning at nine thirty sharp. This rare audience doesn't mean anything good, which is why I guzzled three-thousand-dollar-a-bottle champagne at a gala benefit before burying myself balls deep into the supermodel who happens to be my best friend's little sister.

"Your family have been loyal subjects for over two centuries. Based on this valued relationship, I shall issue a royal decree. Huzzah, huzzah. All hail Catriona, the realm's newest countess." I can't resist a smirk as I tack on, "A new title for her trouble." As if bedding me was a hardship. Which it wasn't. But what the hell? Let her add a castle to her four orgasms. I'm in a generous mood.

"Too kind, Highness." Christian nearly chokes on his words. He wants to beat my ass into Luxembourg, but the microstate of Rosegate has long been a disputed territory with Nightgardin, the country to the north and our ancient foe. The powerful Wurtzer family has been allied to mine for generations, and he knows—without reminder—three salient facts:

I'm an asshole, a leopard can't change his spots, and Edenvale's small but lethal military is the only thing protecting Rosegate against a Nightgardin power grab.

Revenge is a bitch.

Christian and I attended Swiss boarding school together and shared a dormitory room for five years. I love the guy like family, but he recently racked up too many gambling debts playing high-stakes blackjack. My sources say he decided to pay for them by selling titillating gossip about me to the tabloids. I'm not saying banging his hot sister is payback for his betrayal.

But I'm not saying it isn't, either.

A muscle twitches deep in his jaw, the same tic that would act up back when he'd pour over his calculus lessons during late-night study sessions. I'm sure he'd love to order me to "do the right thing" and stick a ring on his sister's finger. But alas, only one of us carries an invitation-only Black Amex card with no preset limits.

Limits are for those who need them. I am no such man.

People can think I'm an arrogant ass all they want.

They're right. But at least I'm a consistent asshole. Fuck with me and I fuck back. No hard feelings. It's how the people on top stay on top. And I can make it good.

Or I can make it hurt.

For those who beg nicely—I can make it both.

Got to say, being a prince is full of perks in all ways but one—I still answer to the king. It's not my throne…yet.

I glance in the gilded mirror on my way out the door. Yep, still me. Bed-rumpled jet-black hair, a roguish mouth and gunmetal gray eyes. I clock in at six foot four and possess stamina for days. Last year I came in number one on a list of the world's sexiest royals. The only thing surprising was that it was the first year it happened. Way I see it, Prince Harry over in jolly old England can eat his ginger heart out.

"For Christ's sake. Wake up, Catriona," Christian orders his sister as I exit the room. I outpace the unfolding drama and stride down the hotel hallway, hitting the button on the penthouse's private elevator. My bodyguard, X, waits in the Rolls. He's been idling there all night. He's used to it.

I slide into the back seat without a word.

A language lesson plays on the sound system—Mandarin Chinese. X collects languages like he does medieval knives. Not my first choice for fun, but to each his own.

"To the castle, Sire?" he asks over the intercom, turning off the stereo. I remove my sunglasses from my pocket. Daylight reflects from the snow on the high mountain peaks. My growing headache isn't in the mood for good weather.

"Home sweet home." I slather sarcasm on my affirmative and slide on the shades to avoid the summer sun.

As X starts the engine, I reach into the minibar and pluck out a handful of miniature cognac bottles. By the time we cross the moat, I toss the fifth empty on the pile by my feet. But the liquor does jack shit to dull the sharp pain in my gut.

Fine. It was an unforgivable move to fuck my best friend's little sister—revenge or no—but I'm sure as shit no Prince Charming.

Kate

I spread my hands across my pleated skirt, then think better of it and rest them atop the leather folder that sits on the table. If I wanted to, I could relax, even luxuriate in the high-backed, cushioned chair, no doubt made of the same buttery leather as the folder in front of me. But it's not exactly easy when you're sitting at a twenty-foot-long mahogany table in one of many rooms at the Palace Edenvale.

It wasn't like I hadn't been here before, but I don't think a prep-school tour counts the same as an invitation that came hand-delivered by a royal herald. The envelope was even closed with one of those fancy wax seals.

Dear Miss Katherine Winter,
Your presence is requested at Palace Edenvale at 9:30 a.m. tomorrow morning. Please come unattended and plan on clearing your schedule for

the remainder of the day. Your audience with the king and queen must be kept private. Tell no one where you are going, and after you've been, tell no one what transpires within the palace walls until—should they request your services further—the king, queen and yourself enter into contract.

The royal family appreciates you honoring your duty and complying with the above requests.

I huff out a laugh, which echoes in the empty room. *Requests.* As if I had any choice once I broke the royal seal. Sure, Your Highnesses, I'll clear my day. Of course, my illustrious rulers, I'll keep my visit to the palace a secret. Not because of any damned duty, though. If there is one thing I value, it's my business and my independence. I am determined to keep the former and as much of the latter as possible, and if that means zipping my lips about my *royal audience*, fine by me.

There better at least be some sort of monetary compensation for this—this—*request*. God knows my sister and I need it. Our savings account has dipped into the red with Gran's mounting medical bills, which has sent my internal stress thermometer in the exact opposite direction.

I glance at the thin gold bracelet on my wrist, an eighteenth-birthday gift from my beloved grandmother, back in happier times. Back when she still remembered my name.

I swallow the threat of tears. This is hardly the time or the place to wallow in my personal woes.

"We won't lose the apartment." The words are a mantra. "And we'll still be able to take care of Gran."

I figure if I say the words enough, they'll be true. So I open my mouth once more to repeat the statements, but the conference-room doors part with a whoosh, and my worry fades into the distance as the same formal-looking man who delivered my invitation steps over the threshold and announces my small country's rulers in a booming voice.

"All rise for His Highness, King Nikolai of Edenvale, and Her Eminence, Queen Adele."

The herald proclaims the royal couple as if they are entering an arena, and I, of course, shoot to my feet. My first instinct is to bow or curtsy, but neither one of them spares me so much as a passing glance. Yet I'm the only one in the room. I've been requested for a private audience with the *monarchy*, and they don't even deign to look at me.

Still, I wait for the attendants who trail behind the pair to pull out two chairs at the head of the table. I wait some more as they lower themselves into the plush leather seats. And as I'm about to do the same, a man wearing half a tuxedo bursts through the doors still tucking in his wrinkled dress shirt.

He winks in my direction, flashing a knavish grin before turning his attention to the king and queen.

"Sorry I'm late," he says, checking a nonexistent watch on his wrist. Then he kisses the queen on the cheek while the king, a salt-and-pepper version of the young man, simply gives his son—Prince Nikolai—a pointed look.

While his parents—make that father and stepmother—take residence at the far head of the table, the prince sits across from me and flips open the embossed folder in front of him.

"So," he says, sprawling in his chair and thumbing through the folder's contents, "what fire are we putting out this morning?"

He runs a hand through his black hair, and I squirm involuntarily in my seat. Sure, I've seen photos of him before. Prince Nikolai's image has graced the front page of the tabloids almost weekly since he came of age. But that sort of sensationalism has never been my thing. I wasn't the preteen with pictures of the teen heartthrob prince on my wall. I didn't wallpaper my computer's desktop with his devil-may-care smile, no matter how gorgeous he was.

And he *was*. Even then.

But he was also a grade-A asshole. Even then.

And from the looks of things—from the colorful headlines that always seem to feature Prince Nikolai's name—it doesn't seem like anything is changing soon.

Still, when those slate-colored eyes look up from the folder and meet mine, I squirm again. He was handsome in photos and the few times I've seen him on television. Not that I watch much of that celebrity crap that's thrown in the public's face on a daily basis. But I'm not prepared for my reaction to the prince in the flesh.

He is nothing short of dazzling.

My lungs revolt, unable to take a deep breath even though I need air badly.

And as if it isn't enough that he has some sort of superpower effect between my legs, I feel my nipples stand at attention against the lace of my bra. Thank God I'd had the forethought to keep my suit jacket buttoned.

"Nikolai—" the queen begins, but the prince holds up a finger as he returns to scanning the contents of the folder—the one I have been waiting for permission to examine myself. Apparently, the rumors are true— stepmother and stepson do not get on as they should. That explains the blatant disrespect.

His shuttered gaze roams the first page, then the second, and several more after that. I watch as his father crosses his arms and humors his son with a look that says no matter what antics the prince displays, the king will have the final word.

Prince Nikolai slams the folder closed and lets out a raucous laugh.

"Please, Nikolai," the king says, steepling his fingers in front of him. "Do tell us what you find so amusing."

The queen rests a hand on her husband's forearm, but the man's icy gaze remains directed at his son. All I do is stare, my head bobbing like I'm watching a tennis match in slow motion.

The prince narrows his eyes, pinning them on me, and my core tightens in disobedient response.

He takes his sweet time scrutinizing me, the corner of his mouth quirked in a crooked grin. Then he splays his hands on the table, leaning forward so that he's close enough for me to smell the tang of alcohol on his breath.

"I find it hilarious," the prince says with an edge to his words, "that you not only expect me to marry but that you think Little Miss Matchmaker-Dot-Com is the one to take care of the job. I mean, why not open me a royal Tinder account and be done with it?"

He has the nerve to sneer at me and my career? Oh, hell no.

Red-hot anger replaces that sensual tightening in my core.

The prince pushes from the table and smooths out his wrinkled shirt. "Father. Stepmother. As always, it's a pleasure to see you both." He doesn't hide his sarcasm.

On instinct, I stand as he rounds the table, my cheeks blazing with repressed fury.

"I—I am not some dot-com organization. My matches are personal, well thought out..." I sputter as it sinks in not only what I've been called here to do but that my client is anything but willing.

"Save it, sweetheart," he says. "I'd sooner fuck you than let you arrange my nuptials."

The queen gasps, and King Nikolai slams his fist on the table.

"Enough," the older man says, the finality of his authority dripping from the word. "Benedict is entering the priesthood. Damien is banished. If you do not marry with the intent to produce an heir, the throne falls out of the immediate family and to your cousin Ingrid. You will not fault on your duty."

The muscle in the prince's jaw pulses. "That's right, Father. I've had enough." His penetrating stare, though, stays on me the whole time. That's when he leans in, hot breath on my cheek. "And you'd enjoy every god-damn second of it," he whispers. "The word *enough* won't even exist in your vocabulary."

He bows toward his visibly shaken parents before making his dramatic exit.

I give myself a mental pat on the back for at least believing the stories.

The prince *is* a grade-A asshole.

My soaked panties, on the other hand, apparently did not receive the memo.

Perhaps they're waiting for one with the royal seal.

CHAPTER TWO

Nikolai

"MARRIAGE? THAT'S IT, Father has lost his goddamn mind," I mutter, ducking into the unobtrusive staircase, the quickest escape route out of the palace. Two floors down a young servant in a black dress and white apron takes one look at me and nearly drops the silver tray she carries, one laden with teapots, fine china and six different cakes. My mood is so foul that I ignore her alarmed squeal and don't even smooth the situation over with a flirtatious wink.

She must have been assigned catering duty for the ambush upstairs, the one where my father invoked the ancient laws of our realm.

Sweat breaks out on my hairline. A sour taste fills my mouth.

My twenty-ninth birthday is just around the corner.

I am the heir to the crown.

The Royal Marriage Decree of 1674 declared that the Edenvale heir must wed before sundown on his or her twenty-ninth birthday or their claim is null and void. Plus, an Edenvale heir had to marry someone of aristocratic blood. My future bride doesn't have to be a citizen of my country, but she does need to be nobility. Other than that, the requirements are simple: free consent.

Sounds easy enough. Except for the part where I'm not the marrying kind.

I reach the bottom of the stairs and draw a lung-searing breath before pushing through the exit that leads to the castle grounds.

Of course I know about the marriage decree. I memorized Edenvale proclamations and laws alongside my ABCs. But this is the twenty-first century. I never dared believe that Father would enforce that arcane law any more than he would the one about how no high ministers could enter the palace wearing purple, or how hunting on royal lands was a hangable offense.

Don't even get me started on the decree prohibiting anal sex.

Hell, I tapped the back door of a hotel heiress in the castle's highest tower last week. Not something I normally do, but she offered, and I sure as shit wasn't going to turn it down. Not my favorite position, but sex is like pizza in Naples. Even if it's not great, it's still damn good.

The castle grounds are perfectly manicured with hedges cut into topiaries of rabbits and swans. Father enjoys indulging his whimsical side.

The morning sun scalds my neck.

"Sire, Sire, please, wait!" a woman cries behind me. Then she mutters under her breath how hard it is to run in heels.

My molars grind with enough force that it's a miracle they don't shatter. I've heard that lilting voice before—the auburn-haired woman from the match-making service that my father hired.

Marriage decree aside, this situation—them hiring a matchmaking service—is the biggest insult of all. As if I need any goddamn help finding a willing woman.

"Sire!"

I should wait. Chivalry and all that. But remember the part about how I'm no Prince Charming?

I veer into the maze, kicking at stones in the gravel path. Fuck being a gentleman. I turn left, then right, then left again. The walls surrounding me are twelve feet high and covered in leaves. This maze might be the largest in Europe, but it was my childhood play-ground. I always know the way out. Time to ditch this tenacious matchmaker and figure out a plan to avoid getting tied in unholy matrimony.

That's when I hear it.

A snap, quickly followed by a sound like someone trying not to cry out.

Shit.

She's fallen over.

Not a surprise. I caught a glimpse of her precarious five-inch stilettos when she crossed her legs upstairs in the castle hall and this path is rocky and uneven.

I also caught an eyeful of a toned calf that con-nected to a perfectly curving thigh. That was the best part of the meeting. Before I glanced at the folder on the table and read the gold-embossed title: Happy End-ings Matchmaking Services: Making Dreams a Reality.

A cool mountain breeze brushes my face. I pause. Debating. I want to keep going. I even take a step. It's not like I asked her to give chase. She saw that I didn't need her advice. That I didn't want her professional services. Yet she insisted on pursuing me of her own free will. This is her own fault. I owe the woman—a total stranger—nothing.

The image of that exquisite creamy thigh flashes behind my eyes, this time draped over my shoulder.

Okay. Correction. I don't want her in a *professional* capacity.

My shoulders slump. No matter what my instincts demand, I can't abandon an injured woman alone in the maze.

Before I know it, I'm backtracking. It takes less than thirty seconds to find her.

She's kicked off that lethal-looking shoe and sits rubbing a swelling ankle. Her toes are painted a glossy classic red.

Okay, damn. I like that.

Her lips are flawless, painted in exactly the same shade. I like that even better.

I'd like it best streaking my shaft.

My cock twitches in agreement.

Fuck. This matchmaker—and maddeningly sexy woman—is the enemy. But try telling that to my ass-hole dick. Sometimes an overactive libido comes with serious drawbacks.

Then her gaze fixes on my face, and with one look at those tear-filled baby blues, my brain fucking flatlines.

Kate

It takes everything for me to hold my prince's fixed stare, not to wince at the white-hot pain in my ankle.

But there is no way I'm letting this guy—prince or otherwise—get the best of me.

"You okay?" he asks.

"Of course not." I glance at my ivory skirt, the side slit ripped even higher. I'm also sure my ass is one big grass stain. And let's not even discuss the hair. I'd gone for professional with the French twist, but now my auburn waves hang in my face, which is probably for the best. His steely gaze is too close.

"Just—show me the way out," I say, attempting to push myself up, but as soon as I put pressure on my bare foot, my knees buckle and I almost hit the ground again.

Almost. Because Nikolai Lorentz, Prince of Edenvale and heir to the throne, catches me.

"Shit," he hisses. "You *are* hurt."

"And you smell like you hit a limousine minibar," I say, trying to cover my reaction to his hands on me with disdain.

But my breath still quickens. He carries me with a concern I can feel in every nerve of my body.

"It was a Rolls, but you're very perceptive, Miss—"

"Winter," I say, having no choice but to throw my arms around his neck for purchase, my broken shoe still dangling from my fingers.

"Aha," he says, that devilish grin taking over his features. "Have you read *Romeo and Juliet*? Doesn't Juliet ask what's in a name?" He begins to walk.

My cheeks grow hot, and the tips of his fingers— his palm where it touches the bare skin of my thigh— sends sparks right through me.

I clear my throat. "You read Shakespeare?" I ask, though it's obvious.

"You're as icy as your name implies."

I huff out a breath and push as far from him as I can while the rogue still has me in his arms.

"I'm no such thing! *You—you're* the one who likened my services to a dating website. My work is nuanced and relies on personal metrics and psychology, thank you very much. You're also the one who just cost me a day's work. So pardon me if I'm not exactly warming to your famous *charm*."

He stops dead in his tracks. We're still in the maze, and I can't tell if we're any closer to making it out of here or if he's taken us deeper.

His eyes dart in every direction, as if he's checking for intruders, before they land on mine. Stone gray and burning with intent, I can't look away if I try.

"I *will not* marry," he says, his voice cool and even. "Is that understood?"

I nod. "And I will *not* walk away from this job."

"Then I guess we're at an impasse."

The air between us is warm, charged with the mingling of our breaths. His skin against mine sizzles. My head tells me that everything I'm feeling is wrong, but the physical need brewing inside me throbs at my core.

I haven't been with a man since my fiancé, Jean-Luc, died BASE jumping in Alaska. He was the love of my life, but he loved the thrill of adrenaline more than me. Afterward, I joined my big sister Madeline's business to devote my life to what I was denied: a happy ending.

It had been two long, careful years of self-denial

and occasionally my own hand. Before that it had only ever been Jean-Luc.

But the hand against me now is big, strong and unfamiliar. All it would take is his fingers sliding an inch more, and he'd *feel* that need, wet and pulsing.

He swallows, and I watch his Adam's apple bob. That's all it takes to let me know that whatever this is, it's not only me.

Maybe this is what it feels like to live in the moment, take a risk, something I never let myself do because I had to be careful for both of us. I had to move in with Madeline to save on rent. Never have I let myself simply *want*.

But this stranger's hands on me are warm. Strong. And for a second I imagine what they could do. It's intoxicating, this growing need and the possibility of satisfying it right here and now. I feel drunk and squirm in his grasp, hoping he'll simply think I'm readjusting myself in his arms, but I miscalculate and my lips brush against his.

He sucks in a breath, and this makes me grin.

"I *don't* like you," I say. Truer words have never been spoken.

"Likewise," he answers, his voice low and rough.

All my life I've played it safe, and where did it get me? Lost and alone. But this man exudes raw power, a power that draws me into his orbit, a pull stronger than gravity. I feel myself inching toward some sort of internal cliff, and the woman I thought I was relinquishes control.

"You said you'd sooner fuck me than let me arrange your nuptials."

He nods. "I certainly did."

I lean close to his ear, nip at his lobe, and step across the line of comfort I've hidden behind for far too long and whisper, "It's *sooner*."

I expect a savage response, but instead I feel him adjust his hands, and then I gasp as his thumb hits the crease of my panties.

That's all it takes. I leap off the cliff with a whimper of need and straight into pure pleasure.

He growls.

"You're fucking soaked." He drops to his knees, still holding me like I'm precious cargo, and lays me gently on the grass. "And I want to drink every last sweet drop."

Without another word, he hikes my skirt up and slides my panties down my thighs, over my knees and then off. I feel them snag on the heel of my remaining shoe but don't care. He shoves them in the pocket of his pants, and I know I'm not getting them back. The thought makes me giddy, and I writhe under his gaze.

"Now, Nikolai," I say, and he levels me with his grin.

The next thing I know, my hands are tangled in that jet-black hair as he licks the length of my folds from bottom to top until his tongue swirls around my swollen clit.

I moan and buck against him as he sucks me between his lips. I relish the feel of his stubble against my thighs, the slight pain only heightening my pleasure.

"Use fingers," I command, and he obeys immediately.

One finger plunges deep while he continues to take his fill with his mouth. Then a second joins the first, and my vision clouds with stars. My body bucks with shivers of reaction.

"God, I wish you could fuck me," I say, daring to voice what I long for—what I've gone without for what seems like an eternity. I try and fail not to whimper as he reaches a spot inside me that almost makes me black out.

Two years. It's been two freaking years since a man has touched me. The thought—coupled with his hands on me, in me—threatens to unleash something more than just the adrenaline rush, but I swallow the impending wave of emotion. Because that's not what this is about. These feelings aren't for the prince.

He peeks from between my legs and slides his fingers from my aching pussy. He takes care in licking each one clean.

"You said it was sooner, sweetheart, and I'm *always* prepared for sooner." From the pocket that does not hold my ruined panties, he pulls a foil packet and holds it up for me to see. "Your wish is my command."

CHAPTER THREE

Nikolai

HER TASTE IS ADDICTIVE—honey, salt and rainwater. I hate the idea of matchmaking. But matchmakers? I take my time drinking in the woman panting on the grass, her conservative blouse opened a button too far, exposing delicate white lace, creamy skin and lush, womanly curves.

Yes. I believe I could learn to like matchmakers.

"Sire. Hurry." She stares through a fringe of dark, thick lashes. Her red lipstick is smudging off her plump lower lip. I'm responsible for that, and the fact draws my balls tight against my engorged cock, clearly outlined through the panel of my tux pants. My muscles ripple with suppressed need.

I fold my arms, making an elaborate show of regarding the condom foil, and set my face into my trademark arrogant sneer. It's my mask. The one the public expects a prince to wear, especially a prince with the world at his feet. It comes easy as instinct, which is good because I am not used to being unsettled. And this woman is—*unsettling*.

"Interesting business you run." I lower my voice to a sensual drawl.

"No, not mine. I mean… I am not… It's not mine… um… It's my sister's…her business," she babbles, skimming one hand over the ragged tear in her prim skirt, the one currently offering me an eyeful of the thighs I'd feasted on. Her eyes darken, pupils dilating at my blatant appraisal.

"And do you provide these *services*—" I clear my throat and raise an insinuating eyebrow "—to every client?"

A dusky rose color flushes the skin of her throat as she catches my insinuation. She's pissed. Angry and turned on, my favorite combination in a woman. Hate fucking has all of the fun and none of the responsibility.

"Of course not," she snaps.

I dip a finger between my lips and give it a long lazy suck. The muscles in my neck cord. It still tastes like her. My mouth waters. "Mmm-hmm. Methinks the lady doth protest too much."

"Damn it." A tear spills from the corner of one gorgeous eye, trickles along her high cheekbone. "I don't know what came over me."

My hands twitch to comfort her. Christ. I did not see that response coming. I should regroup, charm her thighs open and plunge into her from behind, working her fancy hairdo and composure loose in brutal doggy-style strokes. Bet it would make her bum ankle feel a lot better than two ibuprofens and an ice pack.

So why am I pocketing the condom? Or brushing a wayward lock of hair on her forehead.

"Look. It's been…" She flinches from my touch

with a bitter laugh. "A while. And you…well, you're royal sex on a stick. It's a lot for a normal person to take in." She closes the gaping button on her shirt. "An error in judgment that won't happen again."

Looks like I'm not the only one who slaps on a mask when the going gets tough. In a blink of an eye my feisty sex kitten has retracted her claws and is now back to Miss Prim and Proper.

"Pity," I rumble, trying not to appear disconcerted. "Errors in judgment happen to be my specialty." I take my time adjusting my cock, the proud, hard length straining inside my pants.

The point of her pink tongue makes a quick appearance, dabs her lower lip. The kitten reemerges for a second. "You do seem quite…specialized."

"And you have once again proven my long-tested theory correct."

"Which is?"

I tap the tip of her nose with my index finger. "Inside every good girl is a bad girl waiting to get out."

She fingers her pearl choker. "I'm not going to argue with you there." Her laugh is high-pitched—nervous. "I've always been the good girl. Oral in a royal maze is a first and so, *so* not me."

I believe her. She looks like an angel. I might have sucked her sweet clit, but those doe-like eyes speak to nothing but innocence. That's when I'm slammed by a vision of a woman naked in my bed, long legs spread wide, hiding nothing, each pink honeyed fold exposed for my pleasure. Her delicate wrists and ankles bound by thick ropes of pearl.

I blink. My shoulders go rigid. I've never invited a

woman into my royal bed. The west wing of the palace is my personal sanctuary. No one is welcome there save for my brother Benedict. Not my dalliances. And not my father or stepmother. It's the only place that is just for me. Where I can be—*me*.

The world gets my dick. No one has a right to my soul.

"This was obviously a mistake," she murmurs to herself before rising unsteadily. "We got off on the wrong foot."

"*You* got off on the wrong foot." I nod at her bare right foot, the one on which she can barely place any weight, and I offer her my arm. She takes it, but not before rolling her eyes. "We got off on more than that," I add. My cock jumps like a dog hungry for a treat. "At least *you* did."

She sniffs. Who'd imagine this ice queen could melt into such a passionate, bright, fiery lover?

Interesting.

She limps but is able to hold her own now. I like to think it has something to do with my talent between her legs, that my skillful tongue has a healing effect. I guide her out of the maze. Grass stains mar her perfectly tailored ivory skirt, a visible reminder of what we just did, and just like that, I'm hard as a rock again.

"From the tabloids," she says, "it sounds like you won't suffer for long. Tell me, how long has it been since you were inside a woman?"

I shrug with studied nonchalance. "Mouth or pussy?"

She gasps as my words sink in.

I pretend to count my fingers. "Six hours for pussy.

Seven for her mouth. Give or take fifteen minutes. And if her brother hadn't barged in on us this morning, I'm guessing those numbers would be significantly smaller."

"You're a pig." Her brows slam together. "A rutting, depraved boar."

"No. I'm a prince." I draw myself to full height. "*Your* prince."

"And I'm here in service to my king." She juts out her jaw, gaze unbowed, refusing to cave at my power play. "Sire, you are my client. It's been royally commanded by your father and my liege lord, which means we need to get to work. I will return tomorrow to do your personality profile."

"My what?"

"It's protocol for all our clients." There is a note of finality in her clipped tone. She means business.

I click my tongue, half annoyed and half impressed. "You'll never marry me off, sweetheart."

"Tell that to my matchmaking success rate of 100%." She offers a smug smile. "See you tomorrow, Highness."

Once out of the maze, she releases my arm and continues alone. But she's still injured, so her haughty exit falls flat, even as she takes off her other shoe. I bite back a laugh before realizing the joke is on me. Because guess who still has a hard-on the size of the Matterhorn?

Still, I should follow her to the castle lest she goes to the tabloids with some trumped-up story about how poorly she was treated on palace property.

"I am fine to proceed alone," she says, reading my thoughts. An unsettling experience.

"I'm afraid I must insist," I say, taking the few steps needed to catch up to her.

"Please." Her composure slips a notch. The mask not fully secure. "I—I need a moment alone." A sign this unexpected dalliance affected her, as well.

She turns and makes her way toward the palace gates, clutching her heels, only the slightest limp still evident. Miss Winter has spunk. I'll give her that.

A woman like this could bring a less controlled man to his knees. Good thing that I'm no such man. This angel is more dangerous than any devil.

Kate

I don't care if it hurts to walk. Nothing is more important than distance. And by distance I mean space between me and Nikolai Lorentz.

The only problem? When I slip through the gates onto the main grounds, I can't get to the front of the castle without swimming the moat.

Good Lord. He lives in a palace. With a moat. And I almost slept with him in a freaking maze. I begged the prince of our realm to *fuck me* as I lay in the grass with my skirt hiked up over my hips. What the hell is wrong with me? I don't *fuck* anybody. I have lovely, meaningful sex with men who love and care for me— and who put a ring on it. At least, I did have that once.

As I contemplate my next move, an older man— probably in his late thirties—approaches me from a nearby garden.

"Pardon me, Miss Winter, but I have been instructed to take you home."

I shake my head. "No, thank you. That won't be necessary. If you could point me toward the most direct route to the main road, I'm sure I can get a taxi."

I look behind me, expecting to see Nikolai approaching, but he's nowhere to be found.

"Miss, there is no direct route to the main road other than through the palace." He looks me up and down. "And I am assuming you'd like to make a discreet exit?"

I sigh and cling to the last shred of my dignity, holding my head high even as my just-been-finger-fucked hair falls into my face.

"I'm quite content walking through the palace..." But I trail off as I note myself gesturing with my shoes in my hands—as threads from my torn skirt tickle my thigh—and I immediately deflate.

"So...you were instructed to take me home?"

The man nods, the hints of silver in his dark hair glinting in the sun, and it's only now that I realize his impeccably tailored suit, his straightened spine and hands clasped in front of his hips. His jaw is chiseled and his brown eyes are dark and knowing. He is not royalty. I can tell that much. But he exudes an indisputable authority nonetheless.

"Yes, Miss. His Royal Highness the Prince texted me with the order to see you home safely. I can lead you through the kitchen and out the servants' exit to avoid any unpleasant encounters upon your departure."

I hold out my arms, shoes dangling from my index fingers. "I guess I'm not in any shape to run into the king and queen again, especially if I want to keep this job."

The man doesn't even crack a smile but instead offers me a single nod.

"This way, Miss." He motions toward the garden from which he came.

I limp in his direction, trying not to read into the prince's gesture of making sure I get home safely. There is no way Nikolai Lorentz cares what happens between us from here on out other than him opposing my very being here.

"You can call me Kate," I say, once I reach his side and he holds out an arm. I grab both of my shoes with my right hand and take his arm with my left—not because I need to but because it would seem rude to decline.

I breathe in sharply as my hand grips muscle so tight and corded that I can feel it through his suit.

"As you wish, Miss Kate," he says, and I roll my eyes.

"Maybe you could drop the *Miss* altogether? Makes me sound like a prim-and-proper governess." I let out a nervous laugh. What just transpired between me and the heir apparent was *not* behavior becoming of a governess. Or the me I thought I knew, for that matter.

"As you wish, *Kate*," he says, his voice devoid of any hint of emotion.

"You got a name?" I ask as he pushes open a door hidden in the brick of the palace's side wall.

"His Highness calls me X," he says, ushering me inside a small corridor. The servants' quarters, no doubt.

"What do your friends and family call you?" I ask.

He clears his throat. "I have neither, Miss—my apologies—*Kate*."

My stomach sinks at the thought as he leads me through a white six-panel door. But I forget the heartbreaking answer just as quickly as we enter an enormous kitchen and my senses are assaulted in the best possible way. The aroma of garlic wafts in our direction, and my mouth immediately waters. I skipped breakfast this morning because—hello—I was ordered to the palace. Who can eat with that kind of pressure? And now that I'd been satiated in a whole other way entirely, I was famished. There's also something sweet in the air, a richness I can almost taste.

"Would you like one for the road, Miss?" A woman covered in a white apron spins from where she's plating macarons from a baking pan onto a three-tiered plate.

I swallow before I start to drool. "Please," I say, and she grabs a small saucer from beneath the island where she works and serves me *five* of the delicious-looking confections.

"Our secret," she says with a wink and a smile, handing my bounty to X. The man simply nods and continues piloting me toward the exit.

The next thing I know, I'm sitting in the luxury of a Rolls-Royce, a plate of macarons in my lap, and an ice pack on my ankle—also, according to X, ordered by the prince. But the older man speaks no more as he pulls free of the palace gates, out onto the main thoroughfare and toward the apartment I share with my sister in the heart of town.

As I sit here, the breeze of the car's open windows hits me right up the bottom of my skirt, and I'm reminded of the fact that not only am I going commando, but also my underwear is bunched in the Prince of Edenvale's pocket.

Just swallow me up, world, because I am too much of a cliché to exist. I can see the tabloid headline now:

Royal Touch Wakes Celibate Woman's Libido

It isn't that I've ignored the whole libido thing. I have an active imagination and a pretty stellar showerhead. It's not like I've gone completely without. But the first time I go *with* is not supposed to be with my future king, and it certainly isn't supposed to unleash a torrent of pent-up emotion, not when a pint of chocolate gelato is nowhere in sight.

I close my eyes and try to erase the image of him grinning before he went down on me, but it turns out that eyes open, closed, crossed or whatever still draw the same picture—Nikolai Lorentz pleasuring me and taking pleasure in doing so.

And then when I'd called our little maze dalliance a mistake, he'd ordered his driver to take care of me—right down to a ride in his private car and the cool pack soothing the throb in my twisted ankle.

Maybe I am a cliché, something I never thought I'd be. But then again, maybe Prince Nikolai, Duke of Westcraven, isn't what I'd had in mind, either.

I pop a golden lemon macaron into my mouth and moan with pleasure.

Nope. Not what I had in mind at all.

CHAPTER FOUR

Nikolai

NOTHING LIKE A scalding hot shower after a night of rough sex with your former best friend's little sister, followed by impromptu cunnilingus in the palace maze with the matchmaker bankrolled by your father to find your future queen.

It's been a strange twenty-four hours.

I rock my head back. Forget a standard showerhead. I custom designed my own personal waterfall. My groan bounces off the slate tiles as my tense muscles relax in the spray. Shit yeah. This feels good. Almost as good as it did to be on my knees between Miss Winter's sweet thighs. I chuckle to myself. Me. On my knees before a woman. Can't remember the last time that happened.

A visceral memory flies in from the outer reaches of my subconscious and slams my gut with the intensity of an earth-ending meteor.

There once had been a woman who brought me to my knees. But I wasn't much past a boy then. Now I'm all man with a kingdom that's mine for the taking.

I grab a bottle of my favorite Tom Ford body wash and pour a generous dollop in my palm. There's one thing that will relax me. Using the wash as lube, I thrust my cock into my hand in slow, lazy strokes before upgrading to my tried-and-true fist-over-fist technique, my length enough that one hand can never do the job. My ass clenches as I give over to the build.

Here's a fact. No woman, no matter how expert a lover, can touch a guy better than he touches himself. I'm captain of my own fucking ship. Yet here I am, imagining innocent, angel-faced Kate and her beautiful hands—small, delicate, manicured. I picture her grabbing me at the root, and I let out a guttural groan. What is it about this stranger that drives me crazy enough for her to invade my thoughts like this? Every nerve ending in my shaft is ready to burst into flames.

That's when I remember.

I still have her panties in my pocket. I step out of the shower, not giving two shits about getting the floor wet, and yank them from my tuxedo pants. The delicate ivory is pale in my tanned hand. On instinct, I lift them to my face and inhale the elegant French lace. My eyes roll. Beguiling. I'm a goddam pussy connoisseur, and this is the equivalent to uncorking a bottle of Château Mouton Rothschild 1945. I keep a case in my wine cellar, each bottle valued at twenty-five thousand euros.

I clutch the matchmaker's panties in one hand and step back in the shower, working over my cock with increased urgency as her scent overpowers my senses. Sweat breaks out across my chest and is washed away in a torrent of steamy water.

There are those who get intimidated by winery tasting rooms, but it's simple. A good vintage is composed of four things: fruits, acids, tannins and sugars. Young tannins can make the mouth pucker, leave your tongue dry. Left over time it increases in complexity, covering your palate with a signature silkiness. My palate is exceptional, able to identify a vintage by the subtle yet complex notes of coffee, chocolate, blackberry and spice.

Women are much the same. Each with her own nuances. And Kate Winter is in a class all her own. Fruity, with a hint of cherry, but also darker, more intriguing notes, such as to be found in a rich forest floor. She is the fruit of the earth, and I'm starving for the harvest.

A few more strokes and I'm poised on the edge, and then I pitch over, shattering into the most mind-numbing orgasm in a decade. For a moment, I wonder if I'm struck blind. Then the world returns, and I wash my hands, turn off the spray and grab a towel for my waist.

It takes me five minutes to regain my breath. After an intense, almost holy, experience like that, there is only one place to go—my brother, the saint.

Benedict will enter the priesthood. As a virgin.

Fucking crazy, right? My father bursts with pride at the fact he has a son destined for the priesthood and St. Egbert Abbey. To me, it's a fate worse than hell, and besides, it's more pressure. Benedict's put our bloodline at risk given that I'm the heir and he's the spare. My youngest brother, Damien, doesn't factor into the equation as he is banished and thereby removed from the line of succession. If I screw up here, the kingdom could pass from my family to my cousin Ingrid. She is a nice enough girl, and I don't mean that dismissively. She is ten years old.

I shove on a pair of sweatpants, lace up my running shoes and catch my reflection in the window. I look like a debauched lord of the underworld.

Reflections on my banished brother Damien spiral me into a brooding darkness. The latest rumors claim that he resides half-time in London and the rest over in America. He could build a hermetically sealed tower in Madagascar for all I care, and it would still be too goddamn close. My family is like the setup to a bad joke: a commitment-phobic heir to the throne, a virgin almost-priest, and a black sheep all walk into a bar...

I jog through the quiet palace, past row after row of ancient ancestors appraising me from gilded frames. Do they wonder if I'll ever measure up? If I'll fulfill my legacy? Damn these black thoughts to hell. I get outside and run until my lungs are near bursting. On the edge of the grounds, near the Royal River, is the tower where my brother lives. He calls it his sanctuary, and he's not wrong. Poor bastard might not use his cock, but he has peace. And he deserves it because I don't say bastard lightly.

There isn't conclusive proof, but there are many rumors that my mother took a brief liking to the head of her secret-service detail while my father was at a UN summit. The only evidence? My brother's piercing green eyes—neither my mother's nor my father's.

I try the door.

"It's locked, Sir," a formal male voice calls out.

I turn to find X there, watching me with his usual impenetrable expression. One would think that after years of him appearing by my side without setting off so much as a floorboard creak, I would be used to his stealth. But it still unnerves me every time.

"I'm afraid Mr. Benedict was called away on urgent business."

"Where to?" I ask.

"Vatican City."

I laugh without humor. "Of course."

Benedict is the only person that I count a true friend, one I can trust without question unlike recent experiences with Christian. And as far as I'm concerned, Benedict is my *only* brother. If I ever were to cross paths with Damien again, I know Benedict would pass me the knife to gut him.

One happy family.

Looks like I'm not going to be able to get any advice tonight. The only thing I can do is pop an Ambien and hope for a dreamless sleep.

Because tomorrow morning, I'll be facing Kate Winter again. And this time she won't be spreading her legs and offering me a sample of her nectar. She'll be presenting me with a dossier of potential wives.

Kate

It's déjà vu the next morning when I look out my apartment window to find X and the Rolls-Royce waiting against the curb. Maddie peers over my shoulder.

"I still don't get it," she says, and I can hear the disappointment lacing her tone. "Why did they specifically ask for you rather than me? It's *my* agency, after all."

Now that the contract has been signed, I can tell my sister everything. Which is good because that whole secrecy thing won't fly when I'm getting picked up by a Rolls with a license plate that reads *Royal.* Besides, I'd accepted the job—after the king and queen agreed to double my fee for working with such a reluctant client. Well, it was the queen's suggestion. Turns out that despite the business being Maddie's baby, my recent success at facilitating what I thought had been a few discreet celebrity matches had not flown under the radar of the royal family.

"Come on, Mads," I say. "It's a gold star for the business regardless of whether it's you or me facilitating the matches. Plus, you're my partner in crime, so it's not like we can't work on Nikolai's profile together." In fact, the only thing I cannot disclose to anyone other than Maddie is the list of potential candidates.

She is obviously still pouting, but as much as I love my big sister and her flair for business, I am the one with the perfect match record—fifteen happy couples in just the past six months alone. It's all in the interviews. One face-to-face conversation with each potential partner—separately, of course—and I can either feel their chemistry…or not. That, coupled with my limited celebrity experience, I'm sure is why they asked for me, but I don't rub it in. While I'm proud I've taken so well to the business these past two years, what does it say that I can find happy endings for everyone—except myself?

Then I'm reminded that I risked my heart once, and the payoff was total devastation. No, thank you. I'm good with focusing on everything and anything other than that.

I wave to X and hold up a finger, letting him know I'll be right there. Then I turn to face my sister, staring into icy blue eyes that mirror my own.

"Remember, Maddie, we need this fee. We are almost due for another quarterly payment at Silver Maples." Gran's been deteriorating, her Alzheimer's getting worse almost by the week. We're her sole financial support. Actually, we're her sole *everything*. As much as it kills us not to have her at home, caring for her like she did raising us, her condition has declined too much. Silver Maples is a top-rated facility, one of the best in Europe. And it's priced accordingly. It's just out of our financial means at the moment, but I intend to change that.

I don't mention the part about receiving *no* fee at all if I don't get Nikolai down the aisle—if he is my first and *only* fail. I also may have omitted that despite my vow to find him a suitable queen, I already know what it feels like for his stubble to chafe my thighs, for his tongue to swirl around my swollen clit. Or to know that despite the matches that are perfect for Nikolai Lorentz on paper, the only chemistry I'm sure of at this point is whatever happened in that garden maze between myself and our future king.

"Shit," I mutter under my breath and slip past her. I need to stop thinking myself into climax before I've even had my first sip of espresso. "I'm late." I grab my dossier off our small kitchen table and reach for the small cup that should have three shots of my morning wake-up medicine when I realize the espresso machine is unplugged. I never forget my morning shot. Ugh. I am way off my game, which is not an auspicious beginning to day one with my most important client. *"Shit,"* I say louder and then groan my acceptance at another morning with an empty belly. I kiss my sister on the cheek. "Love you!" And then I dart out the door before she has a chance to respond.

Not that I'm expecting a repeat performance of what happened yesterday, but I wear my auburn waves loose today—in case of any mishaps. Better to have my hair down and unfettered than to attempt the whole conservative look only to wind up disheveled and unkempt. Because I much prefer *kempt*.

X holds open the car door, and I enter to find a veritable feast waiting for me on a small table attached to the wall that separates the rear of the vehicle from the front. There's a bowl of the reddest strawberries I've ever seen, a small basket of scones and a stainless-steel travel mug of what I assume is coffee.

My eyes widen as I lower myself into my seat, and I glance at X before he closes the door. He offers me a small bow, and I blush, embarrassed at the royal treatment when my upbringing is probably more common than he can imagine.

"Compliments of His Royal Highness, Prince Nikolai."

While I'm sure my fresh breakfast probably cost him no more than a few seconds of his time, a quick royal order via text, I can't fight the warmth spreading through my veins that he thought of me at all.

"Thank you, X," I say with a smile I'm unable to suppress, and he nods before closing the door.

I settle into the plush leather of my seat, pulling a napkin that's folded in the shape of a swan from the table before me. A pang of guilt rests in my chest for whoever created this small masterpiece only to have me stain it with berry juice or dripped coffee. Yet I shake it out, a swan no more, and lay it across my lap as X pulls smoothly from the curb.

I opted for pants today—a cropped black pair with a green silk blouse. And flats. I'd pretty much taken every precaution to avoid a repeat performance with the prince, and I smile smugly to myself at how easy it will be to keep my panties on today.

I unlock the lid to the mug and breathe in the rich aroma, biting back a moan as I do. Whatever brand of coffee is in there, it's miles above the quality of the espresso I buy on sale at the corner market.

I knock on the window that separates me from X, and instead of him lowering it, his voice pipes through a speaker to my left.

"Can I help you, Miss Kate?"

I roll my eyes at his insistence on formality but decide not to give him a hard time.

"It's kind of lonely here," I tell him. "Can we talk without the intercom?"

I hear him clear his throat. "As you wish, Miss Kate."

The window lowers, and I pop a strawberry into my mouth before leaning toward the open space between us. But the expanse is too wide for my torso, and I end up falling to my knees, a dribble of berry juice on my chin. I wipe it clean and scoot the rest of the way to the window frame, leaning through it so X's strong profile is in view.

"Did you make the swan?" I ask.

His eyes remain on the road as he replies. "No, Miss."

"Did you make the coffee?"

"No, Miss."

"Would you like a strawberry?"

At this I see the faintest tug on the corner of his mouth, and I decide that along with making sure I send Nikolai Lorentz down the aisle, I'm going to make X smile.

"No, Miss," he says, and my shoulders sag.

I follow his eyes to the road ahead and realize we're not headed in the direction of the palace. For a second my heart stutters in my chest.

"Okay, you're not going to ply me with strawberries and scones only to dump me in the river with a backpack full of stones, right?"

Again that twitch of his lip, but it doesn't go beyond that.

"We *are* heading to the river," he says. "But His Highness said nothing about a backpack."

I narrow my eyes even though he won't look in my direction. Despite heading toward the body of water I've avoided most of my living years, I decide to trust my life is not in danger and slide back to my seat, this time bringing a warm blueberry scone with me. Seriously? How is it still warm?

Just as I relax and bring the pastry to my lips, we roll to a stop. X, however, does not leave his seat. Before I can ask him if we've reached our destination, my door opens, and I see the prince—not in a rumpled dress shirt and tuxedo pants but in a fitted black T-shirt and dark washed jeans. I know what I said about not being a preteen fangirl, but holy hell. This man in the flesh is a vision to behold.

He extends his arms wide as if he's brought the world to my doorstep, and based on the breakfast alone, it feels like he has.

"We can't possibly be expected to work indoors on a day like today," he says, his gray eyes shimmering silver in the sun.

He offers me a hand, and I take it, grabbing the dossier with my other as he pulls me into the fresh morning air.

"No," I say, trying to convince myself that the smoldering heat in my core is from the coffee I leave behind in the car. "I guess we can't."

CHAPTER FIVE

Nikolai

"THANKS FOR BREAKFAST." Kate regards me uncertainly.

"Seems only fair, Miss Winter. Especially after the delicious feast you offered me yesterday." Here's hoping that my wolfish smile covers any sincerity that might poke through my veneer. "Nice pants, by the way." They fit slim against her shape, hugging the soft swell of her thighs, tapering at her small waist. I take my time drinking her in for two reasons. One: she looks even better than she did in my dreams last night. Two: it's time to scare her off.

I don't care a whit about ancient marriage requirements. But my father is the king, and Edenvale is a strict monarchy. No constitution. No parliament. His word is absolute law.

But despite his decree, I cannot marry. I *will* not. My heart hasn't been whole for years. To subject a woman to a lifetime of darkness—to a love I cannot give—is anything but fair. I may not play by the rules in my day-to-day—or night-by-night—affairs, but I am straightforward. Each beauty I bed knows full well

I have nothing to offer the morning after other than burying my cock in her one more time.

I do like a proper goodbye, after all.

And I also like to be clear that I will not share my future crown.

Father has to be bluffing about this twenty-ninth birthday bullshit. He can't take the throne from me. He wouldn't. What are his other options? Benedict would yield our sovereign power to the Roman Pope. Damien? My cousin Ingrid, who is still a child? Nightgardin would be licking its chops if that happened.

A hot copper taste fills my mouth. The inside of my cheek hurts from the involuntary bite.

Damien destroyed my world. His scandal nearly brought down our entire lineage. Now he is banished. Not even allowed to claim Edenvale citizenship. No, that bottom-feeder will never be permitted to call himself more than "King of Traitors."

Father has no other choice, if he wants to avoid passing the crown from his bloodline. He will have to relent, to compromise, come around and see things from my point of view. It is that or let the kingdom fall to ruin, and that—he knows—is not an option.

My shoulders relax. I'll indulge in Miss Winter's little game for the time being, but she doesn't know that I'm the one writing the rules, and that I only play to win.

"Ahem, Highness?" Her exaggerated throat clearing breaks my thoughts. "My eyes are up here."

I allow my gaze to slowly rake over the swell of her perfect breasts. "I know exactly where your eyes are, Miss Winter, and might I say that's a fetching color of shadow. Makes your eyes appear deeper than the Bottomless Lake."

Kate sucks in a ragged breath, one evidenced by the rapid rise and fall of her chest rather than heard.

"Can we get down to business?" Pleading fills her voice.

"That all depends. Would getting down to...*business* bring you pleasure?" I dribble innuendo over every sentence. My mask is perfect. I'm every inch the rakish rogue everyone has come to expect. Kate Winter has no idea that my heart accelerates in her vicinity, kicks into fifth faster than my Ferrari 250 Testa Rossa.

And she never will.

She balls her free hand into a fist while the other clutches a portfolio, her fingertips white from her grip. Bet Little Miss Ice Queen would love nothing better than landing a punch right in my arrogant smirk. She can take a number. There are many in the line before her.

Plus she's safer wanting nothing more to do with me than our business dealings.

"X," I call, not breaking my gaze. "The poles."

"Very good, Highness." He clicks his heels and strides to the trunk of the Rolls. Good old X. Familiar as my shadow.

"I'm not really a nature girl." She casts a baleful look at the long grass, swatting away a hovering insect. "But I am excited to get to work. Here is the dossier." She brandishes the portfolio. "I spent last night reviewing suitable prospects and have winnowed your choices to five viable candidates." She clears her throat. "Your parents offered some input as well, wishing the choice to be someone who would buoy your image and thereby the image of the throne. Your stepmother in particular took a keen interest. The queen is a woman of many opinions."

I arch a brow. My hag of a stepmother has many feelings about my existence, none of them good. "I thought we were to do some sort of personality profile."

She breaks eye contact. "Your stepmother didn't think it was necessary to invest too much in compatibility since—well—since you don't intend this to be much of an emotional connection. You've made that point crystal clear. So I've been instructed to provide you with *appropriate* choices."

"Fascinating." A cold front blows over my chest, transforming my tone to sheer ice. I spent last night milking my cock, dreaming of her sweet, soaked pussy, and all the while she'd been reviewing *appropriate* brides. Not once in five years have I given a single fuck what a woman thinks about after I've been with her.

Not once until today.

How much is Father paying her for this trouble? My stepmother would bankrupt the royal coffers if it meant having her revenge. She won't play me the fool the way her daughter did. Victoria made me believe that a kiss meant love, not a fast track to sink her claws into my wealth—or my future throne.

These days the only crown jewels I'm prepared to offer the opposite sex rest between my legs. It's likely she is conspiring with my stepmother. No doubt yesterday's unexpected encounter was part of her carefully constructed ruse designed to disarm me. Being heir to the Edenvale throne means living with an invisible target on my back. The thing is, though, that I already know there's a sniper in my midst, and she sleeps in my father's bed.

My smile is as cool as her name. If Kate Winter hopes to lie in wait to stab a proverbial blade between my shoulder blades, then I hope she has the patience of a saint, because I aim to give her no such satisfaction.

X returns, and her expression morphs from confused to horrified.

"Fishing poles?" She gasps. "Is this your idea of a joke?"

"Fishing is one of my many hobbies," I lie smoothly. "And it seems an apt metaphor given our current situation." I take a pole from X and hand it to her.

She grips it without complaint, understanding the gesture isn't a request, but an order from her prince.

I grab the dossier from her other hand, not bothering to look inside, and hand it to X. "We won't be needing that just yet," I say, then turn my attention to Kate. "After all, there are many fish in the sea, correct? Or should I say…river?" I pivot and stride toward the old Roman bridge. "And how can I be sure of your skills in catching one for me until I see you in action?"

Kate

It's a stone bridge, I remind myself. A sturdy, stone, won't-crumble-beneath-your-feet bridge. There's no need to tell him I can't swim.

Though the swelling in my ankle has gone down, the lingering ache still slows my gait. He walks a few paces ahead of me, not bothering to wait. Decidedly different behavior from yesterday when he carried me after my fall—saw to it that I made it home safe. Hell, he even sent me breakfast this morning. I knew I was stupid to think it meant anything more than feeding the help, that Nikolai Lorentz was anything other than what the media portrayed.

I catch up to him at the center of the bridge where nothing else waits for us other than two buckets, one of which must be bait, the other to hold what we catch. I swallow hard when I note the height—or lack thereof—of the stone wall separating us from the river below. Nikolai perches casually on the low barrier, reaches into the bucket and pulls from it what looks like a small slice of sausage.

"What is that?" I ask, wrinkling my nose.

He shrugs. "X prepared it. Says it's his best recipe for catching trout. You met Beatrice in the kitchen yesterday, yes? Our head cook? Tonight's royal meal depends on what you catch for us today."

His tone is more cold than playful, yet I decide to humor him.

"Well, then," I say. "I've got plenty of suggestions for takeout when this goes *royally* amiss."

He buries the hint of a smile, but I see it nonetheless and take it as a sign that I do have the power to break through whatever wall he's hiding behind today. I remind myself that my livelihood depends on it and let out a breath before reaching into the small bucket and pinching a slimy piece of bait between my thumb and forefinger.

I shudder at the feel of the foreign substance against my skin but do not dare complain. I watch as Nikolai fixes his bait to his hook and mimic his movements precisely. Maybe this won't be so difficult after all.

He raises a brow. "You've fished before?"

I shake my head. "I'm a quick learner," I say, realizing I've nowhere to wipe my hand and opt for the ledge of the wall I don't dare sit on myself.

He casts his line into the river, and again I follow suit.

Piece of disgusting, slimy cake.

He finally grins. "May the best fisherman win," he says. "Not that it's a competition."

I smile. "You're on, Your Highness."

We fish in silence, him still sitting on the wall while I stand a pace behind it. In less than three minutes his line tugs at the pole, and Nikolai whoops in response, standing to reel in his catch.

I can't help but marvel at the ease of his movements, the flex of his biceps as he rotates the crank on the pole. And it's this lapse in my attention, this gravitational pull he seems to have on me despite every bit of logic saying it shouldn't, that causes the tug on my own line to catch me off guard.

My body yanks forward, and I stumble. It all happens in the space of a few seconds. I don't even have time to scream before I knock into the wall and pitch right over it.

The water is cool, yet it burns my lungs and throat as I panic and breathe it in. I cough, but it only makes me take in more water. In this strange, suspended panic, I note the clarity of the river, that I can see through the surface and to the bridge to where it looks like something is falling toward me as I sink.

As quickly as I was yanked off the bridge, strong hands wrap around me and tug me toward the surface. When I break through, I cough up the water I couldn't release seconds ago and gasp for air. Instinct has me thrashing in his arms, but he doesn't let go.

"Kate!" he yells, his voice hoarse. "Christ, Kate! Stop fighting me and put your feet down. It's only five feet deep!"

His words register, and I cease movement, letting my legs straighten below me while I still cling to his arm with my own.

My shoes touch the riverbed, and I stand on my tiptoes, my five-foot-five height keeping my face well above water.

We reach the bank, and I collapse onto my ass, humiliation seeping in as I cough up another mouthful of water.

Nikolai falls onto his back, panting, his T-shirt and jeans plastered to his muscled frame.

"Christ almighty," he says, catching his breath. "Why didn't you tell me you couldn't swim?"

I try to convince myself that this job is worth it, that no matter what other disasters befall throughout the length of this contract, it will be worth it in the end. Because if I fail, it's Maddie and Gran who will pay the price.

"You're my prince," I say dully. "You said we were fishing, so I obeyed."

He bolts upright, brows pulled together. "Is that really—?" he sputters. "You think I would endanger—?" But he trails off again. He reaches for my face, resting a palm gingerly against my cheek, and it's almost as hard to breathe as being underwater. "Are you okay?"

Genuine concern laces his words. This is a Nikolai I've never seen in the pages of a magazine. This man did not exist in the maze yesterday.

"Yes," I whisper, the heat in his palm making me forget I'm soaking wet.

"I told you," he says, his gray eyes darkening to black, "I will not marry."

I nod slowly. "And your father will keep the throne from you if you do not. Nikolai, when you stormed out yesterday, he mentioned Damien…"

A soft, guttural sound emanates from his throat.

"If you want the throne," I continue, "then finding a bride is the only way." And the only way to keep my grandmother getting the best care that our country has to offer. But I don't tell him that. As much as I am drawn to him, I can't get close to another man. Especially not another bad boy who doesn't seem to care about anything other than his next thrill. My heart can only take so much.

He lets out a long breath. "So it is," he says, and my heart tightens at the sound of defeat in those words. "Then we find someone who will play by my rules, who knows she is queen in name only, and that I will govern Edenvale as I see fit when it's my time."

I nod again. "If that is your choice."

He lets out a bitter laugh. "Choice," he says through gritted teeth. "Wouldn't that be a luxury?"

I shiver, the cold setting in and seeping into my bones. He drops his hand to my neck, my collarbone and then to breast, my nipple hard against the cold, wet fabric of my blouse, a trail of heat in its wake.

"What if I choose to touch you like this?" he asks, his lips a fraction of an inch from mine. "Would you choose that, too?" He glances toward the river. Then his gaze burns into mine again. "Because you *have* a choice, Kate. You should have told me that you live along a river yet have never bathed in it."

I feel the prick of tears and try to will them away.

"Maddie and I—my sister—lost our parents when they drove off the road that winds along the mountain's edge. The river was deeper than five feet where their car plunged in." A single tear escapes, and he brushes it away, the gesture too sweet. Too intimate. "I was too young to remember them but not too young to develop a fear of the water. The funny thing is, Maddie says I was an excellent swimmer from a young age, but it's like my mind has blocked that part out. So…here we are."

He runs a hand through his soaked black hair. "You should have told me," he says again, and I startle to see the intensity in his eyes. "*You* have choice, Kate. With me. Nothing is an order. Do you understand that?"

"Yes," I whisper.

He places a hand behind my neck and lowers me to the ground, my body a willing accomplice.

"You will find me a royal bride," he says, hovering over me. A bead of water drips off his skin and splashes near the corner of my lips. It takes all my self-restraint not to lick it.

"Yes."

"I will not love her," he adds.

"I know," I whisper.

"I *cannot* love anyone." His voice is a low vibration, one I feel in his chest against mine.

"I know," I say again, cursing the beating of my heart that seems to speed up the nearer he gets. We might be from two different worlds, but we have that much in common. I *can* love, but I won't. Not when I've known so much loss.

"But I want you," he says, his breath warm against my lips.

"I want you, too," I admit.

He flicks out his tongue, running it along my bottom lip, and I grind my pelvis into his.

"Do you *choose* this, Kate? Do you choose what I'm offering?"

My body has already complied. All that's left is my voice.

"I do, Your Highness."

"Call me Nikolai."

I let out a trembling breath. "I do—Nikolai." His name tastes as delicious as his hungry mouth.

He kisses me, long and slow and deep until my toes curl and my core is on fire.

"Say my name again," he growls, his erection firm against my aching clit.

"Nikolai," I whisper, and his tongue plunges into my mouth again.

I may have the freedom of choice, but I also have the wisdom to know this is a foolish one to make. I'll have to add a note in my planner to regret this sometime tomorrow.

CHAPTER SIX

Nikolai

I BURY MY fingers into her thick coil of auburn hair and pull, not hard, but enough to deepen our kiss. Kate's tears place me on unfamiliar ground. The story of her loss threatens to undo my expertly built defenses. I don't know how to tell her this, but in some ways, I understand her pain. Once upon a time, many years ago, a car accident changed my own world. She and I share an unexpected connection, both forever marked by a tragedy that changed the course of our lives.

Damn it. My pulse thunders in my ears. I don't want to be curious about Kate, to be interested in her as a *person* and not another notch in my belt. I channel my frustration into tangling my tongue with hers, demanding more, demanding everything, and she moans into my open mouth, offering herself freely.

My chest tightens like a vise. I gasp a mumbled curse. This kiss is taking over, filling my veins, replacing the blood. *Slow the fuck down. Keep it physical.* Remember that's my MO—making women cry out my name and wanting nothing more in return than my own

physical release. I reach down to circle my thumbs over
her peaked nipples, hard nubs against her wet, silky
top. She moans again. Louder.

I tear away, one foot in heaven and one in hell. It's
time to get a grip, to calm myself and focus. After all,
getting a woman off is what I do best. My uncertainty
fades as I take charge, increasing the pressure. Not
much, just enough to turn that moan into a gasp, followed by a soft squeak. I break our kiss and nip her
plump lower lip, tasting the hint of cherry lip balm.
Then I continue my leisurely torment down her jaw
to the sensitive place on her neck, relishing her rapid
pulse and trace of perfume that wasn't washed away
in the river. Chanel No. 5.

She is killing me in the best of ways.

"God, you smell brilliant." I give her a soft bite.
Not enough to leave a mark, but enough that I've got
her full attention. She moans. All women enjoy a little
domination in the bedroom. "Like that?"

"Mmmmm," she purrs.

I bite again, wiping away the sting with the flat of
my tongue. "I asked you a question. I am your prince.
I expect you to respond." My tone is authoritative, yet
teasing. I want control, but I also want her to know
she's safe—safe from the river, from the painful memories she buries. I'll erase it all with a swipe of my
tongue. Another nip of teeth.

She presses her hips against me. "Feels so good,"
she murmurs. "If X wasn't close, I'd be on my knees
filling my mouth with your cock."

So my prim-and-proper ice queen likes to talk dirty.

Blood sings through my veins, a pounding chorus, as I thicken in an instant. "Good thing X took a drive."

She stills. "He's gone?"

"I heard him leave while we walked toward the bridge."

She frowns. "He knew you'd seduce me?"

I shrug. "Maybe he wanted a croissant?"

She slides away. My body aches at the gap, and for a moment, I falter. Who is really in control here?

"You seduce many women, don't you, Sire?"

No point lying. *"Nikolai,"* I remind her, my voice firm. I want my name dripping off her lips in a torrent of pleasure. "Call me by my name." Might as well admit there is more to wanting to hear her say it than a simple, sexual ego booster. Every cell in my being craves her closer, wanting to rub against her and smooth away my ragged edges, to see if she is the one who possesses whatever the fuck I need to be made whole.

Good God. I'm pussy drunk.

"You seduce many women, don't you, *Nikolai*?" She bites her bottom lip, and my cock strains against my jeans, but I force my voice to remain steady.

"Yes," I say simply. I'm Mr. Right Now. Not Mr. Right.

"A bad boy."

I crook my lips into an arrogant smile, the mask that she expects her future ruler to wear. I have a rake-hell reputation to uphold. "That seems to be the general opinion."

She shakes her head. "Why not give in?" she murmurs, more to herself than me. "Live dangerously for once in my life." She refocuses her gaze on me. "We can do whatever it is we are about to do and still remain professional."

My brows rise. "Your mouth sheathing my cock is professional?" I swallow hard, and she notices, grinning, no doubt, at the effect she has on me.

She narrows her gaze as if to size me up. "Yes. Once I know what you like, I'll be that much better positioned to find it for you."

"I can think of many positions I'd like to find you in."

She purses her lips. Then a flicker of uncertainty passes over her face. "Tell me how you like it."

"Pardon?" My own eyes widen. "How I like getting sucked off?" She wants a lesson?

"Yes, tell me in thorough detail. If you teach me well, perhaps you'll get a handsome reward." She palms me over the wet denim of my jeans. "I'm a quick study and also quite good at taking direction."

I decide right then and there that despite what she's been hired to do—and how much I detest the thought of finding a bride—I love being around this most surprising woman.

Wait...love? The word doesn't belong anywhere in my vocabulary. This is no good. My heart better go sit its ass in a corner. I clear my throat. "You want to know how to suck a dick? Very well. First, the woman in question needs to crave it. I want her to approach my cock like it's a chocolate fucking fudge sundae and she hasn't eaten in a week."

Her lids flutter. "Go on."

Shit. I can talk dirty in five languages, but I've never

given an explicit lesson in the art of performing a blow job. And believe me—it is a goddamn art. "I need some encouragement," I tell her, my voice growing hoarse with need. "A little inspiration."

She arches a brow. "And how can I do that?"

I pretend to think it over. "Are you wearing a matching set?"

She nods with a shy smile. "I do own the bra to match my pink lace panties," she says, then licks her lips. "But I didn't wear it today."

My throat thickens. And if it's at all possible, my cock grows even harder, and I want nothing more than for her to rip my jeans from my legs. *Mission accomplished, Miss Winter.* The image of what lies beneath her drenched clothing will inspire me for days and nights to come.

What can I say? Kate Winter is my fucking muse. Literally.

"Shall we continue with the lesson?" I ask.

"Please," she says. "It's been a while since—well, I think I mentioned yesterday that it's been a while. Period."

I bury the surge of jealousy at the thought of her mouth on any other man and decide to give her exactly what she's asking for—so that she may give it to me.

"Outside of a sixty-nine, I prefer to stand," I tell her, already imagining her kneeling before me. "Gives me good control and a great view. Hands are important. Use them. I love a mouth on me, but touch is a must. Stroke my shaft. Massage my sac. Gradually increase the tempo. That's when I'll need some tongue on the tip, swirling and sucking like I'm your favorite flavor of Popsicle."

She rolls her eyes. "Cool it with the food references. You're making me hungry." Her tone is teasing, but I can tell from the way her pupils dilate that she is soaked.

"Never use your teeth. Simply lick and swirl until you're ready."

"For what?" She sounds drugged.

"To take me as deep as you can go. A gentleman never crams his cock into a lady's throat. He waits, patiently, but what he wants is for her to suck him down. And all the while, hold eye contact. Trust me on this. A guy loves it when you take it all and let him see how much you love every inch."

She runs a hand over her hair. "And for the end?"

"Swallow," I say bluntly and shrug. She asked, so I might as well give her the truth.

"I've never done that," she whispers. "I've always been too intimidated."

"Well, you don't have to," I tell her quickly. Again it comes, that inexplicable need to make her feel safe. "It's just...you asked what's the best. That is the best, Pet. Nothing like it."

She stays quiet for a long moment. Long enough that I start to wonder if I've pissed her off—or even worse, scared her from even wanting to try.

"Stand, Sire," she finally says, and I obey without question. She stands too, stepping forward to close the narrow distance between us, all the while keeping her gaze locked to my face.

Then she sinks to her goddamn knees.

"I've never mixed business and pleasure." She reaches to undo my fly. "But this is my most important job yet, so perhaps I should ensure you get the royal treatment."

My hands fist in her hair, and I know from the determined look in her eyes that I'm about to be destroyed.

Kate

His jeans are snug against his hard, muscled thighs, and despite them being soaked in the river, it only takes me seconds to pull them to his ankles.

My nipples peak against my cold, wet top, and I wonder if he knows how close to the edge I already am. Just from his words. It was never like this with Jean-Luc, and as soon as the thought enters my mind, I'm awash in a wave of guilt. How dare I compare what I'm about to do to a man I met yesterday to a man I'd planned to be with for the rest of my life?

And yet it's the truth.

I loved my fiancé, but I can't recall wanting him with this sort of hunger. I'd always felt performing oral sex to be more of an obligation than anything else. And he had always finished so quickly that I never knew what he really liked.

But I *want* to taste Nikolai so badly that my pulse throbs between my legs.

I start by placing a soft kiss on his inner thigh, then shift my heavy gaze to his.

"More," he says, and my core tightens at the command.

I kiss his other thigh, this time a little higher up, and I have to grab his backside to steady myself.

He lets out a groan.

"Hands," he says, his voice tight, and I do believe I've made it difficult for my prince to speak.

I look up at him and grin, releasing his ass with my right hand so I can cup his balls. Then, without warning, I swirl my tongue over his tip, the precum salty on my taste buds. We both moan.

His hands tug at my hair, and I move my own to join my mouth, taking him deeper as he slides slick through my palm.

"Fuck," he hisses. *"Yes,* Pet. More. Goddamn, I need more."

My clit swells at the sound of his need, a delicious, aching pulse between my thighs, and I can't hold back a whimper as he sinks deeper into my mouth, as I let the taste of him fill me.

Deeper and faster, my hand grips his throbbing shaft, and I feel his thighs begin to shake. I hold his gaze as I bury him to the hilt, and for the brief moment when he begins to teeter over the edge, I see past the facade to a brokenness that draws me further into his orbit.

He shudders and growls. I swallow his release, an intimate connection I never knew was possible. I back away, ready to force my trembling limbs to stand, but he collapses to his knees in front of me.

His hands cup my cheeks, and he stares into my eyes. Without a word he kisses me so hard and deep I can barely catch my breath. He lowers me to the ground, wordless still, his lips never leaving mine. His hand slides beneath my blouse, and I buck against him as he pinches my sensitive peak.

We are animals, communicating with nothing other than our shared savage need, and I *need* this. I *need* his hands on me, in me—I need Nikolai Lorentz everywhere. And because we speak the same language, he knows, and I find him wrenching my pants from my hips, down to my knees, all the while his tongue tangling with mine.

Finally, when two fingers plunge inside me, immediately hitting the right spot, I call out his name in an overwhelming torrent of sensation.

"Nikolai!"

And then I finally close my eyes and see nothing but stars.

I'm nothing short of a mess when we make our way to the road and find X waiting outside the Rolls. Nikolai, despite his dip in the river as well, looks nothing short of spectacular. Or maybe that's all I can see after what he's done to me.

What *has* he done? I feel satiated yet hungry. Remade but ruined.

X opens the door as we approach, not once letting his impassive gaze give away that he knew Nikolai had planned to seduce me. But when I look inside the car and see my scones and fruit replaced by a small platter of croissants, I can't help but burst into a fit of laughter.

Nikolai's brows pull together, and it takes every ounce of control for me to simply motion toward the open door and say, *"Look."*

He does, and as soon as he sees the pastries, he's laughing too, and I am surprised the way my heart surges to hear such a sound—a genuine emotion from Prince Nikolai, and I get to bear witness.

X clears his throat and raises a brow.

"Your Highness. Miss Winter—I thought you might have worked up an appetite."

I decide not to deny it because damn—I *am* starving. So I reach inside the car and grab a chocolate croissant, tearing off a piece and shoving it into a surprised Nikolai's mouth before tearing into the rest of it with my teeth.

"You're right," I say, mouth full, hair tangled and probably full of sand, clothes still wet and plastered to my body. "I'm famished."

X nods. "Your Highness, I take it there are supplies to collect from the bridge?"

Nikolai swallows his bite of croissant. "Yes, thank you. One fishing pole, the bucket of bait and Miss Winter's dossier. You can throw the trout I caught back into the river."

"Yes, Your Highness," he says, not questioning why we are short one fishing pole.

Once X is out of earshot, I point at Nikolai with my half-eaten croissant.

"Hey, I thought you said tonight's royal meal depended on what I caught on our little fishing expedition."

He shrugs and gives me a sheepish grin, another expression I don't expect, and it disarms me completely.

"I despise seafood, actually," he says. "But I was hoping to enjoy putting you through the wringer."

I open my mouth at an attempt to unleash my fury

on him, but he silences me with a kiss, and I'm caught so off guard that I simply melt into it.

"How about a truce?" he says against me, and I squeak out my answer, the momentary fury dissolving into dust.

"Okay," I whisper.

"Okay," he says.

"But this *cannot* happen again, Your Highness. We have— I mean *I* have a job to do."

He nods. "Of course. Never again, Miss Winter. You have my word."

I sigh. I know he's soon to be my king, that my job is to find him a queen, but right now I don't believe his word for one tiny second. And that impish grin on his face tells me that neither does he.

CHAPTER SEVEN

Nikolai

"My, my, isn't His Highness in quite the chipper mood?" My wicked stepmother, Queen Adele, sizes me up from across the mahogany table. Even when it is just she, my father and I in residence at the palace, she insists on using the formal dining room that can accommodate up to fifty guests. Overhead hang three large crystal chandeliers, and lining the wood-paneled room are suits of armor interspersed with the images of frowning black-haired men, my ancestors, the kings of old.

From the looks of their faces, dark and brooding is a family tradition.

"As a matter of fact, *Majesty*, I *am* in good spirits." I wipe my lips with a linen napkin before crooking them into a smile as fake as her own. The queen's gaze narrows as she tries to see through my mocking mask.

Lots of luck, love.

My father cuts his roast, oblivious as always to the private war that I carry out with the hag. "I understand you met with the matchmaker this afternoon.

She seems a competent woman." He spears the beef with his fork. "Most enthusiastic."

"Quite." An image of Kate Winter flashes, one where she is on her knees, hair wet and wild, sucking my cock like some sort of mythic water goddess, and I suppress a satisfied grin.

"Rather common, if you ask me." My stepmother gives an audible sniff.

"Good thing no one did," I growl, my mouth flat-lining.

She ignores the warning in my voice. "I do admit to having second thoughts on Miss Winter. After all, how can a commoner have the proper breeding necessary to discern fine taste? Edenvale *is* the second-oldest throne in all of Europe. The realm expects certain standards."

White-hot fury builds behind my eyes. This snobby shrew isn't fit to lick the sole of one of Kate's heels, let alone dare to speak her name with such disdain. True, my favorite matchmaker isn't blue-blooded, but she has more natural grace and elegance in one of her little fingers than Adele has in her entire Botoxed body.

Who knows what prompted Father to marry her? I barely remember my real mother, but from all accounts, it was a love match. Queen Cordelia remains well-beloved by her people to this day, no thanks to Adele, who likes to pretend she never existed.

I study the fine lines that groove my stepmother's frown. She has always been a sourpuss, but since her only daughter Victoria's death she's turned downright wicked.

The last vestiges of my good mood vanish. When Adele married my lonely father the only bright spot to the arrangement came in the form of her beautiful and vivacious nineteen-year-old daughter, my stepsister and first love. I was a foolish twenty-three-year-old boy determined to make Victoria my queen. While Father disapproved of the relationship, Adele could not hide her ambition. She might not have liked the idea of me making love to her daughter but persuaded Father to allow the engagement to proceed because it would make Victoria a queen. She even argued that it would strengthen Edenvale's royal ties to have not one but two generations of our royal bloodlines matched. Their aristocratic family has always been one of the wealthiest and most influential in our kingdom. But they've always had a reputation for being ambitious.

Too ambitious for my liking.

Over the years, whenever I indulged in a whiskey too many and allowed my thoughts to wander, it had seemed conceivable that Adele might have masterminded the whole affair, put her only child in my path, advising her on how to best seduce her way into a lonely prince's heart. If Victoria had survived the accident, perhaps she'd have grown to be as calculating and bloodless as the woman sneering down her aristocratic nose at me. The question, though, will never be answered. My youngest brother, Damien, saw to that, ending her life with his usual recklessness, earning his banishment and my everlasting hatred.

"Well, do try to retain your good mood for Saturday evening," Adele says, dipping her spoon into the lobster bisque.

"What's Saturday?" I crook my finger, signaling the butler to bring me more wine. I am tempted to grab the whole damn bottle, get too drunk to dream. I don't want nightmares of Victoria disturbing my sleep tonight.

"Didn't Miss Winter tell you?" My stepmother's lifeless smile is stiff and doesn't reach her cruel eyes. "She has arranged your first date."

Kate

"No," I say, when I open my apartment door to find X standing there. "Absolutely not." Before I can close the door in the man's face—and I would feel horrid doing so, but this crosses the line—Maddie sidles up behind me.

"Who's your friend?" she asks, though I'm sure she can tell by his immaculate suit that he is not one who dwells on Market Street. I glance at my own attire, a freaking Fall Out Boy T-shirt and skinny jeans. I look like an American teenager.

"Maddie, this is X. He works for the royal family."

My sister pulls the door the rest of the way open. She, of course, is in a perfectly beautiful sundress, because *she* has a date. Which is fine because I was very much looking forward to Netflix, and ice cream, and not thinking about the strange events that have transpired this week. But no, the prince has to butt into my plans, my thoughts, my whatever—simply because he can.

X offers my sister a slight bow, and she backhands me on the shoulder.

"*This* is the prince's driver—the guy who picked you up the other morning? You didn't say he was a silver fox!" she whisper-shouts, but the man is standing right in front of us.

X's brows rise, the slightest hint of his amusement. "Miss Kate," he says. "His Highness says it is part of your professional obligation."

I roll my eyes.

"What obligation?" Maddie asks.

"Tell him *no*," I say to X, ignoring my sister.

He pulls a phone from the inside pocket of his suit jacket and glances at the screen.

"Miss Kate declines your invitation," he says, and my stomach drops. The prince has been listening to our entire interaction.

When I hear his voice, my body tingles in response, and I silently curse Nikolai Lorentz.

"Kate," he says. X points the phone toward me and my sister. "I'm going to be late for the date that *you* set up if you don't get down here in the next three minutes."

I huff out a breath and try to ignore my sister's wide eyes and mouth open in a surprised O.

"Your Highness—" I start, but he clears his throat, interrupting me.

"Nikolai," he corrects me, and I repress an exasperated scream.

"*Nikolai*. I think you are confused. This is *your* date. I set it up, but believe me when I say that both you and the Countess of Wynberry will be most put out by me joining you for dinner."

Maddie backhands me again, this time harder, but she still says nothing.

Nikolai's raucous laugh rings out from the phone in X's hand.

"You won't actually *join* us," he says. "You'll be in the car with X. Beatrice has prepared a veritable feast for you to dine on while you wait for my cue."

My fists clench at my sides, and I don't bother stifling my groan.

"You have some nerve," I say.

"I need a wingman."

"No."

"I need to be called to an urgent meeting, an out if things go south. Because if the countess doesn't go for my proposed arrangement, I promise things will go— southerly," he adds, his words laced with amusement.

"No," I maintain.

There is silence for a few long beats, and I hold my breath until he speaks again.

"If I behave *badly*," he says, slowly drawing out each word, "which I've been known to do, I could scare off a potential prospect. But if someone is there to give me a more respectable exit should I need one, well, then, we all win. Don't we?" He pauses to let his words sink in before he puts the final nail in the coffin that is my fate for this evening. "You don't want to chance me *not* making it to the altar. Do you, Kate?"

White-hot fury pulses through me. Does he know the king and queen will refuse my fee—no matter how tireless I work—if he does not marry? How dare he use such leverage against me? But because I cannot let Maddie carry our grandmother's financial burden alone, I say what I need to say to shut him up before he reveals too much.

"Fine," I relent through gritted teeth. "I'll be right down."

X sighs and ends the call as I spin into my apartment. My sister follows.

"You're accompanying *the prince* on his date. Oh. My. God, Katie. Why didn't I get this freaking job?"

I grab my bag from the foot of my bed and sling it over my shoulder. "Right now, Maddie, I wish you had."

I don't even bother looking in the mirror. I storm toward the door where X waits patiently.

"You're not even going to change?" my sister asks from behind me, and I shake my head, answering her over my shoulder.

"You heard the man. He's going to be late, and I sure as hell don't want to keep the prince and the countess waiting."

"Have fun!" she calls, unable to mask her own giddy excitement.

Not likely.

"You too!" I offer, sincerely hoping her night goes better than mine is about to.

"If you succeed then we will have clients pouring in."

I fake a smile. "Yay!" My enthusiasm rings false, but my sister doesn't notice. She is too good to speak the language of sarcasm.

Maddie deserves all the happiness and success. She built our little company from nothing, and when my life fell apart two years ago, she gave me a place to stay and a job to dive into so I wouldn't waste away in my grief.

This is why, despite his behavior, I head downstairs and out to the Rolls-Royce parked at the curb. I'm doing this for *her*. For years I've depended on my sister, and now more than ever she's depending on me. I won't mess this up. She deserves for her business to succeed, and that means lessening the burden of paying for Gran's mounting medical bills. Every day it seems a new one arrives. She tries to hide her worry from me, but I see the dark shadows under her eyes.

X opens the door for me, and I slide into the seat opposite Nikolai. I cross my arms and try to level him with my glare.

"You look—" he starts, but I cut him off.

"Don't, Nikolai. Just don't."

He raises his brows. "I was only going to say *beautiful*. You look beautiful, Kate."

Don't, I tell myself in silence. *Don't let his words have any effect on you.*

"X," he says when the man appears behind the wheel. When did he even get there? I swear he just shut my door. "Do you know what a Fall Out Boy is?"

I snort. "Tell me you're joking." Then I see it again, the ghost of a smile on X's face. We're silently sharing a joke at Nikolai's expense.

Nikolai shrugs. "I'm assuming it is some sort of popular rock band. The music I listen to does not come with a T-shirt."

I laugh again and thrust my phone through the open partition to X.

"It's my top playlist," I say. "Can you put it on?"

The man nods, and seconds later my phone is hooked up to the car's speaker system.

The tightness in my throat loosens as "Immortals"

wafts from the speakers, and I'm shocked once again when Nikolai's shoulders relax, and he cocks his head to the side and smiles.

"It's no Amadeus," he says, "but I quite like it. I suppose I'm learning I like a lot of new things these days, Miss Winter."

A chill runs along my spine, but I will it away.

Do not for one second think that he is charming. You know full well that Prince Charming he is not.

But as the anger subsides I see him clearly, his jet-black hair slicked back from his face, charcoal gray suit to match his eyes, and a royal blue tie for a pop of color. He looks so—*princely*. And gorgeous. And when his smile reaches his eyes, I have to push away the surge of emotion that rises to the surface because I've suddenly lost my grip on the anger.

I shake my head and remind myself why I'm here—to make sure this date goes smoothly. To ensure that Prince Nikolai Lorentz is one step closer to marriage—and becoming my king.

"Thank you for coming," he says softly, and I force a smile.

"Of course," I say, regaining my composure. "Nikolai?"

"Kate?"

"Have you read the entire contract between Happy Endings and your family?"

He laughs. "What's to read? You were hired to find me a wife. You're finding me a wife. I'm not interested in the fine print."

I let out a breath. So he doesn't know the consequences for me—for my family—if I fail. My anger ebbs completely as I realize Nikolai's behavior this evening is simply him being Nikolai.

"Well, then," I say. "Tell me what I need to do to make this date a success."

At this, X pulls away from the curb, and we set off for Nikolai to meet his first potential match.

CHAPTER EIGHT

Nikolai

I MUST GIVE credit to Kate's skillful matchmaker profiling. The Countess of Wynberry fits my usual physical type to a T. Platinum blond hair, come-hither bedroom eyes and ripe breasts that she proudly displays in a low-cut black silk dress offset by a necklace of glittering rubies. Hell, I don't know a guy who wouldn't describe the countess as his type. She could be a sister to that American actress Scarlett Johansson.

We meet in my private room at La Coeur, a three-star Michelin restaurant set in an eighteenth-century manor. The view of the Alps through the wide windows is unparalleled, and the gorgeous woman lounging across the table looks like she'd rather take a bite out of me than the raspberry-and-chocolate confection on her gilded plate. Yet I feel nothing but faint boredom.

Dinner went well enough. The filet was perfectly cooked and the cabernet an excellent vintage. She chattered on and on about her family's approval of our union and then of all the filthy things she planned on doing to me once we left the restaurant. I should have been hard just from her depraved words. Instead all I want is to be in my Rolls beside an auburn-haired woman in jeans who makes me feel like something I haven't felt in years.

Myself.

"You don't talk much, do you?" the countess purrs, taking her time licking her spoon clean. Her bare foot caresses my shin under the table, and I curse my unresponsive cock. The countess could douse the fire inside, the embers burning for a woman who arranged this date, but she'd fail at snuffing out the blaze.

"I do if I have something to say," I answer blandly. Her dessert does look delightful. Too bad I ordered nothing to eat for our final course, just a scotch neat. She needs to stop playing seductive games and enjoy it. But then, I've made my decision, which means she won't have time to finish, so perhaps it is for the best.

She looks curious, missing the warning in my voice. "And do you have something to say?" she asks.

Enough time wasting. "I do." I crumple my napkin on my lap and get down to business.

I say what I must in short, clipped sentences. Her eyes grow slowly wider until the whites are perfectly visible around her nearly violet irises.

Within a minute she throws a glass of champagne in my face. She has more restraint than I credited her with. I expected her to last thirty seconds max.

"You are as they say." She gathers her fur stole and rises in a huff. "A twisted monster of a man."

I blow her a kiss, and she squeals with outrage before storming for the exit.

Kate arrives in less than a minute, exactly as I expected, disheveled from sprinting to my table.

"What happened?" She gasps for air. "I thought I was here to help you to *not* cause a scene!"

I wave my hand in the air. "Trust me when I tell you that what just transpired was *not* a scene. You have read the tabloids, yes? I'm capable of so much worse. Don't you think?"

She must have run the whole way and not bothered using the restaurant's elevator. Her cheeks are flushed to a rosy red, and her chest rises and falls, heaving her breasts against the thin cotton of her T-shirt. The sight captivates me more than all the silk in Spain.

"The countess left in a rage," Kate continues. "She threatened to kick X in the parking lot if he didn't get out of her way. I'm pretty sure that counts as a scene."

I chuckle at the thought of anyone accosting X. I've seen him pin a paparazzo against a wall with one hand while dismantling his camera with the other, the action as simple as flossing his teeth. I have no idea who the hell X was before he came to the palace, but one thing is for certain: he's survived worse than the Countess of Wynberry.

"We weren't a good fit," I say lazily, sitting back in my chair. "And because no photographers are allowed inside—"

Kate lets out a breathy laugh. "Oh, there were photographers outside. I can attest to that." She shakes her head. "I have to admit my surprise… On paper you and the countess were a *perfect* match." Her tone is disappointed even as the relief is plain on her face. Strange how I am in tune to the subtleties of her emotion when we've barely been acquainted for the span of a week.

"She had a hard time hearing key truths," I say.

"Truths?" She crosses her arms and lowers her chin. A wayward auburn strand falls across her forehead. "Nikolai, what on earth did you tell that poor woman?"

Poor woman? Perhaps that was the perfect term for her. While the countess was rich in material wealth, she lacked human qualities like warmth, companionship and kindness, characteristics I can usually dismiss. But for some reason, tonight I cannot.

"Take a seat, Kate." I gesture to the chair opposite me. "I'll tell you exactly what I said *if* you allow me to feed you bite by bite."

Kate

I cross my arms. "I'm quite stuffed," I say, not daring to glance at the dessert on the table. Even out of the corner of my eye it looks heavenly. "Beatrice fed me well with yet another back-seat feast, and I will under no circumstances let you be seen in public feeding a palace employee." Never mind that we are in a private room.

He reaches over and takes a bite of the rich-looking confection, his tongue slowly stroking the spoon, and I swallow. Then I narrow my eyes at him.

"Oh, fine," he says. "Have it your way. I simply told her what we both already know, that whoever my bride will be, it will be nothing more than a business arrangement. There will be no physical obligation other than her providing me with my own heir—however long that may take. And I will be free to satisfy my needs with whomever suits my fancy. Oh, I may have also mentioned that she will under no circumstances have any say in how I rule this country."

I throw my hand over my mouth, but it doesn't stifle my gasp. "Nikolai!" I shout, not caring that his private room is not exactly soundproof.

He shrugs. "Oh, come now," he says. "I explained she'd want for nothing—that she'd be free to dally with anyone she pleased, so long as she was discreet."

I clench my teeth. "I know you don't plan on taking your marriage seriously, but no woman deserves to be spoken to like that. You could have been more—more *delicate*, and you know it. But you care nothing for anyone other than yourself, so you did it the Nikolai way. I should have known this job would be impossible. That *you'd* be impossible. You didn't want me here to help. Did you? You wanted me here so I'd have a front-row seat to the Nikolai Lorentz show."

My cheeks burn as I bunch my fists at my sides. One minute I'm taken aback by how beautiful he is—how he can level me with his gaze. The next I am reminded all too clearly of who he is. He is my prince—and soon, my king. He has the power to behave as he does, and I am nothing more than a subject.

I push back my chair. "I'll call for a taxi," I say, trying to keep my voice even. Anger will get me nowhere. It won't get the countess the respect he should have paid her, and it certainly won't earn any for me. He owes me nothing.

He lets me get as far as the door before he speaks.

"Kate," he says, all pretense gone from his voice. "Wait." Then I hear him let out a breath. *"Please."*

I turn to face him, and he's standing, too. But I don't dare move any closer. Even across the table he feels too near now. Because if there's one word I never expected to hear directed at me from him, it is that last one. *Please*.

"What?" I ask, the fight draining from me as he holds me with his steely, intent stare.

He runs a hand through his perfectly styled hair, loosening it so he looks more as he did on the bridge— or after he'd dived into the river to save me.

"You're right," he says. "About most of it, but you're missing one important detail."

I cross my arms and raise my brows but say nothing.

"Of course I didn't need any help," he says, palms resting on his chair. "I care nothing for my reputation. I leave that to my father, my stepmother, to all those paid to give a fuck. I suppose I'll have to clean up my act a bit once I'm king, though."

He flashes that irresistible grin, but I don't let myself fall prey to it, not this time.

"I know you don't care what others think of you," I say. "But you put my reputation on the line tonight, too, Your Highness." He winces, and the sight is something so wholly unexpected, my heart tugs involuntarily. "You may have nothing to lose, but I do. My *sister* does. Her business supports our family. We have responsibilities. This whole marriage thing that you see as a joke is how we put a roof over our heads. It's how we—"

He steps around from the chair and nearer to where I stand, the movement stealing the words from my mouth. I suck in a breath as he takes a step closer and then hold it as he rests a palm on my cheek.

"I'm an ass," he says, and I nod. "One royal prick,"

he adds, and I don't disagree. "Perhaps I could have been more civil to the countess. But where I truly fucked up was that I wasn't thinking of how this would affect *you*."

I clear my throat. "Wh-what important detail?" I stammer. His brows pull together. "Before, you said I was missing one important detail." I can smell the sweet scotch in the warmth of his breath. I bite my lip to keep from reacting.

He rests his forehead against mine, the gesture far too intimate, and my breath hitches.

"I asked you to come tonight, Kate, because in the span of six days, I seem to have gone from wanting nothing to do with you and what you've been hired for to not wanting you out of my sight."

He braces a palm against the door behind me, and I take a step back so I'm flush against it.

"Nikolai," I whisper. "We can't." My insistence is different than the other day at the bridge. I could take his teasing—could even pretend that we might continue our encounters and leave it at just sex. But now? What he is suggesting now is beyond possibility.

"What if there was a way?" he asks, his lips dangerously close to my own. "What if I could make you truly mine?"

My throat tightens at the thought. "But I was hired to—"

"I know," he says. "And I will continue to see the women with whom you match me. I will even be civil. But I make you this promise. I'll marry none of them."

As much as the idea of him touching another woman, let alone marrying one, already hurts in a way it should not be able to, I need him to do it because my family depends on it. *Irony, you're a cruel bitch.*

"When do you need to be married by?" I'm playing with him because I already know. Maybe if I smile the pain will ebb. One can always hope.

"My twenty-ninth birthday."

"Which is..." As if the heir's birthday isn't a national holiday.

His lids narrow as he tries to figure out what game I'm playing. "Ninety days from now."

I close my eyes and take in a long breath. Then I press my palm to his chest. "I'll make you a wager."

He laughs softly. "Go on."

"I'll see you married by your birthday," I say, my fingers already itching to grab at his tie.

He surprises me with a soft kiss before he answers. "I look forward to disappointing you."

I grip his tie and pull him as close as he can get. "And what's more, I promise you will be happy with the woman." After all, I know exactly what His Highness likes. Who better to find him not just a queen but happiness as well?

I swallow the pang of regret, the one that has me wishing for what cannot be. I do not want for him a life of misery, but I cannot let my own family fall into ruin. I will succeed. For both of us.

"You'd have to be one hell of a matchmaker, sweetheart," he says.

"Trust me." I fight to keep the tremor from my voice. "I'm the best."

CHAPTER NINE

Nikolai

IT ISN'T UNTIL nightfall that I realize that Kate never laid out the terms for our wager. I sit at my baby grand piano, my fingers flying over the keys, weaving a complex, sensual sound. Don't believe classical music can be sexy? Listen to Wagner's *Tristan and Isolde* before dismissing me. Harmony and dissonance. Brutal discord only to be thwarted by soaring passion. Music pours through me as I toy over the many ways I can extract payment from the lovely Miss Winter. Such an interesting paradox that her hair holds hints of flame even as her name promises coldness. She is both fire and ice.

I picture her lips sheathing my cock, taking me down to the root on the banks of the river. There had been a promise in her eyes, a promise that she'd be mine, if I reached out and made a claim. And so I will—at least physically, but the pleasure of the flesh is as much as I can offer. And pleasure I shall give her.

If only she had royal blood…then…perhaps she could make me overcome my vow.

"Who is the lucky lady?" a deep voice says behind me, and I strike a wrong key.

Damn it.

I turn around, ready to bite the head off whoever dares to venture into my inner sanctum, and find my brother Benedict regarding me with an arched brow.

We look so much alike save for the eye color and the goodness that emanates from him just as something wicked brews inside me. I am darkness and shadow. He is golden light. I hear the whispers. I know those that think him a bastard—Benedict himself included. I pay those words little heed. Full brother or half, he is my best and only true friend.

"Welcome home, Bastard," I say. It's a joke between us. We wear our vulnerabilities like armor. It's the way we survive as the lords of the land, all eyes on us.

"That was Wagner, no?" He cocks his head. "You only play that when a woman has you tied in knots."

His memory is keen.

"Dear brother, don't you know? If there is a woman and knots to consider, I am the one doing the tying. Apologies if I offend your holy sensibilities." I eye Benedict's simple clerical garb. My brother is a seminarian, a year away from taking his holy vows and entering the priesthood, much to the eternal pride of our father. When the idea of his virginity is not causing me nightmares, the idea is amusing in the extreme. Benedict is one of the most sought-after men in Europe, and he chooses to marry the church.

I hope God keeps his bed warm.

"What good is the spare to my heir if he is celibate?" Father likes to roar after a drink too many. While he speaks in jest, there is a glimmer of truth.

Benedict takes it all in stride. All he wants to do is

please the king—to prove himself worthy of his lineage no matter what the rumors say. When Benedict declared his life belonged to the church, Father was the first to commend him.

How many times have I wondered if a woman could ever tempt him from his path? But he assures me that his destiny is fixed. That the pleasures of the flesh pale in comparison to the rhapsody of the soul.

I have to say, burying my face between Kate's thighs takes me to the gates of heaven. Imagine what burying my cock in her would do.

"I came to bid you good-night and let you know that I'll be taking up residence in the south tower for the foreseeable future."

Benedict long ago laid a claim to the ancient keep on the far northern border of the palace grounds. He prefers its austere environment for prayer and solitude.

"What happened to the Vatican?" I ask him. "Thought you were off to Italy for good."

He laughs softly. "The Vatican City is its own country," he reminds me. "As you should have learned when studying geography."

"Ah, didn't Mrs. Everdeen tutor us on that subject?"

He inclines his head.

"Well, I was too busy studying Mrs. Everdeen in other ways." I smirk. "She had this trick she could do with her tongue that—"

"You are incorrigible, brother," Benedict says. "And yet it is bloody good to see you."

I cross the room and enfold him in a warm bear hug, slapping him on the back. "You too."

"I hear you are to be wed. Is it your bride who has you playing Wagner?"

I shake my head. "The matchmaker." The words are out before I can stop them.

Damn Benedict. His kind eyes make a sinner like me yearn to confess.

He nods thoughtfully. "Sounds like a dilemma."

A flicker of hope lights in me. "You're the scholar in the family."

"Between you and Damien, it wasn't hard to do."

Benedict is also the only one not afraid to acknowledge our younger brother's existence in my presence.

I ignore it this once. "If there's a loophole to the Royal Marriage Decree, a way for me to make my own damned decisions without losing the kingdom, I need you to find it. I am determined not to wed. You know this."

He appears thoughtful. "Such an action will displease our father."

"Yes." And by extension, that will displease my too-good brother. "And Adele," I add. My lips curl into a grin as I know this point will make Benedict my ally.

He brightens at that thought. He and Adele have no love lost. That witch is the only person to ever make my saintly brother lose his temper.

"Very well," he says, a muscle twitching in his jaw at the mention of our stepmother. "I'll look into it."

"You are truly a glorious human. You'll be canonized yet."

He grins at that, but his normally clear green eyes remain dark.

"What's the reason you are back, brother?" My light

tone doesn't mask the hint of probing seriousness. "You haven't said."

His lips tilt in a smile that only I ever get to see, one that isn't all that angelic. "It appears the Lord's wish is to help prevent your sacrament of marriage." He clicks his heels and disappears out the door.

It takes me a moment to realize that he hasn't answered my question at all.

Kate

What the hell was I thinking, placing a wager against someone as strong-willed as Nikolai Lorentz? If there's anything a man like him thrives on, it's the game, and I've just upped the stakes of the one he'd been playing long before I came into the picture—thinking I will get him to play by his own kingdom's rules.

I pace the length of the conference room, the same one where I first met the prince two weeks ago, and the same one where, afterward, the king and queen called me to a private meeting without their son.

Shit.

The door opens, and I freeze midpace only to find Beatrice and another member of the kitchen staff with a silver cart laden with pastries, finger sandwiches and a sterling teapot. Each woman offers me a quick nod as they begin depositing the refreshments on the table.

"Will there be more than the king and queen joining me in here?" I ask nervously, and Beatrice shakes her head.

"No, Miss. These are Queen Adele's favorites. The king orders Her Majesty's most requested finger foods when she's in—" The other woman flashes Beatrice a look, but Beatrice waves her off and crosses over to where I stand. "It's really not my place, Miss, but I think you should know today is the anniversary of Miss Victoria's passing."

I swallow, and my eyes widen. I am to meet with the queen on the anniversary of her daughter's death—the daughter who was betrothed to Nikolai.

The date hadn't registered with me. Of course I knew of Nikolai and Victoria's relationship. The entire continent did. But it had been years since the car crash. It wasn't the type of thing that made news anymore. Nikolai saw to that—*sees* to that every moment he finds himself in the spotlight. Unless the king has any diplomatic dealings that call for broadcast coverage, Nikolai is the family's media darling.

Why, then? Why have my sovereign rulers called me here today, of all days, for a mere check-in on my list of possible brides for the prince?

A throat clears, and Beatrice and I both look up to see the other kitchen servant nodding toward the entrance of the room where Queen Adele stands in the double doorway, flanked by two guards.

She wears an exquisite black dress, long sleeved with a square neckline, the bodice hugging her womanly curves. I can see why King Nikolai was taken with her so soon after Queen Cordelia's death. The woman is a sight to behold, her golden hair in perfect pin curls framing her face, a ruby-studded tiara atop her head. She is elegance and grace, but there is ice in her emerald stare, and I can't help the shiver that makes my hair stand on end.

"That will be all, everyone," she says, and the two guards, along with Beatrice and her assistant, leave the room, pulling the doors closed behind them.

I bow my head and curtsy as she walks toward the head of the table, and I wait for her to sit. I'm not sure where to seat myself, so like an idiot I ask, "May I pour you some tea, Your Highness?"

"Do sit, Miss Winter," she says, her voice laced with amusement when I expect to hear the remnants of grief. Surely she's come from visiting her daughter's grave. Or perhaps she will be on her way after our meeting.

Our meeting. It's only when I take a seat at the opposite end of the table that I realize the king is nowhere to be seen.

"Will His Highness, King Nikolai, be joining us soon?"

She laughs softly. "The king is away on matters of state business," she says. "It's just the two of us, I'm afraid." She places her palms flat atop the mahogany table. "Don't worry, Miss Winter. I shall be brief."

I nod as the breath catches in my throat. Something about the queen—being in her presence alone—has all my senses on high alert.

"I know how important this job is to you," she drawls, her tone like an animal toying with its prey.

"Yes, Your Highness. It is," I say.

She steeples her fingers before her and grins, the smile not quite reaching her deep green eyes.

"And that you and your sister stand to gain a great deal of fortune if all goes according to plan."

Double my fee *is* a generous offer. "Yes, Your Highness."

She leans forward, and though the length of the table separates us, I flinch at the movement.

"And if you do *not* succeed, your business will be in ruins."

I gasp. To lose the fee promised me would be a devastating blow, but Madeline and I would still be able to come back from it. We'd still—

"Stop trying to rationalize whatever it is you think you're going to say to me, Miss Winter. I'm not in the habit of ruining others—as long as we are on the same side. And I think we both want the same thing, don't we? To see my stepson walk down that aisle and the throne stay in the...immediate family?"

"Yes, of course," I say. I hold her gaze, determined not to flinch again.

Her posture relaxes, but only slightly. "Good. Then all you have to do is keep up business as usual. Seek out all the lovely, appropriate, *deserving* women. Build up Nikolai's image like his father hopes you will."

My teeth grind together in my mouth. Something is off here, but so far she's not asking anything other than what I'm already doing.

"May I ask you a question, Your Highness?"

Her brows rise. She is considering my boldness, no doubt, but then she nods her head.

"Forgive me if I'm being untoward. But are you trying to see to it that I fail or succeed? Because I can't for the life of me figure out why you called this meeting."

This time her eyes light up as her lips curl. "You *will* succeed, Miss Winter."

"How do you know?" I add, deciding to go for broke

in my impropriety of speaking my uncensored thoughts in front of my leader.

"Because," she says, standing from her chair. I stand as well. "*I'm* going to find the woman most deserving of a life with my stepson, and we will present her to him when the time is right."

"But my list—"

She shakes her head, closing her eyes as she does. When she looks at me again, I see something so cold in that stare that I shudder. "My match won't be on any such list, but when I've found the one, you'll know. All you have to do is convince Nikolai she's the one, as well." She narrows her eyes at me. "That boy trusts you already. I've seen the way he looks at you. All you have to do is maintain that trust—keep him occupied while I set everything in place. You'll get your doubled fee and maybe even an additional bonus. I get what's rightfully mine and Nikolai gets what he deserves."

"Rightfully yours?" I ask, unable to stop the question even though I know I should not speak out of turn with her.

But the queen doesn't bother to respond.

She plucks a cucumber finger sandwich from the top of a tiered plate and pops it in her mouth, smirking as she devours it. Then she saunters out of the room, not waiting for me to say another word.

Double my fee. A bonus. Or a ruined business if we're not playing for the same side.

Maybe Nikolai does play his games, but he no longer makes the rules.

I wonder now if he ever did.

CHAPTER TEN

Nikolai

I WAKE TO harsh late-morning light striking my sleep-dry eyes. Crimson silk sheets tangle at the base of my four-poster ebony wood bed.

I'm buck naked.

No big surprise there. I never sleep with clothes. This rock-hard morning wood isn't unusual, either. The only strange part to this scenario is that I'm not reaching for my phone. No mad urge within me craves a speed dial to any of my usual female liaisons. There is no shortage of nubile women eager to serve as my royal lover for the morning. But I have made a great effort to ensure that my personal speed dial is discreet and only includes women interested in keeping things horizontal. Commitment types get deleted.

But today is different.

I close my fist around my shaft, circling the tip with my thumb. It's already slick with a bead of pre-cum. Must have been having one hell of a dream. A flash of it glimmers in the back of my mind, Kate's auburn waves spilling over her shoulders, her milk-white breasts rising and falling with her gasps as I bury myself inside her.

I bite on the inside of my cheek. Even the fleeting memory of the tantalizing dream is enough to make me moan out loud.

As if sensing my need, my phone buzzes. But it's no perfectly timed offer from a casual lover. I stare at the name on the screen as all the extra blood in my brain rushes off to pool in my cock.

Kate Winter: Morning, Sunshine. Ready when you are!

I give myself a few more hard pumps, remember how Kate's tangy sweet pussy tastes, and my hips buck off the mattress. "Oh, I'm ready, Pet."

The phone buzzes again. I'm with X.

X. The mention of my personal guard almost throws me off my game. He is like another brother. We even shared women in depraved threesomes, once upon a time when I was younger and even wilder than I am now. But that doesn't mean I want to share Kate. A muffled growl rises in my throat. I don't want to share her with anyone else in the world.

Strange. Normally I'm a love-the-one-you're-with kind of guy. After I'm with a woman, it's out of sight and out of mind. But with Kate it's different. There is an unfamiliar pull inside me to know more than her body, but I have no idea what to do with this—feeling.

The notion leaves me unsettled. I remove my hand from my dick and text her back.

Nikolai: Still in bed.

Kate: What!?!?!?!? Are you coming?

Nikolai: Not without you...

Kate: Excuse me?

Nikolai: A real man never comes first, Pet.

Kate: OMG

Nikolai: ;)

Kate: You did not just winky face me.

Nikolai: What are you going to do about it? ;)

Kate: I've just eaten my weight in Beatrice's white chocolate scones waiting for you or I'd march up there and drag you down myself.

Nikolai: I have a king-size bed. Perfect place to sleep off a food coma.

Kate: I have an heiress to a screw company waiting at the airfield.

Nikolai: ?

Kate: Your next date is Regina Bjorn. Her father is Vlad Bjorn, owner of Big Bjorn Screws, one of Edenvale's largest exports. We are meeting her at the royal hangar at noon. You're flying her in your personal helicopter.

Nikolai: I'm so screwed.

Kate: ;)

I swing my bare feet to the cold floorboards, my grin from our banter quickly morphing into a sneer. I know Vlad Bjorn. He is titled with a minor barony and is a large man with blotchy skin. He calls himself the Big Screw, but in my opinion he resembles a stick of bologna. I know he has twelve daughters but can't picture any of their faces at the moment. That fact alone leaves me numb. I don't want to fly this Regina anywhere, not when I could be flirting with my feisty matchmaker, who can't learn that my brother Benedict is looking for a loophole to break the Royal Marriage Decree. Until then I must play my hand well by making nice with the dates Kate sets up for me. Not to raise so much as an eyebrow of suspicion.

Lucky for me, I am a most excellent actor.

Kate

My eyes widen as I stare out the window toward the airfield. I knew the palace grounds were substantial, but each time I see something new, it still catches me off guard. My world is so small compared to his.

"Impressed?" Nikolai whispers in my ear, his warm breath sending tingles all the way to my toes.

I nod. "This *car* would barely fit in my apartment. The concept of an airfield is a lot to take in."

"You never listed your terms," he says softly, his voice like velvet, and I know exactly what he means.

I turn to face him, and he barely backs away. My heart races as my eyes meet his.

"Well," I say, keeping my voice steady. "I know money—or anything of material value—is of no consequence to you, which I guess bodes well for me since I have nothing of material value to offer."

"Kate—" he starts, but I shake my head. I don't want him to apologize for his wealth, nor will I apologize for my lack thereof.

"Nikolai. We come from different worlds, and that's okay." His eyes darken at this, and I wish I had the time to ask him what he's thinking, but the car slows, and I know we're approaching the hangar. "And because I'm going to win," I tease, trying to lighten whatever heaviness has taken over his features, "I'll keep it simple."

"Simple?" he asks, raising a brow, painting on that prince of a smile, one I know he is readying for the heiress.

"A favor," I say simply. "If I win—which I plan to do—you do me one favor. If *you* win—which is highly unlikely—then you get to ask a favor of me."

"Are there limits?" he asks. "To what we can ask?"

I shake my head. "No limits on my end. If you are not wed by your birthday, you can ask me for anything you want. Do *you* have any limits?"

"None," he says quickly, his voice suddenly rough. "Ask me anything right now, Kate. Tell me what you'd want from me."

But the car halts, effectively ending our conversation.

"Time for you to fly to Zurich," I say, forcing a smile.

"It's just lunch," he says. "You and X should—"

"I am *not* tagging along on any more dates. If you want to bring X, fine. I'm only here to make sure you aren't late and to remind you to be a gentleman."

He winks at me. "Darling, have you forgotten who I am? I'll do nothing of the sort."

"Nikolai..."

He kisses me on the cheek, effectively shutting me up.

"No worries, Pet. I'll be on my best behavior."

I groan. "That's what I'm afraid of."

Nikolai's door opens, and X stands ready to usher him out of the vehicle and to the hangar.

"I'll be back by dusk," he says on his way out. "And I'd like you here when I arrive."

He doesn't wait for me to protest but assumes I'll obey his every whim.

What if I had plans tonight? I want to ask—even though I don't. As much as it warms me from within that he wants to see me this evening, I can't help but feel like the afterthought that I am and can only ever be.

X joins me in the car, and I watch as Nikolai strides toward Regina Bjorn, a regal, platinum-haired beauty who stands in front of a BMW with windows tinted so black I'm not even sure you can see through them at all.

Zurich was my idea, to have him take her to her mother's homeland, a place I learned she hadn't visited since childhood but had always missed. He'd score points in the thoughtfulness department before they'd even left the helipad, which I glance at in front of the hangar. Nikolai holds her hand as she climbs into the helicopter. Her azure scarf billows in the breeze, floating against Nikolai's crisp white oxford—a picture-perfect couple.

My breath hitches.

I knock on the window in front of me, and X lowers the glass.

"Shall I take you home, Miss?"

The confines of the apartment that doubles as the home office for Happy Endings do not comfort me, especially if it means the third degree from Maddie. If I don't want to think about Nikolai on his date, I certainly don't want to *talk* about Nikolai on his date. So I decide to do something I rarely do—something for *me*.

"X," I say, my mood brightening. "We're going to the cinema."

"Miss, there is a private theater in the palace—"

"Absolutely not. No palace. No royal treatment. Just you and me and that car-chase-with-tons-of-explosions action film that premiered last weekend."

"But, Miss—the palace theater has that film or any other—"

I lean through the open partition. "No. Royal. Treatment."

He clears his throat and starts the engine. "As you wish, Miss Kate."

He backs away from the hangar as the propeller blades begin to spin. And when the helicopter lifts off the ground, I allow myself a few seconds to marvel that the strong hands controlling that beast of a machine have touched me in ways no other man has.

Then I sink into my seat.

"Thank you, X." I hand him my phone. "And maybe my Fall Out Boy playlist while we drive. Crank up the volume so I can't hear myself think." Drowning out my thoughts seems preferable to drowning *in* them. I reach for a bottle and glass from the minibar across from my seat. "And—and I'm going to have some of the prince's cognac even though it's before noon."

"As you wish, Miss."

Seconds later the music blares.

X's eyes remain on the road as we approach the palace gates, but I swear I see a devilish grin take over his stoic countenance. Yet as quickly as it appears, it is gone.

I pour myself a drink and then take a long sip. After a few seconds I tip my head back and laugh.

"No royal treatment," I say with a snort. "I'm in a Rolls-Royce with a private driver and a bottle of cognac. And I have to return at dusk to meet up with the prince." I snort again, but damn it, the laughter feels good.

No royal treatment indeed.

CHAPTER ELEVEN

Nikolai

THE MOUNTAINS EN ROUTE to Zurich are as sculpted as Regina Bjorn's high cheekbones, and yet the experience feels empty. Emotionally at least. Regina has done a damn good job of filling the airspace, making it clear that she knows a thing or two about screwing.

"It is, after all, the family business," she chatters into the microphone with a giggle. We both wear helmets with headsets.

"Nothing about that innuendo is remotely appealing," I mutter and grip the cyclical stick that gives me control of the aircraft.

My surly comment flies straight over her head. As does anything else I say for the rest of our time together—unless it's an attempt to feign interest in her father's company.

Screws.

By the time we return to the Royal Airfield, landing with the setting sun, I'm convinced that I've endured paper cuts more enjoyable than Regina Bjorn.

Kate paired me with this woman through her matchmaking service? What does this say about me and the persona that I have cultivated with such care? Has the shallow, arrogant, vain Prince Nikolai finally become Mr. Hyde, overriding the respectable Dr. Jekyll? Is the facade I've so long shown the world really the man I want to be? I've nearly convinced myself the mask is real. But when Kate looks at me, it's as if she can see someone else. The person that I might have been if life hadn't kicked me in the teeth with a stiletto then had my youngest brother drive it off a cliff.

The thought unsettles me, and I push it from my mind as we exit the helicopter. I escort Regina back to her driver. She still talks of—what else?—screws. In the last hours I've endured lectures about cap screws, machine screws, tag screws, setscrews and—I shit you not—self-tapping screws.

A few weeks ago I would have been able to turn the day's conversation into an activity that required no words at all—unless it was Regina purring my bloody name. Now I hope those self-tapping wonders are Regina's favorite because I don't know anyone who could stay awake through one of her conversations long enough to get it up.

When I wish her good-night, I am not entirely convinced she notices.

The Rolls is parked in my usual spot. As I stride closer, eager to put distance between myself and the Heiress of Screws, I am surprised to hear music playing. It's an American classic, "Sweet Caroline." More to the point, the two people in the car are belting out the words—and X can apparently more than hold a tune. This man… I shake my head. He's full of surprises. Not only is he an expert tattoo artist responsible for all the tribal ink on my body, he's also a ninth-degree Grand Master black belt in Tae Kwon Do, and my on-again, off-again threesome wingman. Now he can harmonize better than Neil Diamond?

Sneaky fuck.

Who the hell *is* X? So often I've asked myself this, but it is to no avail. X has been my bodyguard since I reached maturity. I barely remember life without him. And yet I know nothing of him when he's not in my immediate presence, while he knows all there is of me.

I guess he can add charismatic crooner to his résumé.

I open the door, and he and Kate both clam up, staring at me.

"I didn't know you were back yet," she says, clutching what appears to be a giant bucket of popcorn.

"You didn't hear the chopper blades?" I inquire, lifting an eyebrow. I fly a Eurocopter Mercedes-Benz, the most pimped-out helicopter in the world, able to get high and fly fast. For one not to notice such an aircraft, well—what the hell could pry her interest from awaiting my arrival?

I scowl to myself. Perhaps I *am* the pompous persona I've cultivated.

"Sorry. It's the Golden Oldies Hour on Royal Radio. Our favorite," she said.

"Our?" My eyebrow goes higher.

"Sir." X is matter-of-fact and unapologetic as he starts the engine. "Would you like to take a seat?"

"I'd like to know who you are and what you've done with my bodyguard," I shoot back as an unexpected wave of possessive jealousy rolls between my clenched shoulder blades.

"Was your outing with Miss Bjorn satisfactory?" Kate asks, popping a piece of popcorn into her mouth with wide eyes.

"No. And where the hell did you get that?"

She pops another kernel into her mouth. "We went to the movies. They were showing the live action *Beauty and the Beast* at the discount theater and X had never seen it."

"An oversight he must be happy to have rectified," I snap.

Kate shrugs. "I was prepared to share with him my love of all things fast and furious, but the Disney classic won out. Apparently X is impressed by royalty. Me, not so much." She bites back a grin, and all I can do is bite back my own rage.

X's eyes shoot to mine in the rearview, and I glare out the window. Stupid to be jealous of my bodyguard. But the entire day I suffered with Regina *Bore*, he was with Kate. Enjoying himself. Enjoying *her*. I've shared women with X in the past, but this is one time that I don't want to. I don't want to share her with *anyone*. The idea of her with another man, even if I'm there as well, makes my stomach turn over as my fingers curl into themselves.

I stare back at her as white-hot possession shoots through me.

Mine.

The word is powerful and pure. My blood pounds with the echo. *Mine. Mine. Mine.*

This is the truth. And it's time she knows it.

"X, to the palace."

"I need to get back to the office," Kate protests. "If your second date was another bust, then I need to review lucky number three and figure out a game plan."

"I want to use the back entrance," I continue as if she hasn't spoken. A vague headache pounds in my temples. I want to drop the pretense for two seconds. I will never marry. I'm not made for the institution, and Kate is wasting her time.

That shouldn't be my problem, but I don't want her to leave. At least not yet. I want to enjoy the pleasure of her company a little while longer.

"Sir?" X asks, and I know what he really means. "Are you sure about this?"

No woman has ever accompanied me back to the palace, to my private quarters. Not until now.

I nod my head. "And make it fast."

Kate

"Where are the king and queen this fine evening?" Nikolai asks X as we pull to a side of the palace I haven't seen before.

"In Paris until tomorrow for the queen's—" he coughs "—rejuvenation treatments."

Nikolai grins at me. "Do you need to let your sister know you won't be coming home this evening?"

I cross my arms and narrow my eyes. "I don't have a curfew, *Your Highness*. But I do have work to do if we are going to make the perfect match, so I really should—"

"Stay," he says, the grin fading, those gray eyes

dark with something too intense to deny. Because I feel it too—have felt it since he left for Zurich despite the comfort of X's presence and our day of distraction.

I won't ask him why. Or what this means. I won't let logic override the ache in my belly. I can do this and not endanger the business. I force myself to believe it because the word is already forming on my lips.

"Okay," I answer.

Nikolai's door opens, and X stands at the ready. The man is the epitome of stealth. I didn't even realize he'd exited the vehicle.

Nikolai turns toward the opened door. "Miss Winter will be staying this evening, X."

X nods. "A moment alone with your guest, please, Your Highness. I shall then escort her to your quarters."

Nikolai laughs quietly. "A bit bold today, aren't we, X?"

X nods but doesn't crack a smile. "When it's called for, Your Highness."

Nikolai faces me again, gently grabbing my palm and bringing it to his lips. "See you soon," he whispers, and then he's gone.

Moments later my door opens, and X offers a hand to help me out of the vehicle.

"Let me guess," I say, as he leads me through a small door and into a dimly lit stairwell. "You want to finish our Neil Diamond duet."

No smile or any indication that only several minutes ago the two of us could have turned every chair on *The Voice*. Instead he simply holds out an arm for me to grab as we begin to ascend the steep stairs.

"The prince," he says, "is very private."

I snort.

"What the world sees in the media is what he wants them to see, Miss. And while I am not at liberty to divulge his past, I can say as much as this. Save for Victoria, the queen's late daughter, no woman has ascended these stairs. Not before—and not since."

There is no time for me to respond as we reach a small landing at the top, a tall oak door—partially ajar—before us. He nods for me to enter, and I do. I hear the door click shut behind me and turn to see X standing with his back to it, the faintest hint of a smile on his face. Then, as quick as a blink, he steps to his left, where soft curtains billow beside an open window—and he leaps through it like we aren't on the third story of a palace.

I yelp.

Nikolai rounds the corner, a bottle of Moët in one hand, two crystal flutes in the other.

"Let me guess," he says. "X took the window."

My hand covers my mouth as I nod, imagining my silver-fox companion splattered against the brick pavers below.

Nikolai laughs and shakes his head. "He often prefers scaling the brick to the stairs. Sometimes I wonder who X was before he came here, but I've learned to not question the man's abilities and thank the stars we're on the same team." He moves closer, his feet bare beneath the dark denim of his jeans and his now-wrinkled oxford unbuttoned. "He's fine. I promise."

"I'm not looking out that window," I say, goose bumps raising the hairs on my bare arms. The sundress was perfect for the day, but now that the sun has set, I shiver in the open-air breeze. "I'll take your word for it."

Nikolai nods toward the direction from which he came.

"You're cold," he says. "Come. Let me warm you up."

I follow him around a corner and note a small galley kitchen with dark marble counters, a sturdy wooden table—round—with four high-backed chairs beyond the breakfast bar. I don't have time to take in the modest living space other than a baby grand piano against a floor-to-ceiling window beyond a leather couch. The next thing I know, I'm walking through another door and into my prince's bedroom.

He sets the bottle and flutes on a night table and turns back to me. His strong hands run the length of my arms, warming me from the outside in. I let out a breath.

"Why am I here, Nikolai?" I can't hold out any longer, my curiosity getting the best of me. My chest tightens at the thought of his answer.

He kisses my neck, and my head falls back. A small sigh escapes my lips.

"I don't want to share you," he says against my skin, his lips making their way up to my jaw, then my cheek.

"But I haven't been—" I stop myself before telling him that I have not been with any other man since he first laid his hands on me—that for two years before that there hadn't been anyone, either.

His mouth finds mine, and my lips part, inviting him in—craving the taste of him like I didn't know I could.

"I don't like that X got to see a side of you today that I've never seen."

The sentence comes out almost as a growl, and my breath hitches.

"It was a movie," I whisper. "Not a helicopter ride to another country for an intimate lunch." I don't regret the words—or laying my jealousy out before him, not when he is blatantly doing the same. I want him, more than I've been able to admit, and right now I'm ready to give him all of me in return.

He backs toward the four-poster ebony bed, red silk sheets pulled back to reveal the space where his body last lay. I grin against his lips.

"What?" he asks, feeling the change in my expression.

"No one comes in to clean? To make your bed, Your Highness?"

He sits on the edge of the mattress, pulling me close so I straddle his lap.

"No one enters other than those closest to me," he says, his eyes dark with need. "And I want you closest, Kate. Tonight I want you more than anyone else."

I answer him by unbuttoning his shirt the rest of the way and sliding it down his arms. He closes his eyes and breathes in deep as my fingers trace the lines of ink on his shoulder, as they circle the tattoo of a compass that rests above his heart.

"It's beautiful," I say, a slight tremor in my voice. "*You're* beautiful, Nikolai."

He opens his eyes and wordlessly lifts my dress over my head so I'm left in nothing but my white lace panties.

"You're exquisite," he says. Then he takes one of my breasts into his mouth. I arch against him. "Finer than any woman who bears a title." His tongue swirls around the peaked nipple of my other breast, and I gasp. "Open your eyes and look at me," he says, and I obey. "No matter what I do, you *see* me."

I cradle his beautiful face in my palms. "I do."

"And you *want* me," he says.

I nod.

"*Only* me."

I nod again, taking each of his palms in mine and pressing them to my breasts. "Only you."

"I'll win our wager," he says with a grin. "I will not walk down the aisle."

"You *will* marry," I remind him and swallow back the reality of what that means.

"Not tonight, though." He falls onto the bed, pulling me over him.

"No," I say. "Not tonight."

CHAPTER TWELVE

Nikolai

FOR HOW LONG has my soul been trapped in a vise of loneliness? For years I have passed through countless nights as restless and insatiable as a vampire. Instead of feeding on mortal blood, I devoured what distraction and comfort was available in the form of sexual release—the more depraved, the better.

I take and take and take with a relentlessness matched only by my many lovers who are eager to use me in turn for the proximity to limitless power and wealth.

But tonight? All I want is to give. Kate Winter shall experience nothing less than absolute, exquisite pleasure.

She is stretched above me. My hands roam the soft swells of her body, the dip of her small hourglass waist. Her loose curls tumble over my face, forming a curtain of fire. Again I am stricken by the paradox—Miss Winter, whose hair burns brighter than the sun, whose undeniable beauty burns my heart.

"Are you sure this is a good idea?" she whispers,

and as her lips part, I catch a glimpse of her teeth, her tongue. Oh yes, that pink clever tongue, which swirled around my cock until I nearly forgot my birthright. And that was in a hurried riverside tryst. Tonight the hours spread before us, and I intend to put each one to good use.

"A good idea?" I give my head a single shake. "No, Pet. It is *the best* idea."

A hitched breath escapes her perfect lips as I cradle her face in my hands. My mouth finds hers, and our groans collide. I place my palms over her breasts again, and her heart careens against my hand. My thumbs circle her nipples before teasing them with a flick. She gasps in appreciation, sinking her nails deep into my biceps. I coax her forward.

Her breasts tumble into my face. I suck one gorgeous nipple into my mouth, then the other, feasting as if she is languorously feeding me champagne grapes. One small press of my teeth against her sensitive flesh, a teasing nip, and she arches, her pelvis rocking over mine.

I snarl from need mixed with acute frustration. Tonight I had planned to take it slow, savor every last inch of her body, worship her skin with my tongue. But animal that I am, lust consumes me, and a deeper feeling, an urgency comes over me to be *home*, as if her body is the safe harbor in the violent black storms that have rocked my world for so long. Turbulence has since become my new normal.

"My turn," she whispers, moving over me, traveling the ridges of my flexed abdomen with her pouty lips. Then lower, until she reaches my belt buckle, unhooks it, and with a pop of a button and the grind of a zipper, my entire proud length is revealed.

She takes me by the root and swirls her tongue around the end. "Mmm," she murmurs. "So good."

I prop myself up on my elbows, letting her take me for a few wet strokes. "Fuck," I groan.

"You like that?" she asks in a flirtatious tone, before adding, "Your *Majesty*."

Naughty minx.

"Hell yes, I do, Pet. And you know what I'll like even more?"

She arches a brow in question.

"Tasting you at the same time." I reach down and with one deft motion flip her around so her pert ass is in my face. "Spread those thighs for me," I growl, slapping one cheek, and she moans loudly, parting her legs wide enough to let me see the sheen on her intimate flesh.

"You are so goddamn gorgeous," I groan and slam her against me. With both hands I give her hips a firm rock, encouraging her to fuck my face, seizing her pleasure as she works over my cock, taking every inch that I have to give.

I flex my tongue over her swollen folds, making sure her clit is well-attended, and when her breath grows ragged, I press harder, giving her hearty licks, writing my name on the soaked, silky skin, marking my territory with flourishing circles and swirls, an intimate calligraphy.

As she falls apart, I plunge my tongue deep inside her tight hole, ravage her with smooth strokes, hinting at the delirious euphoria that is about to be hers.

"Nikolai, oh, God, Nikolai," she gasps, rising up to sit on the back of her heels, spastically jerking then grinding over me in a slow, rhythmic, figure-eight fashion. "Oh God! Your Highness!" She gasps. "Fuck me harder!"

I could come this very second. Sweet, sweet Kate has one filthy mouth. And I obediently comply. The bed shakes. Someday I'll control this entire land, but right now this firecracker is begging to be ruled. Before I take what is mine, I plunge my full face against her pretty pink pussy.

Tonight is about the journey, not the destination. I lick and fuck her until she is dripping and on all fours, hot, tangy juices running down my chin. Two orgasms. Three. Fuck. I lose count of how many I give her. But now my cock is so thick, the need so intense, that I need to join her in this mad passion. Ours won't be a mindless rutting. A fleeting pleasure.

I freeze as the realization takes hold.

There is a chance that entering her will tear asunder the very fiber of my soul.

Kate

I don't know what's come over me. I've never spoken like that. Not to Jean-Luc. Not to anyone. But this man—this man turns me into my basest self. A woman in need who will do or say whatever it takes to satisfy the hunger. And I hunger for Nikolai Lorentz, with everything that I am.

He lifts his head from between my legs, his dark hair a beautiful mess of ravaged waves.

"I need you," he says, his voice strained. "Fuck, Kate. I *need* you."

There is something akin to pain in his words, an ache I'm not expecting, and the animal in me gives way to something else entirely so that all I can do is nod.

He stands from the bed, and despite how hard I already came, I need him inside me. I need *him*, too.

How can any good come of feeling like this?

He disappears into the bathroom, and I hear the faucet run. When I can't stand not knowing how long it will be until he returns, I follow him in there, not caring that he knows how desperate I am to keep him close.

His head dips toward the sink as he splashes water over his face again and again. I rest my palm on his back, and he shudders.

"Nikolai," I say softly.

He straightens enough for me to see his beautiful face in the mirror.

"I thought I could clear my thoughts. I thought I could cleanse away this feeling." He shakes his head. "But I *need* you," he says again to our mirrored selves. "I'm not supposed to *need* anyone."

I see the foil packet on the counter, grab it and tear it open.

"Look at me," I say. "No hiding behind a reflection."

The muscles in his shoulders and back flex as he moves, and when our eyes meet, I don't hesitate as I roll the condom down his thick, pulsing length. He sucks in a breath.

"Remember," I say. "No matter what sort of mask you give to the rest of the world, I *see* you."

As much as this man turns me to animal, I shift to caring lover just as quickly. Because who truly takes care of a prince?

He dips his head toward mine but stops before our lips barely touch.

"You're the only one who can."

And then he kisses me with such tenderness I have to fight back tears. I rise to the tips of my toes, and he nudges my entrance. I grab the base of his shaft and urge him inside. His palms clamp against my thighs, and he lifts me. I wrap my legs around his waist as he sinks into my warmth, and a growl tears from his lips.

Nikolai walks with me like this until we're back at the bed. He lays me on the elegant silk sheet and climbs over me, burying himself as deep as he can go.

I cry out. Not from pleasure or pain but from the undeniable ache of both. The walls around my heart crumble to dust, letting my prince inside.

My prince.

"My prince." This time I say it aloud as he slides out and back in again—slow, controlled, deliberate. He claims me with each thrust. Heart and soul.

My prince.

My prince.

My prince.

His lips are strong and fierce against mine. Each sweep of his tongue is a taste sweeter than any confection and richer than the royal coffers.

The pressure builds, and his momentum picks up. My muscles throb around him as I feel him pulse inside me. So close. He's so close. But I know he's waiting for me.

And because he knows me like no man ever has, he knows what is necessary to send me over the edge.

He slips a hand between us, at the place where two bodies become one, and presses his thumb to my swollen clit. I cry out again and again and again.

He roars as he tumbles off the cliff with me, shuddering above me until we both shatter into a million pieces.

He opens his eyes and traps me in his steel gaze.

"My *queen*," he says before collapsing beside me.

I stroke his sweat-dampened hair as he peppers my shoulder with kisses so achingly tender. I try not to take his words to heart. What we have is only temporary, until I find him a proper bride.

He combs my hair out of my face, his fingers grazing my chin. "My beautiful, fiery winter queen," he says, and I start to wish those words to be truth, though I know full well they never could be. Even if he would marry, a commoner like me could never be in the running.

"Your *what*?" I hear, and gasp when I see a figure looming over us where we lie.

Nikolai turns his head lazily toward our intruder.

"Fucking hell, Christian," he says with nothing more than mild annoyance in his words. "How in God's name did you get in here? And do you ever bloody knock?"

The man steps closer, a muscle ticking in his chiseled jaw. "Give me one good reason why I shouldn't lay you out like the bloody prick you are. Royal law or not, you know I can fucking do it, and it looks like your shadow isn't here to stop me."

I suck in a breath. Am I about to witness a royal

brawl? Or worse—get caught in the middle of it? Regardless of my ability to do so or not, a fierce urge to protect my prince takes hold.

"Who are you?" I ask, but the man ignores me, his gaze still fixed on His Royal Highness.

Nikolai sits up, not at all concerned that he's conducting this conversation completely naked. In fact, he uses his other hand to free his princely cock from its condom.

"Come now, Christian. Answer the lady's question as you know I'm too bored to keep answering yours."

The man clenches his teeth. "Lady?" he says. "I'll do no such thing. But you can bloody tell me why you called this commoner *queen*."

Nikolai glances back at me and winks, and with that tiny gesture the intimacy of our connection falls away.

He laughs. "If you'd been given the royal treatment like I had, you'd bow to the woman who performed such a deed and call her your sovereign, as well."

I know this act. Something about this man—this Christian—instills a quiet fear in the prince, one that causes him to protect our connection. To protect *me*.

"I'm hungry, Your Highness. Can I fix you a snack?"

I slide off the edge of the bed, taking the sheet with me as a robe as I brush past our visitor.

"That would be lovely, Pet."

I grin at the term of endearment as I make my way to the kitchen. Only when I'm out of the room do the pieces start to click in place.

I know that man. Christian. Christian *Wurtzer*.

He is the Baron of Rosegate, the disputed land between Edenvale and our ancient enemies to the north, the Kingdom of Nightgardin. For now Rosegate is under King Nikolai's protection and rule. I squeeze my eyes shut, remembering that the baron also has a supermodel sister. Her face has been splashed across the tabloids almost as much as Nikolai's. Sometimes *together*. Whatever his visit entails, it cannot be good.

And despite what just occurred in Nikolai's room before our interruption, it's only now that I feel royally screwed.

CHAPTER THIRTEEN

Nikolai

"Jesus." Christian paces my room, disgust marring his features. I find a pair of trousers and yank them on. "I'm a fucking idiot. How much time have I wasted worrying that I'd been an overhasty judge, that maybe my little sister, as shallow and conniving as she is, and as depraved and arrogant as you are, had made an unexpected love match?"

He tears a hand through his clipped blond hair. "Instead you're up to your usual tricks, except now you're bedding women in the prince's wing. So much for all your high-minded talk about keeping your chamber as a sanctuary. Now any gold-digging sex kitten can—"

He ceases speaking. Mostly because my hand closes on his throat and squeezes. X once told me he could break a man's neck with a simple flick of the wrist. Good thing he refused to share the trick because, so help me, I would use it against my old friend for besmirching what happened between Kate and me in this room tonight. Our lovemaking was by turns savage and sensual, raw and romantic, two sides of a single emotion, one that hums through me like liquid gold.

I don't dare give it an official name. I don't even think too hard on the word's existence because it feels so fragile, like a soap bubble that could pop in a brisk wind.

Christian's feet kick at the empty air because even as my feelings toward Kate beckon from a place of light, darkness still owns my soul. And my friend dares to condescend an amazing woman such as she.

"Please," he wheezes, hands clawing uselessly at my strength. "Nikolai." He may be skilled in a boxing ring, but I have undiluted fury on my side.

"I don't need a goddamn bodyguard to deal with you, *Baron*. I could break your neck as easily as I could break the alliance with Rosegate," I grind out. "How many hours would it take for Nightgardin to invade if I call off our military protection?"

There is the sound of wood sliding along a groove. Then a warning hand on my shoulder. "Put him down," X's quietly authoritative voice insists.

"Thought I told you to quit using secret passages," I say, releasing Christian and letting him tumble to the floor, gasping for oxygen.

X shakes with noiseless laughter. He doesn't so much as smile, but I know he is amused.

"Don't you get claustrophobic in there?" I ask. The palace is riddled with secret chambers, a veritable rabbit warren within the walls. X seems to liken them to his own personal sanctum.

"After the month I spent as a prisoner in the Russian nuclear sub in the Arctic Sea, the passages here are as roomy as a Versailles ballroom, Your Highness."

"Jesus. Who are you?" I ask him, and not for the first time. I'm never entirely sure if the guy is joking.

"What are you going to do with him?" Per usual, X evades my question to gesture at Christian, who now pushes himself to standing.

"He disrespected Kate," I snap.

Christian stares at me, eyes wide. "Your face, when you say her name. You *feel* something for this woman. Don't you? I never thought it possible."

"I don't owe you—or anyone, for that matter—any explanations," I remind him. I might sound arrogant as hell, but I never denied that I am a royal prick.

"Your Highness," he says, bowing his head. "I apologize for barging in on you. And for assuming the worst. I actually came to warn you about Catriona, in the vain hope that you and she had forged a connection. After you didn't call, it appears she has gone sour. She had delusions of herself on the Edenvale throne. And I thought that if there was any chance you *did* feel something for her... But I know the truth, that Catriona is only capable of loving herself. Still, she is my sister. When I saw you with—"

"Kate," I say, before he calls her a commoner again and I *do* rip his throat out.

"Of course," he says. "Kate. I just wasn't expecting you felt something for another."

"Thank you," I say curtly. I am not yet ready to forgive, but I appreciate the warning.

I don't have time for Catriona's petty scheming. What I said to Kate tonight was the truth.

She is my addiction; I can't stay away. Every kiss, every caress, every damn moment in her presence hits my body like a drug. I can't seem to get enough and crave fix after fix. It's not that I want her so much as I *need* her. There must be a way to make her my queen and keep my royal inheritance.

Kate

I open the stainless-steel refrigerator in Nikolai's kitchen to find nothing but a bowl of strawberries that look freshly cut.

"They go perfectly with the champagne."

I yelp and almost lose my sheet—the only thing covering my naked body—to find X using a pocket square to clean what looks like berry juice—or possibly blood—from a small knife. I opt to believe it is the former. When he's done, he slips the knife into a sheath inside his suit jacket.

"How did you...? I mean, where did you...?" I glance toward an open window near the grand piano across the great room, but X shakes his head.

"Not tonight, Miss. My travels are *within* the walls this evening rather than without."

I shake my own head and decide not to press the issue. Instead I tuck my sheet tight around me and remove the bowl of berries from the fridge, cradling them against my body. I inhale and sigh.

"How do these smell so good?" I ask, my mouth watering. "I can already taste them."

X reaches into another coat pocket and hands me my cell phone.

"The reason I left the prince alone with the baron. You seem to have missed a call. Also, my apologies for him interrupting you and His Highness. Save for his brother Benedict, Christian Wurtzer is the only one with unrestricted security clearance to the annex, an oversight that will soon be remedied." The corner of his mouth twitches into the ghost of a smile. "The strawberries are a gift. I thought you and the prince might need a bit of—sustenance."

X dips his head in a mild bow and disappears around a corner. I hear the sound of what must be a sliding door on a track and then what I swear is a chuckle coming from within the very walls.

Who is that guy?

The caller identification on my phone steals my attention from the mystery of X. My sister. It's not even eight o'clock. I know I told Nikolai I don't have a curfew, but maybe Maddie is worried after all. I ignore her voice mail and move straight to calling her back.

"Oh, Katie, thank God," she says when she answers.

"I'm okay," I tell her. "I guess I should have called. I'm with Nikolai and—"

"It's Grandmother," she says, and all the air rushes out of my lungs with her utterance of those two words.

"Is she—?"

"She's still with us," Maddie says quickly. "But do you remember the cough she had last time I visited? It turns out it was the onset of pneumonia. They started her on medication, but she wasn't responding. We're at the Royal Hospital. She's on a respirator and IV meds. They say she can recover, but, Katie—the money it will cost for all of this. We're barely making our rent at the moment. Can they not pay you a small advance?"

I swallow back the lump in my throat. "Can we get by for two more months?" I ask.

"If we're very careful," she says. "Maybe." Her voice sounds ready to crack. Poor Maddie. She's shouldered so much responsibility since our parents died. Too much.

I take a deep breath and back myself into a corner of the kitchen, a feeble attempt at privacy.

"As long as I get Nikolai down the aisle, we get double our fee."

I hear her gasp. "But what if you don't?" she asks.

I shake my head. "That won't matter. He will marry. I'm sure of it."

Nikolai won't let the kingdom slip away from his family. As much as he embraces the part of the careless playboy, I know deep down he is a man of duty, which means he *will* have to choose a bride—one who is fit to rule beside him. There is no one better than me to find his perfect match, even if it's only perfect on paper.

As much as the thought kills me, I can't let down my own family. My grandmother was there for me and my sister in our darkest hour. She deserves nothing less from us in kind. To see out her final days in peace and comfort.

"I trust you," Maddie says.

"I won't let you down." I step out of the kitchen and glance toward Nikolai's room and see our uninvited guest on his way toward me. "I have to go," I say.

"Okay. I'll be with Gran all day tomorrow. Only one visitor is allowed at a time. Relieve me in the evening?"

"Of course," I tell her. "I'll be there by five. But I won't be home tonight," I add. "Love you, Maddie."

And then I end the call before she can question where I am—before the guilt for not being with Gran now can set in. Because I know what happened between Nikolai and me wasn't just sex.

He called me his queen.

Christian offers me a slight nod as he walks by but says nothing before letting himself out the apartment's front door.

I pad into Nikolai's room, strawberries in hand. He sits on the edge of his bed, hair rumpled and jeans on but unbuttoned. He pops the bottle of champagne and fills the two flutes.

"Sorry about that, Pet." He offers me a glass.

I set the strawberries on the night table and take it willingly. He pulls me onto his lap and then lifts his own glass, tapping the crystal against mine.

"Stay the night," he says.

I nod, and when I lift my glass to drink, the sheet loosens and falls below my breasts.

"My God, you are beautiful," he says, and I don't bother covering myself again.

He sets down his flute and plucks a strawberry from the bowl, bringing it to my lips. I bite, and juice dribbles onto my lips and my chin. Nikolai kisses me, licking my skin clean. I swallow the rest of my champagne in one sip, the bubbles tickling my tongue, and I'm swept away in a giddiness I've never felt before.

He lays me out on the bed, unwrapping me from the sheet as if I am a gift.

"I'm yours," I say. And we make love again, this time achingly yet wonderfully slow, and I know when he buries himself in me again and again that I'm in trouble. *Big* trouble.

I must help him marry another.

Both of our futures depend on it.

In the morning I slide out from the crook of his arm. I kiss the inked compass above his heart and silently wish for it to point us both in the right direction.

X is surprisingly absent this morning, so I exit the prince's quarters as discreetly as possible, leaving him a note that I've gone for a walk.

I need to clear my head.

Soon after I leave the secluded wing, I find a chapel on the outskirts of the grounds. Perhaps someone inside can offer guidance when I have no direction of my own.

I enter to find the place empty but for the rows of pews. A few moments of silence will do me good, as well.

When I take a seat in the rear, I bow my head and close my eyes.

So... I've never actually done this, I think, rationalizing that if there is some higher power, he or she can hear my thoughts. No need to speak them aloud. *But I have loved. It was a good love, but not a great one. I know that now. Because my chest—my body— doesn't feel like it can contain what I have for Nikolai. But whatever this is will fade. It must. We've only known each other for a few short weeks. And he must marry another.*

"I'm frightened of what I feel," I say aloud.

"That which scares us is the most important to face."

The deep voice comes from behind, and I suck in a breath.

"God?" I ask, afraid to face whoever is chuckling. But I'm being a fool, so I turn.

"Not exactly the risen Lord, but I like to think we're close." A dark-haired man, dressed head to toe in black, stares at me with the loveliest green eyes. He wears the white collar of the seminary.

"Oh! Father!" I stand quickly, bumping my knee on the pew in front of me, and hiss out a curse before covering my mouth. "I'm so sorry," I say.

The man smiles, and his kind eyes put me at ease. "You should hear some of the phrases that come out of my brother's mouth when he's here. I assure you none of them are accidental."

My eyes widen. It has been quite some time since any photographs of him have shown up in newspapers or magazines, but I recognize him now.

"You're Prince Benedict," I say, but he shakes his head.

"I prefer Father Benedict, if that's okay with you, Miss—"

"Kate," I say, extending a hand. Though I'm not sure that's the appropriate gesture. He obliges me nonetheless.

"The matchmaker, I presume?"

I swallow. "How did you know?"

"Come," he says, nodding toward the exit. "It's such a beautiful morning. Let us sit in the sun."

I follow him to a small garden where we settle on a stone bench. He tilts his head toward the sky and closes his eyes, breathing in the morning air.

"Has Nikolai spoken of me?" I ask, ashamed at my boldness, but I don't have time to beat around the bush.

Benedict folds his hands in his lap and simply nods.

"Do you truly care for my brother, Kate?"

My cheeks grow hot, and tears prick the backs of my eyes. I have not even told Nikolai of my feelings. Caring for him is not allowed. He is destined for another woman.

Benedict smiles again. "Your reaction is answer enough," he says. "So I will tell you two things. The first is that I love Nikolai, and I will do anything I can to protect him—and anything I can to help him find happiness, something I don't believe he's been capable of feeling for quite some time."

I swipe a finger under my eye, clearing away an escaping tear.

"The second is that if his happiness lies with someone who does not fit the parameters of the Royal Marriage Decree, I will do all that I can to find a way around it if Nikolai is ready to stop playing his games and fight for something real. Do you understand this, Miss Kate?"

I nod and fight the urge to hug him.

Nikolai and I have an ally. It is not a solution, but it is hope.

"Thank you," I whisper instead, but I grab his hand, pressing it between my own. "Thank you so much."

I decide not to overstay my welcome. I don't want to worry Nikolai if I'm gone too long. But as I'm walking away, Benedict calls after me.

"You may very well secure his heart," he says, and I

pause midstep. "Just remember that if you do, it is not only yours to cherish, it is yours to protect."

I don't turn around or respond but instead continue on my way.

He knows I heard.

He knows I understand.

He knows Nikolai might just secure my heart, as well.

CHAPTER FOURTEEN

Nikolai

KATE RETURNS FROM her walk in a pensive mood.

"Everything okay, Pet?" I ask with no small concern. Her cheeks are white as marble.

She presses her lips into a grin, but it doesn't quite reach her eyes. So I make that my singular purpose for the hours ahead, to wash away whatever plagues her and get her beautiful blue eyes to smile again.

Today is the sole day in the month when tourists flood the palace and our extensive grounds. Social media shall soon be filled with #royalday #palacelife #princenikolaiwhereareyou #princenikolaihereicome posts.

And the women who flock inside aren't lying.

Invariably, a few overenthusiastic subjects attempt to break into my royal suite. Once, a coed from the University of Edenvale evaded the guards and made it all the way to my door wearing nothing but a yellow rain slicker and a pair of Wellingtons. Luckily, X was brushing up on his Japanese ninja star throwing skills in the antechamber off my residence, and the sight of him clutching a deadly iron *shuriken* halted her explorations and sent her fleeing for friendlier environments.

But today, I don't want to mix among my subjects. Nor do I want the public world to have a peek at the intimacy developing between me and Kate. All I want is to whisk her somewhere far away from prying eyes, and thanks to my helicopter, this is an entirely plausible option.

"I have a surprise," I tell her, picking up a woven brown picnic basket. X would normally be happy to carry such items, but I want this date to be all from me. For the next few hours there won't be any sign of bad boy Prince Nikolai putting his signature moves on a woman. Instead, she will be with a man who is taking a wonderful woman to a place that couldn't match her vibrant beauty, but comes close.

"We're having a picnic?"

"I made the sandwiches myself…and got lost trying to find the palace kitchen," I admit with a rueful grin.

She giggles, half in horror and half in amusement. "Please tell me you are joking."

I shrug. "In my world, you ring a silver bell, and whatever you need appears."

She stares at me with her signature intense gaze for long enough that my heart pounds. Does she see me as nothing more than a spoiled, overgrown brat?

"So if you tinkle your little bell, your wishes all come true."

I nod. "The palace staff pride themselves on this point."

She glances around the room. "Would this magic bell work for me?"

A thought scuttles through my brain like a menacing cockroach. *Does she value your worth more than you?* I stomp the passing notion into a million unrecognizable pieces. This is Kate. She isn't a gold digger. She could never be. "But of course. It's there on the table, beside the chaise lounge."

She eyes it and gives her chin a musing rub. "What if I ring for Hugh Jackman? The Wolverine version."

I choke on my breath, coughing into my fist.

"What can I say?" She stares with wide-eyed innocence. "I like my men with a sharp edge."

I cross the room, settle my hands on her hips to pull her as close as possible to me and my rapidly thickening needs. "You want me to snarl?"

"Maybe," she says, her voice lilting, teasing, driving me mad.

"You are playing with fire, Pet."

She nods. "Are you saying that I make you burn?" She rocks herself against me with a wink.

I nearly groan aloud. "Come, before I ravish you here and waste all these Nutella sandwiches."

She claps her hands. "You made *Nutella* sandwiches?"

I grin. "With bananas from Hawaii sliced over sourdough imported from San Francisco."

Her eyes brighten, finally, and the sight of her unencumbered joy makes my heart race.

"Nutella sandwiches with banana are my favorite. How did you know?"

"I may or may not have perused your Facebook account. You don't post often. I was hoping for a few more selfies."

Her mouth makes a perfect O, utterly adorable and unassumingly sexy as hell.

"The profile *About Me* section says…" I clear my throat. "'The quickest way to my heart is through a Nutella sandwich.'"

"Guilty as charged," she says with a giggle. "If you read the rest, you'd see it says you'd capture my heart forever if you added bananas." She raises a brow.

"Does it now?" I ask, and she merely shrugs.

We start to walk before I hold up a hand. "Wait, I need to get you something." I open the hallway closet door and pull out two hangers, one with a brand-new sundress and another with one of my jackets. "X procured you fresh garments for our journey, and I want to make sure you don't get cold on the way."

She smiles at the floral printed dress, but her brows knit together when I hand her the jacket. "You're planning on blasting the air-conditioning in the Rolls?"

I click my tongue. "No, we'll be flying at ten thousand feet." I smile into her uncomprehending face. "We're taking my helicopter to a little place I know." I lean over to kiss her forehead. "Me, you and the most beautiful place on Earth. What can go wrong?"

Kate

Nikolai fastens my seat belt and affixes the helmet strap.

"Are you shaking, Pet?" he asks, planting the sweetest of kisses on my nose.

I inhale a trembling breath. "I guess now wouldn't be the *best* time to tell you I've never flown before?"

He grins. "In a helicopter, you mean."

I shake my head. "I've never gone farther than a train could take me, and even then I never left the out-skirts of Edenvale," I tell him, almost ashamed of my words. My fiancé was the adventurer, but he always took that to the extreme. It was never my desire to join him. Plus, Gran's health has been declining for years. "I don't know," I say, not wanting to burst Nikolai's bubble of excitement. Then I shrug. "I guess I'm the kind of girl who plays it safe."

Until I let my country's future king pleasure me in the royal gardens.

My head spins. My world is so small compared to his, and each revelation of my upbringing must re-mind him of this.

He rests his hands on my hips, so strong and reas-suring. And as ridiculous as I must look in this hel-met, he kisses me, his lips a promise that he will keep me safe.

"I want to show you so much," he whispers against me. "I want to give you the world."

I suck in a sharp breath. "I want that, too," I tell him. And with one more kiss, he hops from my side of the helicopter and makes his way to his own.

His helmet on and seat belt fastened, he flips a few switches and grips what looks like a very complicated gearshift. And then my stomach plummets from my body and probably through the cockpit floor as the ground drops out from under us.

I yelp.

"Shit. Are you okay?"

Concern laces Nikolai's voice as it pipes through

the small speakers close to my ears. It's then that I start giggling.

"This…is…amazing!" I squeal as the palace shrinks beneath us—as all of Edenvale, the only home I've ever known, begins to disappear. I turn to him, eyes wide in amazement. *"Nikolai."*

He nods. "I know, Pet. I know."

We rise above mountains and valleys. The outskirts of our country's rolling green hills spread out before us like an emerald blanket.

"Grab the cyclic," he says, nodding toward the joystick next to my leg.

I shake my head violently.

"Don't worry. I won't let us fall."

I swallow and do as he says. He flips another couple of switches and then grins at me.

"Now—tilt it ever so slightly to the right."

I do it, my hands shaking yet gentle on what will either fly us in the direction he wants or be the instrument of our doom. To my surprise, the helicopter veers right, and I squeal with delight.

"I'm flying it!" I cry.

"You're flying it, Kate."

My heart surges at his utterance of my name. Though I enjoy his term of endearment, something about him calling me *Kate* makes whatever today is all the more real.

Nearly two hours later we land in an open field that is lusher and greener than any I've seen. Nikolai leads me several yards away to a country road, a motorbike parked on the gravel beside it.

"How did you—?" I start, and Nikolai answers me

with a kiss so deep and full of need that my knees buckle.

"Careful there, Pet. The day's only just begun."

My grandmother, I think, the real world intruding on the fantasy about to begin. "Nikolai, I need to get back—"

He kisses my nose. "Let go of home, if only for today. I promise to get you back to your life…and me back to mine." There is regret in his tone. "Just give me this day."

I nod and swallow back the threat of tears.

He fastens the picnic basket to the back of the bike and once again fastens a helmet to my head. He helps me onto the seat and then hops on in front of me.

"Don't let go," he says as I wrap my arms around his waist, and I squeeze him tight, my silent promise to obey.

The hills we ride are bumpy, on the verge of treacherous at times as we wind through the mountains. Nikolai has not told me where we are, but when we arrive at our destination, I know without the day having really begun that it will be the best one of my life.

"Nikolai," I say again as he helps me off the motorbike. I open my mouth to say more, but tears prick at my eyes, and I am left speechless, staring out over white rocks and turquoise water, a small bathing pool with a cascading waterfall at its end.

He removes his helmet and then my own as I continue to gape at the site before me.

"I wanted to bring you somewhere as beautiful as you," he says. "Such a place doesn't exist, but I do believe this is the closest I'll get."

This time I'm powerless against the few tears that fall. I don't recall knowing happiness like this.

He pulls the basket from the bike and then lifts a small hatch beneath the basket's perch, pulling out a pair of socks and hiking boots.

I laugh as I look at my ballet flats. Sensible shoes, yet not sensible enough for the terrain we are about to traipse.

"Your glass slippers, Cinderella," he says, and I lean against the vehicle, allowing him to lace me into the boots. On the second one, his hands travel up the length of my leg, and his lips trail sweet kisses in their wake.

I give his head a playful tap. "Not until I get my Nutella sandwich," I say, though if he truly wanted to, he could have me right here on the side of the road.

We make our way to the pool, and Nikolai spreads a blanket upon an embankment.

"Are we the only ones here?" I ask. "And by the way, *where* is here?"

He retrieves a sandwich from the basket, removes it from its parchment wrapper and tears off a small piece.

"We are in the secluded hills of western Rosegate." He pops the sandwich bite into my mouth, and I hum my approval as chocolate, hazelnut and banana converge upon my tongue. "And I can assure you that *no one* will be visiting this pool today."

I swallow. "How—how deep is it?" I ask, and Nikolai's eyes soften.

"Not more than four feet, even at the deepest end. We don't have to go in. I knew you might not want to, but I also knew I couldn't *not* show you this place."

I shake my head, wanting to be brave for him—to

be brave for *me*. I've been in water before—willingly. I just don't remember knowing how to swim.

"You'll keep me safe?" I ask.

His hands cradle my cheeks. "God, yes, Kate. Of course. *Always*."

His gray eyes bore into mine, and I know he's telling the truth. It's that last word, *always*, that seals the deal.

I back away from him and kick off my boots. Then I pull my dress over my head, revealing my one surprise for him today.

"Where—where are your undergarments?" he stammers, and I beckon for him with my index finger.

"You've already given me the world today. I wanted to give something to you." As he steps closer, I begin to unbutton his shirt. "I want to tell you something. I—I hadn't been with anyone else for a couple of years before you." I squeeze my eyes shut and wait for the embarrassment to subside. When I feel his fingertips caress my cheeks, I open them again to see nothing but pure adoration in his gaze. "I was engaged and—he died. I didn't say anything before because—"

"It's okay," he says, surprising me with his reassurance as his hand still cradles my face. "I guess we are more alike than we thought."

He means Victoria. And maybe he's right. Maybe our worlds aren't so far apart after all.

I nod. "What I'm trying to say is… I've been on birth control the whole time. Because it was easier… because I hoped that maybe someday…"

He grins. "I'm clean," he says, knowing what I'm trying to ask. "I may be a wicked rake much of the time, but I'm always careful. If you want to know how many times a year I get tested…"

I shake my head, deciding to trust him rather than wonder how the frequency of doctor's visits factors into the ratio of women he's been with.

"I want to *be* with you, Nikolai. Like this. If you want to be with me."

"There's only been one other I've been with—like this." He growls softly in my ear. "And there is *nothing* I want more right now."

So I free him of his clothes, marveling at his naked body—each ridge of his muscles, the black ink of his tattoos.

"Tell me what it means," I say, tracing the compass with my finger as I've done before.

He brings my hand to his lips, pressing a kiss into my palm.

"It means I was lost," he says. "But I'm not anymore."

I nod, unable to speak. So we step carefully from our perch, down the rocks and into the warm crystal waters below.

"Make love to me," I say, wrapping my arms around his neck, his hard cock already nudging me open. I am slick and ready—just from his words—to take him in.

He pushes inside, and I cry out as my legs wrap around his hips. I am weightless in the water. Weightless in his arms. Gravity no longer exists.

And I never, ever want to come back down.

CHAPTER FIFTEEN

Nikolai

MY COCK SHEATHES itself inside Kate, her intimate muscles clenching my length, and a single word hits like a punch to the soul. *Home.* I have traveled the world, set foot on every continent, skied sky-kissing alpine slopes, explored tiger-filled jungles and indulged in exclusive VIP sex clubs in most major cities, yet I've always felt adrift, empty, as if I live my life surrounded by an invisible moat.

Kate might never have set a single stiletto beyond our small kingdom's borders, but when we lock gazes, it is as if the whole fucking universe is in her eyes.

She is my home.

I withdraw, take my hard cock in one hand and press the tip to her clit, stroking her hot wet center in a slow, hip-grinding circle. This realization makes me dizzy. I knew she'd attracted me, then entranced me. But this feeling requires me to get out a thesaurus, search for superlatives. And yet it might be simple. So goddamn simple.

Her lips part as her pupils dilate.

"Good, Pet?" My voice is husky with emotion. I want to make her come so hard that the memory of the pleasure imprints on her skin, engraves in her bones.

"Amazing, but…" She trails off, lowering her lids.

I smooth a strand of fiery hair from her cheek. "No secrets between us. No barriers. I am here, raw, skin to skin. I demand no less from you."

"I need you back inside me."

The urgency lacing her plea is almost my undoing. "Your wish is my command, m'lady."

I hike her off her feet and position her slender thighs around my hips. She tries to wiggle lower, but I hold her firmly as I begin my trek toward the waterfall.

"Please. Nikolai. In me. Now."

I intend to bury myself in her so deep that I no longer know where she ends and I begin. But first she needs her surprise.

We pass under the fall, and the intense pounding rush is nothing to the thundering pulse of my blood in my ears.

Inside the cave there is a small crack in the ceiling, and a shaft of perfect buttery sunlight sparkles over the crystal walls.

Kate gasps. "What is this magical place?"

I bury my face in her porcelain neck and breathe in her essence, the faint hint of Chanel No. 5. "The Grotto of Diamonds," I rumble. "Stunning, isn't it?"

Her chest heaves against me.

"Absolutely breathtaking," she says.

I cup her chin, refuse to let her grow demure, to be shy. "Wasn't talking about the grotto."

With a pump, I am back inside. Fucking Christ. My

ass muscles clench. She feels softer than spun silk, tight, wet and perfect. As much as I want to lose myself in a series of punishing, dominating thrusts, this is for her. This day. This trip. This moment. So I take the time to ensure every stroke glides over her clit in the slow, steady rhythm that she craves. When I settle her ass against a smooth rock, she hisses with pleasure.

"There's a hot spring running down the wall here," I rasp.

She hums. "This feels amazing." The warm water seeps between her legs, splashing my own thighs.

She arches with pleasure like a naughty kitten and I slide the final inch. Fuck. Her pussy milks me in micropulses. Savage pleasure claws my chest. She is so close already. My darling Kate is responsive as hell. But I won't find my release until she gets hers.

I dip over her sensitive nipple and trace the rosy bud with the flat of my tongue while I enter her over and over, deeper and deeper. Her nails claw my back helplessly. Those micropulses become quakes.

"Watch me, Pet. Watch *us*. Watch your sweet pussy take all that I have to give."

We stare through the crystalline water, hypnotized at the erotic sight of my thick root working through her pink entrance. It's the most goddamn beautiful sight that has ever existed.

"This is where I belong," I say. "In you. Giving you everything you deserve."

"I love watching you take me," she gasps.

"Love watching you get it."

Then her dizzy gasp turns to a small cry. "It's so good. It's too much. I'm coming."

"And who is giving it to you?"

"Nikolai."

As she breathes my name I shoot inside her, my own groan losing itself in her mouth as I taste the ecstasy on her tongue.

We spend the day like this. Lovemaking in the Grotto of Diamonds. Nibbling Nutella sandwiches. Sharing funny stories about our childhoods. Each moment is the best one of my life.

When at last I fly us home, she falls asleep in her seat, too satiated to fear the helicopter, and among the night sky, I tell the stars my secrets, the truth that's burning a hole in my heart. The one that I am not yet ready to confess to her face.

For now, the truth lies in the sky above—and buried deep within my long-darkened soul.

Kate

I feel his fingertips softly caress my face, and I stir in my seat. I'm vaguely aware of my surroundings—a helicopter, I think—but I don't want to leave the dream, one where Nikolai tells me he loves me.

"We're home, Pet. Time to wake."

His voice is soft in my ear, and my body betrays me as my eyes flutter open, exiting the fairy tale I so long to stay in. Because of course he never spoke those words, and I'm not the princess who gets her happily ever after. Yet after this day, I can't help but hope for the possibility that one day I will be.

The propeller blades are still, and Nikolai no longer

wears his helmet. I reach a hand to my own head and find that neither do I.

"Wow," I say. "I was really out. What time is it?" It's only then that I realize the setting sun—that I remember Maddie spending the day at the hospital with Gran.

"It's nearly six," he says. "Is everything okay?"

I fling off my seat belt and fidget with the door. "I'm sorry. Today was—it was everything, but I'm late. It's a family thing. I—I have to go."

I must sound as frantic as I feel because he rushes from the helicopter and around to my side, helping me out.

"Whatever you need. Where do you have to go? I'll take you there myself."

We race from the helipad where I expect to see X waiting with the Rolls-Royce, but instead I find two guards along with Queen Adele. Christian Wurtzer. And a young woman I recognize from the covers of various magazines—Catriona Wurtzer. She stands with a self-satisfied grin plastered on her face and one hand distinctively rubbing her flat belly.

"What is all this?" Nikolai asks, more annoyed than concerned.

Christian's jaw is tight, and I can tell he is using monumental restraint. Whatever is going on, this man looks at Nikolai like he wants to tear his throat out.

The queen purses her lips and narrows her eyes at me. "Come now, Nikolai. Really. Dallying with the hired *help*. I'd like to know how she plans to earn double her fee for getting you down the aisle if she can't keep her legs crossed in your presence." She sets her cold gaze on me. "And *you*." The queen raises her brows. "I know I told you to earn his trust, but I had no idea you'd seduce him, as well. I guess that *is* one way to go about it."

Her lips part into a satisfied, victorious grin.

"Double fee? What the fuck is this about a double fee?" Nikolai asks.

The world seems to spin around me. I might be sick.

Christian's jaw ticks. Catriona stifles a laugh. And when I look at Nikolai, the light in his eyes snuffs out as I watch his gaze cool and then turn completely to ice.

"Double your fee?" he repeats, his tone achingly bitter.

"The contract," I say, but it comes out as a strangled sob. "You have the copy. The money wasn't a secret." But he told me he hadn't read it, which means I let the lie of omission stand. I let myself believe that what he didn't know wouldn't hurt him. I let myself believe that we could beat the queen at her own game, but I never really stood a chance. Did I?

"I trusted you," he says. "But I guess that was just part of your job too. I didn't think I needed a contract to prove to me that you weren't like every other woman who's schemed to get in my bed. If it wasn't meant to be kept from me, then why not say something?" he asks, his words biting and bitter. "Is this why you challenged me? Why you were so confident you'd succeed? Because you were allied with the person who despises me most?"

He steps toward me, his face inches from mine, but I don't for one second think he will kiss me, not with his teeth clenched. Or that vein in his neck throbbing with the hot anger rising from his body.

"Was. Any. Of. It. Real?"

Each word stabs me like a poisoned dagger.

"Nikolai, you *know* it was real," I say, but how can he trust me now when the queen speaks the truth? She didn't request my help. She demanded it, under veiled threats. I *was* her ally. I had no choice but to comply. And even though I gained his trust, I never really gave him mine. Or I'd have been brave enough to tell him everything.

I knew I was falling for him today, and the possibility of us made me think I wasn't afraid of her anymore—that I could tell Nikolai about Gran. About why I needed to succeed even if it meant breaking my own heart.

She played me. She played him. And now she is going to win.

"Money," he says, his voice so distant I almost don't believe it's the same man who woke me moments ago. "That's what you really hoped to gain. Wasn't it?"

I shake my head, refusing to believe things can change with one utterance from the queen. "You know that's not true. She *made* me agree. I had no choice. I should have told you everything, but that doesn't mean—"

"Stop," he says. "Just stop. Why would you say anything if *seducing* me could earn you double your fee?" His eyes flash to the queen and back to me. "Do you want to know why I refuse to marry?" he asks, but he doesn't wait for an answer. "Because the last woman I asked to be my queen was willing to accept my hand even though she loved another. All because she thought the title more important than all else. Now she is gone, my brother banished, and I right back where I started, fooling myself that any woman could see past the facade."

He takes another step closer to me, and I flinch. I do not know this Nikolai. *This* is not my prince.

"I told you. I will. Not. Marry."

Laughter bubbles from the queen's lips, and she claps her hands slowly.

"Lovely speech. Really. Lovely. But here is the thing. It was only a matter of time before your—dalliances—got you into trouble. Thankfully, the countless times you've *dallied* with the baroness seem to have worked in your favor." Her lips curled into a malicious grin. "Catriona is pregnant with your heir. You *will* marry and secure an alliance with Rosegate...or lose the throne."

Nikolai's eyes widen as his gaze meets that of his former lover, and then falls to where her hand rests on her belly.

My tears fall hot and fast because I know now we never had a chance—Nikolai and I. The queen had said she would find his match and that I would support it. Benedict searching for a loophole was nothing more than a distraction. This was always going to end.

"Take her away until I decide what to do with her," the queen says.

And before I can comprehend that she means me, both of her guards appear at my sides, my arms firm in their grip.

"What are you doing?" I cry.

"Your Highness," Christian starts. "You never said anything about locking her up!"

But the queen waves him off.

"Take. Her. Away," she says again, and the guards start dragging me toward a car at the edge of the grounds.

"Nikolai!" I call. "Listen to me. You know it was never about the money. I know you do."

But he doesn't respond as the guards pull me farther and farther from him.

I want to cry out again, but for whom? Nikolai stands there, dumbfounded and shattered. I have no ally.

As I collapse into the back of the car, my eyes blur with tears—so much so that it takes me several seconds to get my bearings.

A minibar. A bottle of cognac. And when I look up, the window between me and the driver lowers.

"To the dungeon, then, Miss?" the driver asks, and I dare to let myself hope.

"X?"

CHAPTER SIXTEEN

Nikolai

"Tsk, tsk." Adele clicks her tongue. Her mouth's sympathetic purse only serves to make the triumph in her eyes more grotesque. Not for the first time I wonder just how she managed to capture my father's heart. She hails from an old Edenvale family, aristocratic to the core, but besmirched by a long line of traitors who over time have betrayed our throne's integrity to cut lucrative deals with Nightgardin, hoping to profit in the destabilization. A few of her ancestors' heads decorated the palace bridge as a warning to other transgressors.

I flex my fist, wishing for an ancient ax and a chopping block.

"Naughty, naughty, Nikolai, leading that pathetic matchmaker on. I hope you had fun with your little game. I'm sure she'll get over it in, oh, ten or twenty years." She glances to Catriona, and they share the same tinkling, malevolent laugh.

I don't know what the fuck to think. Two hours ago I was making love to a woman who I'd have sworn looked into my pitch-black soul and saw a man worthy of her heart. Now I'm being told it was a lie? That she was in it for a double fee. It's not even the money that gets me this time. It's that she kept her alliance with the queen rather than me. I've been enough of a royal idiot to be duped into thinking Kate had grown to care for me for my own sake.

Idiot.

Self-disgust roils through me. But I don't allow a trace of feeling to reveal itself on my face.

Instead, I twist my own lips into a sneer. "Pity." I ensure my words are ice, that they drip with scorn. "For a commoner, she was uncommon good fun." I allow my gaze to fall on Catriona. Her white-blond hair. Her porcelain perfect skin and pale blue eyes nearly the same shade of water. Nothing warm or welcoming. No. Twin pools of an Arctic lake. I take my time scanning every inch of her perfect body. "Darling," I drawl. "You didn't need to fake a pregnancy to keep my interest. The way I recall, we have unfinished business. You promised me a backstage pass and never delivered." I arch a brow.

"You bastard," Christian says, lunging for me. The two guards, already returned, restrain him.

"I think you meant to say Your Highness." I dust off my shirtfront. "I do believe the proper terminology in addressing your liege lord is Sire, Prince, Majesty. You could go for Your Most Exalted Worshipfulness for extra credit. You always were an ass kisser back in school."

And he was. Perfect grades. Awards for chivalry. While my extracurricular activities consisted of fucking Miss Teatree, the student French teacher, in the back of my Rolls-Royce during lunch breaks.

"I am going to cut out your disgusting tongue," he hisses.

"Your loyalty to your sister is commendable," I answer easily. "But problematic. Because either she is lying, in which case you are a fool, or she is telling the truth, and you are threatening violence not only on your future king but also the father of your nephew. A child who will be the only one to carry on your noble line given your...dilemma."

Christian stares at me with fire in his eyes. He contracted mumps during our school days, and the nurse told him he was probably sterile. A pity as it puts his small but highly coveted territory in jeopardy. Rosegate needs an heir. Edenvale needs to solidify the alliance. Despite the circumstances, it would be an advantageous match.

"My money is that you are a fool," I say, turning back to Catriona. "How do you know that you are pregnant? Will you have me believe you are some sort of modern-day Princess and the Pea? That you can magically sense if my child is growing within you?"

"Don't be ridiculous," Adele snaps, beckoning to a butler who stands off to the side, holding a silver platter covered by a swan-shaped lid.

He hurries over and removes the lid with a flourishing bow. On the tray lies a pregnancy stick with two lines.

"I do not read hieroglyphics," I mumble.

"Idiocy doesn't become you. It's obvious that's a positive sign." Victory is stamped on my stepmother's every smug feature. "You coated her womb with your depraved seed. Time to do your duty."

"A little baby," Catriona says, her mouth curving into an uncertain smile. "A future king or queen. Plus, Rosegate will unite with Edenvale at last, and Nightgardin won't ever have a chance of taking it over."

My stepmother inclines her head as if truer words had never been spoken. What is her poisonous endgame? I have to think, but my brain is flatlining, my neurons only able to process one thing. That I let another woman pretend to care for me. That I let down my defenses and gave Kate entry into my inner keep.

My stepmother hates me, blames me for her daughter's death, but why the fuck is she so intent on marrying me off to Catriona, or marrying me off period? I am not buying her giving a flying fuck over solidifying ties to Rosegate.

The cogs in my dulled brain begin to creak back to life. Doubt slides up my spine like a serpent. I used condoms with Catriona. She said she was also on birth control. If Kate was working with Adele, why not Catriona, too?

If it looks like a duck and quacks like a duck…

"The wedding will be in three days' time," Adele says. "A very private, very legally binding ceremony."

The queen might be crafty, but she isn't exactly a rocket scientist. And about as subtle as a doorpost.

"I don't think so." It takes all my strength not to gnash my teeth. "I know I've been nothing but a crushing disappointment to your selfish motives, so just add this latest mistake to my tab."

I turn away, thoughts reeling. If Catriona is carrying my child, I can't abandon her or the innocent baby, but I can't marry her. I'll order a blood test and then figure things out. Even if the ache of betrayal floods my body as I think of the woman who just disappeared into the night, I know it was real for me, so much so that I can barely breathe thinking it was all a game for her. I want to fall to my knees and scream. I want to find a wall and punch it until my fists run with blood.

Love is my curse, never my salvation. When Father dies, I will sit on the Stone Throne, but my heart will be as impenetrable as a block of uncut granite. Perhaps Catriona will bear my bastard, but she will never be my queen.

X. I need X. He'll know what to do. Even if it is to get me mind-numbingly drunk until today is blacked out of memory—he'll know.

"I will make you happy," Catriona says, putting the perfect quaver in her voice. She's such a drama queen that I'm half tempted to give her access to the throne, just to watch the spectacle.

"Sweetheart, there is only one reason why I stuck my dick in you. Fine, two. But the primary reason was this... I was trying to find out if your brother was selling me out to the tabloids again."

"What are you bloody talking about?" Christian yells.

"Every time I went out in the past year, images would appear of me online and in the print media. Despite my reputation, I do value discretion when it suits me. I knew someone in my entourage was spilling the proverbial beans. Squeaking to the press. But it was you all along. You were the little mouse." I'm unleashing the asshole attitude that's made me infamous, going full scale royal prick.

There is no one that I can trust. I am as I have always been—alone.

Catriona presses a hand to her heart. "How could you accuse me of such base behavior?"

My shoulders shake with my cold laugh. "The minute Christian found me with you, I knew it wasn't him. He was so upset. Then nothing leaked afterward. Except there was an attempt to sell something to a national magazine, wasn't there?"

She blanches. If she was pale before, now Catriona is a living ghost.

"X intercepted the messages. You were going to sell a tell-all exposé to the highest bidder. Did you think that texting your brother to come find you in my bed was going to force him to badger me to marry you? Or that you'd achieve notoriety as my lover?"

Catriona draws her hand back and slaps me hard on the cheek. "You are a monster. No wonder Victoria ran off with Damien. You can't love. Your heart is complete and utter stone."

"Enough!" Adele commands in her usual imperious tone. "Someone escort my sniveling future daughter-in-law back inside the palace. And her brother, before he murders the heir to the throne."

The crowd clears, and within minutes it's just my stepmother and me.

"Why are you doing this?" I ask at last, breaking the silence. No more pretense. I just want answers.

"I've waited for this moment a long time," she purrs. "Ever since I buried my daughter in the cold, hard ground."

And I believe her. I just don't believe that is the

whole truth. But do I trust this inner voice, the same intuition that whispered that I should take a chance on Kate? The one that has led me back here, to this black place of pain and bone-crushing loneliness? Victoria hurt my heart. Kate detonated it with the precision of a lobbed grenade. It will never be whole.

As I begin to search for answers, one truth is certain. Not only will I never marry, I will never love again.

Kate

A heavy gated door scrapes across stone as it slams shut behind me. I stumble into the cold, dank cell and stare with wide eyes back at the man who just threw me in here.

"X," I say, my voice shaking. "Why?"

He stares at me without expression, and my fear starts to morph into something fierce. I throw myself at the bars separating me from him, shaking them to no avail.

"I care about him—so much! You know I do."

My heart beats wildly in my chest. I can't even say it to X, that I *love* Nikolai. But he watched me get carted away thinking I betrayed him because I was too afraid to tell him the truth.

Because I'm a fool to have ever thought I could bridge the divide between his world and mine.

"This—this is all the queen," I continue. "She told me she would choose his bride, that if I didn't comply my sister's business would be ruined. You know she has the power to do that. You know she set this whole thing up!"

Still he stands, arms crossed, impassive as ever.

I pace, shivering in the damp air, tears pouring along my cheeks. When X says nothing, I collapse onto a stone bench at the rear of the cell and let out a bitter laugh.

"I didn't think places like this were real, you know. Castles? Sure. But dungeons? This is the stuff of fairy tales," I tell my emotionless captor. "But I never expected to be the princess. I only ever wanted to take care of my family."

I meet X's stare. There is no sign that he's even heard a word I've said, yet I swear I see a twinkle in his eyes that wasn't there before.

"The money?" I say, my voice steady now because even if Nikolai won't hear me out, he will know the truth. "My sister and I live and work out of our small apartment. Every cent that doesn't go toward our monthly payments, toward food or keeping the business afloat—it goes to the elderly care center where our grandmother lives. And now it will go to the hospital that's keeping her alive. That's where I'm supposed to be now, X. *Please*. Let me go to her."

X's jaw tightens, the only sign that any of this is getting through to him.

I open my mouth to say something more but am interrupted by what sounds like a sack of potatoes hitting the stone floor.

X looks to his left, and his features finally relax.

"You have three minutes to decide if you trust me,

Miss Kate. Three minutes to decide if you are willing to put your life in my hands."

I rise from the stone bench and make my way to the iron gate that separates me from him, pressing my face against the bars so I can see what X sees—a burly palace guard slumped on the floor next to a stool, an empty beer stein tipped over next to him.

"Yes, I drugged his ale." X waves a hand. "It won't be the first time he's fallen asleep on watch, but it is the first time it's of my doing. He'll be lucky not to piss himself with relief when he wakes to find he hasn't been caught."

The corner of his mouth quirks ever so slightly into the hint of a grin, and my heart surges with hope.

"You don't need to prove your love, Kate. Not to me," he says, his voice a firm whisper. And just like Nikolai calling me Kate somehow made me know that what we had was real, X doing the same—dropping that ridiculous *Miss*—tells me I can trust him, too.

"I've known of your family's situation since the king and queen hired you," he goes on. "But the prince—he has been in the dark, and you are one of those responsible for keeping him there."

My breath hitches, and I swallow back a sob. He is right. Nikolai hid nothing from me, but I hid my life from him. Even if it was for my own protection, I betrayed his trust in doing so.

I nod. "This isn't my world," I tell him. "I'm out of my depth. And as much as he means to me—as much as my silly secret wish has been for him to choose *me*—I knew it was a fool's errand to think he could ever truly be mine. I must think about my family right now. And Nikolai—" I stutter on the next thought, but it is the only way. "Nikolai must marry Catriona. If she's carrying his baby, he must." I swallow hard against the ache in my chest, against the cavern that will replace my heart after my next words. "Tell the queen I forfeit my fee. Tell *Nikolai*. I will not cause trouble for the prince. I just need to get to my family."

X nods somberly at me. "Queen Adele plans to leave you here until after the wedding." My whole body begins to shake as his words sink in.

Another tear slides down my cheek. "When will that be?" I ask.

X clears his throat. "Three days' time," he says. "I hope you understand I *had* to bring you here. The prince's safety depends on it."

I glance around my cell and shudder not just at the thought of being locked here for three days or of losing Nikolai—but that such cruelty exists in the queen's heart.

"Father Benedict is working tirelessly to find a loophole," X continues. "If this baby is not Nikolai's—and if there is a way out of the decree—he will find it within these three days. If I let you go, though," he says, "the queen will expedite the wedding, and Nikolai will have no chance at true happiness. But if you trust me—if you trust that my one and only mission is to protect my prince—then you can leave here tonight."

I wipe the tears from my face, my hands now covered in dirt from the filthy cell bars. I'm sure I look as frightened as I feel, but I don't care. I don't care about anything but protecting my family and the man that I love, even if he will never know my true feelings.

Everything inside me trembles so hard I fear my bones will shatter. But I hold my head high and look straight into X's unwavering stare.

"I trust you," I say. "For Maddie. For my grandmother. For Nikolai, all whom I love. I trust you, X."

He pulls a small vial from his coat pocket and hands it to me through the bars.

"Then drink."

CHAPTER SEVENTEEN

Nikolai

"WALK WITH ME." Adele gathers her crimson skirts and strides toward the gloomy entrance to the maze.

I follow as if in a trance. My head pounds, and my brain is reeling. Too many questions. Too many years living with lies and pain and never knowing who to trust. Who, if anyone has, ever loved me for me?

Maybe no one.

A feeling of utter loneliness swallows me.

Do I want to be king? It's never been a question that I've consciously asked myself before. It's as inevitable as drawing a breath. The next beat of my heart. Someday I will sit on the Stone Throne in the Reception Hall and lead my people into what I have always hoped in my deepest heart would be a prosperous and bright future.

But I don't want to be king at this price. My birthright isn't worth letting Adele win at her twisted game. But I don't know the rules. I don't know how to beat her when she holds all the cards. But the worst thing that can happen is to let her sense my uncertainty. That would be like slicing my wrists in a shark tank. Better to square my shoulders, set my jaw and figure this the fuck out. She will make a mistake. I just need to stay sharp, be ready to pounce at the first misstep.

"So quiet, no? As if the world holds its collective breath." Adele runs her fingers over the hedgerow. "Why the long face? I'd think you would enjoy taking a stroll down memory lane." Her voice is steeped in innuendo.

I ball my hands into tight fists. "I don't know what you are talking about."

"Now, now. Coy's not a good look on you, Nikolai," she croons. "We might *dislike* each other, but do let's be frank. I know how you ravished the lovely Kate Winter here on the ground of the maze. You feasted and rutted on her with your face like the wild beast that you are, depraved by lust. Disgusting and yet fascinating."

I stare at her, blinking slowly.

"How do I know your...*activities*?" She leers. "Please. You think your father runs this place? Why do you think I encourage all of his travels for diplomacy? This is *my* kingdom, and I have eyes *everywhere*." She enunciates each syllable of that last word. "A mouse doesn't so much as shit in this palace without me getting an update." She shakes her head in mock sorrow. "Now don't get all pouty. No one likes a sore loser." Her eyes gleam. "And you've lost, my sweet prince. You have lost so much that I'd be tempted to pity you if I wasn't so absolutely delighted."

Her laugh cuts my skin like glass shards before it morphs into a hysterical sob. "My daughter should have been queen!" she snaps. "It was *her* destiny to save Rosegate, not that dimwit Catriona."

My jaw clenches. "I *loved* Victoria." I choke out the bitter truth. "But she was sleeping with my traitor of a brother."

She scoffs, sneering as she looks me up and down. "You are unfit to be king. A real man worries about affairs of the state, not of the heart. You are nothing but a weak fool. So what if Victoria didn't love you? She would have bedded you, born you an heir. She knew her duty. And your duty was to keep her safe! There were greater plans at work."

Every cell in my body recoils. "Wouldn't you want more for your daughter than to serve as a broodmare to a man she didn't love?"

"I wanted her to be queen," she hisses. "And to… and to… It doesn't matter! There is no more worthy goal than the pursuit of power. *You* took that away from her. And now I get to take your happiness from you."

Bile rises in my throat. "She loved my brother! *He* took her life, Adele. And he's been paying the price for years." An unexpected twinge of sympathy pierces me. I loved Victoria and lost her. Damien loved her and lost everything. I will not forgive my youngest brother, but only now when I have lost Kate—when I stand to lose everything if Adele has her way—do I have the slightest idea what life might be like to be banished.

"Damien was third in line to the throne." She speaks so forcefully spittle flies from her mouth. "You ran her off so she could be what? An insignificant nobody? Do you know who my family is, that we are a bloodline even more ancient than yours?"

I swipe my cheek, not having the slightest interest in getting into a snobby pissing match over who is the most royal. "I ran them both off after discovering them fucking like dogs in the Royal Library. And do you know what I think? I think she wanted me to catch her. I think she wanted me to *free* her from a future she never wanted as much as you did."

My chest heaves. I have to squeeze my eyes shut as the memory takes hold. It's not as if I don't hold some of the guilt. For years I've wondered if it could have gone differently. If there was something I could have done that would have set in motion a different course of events that did not end with Victoria dead. But the fact remains that she loved another, that she betrayed me and was all too happy to leave once she was caught.

"She'd still be alive if it wasn't for you." Adele flies at me, claws outstretched, grief taking her to the point of insanity.

This is my moment.

I've been waiting for a misstep. If she was playing a political game, her feelings for Victoria, the grief at losing not only a daughter but also a future meal ticket, muddles her thinking. She isn't calculating now. She is ready to tear me apart limb from limb, unleash her long-simmering resentment, the fact that she has had to kowtow to the Lorentz family to wear the crown, and now the best she will ever get is a puppet in Catriona, a weak-minded, selfish woman easily manipulated to do her bidding.

As for me, I'm ready to go to hell and bring Adele along for the ride. I am at the brink of endurance, and below me lies the bleak roiling blackness, the void that is there, always there. I'm done resisting. I'm ready to give myself over to the void.

She is right.

I've lost.

I've lost everything that matters.

The world goes crimson before a strong steady hand clamps my shoulder.

"Sire," X says in a grave voice, pulling me back. "Come quick. There is no time."

Kate

You will be able to hear all too clearly but see nothing. You'll feel the touch of others all too keenly but will be paralyzed from any movement yourself. You will be alive, but to anyone without sharp medical training, you will appear dead. Heartbeat too slow to detect, breathing too shallow to recognize.

This is what X tells me before I drink. There isn't time to ask him how he knows of such a drug or if he's seen it work before. I have mere seconds to decide that I trust him before everything goes black and I lose myself completely.

I feel the cold stone beneath my cheek but see nothing at all. I hear the frantic scuffle of shoes in the distance. The sound grows louder, and then there is nothing but silence for several long moments before the unmistakable click-clack of high heels approach.

"She was delirious. Screaming nonsense about how the queen threatened her livelihood if she did not get you down the aisle. Of course it was all rubbish," X says. "After her tirade she complained of shortness of breath. I knew she was just looking for a way out, so I ignored her pleas. And then she just—collapsed."

Metal clangs, and I swear the ground beneath me shakes.

"You *ignored* her?" His voice is hoarse, frantic, and I can feel his pain. It is as tangible as the stone against my cheek.

Nikolai! I want to cry out his name, but I'm stuck in this blackness, forced to do nothing but listen and to trust that I will be out of here soon.

"You bastard!" he growls, his voice wild. "I will kill you, X. I will fucking kill you!"

Laughter trills through Nikolai's madness. The queen. They are all here, staring at my prone body. And Nikolai thinks— Oh God. X. What have we done to him?

"Oh, this is too good," Adele says. "Not even in the plan, but it certainly makes things much easier for me. Tell me, X. Is she dead?"

"Unlock the fucking cell!" Nikolai bellows, interrupting her question.

"Oh, very well," the queen concedes. "Have your last look if you must."

Metal grates over stone, and I feel the faint warmth of skin against my own.

"There is no pulse," X says gravely. "Sire, my deepest condolences."

I hear a sickening crack and then Nikolai's broken voice. "I *will* kill you for this," he says again, and I'm not sure if he's speaking to the queen, or X, or both.

The scraping of heels comes nearer, and icy fingers touch my neck. If I wasn't already paralyzed, the queen's cold touch would do it.

"You didn't actually think I'd trust your word, X. Did you? But it looks as if you're being truthful. The girl is dead."

Her skin leaves mine, and I fight to claw my way out of my body, out of this cell and away from her even though I know there's nothing more she can do to me—so long as she thinks I'm gone.

Seconds later I am weightless. No, I'm in someone's arms. I feel warm liquid splash on my cheek and know that it is my prince who cradles me.

"I'm so sorry," he whispers, and I feel his trembling lips press against my forehead. "I believe you," he whispers. "I trusted you, and I know in my gut it was the right thing to do, but I let the goddamn past get the better of me. I will never forgive myself for doubting you. I don't deserve your love, but I know you gave it to me today. I let my fear blind me to the truth, but know this, Kate. I love you. And I promise you this—I will *not* love another." And then in a voice so soft I almost miss it, I hear, "I win our wager," he says, his whisper cracking on that last word. "I will not marry—not if it means the woman beside me is not you. You owe me a favor, Kate. Those were our terms." I hear him take a shuddering breath. "Please. Come back."

My body rocks in his arms. Again and again warm drops of liquid splatter my cheek, and my heart cracks wide-open for the broken man who holds me. "Come back, Kate," he pleads, louder this time, and then his lips are on mine.

I taste the salt of his tears, and if I wasn't sure

that I was, in fact, paralyzed, I would swear that my eyes leaked tears of their own. Kiss after soft kiss, he doesn't let go of me, not even when the queen groans.

"Enough already," she hisses. "You'll never know loss like I do, Nikolai. But now you will live with yours for a lifetime. Now, X. Wipe the blood from your lip and do something with Miss Winter's body. I'm sure you can conjure a reasonable explanation for the Royal Guard, and I trust it will be kept from the papers."

"Yes, Your Highness," I hear X say.

I feel Nikolai lift my palm to his cheek, and my fingers twitch against his tear-soaked skin.

A throat clears. "Your Highness," X says, "is the king not arriving back at the palace shortly? Surely you want to be the first to break the news about the prince and Catriona. I will—take care of things here."

"Yes. Fine," she says. "Nikolai, clean yourself up and join us in the grand dining hall for dinner. You can announce your impending nuptials yourself."

Nikolai says nothing, only holds my palm flat against his cheek as I listen to the piercing blows of her heels against the stone until the sound grows farther and farther away. Finally, I hear the far-off clank of the heavy cellar door closing.

Nikolai lets go of my hand, but it doesn't fall. My fingers twitch against his skin again, and I hear a sharp intake of breath.

"X?" He draws out his servant's name.

"Really, Sire," X says, the slightest admonishment in his voice, "I thought you had more faith in me than that."

My eyes flutter open, and Nikolai's head is turned

toward the man who hopefully saved us both. I gasp as my sluggish lungs gulp at the air while my heartbeat feels like it's increasing at an exponential rate.

Both of their heads snap toward mine. X stares at me with a satisfied grin on his face despite a split lower lip. It's the first genuine smile I've seen from him, and I can't help but feel the slightest bit victorious. I vowed to make the man smile, and I did, even if I had to nearly die to do it.

Nikolai still holds me, his eyes wide and red rimmed.

I regain movement in my other arm and cradle his face in my palms.

"I *love* you, Nikolai," I say, my thumb swiping at a remaining tear on his cheek. "The money was never—"

But his lips are on mine before I get a chance to explain, and that's when I realize that I don't have to. He trusts that my love is real, and it is. God, it is. He pulls me closer, deepening the kiss as my lips part for him. My limbs are still weak, but he holds me so tight I know I won't fall.

"Sire," X interrupts. "We don't have much time. The drug was supposed to last longer. Perhaps I measured incorrectly in my haste. We must get Miss Kate to the hospital."

Nikolai pulls away. "But I thought—" he stammers. "I thought she was okay," he says to X and then turns back to me. "You cannot leave me again," he says.

I shake my head. "This is all X's doing," I say. "I trust I will be okay soon. But my sister. My grandmother." A tear escapes. "I need to get to them."

In the distance the cellar door grinds open again.

"I will explain everything in the car, Sire," X says,

an edge in his voice I do not like. "But we are out of time!"

"I can't walk," I whisper, fear lacing my words. If Adele was happy to find me dead, what will she do if she finds me still alive?

Nikolai stands with me still in his arms, and I wrap mine tight around his neck.

"We cannot exit the cell without being seen," he says.

X raises a brow. "Of course we can, Your Highness. Just not through the door."

CHAPTER EIGHTEEN

Nikolai

X PRESSES A moss-covered stone on the dungeon wall, and it sinks back like a button on a keyboard.

"This palace is full of surprises." He turns with a wink. "Designed that one myself."

Of course I've wondered about X's background story. He is so tight-lipped that it is possible to believe he is anything or anyone. When I came of age he was assigned as my personal bodyguard and soon became my most trusted friend and adviser. I have given him free rein to indulge in any number of curious hobbies from Kenjutsu Japanese swordsmanship to breeding poison dart frogs. But it appears secret passages have also been a keen interest, for I thought I knew them all, and I have just been proved wrong.

"It's a tight squeeze, but it will bring us out at the Gates of Victory," X says.

"And from there we can proceed to the back entrance," I say, unable to believe Kate is still alive in my arms. That this nightmare has turned into a dream.

"The guards in the back keep were sent a flagon of ale from you tonight, as thanks for their service."

"I ordered no such thing," I tell him.

X arches a brow. "I did. And saw it dosed with six seeds of the Evernight Poppy before delivery. The men should be dreaming of busty Edenvale milkmaids this very moment." He glances back at us. "Miss Kate here, however, consumed one entire blossom. She *should* have been out for at least twenty-four hours. I do wonder about that kiss, though…" He trails off.

"What about the kiss?" I ask.

X shakes his head. "Even I don't believe in such tales," he says. "True love's kiss being more powerful than poison? There just is no logical explanation for her early rousing."

I open my mouth to respond, but Kate interrupts me.

"I've never heard of an Evernight Poppy," she murmurs, rubbing my bicep and attempting to shift her body in my arms.

"Of course not," X snaps. "No one outside of a nomadic tribe of Kazakhstani master poison makers knows of the flower's existence." His mouth quirks. "Except me."

Kate attempts to lower herself and take a step but immediately crumples. I sweep her off her feet once more.

"What's happening to me?" Her eyes cloud over with fright. "Why won't my legs work?"

"You were mostly dead. Intermittent paralysis is an unfortunate side effect from the poison."

Kate moans.

"Damn it, X, for how long?" I snarl, hating Kate's fear. She moans again, this time more breathless. "For how fucking long?"

The voices in the corridor grow louder. Whoever is coming for Kate's supposed dead body is almost here.

X beckons me forward and we slip into the secret passage. He pulls a crank and the door slides effortlessly closed. "Not long," he says at last.

"Then why do you look unsettled?" I rumble. The idea of Kate suffering another second more has me in agony.

We wind through the complex twisting labyrinth that X has built through the ancient walls. The corridor is pitch-black except for the powerful flashlight beam that X shines from his wristwatch.

"There is another side effect," he says in a tight voice.

Kate writhes in my arms. "Oh, God," she breathes in a husky whisper unlike any I've ever heard. "Oh, my Jesus God."

I freeze, unwilling to take another step until X fills me in on every last fucking detail.

X sucks in an audible breath. "Unbridled sexual desire is the other effect."

"I need you inside me or I'll die." Kate licks the side of my neck while sliding her hand to cup my bulge. "Feed me that gorgeous royal prick, Your Highness. Inch by majestic inch."

"This side effect, Sire… It won't abate on its own," X says grimly. "It's the poison attacking the part of her brain that controls pleasure."

"I need it so bad," Kate moans. "It hurts. It hurts to want this badly."

My eyes widen. "What do I do?" My cock is granite hard the instant Kate's palm caresses it through my pants. We need to escape, but Kate's sensual moans are making me mad with roaring lust, and soon others will hear her pleas on the other side of the wall.

X turns to regard me in full. His normally inscrutable expression is even harder to read than ever before. "The only cure for this side effect is for someone to bring her to orgasm."

Kate

"X," I growl. "You said I would feel things more keenly in my sleep state." I writhe in Nikolai's arms as we slide through the narrow corridor. "I'm not asleep anymore, and I can't turn it off!" I cry. "The pain is going to kill me!"

I thrash and grind against my prince's hands. "Touch me, Nikolai. God, please, touch me!"

"My apologies, Miss," X says as he leads the way. "The sharp awareness of your senses—of your needs— it is more intense when you wake. And you woke early. You still have much of the drug in your system. Sire, you must pleasure her at once."

"Kate," he says. "I need to know it's not just the drug. I need to be sure that after everything that's happened, you still truly want me like this."

His tortured eyes bore into me, and for one short moment, everything is clear.

"I love you, Nikolai. Of *course* I still want you like this."

"Very well," he says.

My prince repositions me in his arms so that one of his hands is now underneath my dress where I'm wearing nothing at all. A finger grazes my clit and I nearly black out as I scream from the sensation.

"Silence is of the utmost importance," X says, reminding me of our predicament…and that Nikolai and I have an audience.

"Fuck you, X," Nikolai hisses. "You saved her only to torture her?"

We come to a screeching halt, and Nikolai's finger slips inside me. I buck and moan. Nikolai kisses me, no doubt to quiet me, and I'm ravenous for him, teeth gnashing and tongues swirling. I nip at his bottom lip and draw blood, the copper tang filling my taste buds.

A stone door slides open, and we burst into a stairwell and then up and out into the night air.

"Hang in there, Pet. I'm going to take care of you."

But I can't even answer him. I am an animal, biting and scratching in his arms as X flings open the door to the Rolls and Nikolai practically throws me inside. I lie sprawled on my back when he climbs in and kneels beside me. He glances up to the open window where X climbs into the driver's seat.

"Drive!" Nikolai yells, and I feel the car lurch forward. Tears stream. "Now, Nikolai! Fuck. I need you *now*!"

"As you wish, my lady," he says with a wicked grin.

He shoves my dress up past my hips, spreads my legs wide and plunges two fingers inside me. I cry out in such exquisite agony I think I may burst at the seams. His face disappears between my legs as his tongue assists his fingers, lapping the length of my folds and swirling around my aching clit.

I tear at my hair and writhe along the seat of the Rolls.

"Don't stop! Oh, my God, Nikolai. Don't you fucking stop!" I growl and moan and buck into his face.

And he doesn't stop. He is relentless in his savage feast—lips, tongue, *teeth* working me to the brink of insanity while his fingers pump inside me.

One of his fingers hits the spot, and his tongue sends me straight over the edge.

I cry out my prince's name as fresh tears stain my cheeks. The relief is overwhelming.

His head collapses between my knees, and for several long moments, no one says a thing.

The car rolls to a stop and X announces our arrival through the still-open divider. "The Royal Hospital of Edenvale," he says. "Shall I give you two a minute?" he asks, not even trying to hide his amusement.

Neither Nikolai nor I say a word. I'm not even sure I've retained the ability to speak.

"And, Miss," X adds. "Congratulations. You're cured."

I wiggle my toes and note that I am no longer paralyzed *or* in sex-starved agony. It would appear that X is correct on all accounts.

"Nikolai?" I say softly when I find my voice again.

He finally lifts his head. His hair is wild and his eyes glazed over.

"Are you truly okay?" he asks.

I push myself to a sitting position and slide my dress back down.

"I'm okay," I assure him. "Thank you."

He runs a hand through his black hair, and I note the weariness in his gray eyes. It finally hits me that I'm not the only one who's endured today.

"I want to make sure *you're* okay," I say. "But—I

have to get inside. My sister must be worried sick, and my grandmother…" My voice catches on the word. "She's the reason we needed the money. This was never about deceiving you, Nikolai. Only about saving my family. I should have told you." Tears prick at the backs of my eyes once again.

"Don't worry about me," Nikolai says. "I understand. And I never should have doubted you." His eyes are so tender and full of love. "Whatever you need, Pet. And I'm coming with you."

He reaches for my hand, and I see that the knuckle is split on his own.

"Did you really punch X?" I ask.

His gaze grows dark and all too somber for a moment. "I thought you were dead."

The door opens to my right, and X stands there extending a hand.

"I've a salve for the wound when we get back to the palace, Your Highness." X grins at us, patting his bloodied lip with a silk handkerchief. He closes the door after Nikolai and I exit the vehicle. I marvel at my ability to stand after being paralyzed minutes ago. Then I catch sight of myself in the tinted window of the Rolls and gasp.

Dirt streaks my face, and my hair? I look as if I've been living in the forest like a wild animal.

"You're the most beautiful woman I've ever seen," Nikolai whispers in my ear.

I decide not to chide him for lying because time is everything.

"I have to get in there," I say.

Nikolai laces his fingers through mine. "Let's go."

X leads us inside the main entrance, and it only takes seconds for the gawks and whispers to begin. Before we even make it to the information desk, a camera flashes violently in my face.

"Look!" the paparazzo cries. "It's Prince Nikolai and his latest conquest! How about a quote, Your Highness? Who's the flavor du jour?"

In a flurry of movement, Nikolai has the man by the throat and shoved up against a wall.

"Be careful with your words," he hisses through gritted teeth as the man drops his camera to the floor, his face turning blue.

My eyes widen, and X leans in close, whispering in my ear. "I taught him that."

Before I have time to react, Nikolai lets the man go and is by my side again. In seconds, we've obtained my grandmother's room number. We bypass the elevator and race up the stairs to the fourth floor and stop short just outside her room.

Standing in front of the door are the queen and three guards, Christian and Catriona Wurtzer, and Brother Benedict.

"I almost trusted your little charade," the queen says with a self-satisfied grin. "But imagine my confusion when the prince failed to show up to dinner and I tracked the Rolls to the hospital. Surely X wasn't going to *dispose* of Miss Winter here." She raises a brow. "I suppose I'll have to take care of the disposal myself."

"What the *hell* is this, Adele?" Nikolai growls.

The queen simply nods in our direction. "Arrest them all for treason."

CHAPTER NINETEEN

Nikolai

ONE OF ADELE's thuggish goons lunges at Kate. But before the oversize gorilla with the neck tattoos can set a single finger on my love's skin, I lay him out with a swift uppercut to the underside of his mean jaw.

"Oof." He hits the floor like a sack of rotten potatoes and doesn't move again.

"That's going to be one hell of a migraine when he comes around," X says with approval, rolling the henchman over with his toe. "Well-played, Sire."

"Who's next?" I roar at the remaining guards. They forget what blood pulses through my veins, that of generations of fierce warriors and plunderers. I am descended from a long and noble line of men and women who got and secured what they wanted by any means necessary. I call on them now to aid me in this hour of dire need. My gut tells me that Nightgardin is using her as their puppet, but I don't have the proof to make an accusation now. Better to wait and watch. For now, the threat is neutralized. She is going down, and Kate will be protected.

Adele snaps her fingers. Sven and Sval, giant twins who reportedly did time in a Siberian prison as hit men for the Russian mafia, swagger forward, cracking their scarred knuckles.

"Want to tag team, X?" I call out. "A little fun for old times' sake?"

"Only if we challenge ourselves to taking these amateurs in under ten seconds." My bodyguard's wager enrages the twins.

"We *amateurs* eat little worms like you for breakfast." Sven opens his mouth to reveal a row of gold-plated teeth.

"Scared, pretty boy?" Sval jeers.

"I am, actually." I yawn. "Scared that by the time X and I finish with you, there will be nothing left to interrogate."

Sven slowly blinks. "But the queen—"

"Is not heir to the throne." I draw myself to my full height. "And is acting without a signed decree from the royal liege and is therefore in breach of the law. She doesn't have a leg to stand on legally with this attempt at a coup. Treason is being committed here, but it's not by me. With whom do you want to align loyalties, gentlemen?"

"Catriona is not with heir, either!" Christian says, stepping forward, his sister's upper arm in his grasp. "I mean, she's not carrying *your* heir. She made the mistake of confiding her and the queen's little scheme to me. My sister actually thought I'd be party to her own treason to further Rosegate's interests alongside Adele's bigger and more diabolical ambitions. But it's not your child she carries, Nikolai. She has said so herself."

Catriona wrenches from her brother's grasp and slaps him across the face. "You spoiled everything for me. Everything! The queen will make you pay. *All* of you!"

"I will ruin you," Adele says to my friend, her voice as threatening as the hiss of an adder.

"So be it," Christian says. "But you will *not* ruin the prince." He turns to me. "I'm so sorry, Your Highness. I will never doubt you again." Then he grabs Catriona's arm again and hauls her away.

"Well," I say, eyeing the queen. "That solves the problem of my upcoming nuptials, X. Wouldn't you agree?"

X steps beside me, removing a deadly-looking blade with a jewel-encrusted handle from his black boot. He uses it to casually clean his nails. We are in a hospital, after all, and do wish to remain civil.

"Don't be fools, my good men," I order Adele's remaining brutes. "I am prepared to be reasonable based on the fact you have a combined IQ that is smaller than today's date, but if you come one step closer to Kate, you will be dead." I'll resurrect Edenvale's old beheading customs and do the deed myself.

"Blood doesn't need to be spilled," Benedict breaks in with his deep, commanding voice, as if sensing my murderous urges. A crucifix dangles from his wrist beneath his black clerical habit.

But I am not to be reasoned with. "Anyone here who makes the mistake of touching a single square inch of

Kate's body will be chewing on my boot." My voice echoes through the hospital corridor.

The door behind us creaks open.

"Kate?" A fiery-haired woman with creamy skin and a smattering of freckles peers out. "What's going on? You brought company?"

"Maddie!" Kate sounds on the verge of tears. "Is Gran—?"

"Still touch and go," Maddie says, hugging herself. "She has moments of consciousness, but they are few and far between. Where have you been? You were supposed to relieve me hours ago. I need to step outside for five minutes. Feel fresh air on my face."

"I said arrest them!" the queen shouts to Sven and Sval, but they remain motionless. "Or I shall make sure you are both the first volunteers in my new all-eunuch squadron."

"I must insist that everyone listen to me," Benedict says in a calm voice that silences the chaos. He has always been good at that. "Nikolai has been ordered to marry according to the proclamation, but I have recently learned of the Wagmire Defense."

"The what?" Adele waves her hand. "Never mind— I don't care. Arrest them all."

"If true love can be proven…" Benedict catches and holds my gaze as if the queen hasn't opened her mouth. "Then the marriage may proceed."

Kate gasps behind me.

"Is this true?" I ask, unable to grasp the fact that I might be able to somehow get everything I want.

"I read all eight hundred pages of *The Lesser Known Edenvale Royal Bylaws and Subcommands*." Benedict raises a finger. "There is one catch. To prove true love the couple must swim unassisted across the Bottom-less Lake to the Island of Atonement, in accordance with our ancient customs, thereby passing a test of the heart."

I flex my jaw. A mighty challenge awaits us, but I am determined we shall prove our love's worth. After so many years in the darkness, I am ready to fight for this shot at the light.

"Did you just say swim?" Kate asks in a tiny voice shot through with fear.

An ominous medical device alarm sounds from the room Maddie has just emerged from. Two nurses run up the hall. Kate steps forward, the panic on her face from her fear of water twisting to an expression of pure anguish.

"Gran, no!"

Kate

The nurses rush past me and nearly knock Maddie out of the way. The queen and her two guards are forced to move as well. Nikolai doesn't waste a breath, grabbing my hand and spiriting me inside the room.

I can't see anything other than the nurses, a flurry of movement around my grandmother's bed. My breathing hitches as I prepare myself for the worst.

"Sophia," one of them chides, calling Gran by her first name. "You gave us quite a fright. Next time press the call button, and we'll be in as soon as you need us."

One of the nurses turns to face my sister and me, and her eyes widen when she recognizes Nikolai.

"Your—Your Highness. I didn't realize—"

"Ignore me," he commands. "Let the two Miss Winters know what has happened with their grandmother at once. That should be all that matters here."

Her cheeks redden with embarrassment. "Of course, Your Highness." She turns to Maddie, the one who's been here all day. I swallow back the guilt. I should have come last night when she called. I should have thought about something other than my own fleeting chance at happiness. Then half the ruling body of Edenvale wouldn't be waiting in the hall to take me from my family for good.

"Miss Winter, it seems as if your grandmother is ready to breathe on her own, and she took to telling us by turning off her heart monitor."

Maddie gasps and covers her mouth. I let out a strangled sob.

"She's—she's okay?" I ask, tears of happiness overpowering whatever awaits me when I walk out this door.

The nurse nods, her warm brown eyes immediately setting me at ease. "Please, if you all step out for a few minutes, we can get the doctor in here so we can remove the tube and check her vitals. We'll call you as soon as she's ready."

I nod eagerly, grabbing Maddie's hand. Nikolai holds my other one, and I squeeze them both, two people I love dearly standing beside me.

We step out into the hall, where I find the Royal Police leading away the queen's brutish guards.

"I've spoken with Father," Benedict says to Nikolai. Both men shoot a glance toward Adele, who is also being detained by two officers. "It sounds as if much has gone on tonight that he was unaware of. He'd like to see you for a full statement when you're through here."

Adele growls at us and spits at Nikolai's feet. "You don't deserve happiness," she says. "Not after any chance of it was taken from me because of you and your miserable family. I know people. Powerful people. This is *not* the last you'll hear from me, Prince Nikolai," she vows, her words dripping with both anguish and disdain.

"I'm sure it's not," he says. "But for now I want you out of my sight." He eyes the officers. "Detain her somewhere safe—where she cannot harm others or herself. My father will be in contact with further instructions."

The men nod and take hold of her under the arms, leading her away with heels dragging.

I understand her sadness. I've known great loss, too, as has Nikolai. I'd even shut myself away from the prospect of happiness again after Jean-Luc. For two years I played it safe, afraid to move on. But the queen—she is stuck in a cycle of hate and blame so big that it's blinded her to the world around her.

I shudder.

"No, Pet," I hear Nikolai say. Then my eyes meet his. "I know what you're thinking, and no. I would not have ended up like that."

A tear rolls down my cheek, not only because he's read my thoughts but that he knows what I was thinking about him.

He cups my face in his palms. "It could have been me. I admit that wholly and completely. But it only could have happened had you not walked into my life—or had Adele truly sent you to your death."

He kisses me, his lips fierce and insistent against mine. I can taste the salt of my own tears.

"No," I say. "Your heart may have been dark, but hers is black and cruel. Yours was always salvageable."

"Only by you, Kate."

I smile. "Only by me."

Benedict clears his throat, and I'm reminded that we are not alone.

"The Wagmire Defense," he says.

My grandmother's door opens, and the nurse ushers us in.

"Did someone just say the Wagmire Defense?"

Her voice is like the sweetest music. I keep from throwing myself on her frail body, but I grab Gran's hand and press it to my cheek.

"Yes." I laugh through falling tears. "The Wagmire Defense. Do you—do you know something of it?"

She huffs out a breath as if whatever she's about to say she's told me a million times.

"I knew your mother," she says, and I frown as I realize she's not lucid after all.

"Yes, Grandmother. I know. My mother was your daughter-in-law, remember?"

She waves me off, and the focus of her gaze fixes not on me, not Maddie, but—Nikolai and Benedict.

"I knew *your* mother," she says to the two men. "Knew her when she was a commoner and even after she'd met the terms of the Defense. A great woman, she was—your mother. Pity her history couldn't be shared, sworn to secrecy as we all were."

Nikolai's normally golden skin blanches while Benedict's expression remains impassive.

"She did what she had to do to protect her sons," Gran says, and her gaze returns to me. "And you, my Katie. Love will carry you across the Bottomless Lake. I am sure of it as I'm sure their mother isn't—"

She pauses, and a far-off look takes over her features.

"Nurse," she says, eyeing the woman who's wheeling the ventilator to the other side of the room. The woman turns to face us. "Nurse, would you introduce me to my visitors?"

"We're just volunteers," Maddie says, understanding that Gran's memories have left her. We are once again strangers to her. "Happy to see you're feeling well."

Maddie puts an arm around my shoulders and backs me away from the bed.

"She's gone for now," she whispers. "But it looks like the worst is over."

I nod and swallow back any more tears, for Gran's sake.

"She knew Mother," Benedict says, and I don't miss the hint of bitterness in his voice.

"If your grandmother is telling the truth…" Nikolai starts, but I cut him off.

"She's ill," I tell him. "She could be confusing your mother for someone else."

He shakes his head. "Confusion or not, she knew the Wagmire Defense. Our very own mother found the loophole," Nikolai says softly. "And now Kate—"

I shake my head. "I can't swim," I remind him.

"You can," he says and kisses me. "We can together. And then you'll be my bride."

"I'm terrified," I admit. "And also, that was a terrible proposal. If we survive this Bottomless Lake, I want a real one," I tell him.

He laughs. "And then you'll say yes?"

I shrug but can't fight the giddy smile taking over my face. "I guess we'll see."

He whisks me into the hall, where we hardly have any more privacy, but then, Nikolai loves to put on a show when he has a proper audience. He surprises me, though, with nothing more than a sweet, tender kiss that makes me positively melt.

"I love you," he whispers. "Just so we're clear on that."

I swallow as the words sink in, the words I never thought I'd hear, words he now cannot stop saying. "I love you, too."

"Then that settles it. You *will* be my queen."

I can't help but laugh.

"Still not a proposal," I say.

But yes, I think quietly to myself. *My answer is most certainly yes.*

CHAPTER TWENTY

Nikolai

My STEPMOTHER IS sent to recuperate on a private thera-peutic island in the Indian Ocean. Father is still blinded by his love for her, trusting that her betrayal comes only from a place of grief. But I know better, as does X. He promises to continue a private investigation into Adele's past. Something will turn up.

X briefs me on all the particulars as we race home at top speed. The Rolls-Royce screeches through the palace gates. It is time to face Father.

"Pet." I take Kate's hand between mine and kiss each fingertip. We step out of the car and into the pal-ace's grand entrance. "X can escort you to my cham-bers. Ensure you get a proper shower and that the cooks prepare a batch of fresh scones."

Kate spent some time with her grandmother before we left the hospital. But now that she is off the venti-lator, she and her sister no longer have to remain vigi-lant at her bedside.

"I don't want to leave you alone to confront your

father," she says, setting her jaw in the stubborn manner that I love.

"I don't need anyone to fight my battles for me," I snap, harder than I intend to.

She is unmoved. "Of course you don't. But you deserve to have the woman who loves you by your side no matter what. In good times and bad."

"My father's temper is worse than mine," I warn.

"I don't scare easily," she says with a small smile. Given that she is still beside me despite everything that has happened, I can only choose to believe her. Love for this amazing woman ignites my veins. She is a spark of everlasting fire. When I am beside her the darkness doesn't stand a chance.

X clicks his heels. "I'll inform air traffic control that we intend to depart for the Bottomless Lake within the hour?"

I nod. "Yes. The sooner the better." I squeeze Kate's hand. "I want you to be mine."

She squeezes back, but then I feel her go rigid.

"Something is wrong," I say.

She worries her bottom lip between her teeth. "Won't it—won't it be dark when we arrive?"

The sun already dips beyond the horizon.

I nod. "Yes. But X will see to it that torches are lit so we can find our way. We can wait until morning, though." I kiss her. "Patience is not one of my finer traits, but I can do it—for you."

She shakes her head. "You're right. The sooner the better. I don't want to chance anything else getting in the way of you being mine, as well." She offers me a nervous smile, and my whole being is set ablaze.

What this woman has already risked for me—what she's willing to still chance on my behalf—knocks the air straight out of my lungs. I've never known love like this, and I'm still not sure what I've done to deserve it. She needs to know I'd do the same for her.

I turn her toward me and settle my hands on her shoulders. She seems so delicate. Yet behind that fragility is a strength that threatens to bring me to my knees. "The lake, it is deep beyond measure."

She mashes her lips. "Hence the name."

"I will not force you to swim for me. This kingdom isn't worth making you feel like you're in danger for even a moment."

She swallows. "You'd walk away from all this for me?" Her face is pale even as her blue eyes shine bright.

"Without a second thought," I rumble. "Outside of telling you that I love you, these are the truest words that I have ever spoken."

She dips her head. "You think I'm strong enough for this?"

I tilt her chin up and fix my gaze on her. "I think you are strong enough for *anything*. Never doubt that, Kate. Not for one second, my beautiful, courageous *queen*."

Her eyes glisten, but she holds her head high and smiles. "Then I won't back down. Not an inch. You and I shall rule this kingdom, and I will start demonstrating my future courage as a queen by not letting the Bottomless Lake stand between me and my dreams."

She wraps her arms around my neck and presses her lips to mine. There is the sound of slow clapping.

I glance over, and Father stands in a nearby doorway, studying us with a sardonic expression. "Touching," he says in his deep voice. "The best performance I've seen in years."

Kate

I freeze. Yes, I've spoken to the king before, but it was for business purposes only. His voice hadn't sent ice flowing through my veins then. It does now.

"Don't, Father," Nikolai says, his voice firm, but I'm so attuned to him now that I can hear the strain. The worry.

The prince has his father's eyes, but King Nikolai's irises grow dark as he takes a step toward his son. His salt-and-pepper hair is perfectly in place, his suit tailored to an older yet still ruggedly fit body. If he's any indication of what I have to look forward to as Nikolai ages… I shake my head, banishing the thought. Because other than his distinguished good looks, the king stares at me with utter condescension and disapproval, his own gray eyes mired in distaste.

"How dare you speak to me as such," the man says, standing inches from his son. "How dare you bring your whore into our home when you've broken it beyond repair. The queen is *ruined*, you selfish, ungrateful child."

I gasp. The king opens his mouth to speak again, but Nikolai cuts him off.

"Enough, Father!" he roars, enough so that the man takes a step back. Nikolai's hand still grips mine fiercely, enough so that I feel pain, but I stand my ground along with him. "The true *queen* was my mother. And I know everything. I know about the Bottomless Lake, about the Wagmire Defense, and that my own mother was not of royal blood." He holds up his arm. "Look, Father. Take a good look at where common blood flows through my veins all because you wanted to marry for love. And you dare to deny me the same?"

Nikolai's chest heaves with every breath. All of his words, his passion—it's for *me*.

The king's eyes widen. His skin grows pale, and he stumbles back another step. Yet he says nothing.

"If you ever, *ever* refer to Kate as my whore again, I won't be so kind with you as I was with Adele. She is not fit to be queen, Father. And I think, deep down, you know it. But also know this. If you loved my mother enough to risk the kingdom for her, then you might understand a fraction of what I feel for Kate. We will swim the lake. We will make it to the Island of Atonement. And I will prove that I am worthy of her love."

I take in a sharp breath. "No," I finally interrupt. "Nikolai—I must prove myself to *you*."

He lessens his grip on my hand and brings my palm to his lips, pressing a soft kiss against my skin.

"You never had anything to prove," he said. "You and your sister have given everything of yourselves to take care of the only family you have left. I know this was never about money for you but about unconditional and unwavering love. I've spent too long surrounded by people who are with me for their own gain that I forgot what love was. Perhaps this test of will is meant to prove something to the rest of the royal court, but know that whether we make it to the end of this quest or not, we've already won."

I let out a hiccuping sob, yet my smile is as broad as my love for this amazing man.

I cup his hands in my palms. "We've already won," I echo.

X appears in the doorway behind the king, which is odd considering he should have had to walk past us to arrive there. Then again—as I'm beginning to learn—X is capable of far more than we know.

"Sire. My Lady," he says. "The jet is fueled and ready to go. Are you ready?"

We both nod without hesitation, but the king approaches his son again, this time planting his hands on Nikolai's shoulders. Nikolai stiffens.

"You really love her," he says, and then he begins to laugh. "You *love* her!"

"Father, have you gone mad?"

The king laughs again, his head tilted toward the ceiling. "How," he says, "after all these years, could you expect me to believe your feelings were true? You've never so much as brought a woman to dine with us, yet you are willing to swim the lake for a commoner."

Nikolai's jaw tightens, and his father's laughing ceases.

"Commoner or not, your mother had more royal blood than any queen before her. No one—and I mean *no one*—shall ever be her equal."

Nikolai swallows hard, understanding what I know to be true, as well.

Theirs was a great love—Nikolai's mother and father's. Perhaps that is why someone like Adele was able to manipulate her way to the throne. No one could ever replace the love the king lost, but the kingdom needed a queen. Adele must have been the perfect aristocratic fit—on paper.

But there is so much more to finding the perfect match, as I've found mine in the most unlikely of places.

"I know the feeling," Nikolai says, the slightest tremor in his otherwise determined voice.

"How did you know?" the king asks, scrubbing a hand across his jaw. "How did you know about your mother?"

I clear my throat. "My grandmother, Your Highness," I say, taking a steady breath. "She's not well, mentally speaking, but she has moments of clarity. I believe she might have known the late queen many years ago."

The king pulls both Nikolai and I into an unexpected embrace, and I respond on instinct, wrapping one arm around each of the men at my sides.

"Go," King Nikolai whispers to us both. "Go prove your love to the rest of the world. You've already proven it to me."

He releases us, and both Nikolai and I bow our heads to our respected ruler.

"Why, though?" Nikolai asks. "Why did you never tell us?"

The king shudders his expression, and I wait for him to repeat what Gran said, something about protecting her sons.

"My father wasn't so understanding," he simply says. "So we were forced to live a lie, to tell all that she came from an ancient royal line only recently uncovered. And because I loved your mother, I didn't fight him on it. She was my queen. That was all that mattered."

It's a nice enough story, but for reasons I cannot explain, I think he's lying. Maybe it's that Nikolai is so much like his father, that being able to read one allows me to read the other.

But Nikolai's beautiful smile is his acceptance, so I let it go. Because Nikolai is my prince. And that's all that matters to me.

"Thank you, My Liege," Nikolai says, and it's in this moment I know he will be the king this country needs…and the man I cannot live without.

As X leads us toward the doors from where we came, Nikolai stops and turns toward his father once more.

"I'd like to move Kate's grandmother—and sister, if she chooses—to the palace after the wedding. Her grandmother will need constant care, so I'll be hiring nursing staff, as well."

His father nods. "Tell me her name, and I'll see to it the preparations are made."

"Sophia Winter," Nikolai says before spinning back toward X so that only I see the look of complete and utter astonishment take over the king's countenance. But it lasts no longer than a second before he is a mask of calm again, so much so that I believe it must have been my imagination playing tricks on me.

"Consider it done," the king says, and before I know it, I'm spirited out the palace gates and to the airfield once again.

"It's time to claim our future," Nikolai says as we stand before the steps leading up to the aircraft.

And then he kisses me until I forget that I almost died tonight, until I forget the king's strange reaction to my grandmother's name, until I forget that I have anything to fear.

I will claim my future, I think, as his tongue sweeps past my lips and I taste victory already.

And then I whisper against him. "My future—is *you*."

CHAPTER TWENTY-ONE

Nikolai

THE BOTTOMLESS LAKE is located in the most remote region on the eastern borders of my kingdom. We fly over fifteen-thousand-foot mountain peaks until we reach a high-altitude meadow with a runway. Long golden grass waves in the wind while white flowers bob as if in greeting. After we disembark the jet, I take Kate's hand in mine, leading the way along the narrow trail. No words pass between us. At least nothing that can be spoken aloud. The trail swings out onto a cliff, and I hear her gasp. Not because of the sheer granite wall and vertigo drop-off. But because of what lies so far down below.

It is the deepest lake in the world. There are rumors of ancient creatures trolling these mysterious waters— sea monsters, mermaids and other such nonsense. But I don't take much stock in the old storytelling.

Still, it's disconcerting to peer into water that blue, visible even in the luminescence of the moon, that piti- less color that seems to attract all available light, to suck it down into its icy heart.

I lace my fingers with Kate's, let our palms slide in a gentle caress, a delicious promise of later. Heat ignites my veins. Soon, so soon, this beautiful woman will be mine.

X guides us down the stone steps to the lakeshore, and as he sets to work lighting floating torches to blaze our trail, I strip from my clothing in easy, unconcerned movements. As I remove my pants I smile as she stares at my cock.

"See something you like, Pet?" I ask her with a wry smile. I love that my body gives her such wicked, carnal pleasure.

She opens her mouth, and I expect a witty insult. Instead, she sucks in a breath and falls to her knees, bracing her hands on the gravelly beach.

My flirtatious instincts evaporate as I slip into pure protection mode. "What is it?" I drop into a low crouch.

"It's a stupid thing to be this afraid of water, isn't it?" She lifts her gaze, and the pain stamped there almost levels me. "But try rationalizing that with my body."

"Kate, my love, I have told you before, I don't require you to do this. My kingdom pales in comparison to your safety and happiness."

"I want to be brave for you, for me, for us, for love. But it's not the memory of what I've lost at the depths of a river shallower than this. It's what I could lose. I don't just mean us losing our freedom to marry, Nikolai. What if something happened? What if I lost *you*?" Kate shakes her head, and then her jaw takes on that determined set that makes me want her all the more. "Promise me you can do this, and I won't let fear win." She removes her dress and is bare before me, all creamy skin and soft angles. Her perfect breasts make my mouth water.

I step forward. "I can do this, Kate. *We* can do this. Though I can't help feeling that I don't deserve you."

She presses a cool hand to the side of my cheek, skimming my stubble. "We could stand here debating that claim, or we could swim to the Island of Atonement and get on with the rest of our lives."

We stare out to the middle of the lake, now dotted with small licks of flame, to where a modest, heart-shaped island is covered by a thick blanket of trees. In the middle is a tall stone tower, glittering in the brilliant moonlight, that looks as ancient as the mountains.

"What is waiting for us out there?" she whispers.

"I can't say for certain." I cover her hand with mine. "But whatever dangers or mysteries we are about to face, we'll face them together."

"Just as we will anything else in life."

She nods and wades into the water, and I've never seen anything more stunning. This woman is willing to sacrifice anything for me, for us.

I feel the same way.

And so I follow after.

Kate

The water is surprisingly warm, yet I inhale a shuddering breath. Nikolai's hand is still in mine as we wade deeper, following the line of X's torchlights, though X himself is nowhere to be seen.

Because we must do this alone.

Nikolai suddenly halts.

"What is it?" I ask.

He squeezes my hand. "The bottom will drop out soon," he warns, and I can tell he fights to keep his voice even. "You said once that your sister said you could swim, that you'd just blocked it out. I can't let you go any farther, Kate. Not if you are putting your life at risk."

I nod, knowing what he is asking of me—what I am asking of him. The water is halfway up my torso, my breasts nearly covered, and despite the balmy air, I tremble. Then I squeeze my eyes shut and drop beneath the surface, letting go of Nikolai's hand. The last thing I hear is him frantically calling my name.

I force my eyes open. The water is clear but dark, and in the places below a floating torch, I catch the movement of a fish or whatever else dwells beneath the surface. My heart races as panic threatens to take hold of my senses, but I remind myself that there is clean air above me, that I am not alone, and that I am not trapped as my parents were.

I am not trapped. But Nikolai is. And he is depending on me to set him free.

I kick my legs out behind me and push my palms and my outstretched arms through the water. And then I burst through the surface. My feet no longer reach the ground, yet I am still here. I am in control.

I am triumphant.

"Kate!" Nikolai cries, his voice hoarse as he swims out to meet me. "Fucking hell, Kate. What are you doing?"

I grin as my arms and legs make circles through the

inky blue. "I'm pretty sure I'm swimming," I say, and my heart thunders in my chest. "Oh, my God, Nikolai. I'm swimming!"

His eyes gleam silver in the moonlight, and the terror I know I caused washes from his face.

"You did it," he says. "Jesus, fuck, you did it!"

I narrow my eyes. "Don't let Benedict hear you speaking like that."

He lets out a broad, bellowing laugh and kisses me as he keeps himself afloat.

"Let's go get our future," I say. He nods, and we set out for the island.

We swim from torch to torch, each one a beacon. As my adrenaline wanes and the long minutes set in, my limbs grow weary.

"Just make it to the next torch," Nikolai says, when he senses my exhaustion.

And so I vow to make it to the next torch. And then the next one. And the one after that until I stumble as my toes unexpectedly dig into sand.

I straighten and stand as tears spring from my eyes. Nikolai doesn't waste a second as he scoops me into his arms and kisses me hard, unrelenting, and I realize my only fear now is that I will never be able to get enough of this man.

He doesn't let go, doesn't release me from the kiss as he strides onto shore, his strong arms holding me close. It is a mirror image of the day we met, when he carried me to safety in the maze. Then I was determined to marry him off to another. But today I risk everything to make him mine.

I cling to his solid, naked form as he marches

straight for the stone monument, and he only releases me when we stand before a carved-out doorway that beckons us to enter.

We do.

I gasp as Nikolai whispers, *"Look."* His head tilts toward the ceiling—or at least where there should be one. But instead the stone opens to the star-speckled sky, to the full moon in all her brilliance, lighting us from above. I spin, my eyes taking in the walls that surround us, and see that they are covered with rich, painted murals, all different versions of two lovers discovering this land.

"Oh, Nikolai." Those are my only words, though. I am not sure I have breath to give life to what I wish to say.

"I know," he says, relieving me from the burden as we simply marvel and stare.

I run my hands along the painted stone walls until I come to a spot of empty canvas, a section of a wall waiting for the next painting. It's then that my fingers nick a loose stone, sending it crashing to the floor.

I gasp. "I'm sorry! Oh, my God. I broke the monument. I survived that swim to come here and ruin this sacred place, and I—" But I gasp again as Nikolai, without hesitation, reaches his arm inside the shadowy opening. This is the thing horror stories are made of, and I brace myself for him to cry out as some deadly creature takes his hand, but instead he pulls out a blue wooden box no bigger than a schoolchild's pencil case. A piece of parchment is wrapped around it, fastened with a waxen seal.

Now it is Nikolai who gasps.

"What is it?" I ask, and he stares up at me, his gray eyes glistening.

He smiles as a tear escapes down his beautiful, chiseled cheek.

"This is the royal seal," he says. "I think—I think this is from my parents."

I step into his grasp, wrapping my arms around his torso. Then he breaks open the seal and unfolds the parchment, holding it up for both of us to see.

"Read it to me," he says. "I'm too fucking nervous."

I swallow and do as he asks, reading the letter aloud as my own eyes well with tears again.

To Our Dearest Nikolai,

Generations have gone before us, those that have abided by the ancient decree. And should you go that route as well, we pray that you are happy. That if and when it is necessary, this finds your heir; that generations do not pass before Edenvale is rewarded once again with a king and queen who are pure of heart. For we have found the way to true happiness.

Our only hope is that you are able to do the same. Should you find the one who fills your heart, then she shall also be the one to fill your soul. There is no room for blackness, for hate, for anything to cloud the mind of a king who shall rule with a just hand if he has true love in his heart. If you've found this gift, do not take such treasure for granted. Populate the palace with heirs, with products of a love immeasurable, and the kingdom will prosper as does your devotion.

To love and be loved in return—there is no greater reward we can bestow upon you. But take what is in this box and use it as a token of that love. Then, when the time is right, come back to this place and paint your story upon these walls. Leave a token for those who come after you.

With all the love in our hearts,
King Nikolai and Queen Cordelia

I wipe away tears as I finish, my arms still around my prince. He says nothing as he opens the box and removes a glorious sapphire-and-diamond ring—a ring fit only for a queen.

He pulls away and stares down at me with shining eyes, his beautiful naked body bathed in radiant moonlight. He lets the box and parchment clatter to the stone floor as he drops to his knee.

"You said you wanted a real proposal," he says, no hint of the rogue I met barely a month ago in his gaze or in his tone.

I cover my mouth and nod, unable to speak without the possibility of sobbing.

"Then here it is, Kate. There is nothing more real than my love for you. Words cannot capture it. The entire kingdom cannot contain it. It is as deep as a lake with no bottom and as vast as the infinite universe. I would have given up my birthright for you, but instead you gave up your fear for me. I can think of no greater act of love than the one you have performed. I beg you to give me a lifetime to repay you. Be my life. Be my love. Be my queen."

I sink to my knees in front of him, pressing my lips together to keep from falling apart. Then I stand and take his face in my hands.

"Yes," I whisper, and I kiss him again and again and again. "Yes, Nikolai." He kisses me back, pulling my left hand free so he can slide the ring onto my finger. It is a perfect fit. "Infinite times—*yes*. But wait. First we have to take care of one pesky detail."

His face blanches. "What. What more do you need? Kate, I'll do anything to win your hand."

I take a step toward him, splaying my palms against his chest. "We had a wager."

And there it is, that feline grin of his that tells me he wants to devour me whole. I might let him.

"Why, yes, my love. We did have a wager. And I do believe you won. Didn't you?"

I nod. "Do you remember the terms?"

His brows furrow, and he scrubs a hand across his beautifully stubbled jaw. "I owe you nothing more than a favor. Would you like me to make payment? What is your price?"

I nod again then stand on my toes and whisper in his ear. Nikolai's eyes widen, and he lets out a guttural sound.

"As you wish, Beloved," he says.

My skin is pebbles of gooseflesh. I'm wearing nothing but the glittering jewels on my finger. I marvel at his stiff length, ready for me as the heat coils in my belly, so very ready for him. I let him guide me back into the water. He speaks no words at all as he pulls me over his beautiful body.

The lake water is cool against my skin, but his tip

is warm and wet at my opening where he nudges until slick heat envelops his perfect, thick erection. I sink over it, burying him to the hilt.

He bites my shoulder and growls.

I slide up slowly and let him swirl around my swollen center before plummeting over him again.

He cradles my face in his hands and stares intently into my eyes—eyes I know are reddened from tears of disbelief, of love, of complete and utter joy.

"We may rule this kingdom for a lifetime, but you—my future wife and my future queen—shall rule my heart for eternity. Just as those paintings on the island's tower wall, my love for you lives beyond this life and beyond this world."

"Nikolai," I gasp as he moves inside me. "I love you, too."

"But," he says, flicking his tongue against my lips, the devil in his stare, "just because you rule me doesn't mean you'll ever tame me."

He pinches my pebbled nipple, and I shriek at the exquisite pleasure and pain.

"After all—I'm still one royal prick."

And he is my royal temptation. I will never, ever get enough.

EPILOGUE

X

I WIPE REMNANTS of drywall from my shoulder as the sound of drilling whines through the ceiling.

"You're getting sloppy, X," she scolds from the shadows. "You've been followed."

I step to the left and watch the drywall dust on the carpet to my right.

I raise my brows, knowing that she can see me even though I cannot see her.

"Really?" I ask. "Because if that were true, why are they a floor above?" I nod toward the flashing blue light on the desk in front of her. "Perhaps they have no idea *I'm* here. Perhaps they weren't even looking until a server signal popped up on their screen." I imagine her dark eyes boring holes through me.

She lets out a sigh. "You are still as arrogant as ever."

I grin and take a step forward. She doesn't stop me because she knows I'm still not close enough to see.

"And you're still as easy to ruffle as ever. And, my Lady, I do enjoy ruffling you."

There is a long silence but for the drilling overhead. They will break through soon. We're on borrowed time, but then again, we always are.

"Tell me," she says, her voice firm, though I detect the slightest tremor. Our parrying is over. "Is he safe?"

I open my mouth to say her name—or maybe her call sign, *D*. But I stop myself as I always do. If I don't speak it aloud, no one else can hear. If I don't see her in the flesh, they cannot torture her existence from me.

I bite back a self-satisfied grin. I've survived the worst any captor has had to offer—whips, brands, knives sharp enough to draw blood yet small enough that bleeding out would be a long, slow death.

Much to the disappointment of all who've tried, I'm not dead. Unfortunately for them—they are.

"X," she pleads, as if I'd ever falter on a mission.

"He is safe," I say. "He and the princess are enjoying an extended honeymoon on a private island off the coast. They will return soon, but plans for the celebration have been postponed until the king decides what to do with the traitorous queen. The prince, though, will rule at his father's side, and the princess will serve as ambassador to our neighbors."

"And Rosegate?" she asks.

A chunk of ceiling falls to the floor.

"We don't have much time," I say. "They *will* break through. And Rosegate is secure for the time being, but we're still trying to figure out if the queen's motive was merely to take the throne or to aid Nightgardin in Edenvale's fall."

She pulls the thumb drive, the source of the flashing light, from the laptop's USB port.

"We won't be here when they break through," she says, and I hold up my palm, my hand curling into a fist to catch the small projectile. "I want the oldest prince to remain under surveillance, but you are relieved of immediate duty when it comes to him."

I nod. More drywall falls. I clip the carabiners to the belt loops on my trousers and wonder for the first time if the material will hold. I guess we're about to find out.

"What is the next mission?" I ask, knowing there is one.

I hear the wheels of her chair roll and can tell from the cadence of her breathing that she's now standing.

"It's all on the drive," she says.

I look down at the blue light in my palm. "The heir spare," I say, knowing without a computer monitor in front of me to corroborate. This is exactly what Nikolai wanted anyway. He will be none the wiser when my attentions shift.

"He is lost," she says, "the second son." Her voice grows distant as she does what she does best and disappears into a world that used to recognize her in seconds—one that now knows nothing of her existence.

Lost, I think. *What if he doesn't want to be found?*

The ceiling caves in, and because being found is not on *my* agenda for the day, I unhook one of the carabiners and leap from the fifteenth-floor window.

I throw the bungee cable over the line and let gravity and the southerly wind do their job.

I skim over taxis, buses, locals and tourists, none of them aware of my existence overhead.

When I land on the hotel balcony, I make a mental

note to thank the tailor of this suit. The strength of the belt loops is exquisite.

I brush away any further signs of ceiling dust and pick up my tumbler from the balcony ledge, draining the rest of my scotch. Then I thrust open the balcony doors to find a delicious brunette naked on the bed, a blindfold over her eyes and her wrists still bound to the bedpost. She purses her luscious, red-painted lips into a pout.

"You said you were running out to grab your drink. You've been gone for at least five minutes, X."

I check my watch. "Seven, darling."

She writhes against the satin sheet and bites her lip. "Well, I'm counting the minutes until you fuck me."

I tap my breast pocket and make sure the flash drive is stored securely. Then I tear off the jacket.

"Spread your legs and count down from three," I command, and she writhes again.

I unbutton my shirt.

"Three," she moans.

I lose the pants.

"Two."

I press my knees into the edge of the bed and run a hand up her thigh, my thumb teasing her folds where I left her drenched with anticipation.

"One," she whimpers.

Time's up.

* * * * *

*Keep reading for a sneak peek at
Benedict's story
MY ROYAL SIN
Coming soon!*

Ruby

YOU HAVE ONE month to break him, to make sure he does not take his vows still a virgin.

The door from the stairwell starts to slide open, and because I have no choice, I sneak past the pews and into a confessional. I'm still trying to calm my breathing when the shadow of a man appears on the other side of the lattice.

"Have you come to make confession?" a deep, gravelly voice asks.

I stopped believing in any higher power long ago. But I know why I'm here and what part I need to play. "Forgive me, Father. For I have sinned."

I open the screen on my phone that has my script for the evening and hope on my brother's innocence that giving up my own will set him free. If I can earn the money Madam promised, then I can buy the best legal representation in the kingdom and set my brother free.

"You may proceed, child," he says. "The Lord is ready to forgive your sins."

I stroke a finger along the lattice grate and remind myself to play the part for which I'm being paid.

"What if I want to keep sinning?" My voice is breathy and soft as I infuse it with the need a client would ache to hear. I glance at the screen in my palm.

"What if all I want is to relieve you of that desire pulsing between your legs?"

He hisses in a breath. "Who sent you?" I can tell he speaks between gritted teeth.

"Let me taste your thick, aching cock, Father," I say, my voice sweet as an angel as I try not to sound like I'm reading. "Let me take you so deep. I want to feel you throbbing, salty sweet against my tongue—"

"Who. Sent. You?" he interrupts, but I will not be deterred, not when my only choice is to succeed.

I scroll through the preplanned dialogue on the screen. "Think of all those times you've come alone," I tell him. "Every fantasy you've ever had, every sinful act you've dared let yourself imagine—I can be that for you."

His breaths are ragged, but he does not speak.

I let go of the lattice and slip my free hand under my skirt.

"Sire." I moan, as I slip a finger beneath my thong, working myself until I'm wet. "Do you hear that?" I ask, plunging two fingers into my now-slick heat. "That's my pussy, so ready for you. Don't you want a taste, Sire? Just a little lick?"

You need the money.

This silent reminder plays in my head as I try to lose myself in pleasure.

This is for your family.

I swirl a slippery finger around my clit and gasp,

the phone clattering to the floor. "Don't. You want. To make. Me. Come?" I ask between gasps, the words all me now. I am lost in the moment. "Is your hand on that cock, Sire? Is it daring you to bury yourself inside me? Because all you have to do is step outside that booth and sheathe yourself to the hilt."

I try to bring myself to climax, but even I can't forget entirely where I am or why I ended up here. So I embellish, crying out in feigned ecstasy.

"Oh... Your Highness. Oh God! Your Highness, I can't—" I add a few more gasps before yelling, "Benedict!"

"Enough!" he growls, and I collapse back onto my knees with a satisfied grin.

Yes. That was quite enough.

He waited until he thought I was done, which means he didn't want me to stop. If that's all that comes of tonight, I have succeeded in the first step.

Because this is not just any client on the other side of the wall. He is a prince, second in line for the throne and brother of our future king. I startle to see him standing in the opening of my booth.

"Forgive me, Father," I say, straightening the skirt that barely covers what lies beneath. The air smells of sex, and the man looming before me stares with beautiful green eyes. "Did I make you sin?"

RUINED

JACKIE ASHENDEN

MILLS & BOON

To Jenny.

You've been waiting so patiently for the end of Cat and Smoke's story

and here it is at last.

Hope you like it. :-)

CHAPTER ONE

Cat

IT'S ALWAYS BAD when you're in the kind of trouble that requires the help of an outlaw motorcycle club. It's especially bad when you know you'll do anything to get that help.

But what do you do when your kid's in danger? You fight any demons, slay any dragons. It's hard when you can't slay those dragons on your own, though. When you have to pay in order to have them slain for you.

I would have paid anything to get Annie away from her father.

Which was why I'd ended up standing outside the Knights of Ruin MC's clubhouse, in the rain, at midnight on a Saturday. In the middle of one of the loudest parties I'd ever heard.

I didn't want to go in. I always swore I wouldn't.

But when the devil has your kid, and the cops think everything's fine, what the hell are you supposed to do? There was only one person who could help me, and unfortunately he was inside.

Dane Kingsolver, aka Smoke, my best friend since I was a kid and a Knights enforcer.

Who was not answering his goddamn phone.

The Knights' clubhouse was in an old brick warehouse on the outskirts of Brooklyn. There were hogs lined up like toys outside, a couple of prospects hanging around looking after them, a couple more on the door. Music blared—the hard-driving beat of heavy rock. A bunch of girls were talking to the prospect on the door, their hair in artfully styled manes, their skirts up to their navels. All looking for a piece of danger, of wildness.

Idiots. They didn't know the real danger they were getting themselves into, and I almost wanted to go over there and tell them. But I didn't. They wouldn't listen. I'd done it enough times to know that.

As they disappeared inside I walked up to the prospect, who was standing with his hands in the pockets of his low-slung jeans, probably thinking he was God because he got to say who got in and who stayed out. He was young, with pretty blue eyes and still a hint of softness around his mouth.

That wouldn't last long. Soon he'd be a monster like all the rest.

He eyed me suspiciously, clearly not knowing who I was. Not that he would. I never came down here if I could help it.

I met his gaze—never look away from a snarling dog. 'I need to see Smoke.'

My voice sounded flat and definitely don't-fuck-with-me. Don't give them an opening, because the next thing you know you're on your knees with two black eyes, your dignity and strength in pieces on the floor.

Never again. Never *fucking* again.

The prospect looked even more suspicious. 'Who's asking?'

'Cat. Cat Livingston.'

The kid's gaze took me in and I knew what he was seeing. A frazzled-looking older woman in skinny jeans and a faded Ramones T-shirt. No make-up. Stained sneakers with the rubber coming off at the toe.

Unimpressive. Deeply unimpressive.

I didn't give a shit. I wasn't here to impress him. I was here to see Smoke. To save my kid. Because if there was one thing I knew, it was that Smoke loved that kid nearly as much as I did and he'd do anything for her. He'd do anything for me, too—we had each other's backs like that.

'Yeah… See, I don't know you,' the prospect said, 'And I don't fucking think—'

'I don't care *what* you think.' I cut him off curtly. 'I'm Smoke's best friend, and he's going to be pissed if you don't let me in right now.'

I didn't want to tell him about Annie. I felt like a big enough fool as it was, without this asshole knowing all about my business.

'Hey, watch your mouth,' the prospect growled, full of his own self-importance. 'Show a little goddamn respect.'

Great. So I was going to be put in my place by a teenage asshole while my violent ex had my kid. And all because of a little 'respect'. Typical biker.

I'd opened my mouth to tell him what he could do

with his goddamn respect when Tiger came out through the doors, cigarette in one hand, beer in the other. Tiger was one of Smoke's best buddies, tall and leanly muscled like Smoke. He had dark, almost-black hair that glinted with copper in some lights and strange amber eyes that had apparently given him his road name.

Tiger was an asshole, but he was less of an asshole than this idiot in front of me.

'Hey, Cat,' Tiger said as he spotted me, his deep voice rough. 'What's brought you down here?'

Ignoring the prospect, I looked over at Tiger, who was standing at the top of the steps. 'Is Smoke around? I need to see him. It's urgent.'

I didn't particularly want to talk to Tiger about Annie either. He was opinionated about a lot of things, and kids was one of them.

Tiger leaned against the doorframe, lifted his beer and took a sip. He looked casual, but the gleam in his amber eyes was anything but. 'Yeah, he's around. But I don't know if you'd want to see him right now.'

'Why not? Like I said, it's urgent.' I shifted on my feet, not wanting to give away too much. 'Like…life or death urgent.'

'Uh-huh.' Tiger's gaze sharpened, though he kept on leaning against the doorframe lazily. 'Well, he's down the corridor. By the bedrooms.'

That was all I needed to hear. Not wanting to waste any time, I didn't spare the glowering prospect a glance as I went quickly up the steps. 'Thanks, Tiger,' I murmured as I slipped through the doors past him.

He gave a low laugh. 'Don't thank me. Just remember that this is a party. Don't blame me if you run into something you don't like.'

I should have listened to him. But I didn't. My head was too full of my kid and the asshole who'd picked her up from school and hadn't brought her back like he'd told me he would. Who wouldn't respond to my texts or calls.

Fear sat heavy and cold in my gut, but I tried to ignore it as I stepped into the clubhouse. Panicking wouldn't help anyone—least of all Annie.

'Watch out for yourself, Cat,' Tiger called behind me. 'You know what a Knights party is like. An un-spoken-for woman is fair game.'

Actually, I *didn't* know what a Knights party was like. I'd never been to one. But Smoke had told me enough about them. Lots of drinking, smoking and loud music. Drugs. Public sex.

Sounded hideous to me, but then again, I wasn't a Knight and I didn't go to parties, so it wasn't my place to judge.

Still, as I made my way down the corridor I realised I was in the thick of it now. And, yeah, I was damn well judging.

The common area of the clubhouse looked like a group of frat boys had gone wild in a huge draughty warehouse—fat black leather couches, pictures of bikes and naked women on the wall, a couple of tables covered in beer bottles. The air stank of cigarette smoke, joints and spilled beer.

There was a bar down one end, where a guy was pouring shots onto the stomach of a mostly naked girl who was laughing and in danger of overturning the shot glasses.

I headed straight through the doorway without stopping or looking around, trying not to draw the attention of the mass of leather-clad bikers sitting on the couches or standing around near the bar. There were a couple of guys over by a pool table with two very naked women who carried cues, and a few who looked like they were having a serious conversation in one corner—except the woman had her head in one lap while her hand worked the guy next him.

Jesus. Smoke hadn't been kidding about these parties.

I'd only been in the clubhouse a couple of times, but I knew where the bedrooms were and I headed straight there, with my attention firmly on the doorway that led to them. Only to be stopped by a massive dude with tats everywhere, a heavy black beard and the weirdest pale green eyes I'd ever seen.

'Big Red' the name on his cut said. The VP. I hadn't met him before, but Smoke had told me about him. Meanest motherfucker this side of Genghis Khan, apparently.

Just my luck to run into him.

'Hey, darlin', whatcha doing here?' he asked lazily. 'I ain't seen you before.'

I gave him a smile, trying to be nice. 'I'm looking for Smoke. Tiger said he was down this way.'

'Aw, you don't need to see Smoke. You can see me.'

Great—first the prospect, now this guy. Could this night get any better?

I widened my smile. 'Perhaps I could come see you afterward?'

He laughed, raised a hand and gave my chin a pinch—which I did not appreciate. 'Smoke's kinda busy at the moment, sweetheart.'

'Why? What's he doing?'

Big Red laughed again. 'He's with Hannah. He won't want to be interrupted.'

Of course. Smoke was with a woman. Well, every other guy appeared to be, so why not him?

Simmering anger coiled tight in my gut. So, not only had I been forced to come down here to beg for help during a goddamn party, I was now being forced to interrupt my best friend having sex. And all because my asshole ex, Justin, hadn't brought Annie home when he'd promised.

I caught that anger, held fast to it—because it sure as hell was better than the cold fear that lay beneath it.

Keeping the smile plastered firmly to my face, I sidestepped the massive VP. 'Oh, I think he'll appreciate an extra,' I said as I moved past him, giving him a wink.

Leaving Big Red safely behind me, I stepped through the door into the corridor beyond. It was quiet back here; the only sounds were the beat of some kind of heavy house music coming from behind one door and the groans coming from behind another.

Oh, God, please don't let him be behind *that* door.

I moved down the corridor and was wondering where the hell he was and whether I needed to start knocking on doors and embarrassing myself, when I rounded the corner.

And stopped.

Dead.

A tall figure leaned against the wall. A familiar figure. Six three. Wide shoulders. Lean hips. Hair the colour of black ink cut short and close to his skull. Cheekbones God himself would envy. A strong, hard jaw. Straight nose and straight black brows. A mouth that apparently had *sin* written all over it—at least it did according to some of my friends.

Smoke. The person I knew best in the world and who knew me best, too. Whom I'd met when I was five and he was seven and we were next-door neighbours. I was his friend the moment he jumped on his skateboard, a skinny little kid in torn jeans and scraped knees, showing off for the new girl next door.

He'd done magic on that board. He'd been like the wind—smooth and fluid and powerful. Even at seven. Right then and there I decided I was going to marry him.

I didn't, of course.

Because if I had I certainly wouldn't be here, standing in a bikers' clubhouse, watching him with his long fingers buried in the dark hair of the woman kneeling in front of him. Obviously getting a blow job.

A wave of the weirdest heat went through me. He always had women hanging around, and I'd seen him making out with them on more than one occasion and it had never bothered me. But there was something about *this* that hit me like the flame from a blowtorch.

He'd always been a quiet, guarded kind of guy. Never let anyone see what he was thinking, kept everything locked down. Even with me. And if you tried asking him about himself he'd give you a couple of sentences then turn the question back on you—which made him a great listener.

But that's why they called him Smoke. Because it was just a smokescreen, a distraction so he didn't have to talk about himself.

Yet there was no smokescreen now, and the expression on his face...

I couldn't look away.

I'd always known he was a beautiful man, but I'd never *felt* it before. Now, though, I was mesmerised by the intensity that burned in his features. By the fierce hunger that drew his impressive jaw tight and made the powerful tendons of his neck stand out.

He had his attention on the woman as if every movement she made was incredibly important, and his mouth was moving as he whispered things I couldn't hear. I found myself wondering what kind of expression would be in those dark eyes of his. Whether they would be burning with hunger, too.

And what it would be like if he looked at you that way, too.

Shit. I shoved the thought away. Hard. Smoke and I had never gone there and never would. Once, when I was about sixteen, I'd had a major crush on him, but he never gave me any hint that he felt the same way—not once.

So I'd pushed it aside, forgotten about it. And I definitely didn't want all those old feelings bubbling up again now. No fucking way.

I loved Smoke—he was my best friend. But when

it came to sex, men were nothing but trouble, and I didn't want anything to do with them. Perhaps forever.

As if he'd sensed my presence, Smoke's head came up sharply, his black eyes slamming into mine.

And the weird heat that had me gripped intensified.

Holy shit. There was something in his gaze that made my knees weak for a second, that made me dizzy. Made me forget who I was.

As if he was looking at me for the first time in his life and really seeing me.

It was wrong and strange, and I didn't know how to deal with it. So I looked away, my face feeling like it was about to go up in flames.

'Cat?'

His voice was usually quiet and deep, but now there was an edge to it, rough and husky, that made something inside me shiver.

'What the fuck are you doing here?'

I stared fixedly at the wall opposite. 'Sorry. I didn't mean to interrupt. But…I need you.'

'Christ, I'm a little busy—'

'It's Annie.'

He went silent. After a moment he muttered something to the woman kneeling at his feet. There was the sound of rustling fabric, the jingle of the chains attached to Smoke's low-slung jeans, a zipper being done up.

I tried to will the blush in my cheeks away, tried to calm the fast beating of my heart. I had no idea what was wrong with me, but whatever it was I didn't have time for it.

The woman hurried past me, giving me a pissed-off look. Clearly she didn't like being interrupted either.

'Talk to me,' Smoke said shortly.

I took a moment to calm myself, then looked back at him.

The expression on his face was the same as it always was—guarded, wary. The walls behind his dark eyes were impregnable. That fierce, hungry look was gone as if it had never been. And there was a part of me that couldn't help but be sad about that. A part that wanted to see it again.

Getting a hold of myself, I ignored that part. 'I'm sorry—I really didn't want to come out here. But it's Justin. He picked Annie up from school and was supposed to have dropped her off four hours ago. He didn't. He's not answering his phone or his texts or...'

I stopped, feeling a bubble of panic welling up inside me. I didn't want to go to pieces now, and there was something about knowing Smoke was here, that he had my back, that made the tension inside me relax.

'Hey,' he said quietly, and his familiar, deep voice eased the panicked feeling. 'It's okay. We'll get her. You tell anyone else about this?'

'No.'

'How did you get here? You got a car?'

'Yeah.' The short, flat questions calmed me even further.

'Good.' He ran one long-fingered hand over his shorn head. 'Fuck. Okay. I want you to go home and stay there. I'll go get Annie.'

I knew he'd help because he always did. Still, relief had me leaning against the wall to stop myself sliding down it. But that was the way I dealt with things. If something needed to be done I tended to focus on that to the exclusion of everything else—even my own feelings. Because feelings just got in the way.

The downside was that when I'd done what I needed to, I tended to get overwhelmed by the inrush of the emotions I'd managed to block. It probably wasn't a healthy way to deal with things, but it had got me out of a lot of bad situations in the past so I wasn't knocking it.

Smoke's gaze sharpened, his dark eyes glittering. He knew when I was crashing.

'You need a lift home? I'll get Tiger to take you.'

Part of me wanted to go with Smoke, but I knew he wouldn't want me getting in the way. Still, I wasn't going to collapse like a complete loser.

'No, it's okay. I've got my car.' My throat tightened, a wave of fear hollowing out my stomach. 'I just want her home, Dane. Please.'

Panic had made me use his given name, and even though he hated it when I did, the look in his eyes softened.

Lifting one of those large, warm hands, he touched my cheek—light, fleeting. 'It's okay, kitten. I'll get her back.'

Kitten. When I called him Dane he called me kitten. A stupid joke.

Yet for the first time ever the touch and the dumb pet name sent a strange shiver straight through me.

He didn't seem to notice as he dropped his hand. 'Jesus, why the fuck is he doing this? He knows I'll fucking kill him if he so much as touches you or Annie.'

I dismissed the shiver. I really didn't need any more weirdness tonight.

'I don't know. He seemed fine when he dropped her home last week.'

Justin had been quiet for weeks, with the threat of a restraining order keeping him in line. He was a lawyer, and he was always talking about how he could get around it, but he hadn't done anything—much to my relief.

Then again, if Smoke went and got Annie and some shit went down...

'Don't do anything stupid, okay?'

I hooked a finger into one of his belt loops, holding him in case he decided to take off without listening to me. He never had before, but I wanted to be sure. He viewed Annie as a surrogate daughter and was hugely protective of her.

'I know Justin's a dick, but he could make life difficult for you.' I didn't add that he could also make life difficult for the rest of the Knights, too, but I didn't need to.

Smoke looked down at me, his face unreadable. 'He'll get what's coming to him, Cat. Nothing you can do to stop it. Especially if he tries pulling any more of this kind of shit.'

I swallowed, my throat dry all of a sudden. 'It's not him I'm worried about.'

Something shifted in his guarded dark eyes, but I couldn't tell what it was.

'Yeah, I know. Don't worry.'

He smiled. and I knew then that he was furious. Because he only ever smiled like that when he was angry.
'I'll let him live.'
And for the second time that night I shivered.

CHAPTER TWO

Smoke

I'D KILL FOR that kid. I'd kill for Cat.

And as I headed out of the clubhouse and got on my bike I wanted to. Wanted to wrap my hands around that motherfucker Justin's neck and choke the living shit out of him.

He'd never pulled anything like this before, and I knew it was a bad sign. So far he'd kept his hands off Annie, but it was only a matter of time. Pricks like that were all the same—and I should know since I'd grown up with one.

As I slammed up the kick stand Tiger came over. He looked stoned, which was unsurprising given the smell of weed wafting around the clubhouse entrance.

'Whatcha doing?'

'Cat's got a problem with Annie,' I said shortly. 'Going to deal with it.'

'Need a hand?'

'Nope.'

The fewer people involved with this the better. Especially if that fancy-ass fucking lawyer was going to start throwing his weight around. He was the son of the local police chief, and that was the only reason he was still walking around and breathing.

Keep, the Knights' president, didn't want any situations escalating with the cops since the Knights had got them sweet a year or so ago. A few favours here, a few favours there and they left us alone.

The chief's son ending up dead would kill that arrangement.

Which was a big fucking pity for me.

He'd hurt Cat once before—hurt her real bad. I'd have killed him for that alone and screw the fucking peace agreement if she hadn't told me to back off.

I'd never understood that. But she was my friend and I didn't want to fuck up her life any more than it was already.

'Sure?'

Tiger liked to be involved when shit went down, but tonight he could stay here. He'd had too much to smoke anyway.

'I'm sure.' I started up my Harley, the roar of the pipes filling the night air. 'But keep an eye on your phone in case I need backup.'

He gave me a salute with two fingers near his forehead and I took off, heading out onto the streets.

I knew where Justin lived. Sometimes I used to ride past his townhouse just to remind him that I was out there, looking for an excuse to end him. A warning to stay away from the two people I cared about most in the world.

What the fuck he was doing with Annie tonight, I

did not know. But one thing was for sure: he'd made the biggest fucking mistake of his life.

I must have got lucky or something, because as I pulled up to the kerb outside his house, the door opened and out the prick came—Annie in one arm, the handle of a giant suitcase bumping down the stairs in the other.

He didn't see me at first, obviously in a hurry to get both the kid and the suitcase into the back of his fancy BMW. So I gave him five minutes to let him think he was going to get away. Then I got off my bike, walked up to the car as he was closing the door after him, and wrenched it open before he could get it shut.

'What the hell?'

He looked up at me from his place in the driver's seat, his face a mask of rage. That soon turned to fear as I leaned an elbow casually on the roof of the car, my other arm on the open door to stop him from getting out.

'Hey, Justin,' I said, smiling. 'Going somewhere?'

His mouth twisted. 'Get away from the car or I'll call the police.'

I laughed. 'Yeah… See, I don't think you want to do that.'

'Smoke!' Annie was wriggling in her car seat. She was six and didn't know her daddy was an asshole. 'Why are you here? It's really late and we're going on a trip. Just Daddy and me!'

'Hey, kiddo.' I kept my voice low and friendly, at the same time giving her a quick scan. She looked fine, grinning at me in that way she always did, like she was having the time of her life. 'How's it hanging back there?'

She giggled. 'Nothing's hanging. Is Mom coming soon?'

'Soon, honey.'

I glanced back at her father. The guy was furious, his mouth gone tight and mean. Cat had told me once that she thought he was good-looking, but I couldn't see it.

'Annie needs to come home now,' I said flatly. 'You unstrap her, give her to me, and nothing else'll happen.'

'Like hell.' Justin reached for the keys. 'She's *my* goddamn kid, and I'll do what I goddamn like with her!'

Fuck. The prick just didn't listen, did he?

I leaned in and grabbed the keys before he could move, pulling them out of the ignition and throwing them as hard as I could over to the other side of the street. 'Go fetch, motherfucker.'

Justin looked like he was going to explode. 'Touch her and—'

'You'll what?' I cut him off, sick of this bullshit. 'Go running to Daddy? Hide behind your fucking laws? Or are you actually going to man up and take a swing at me?'

I wished he'd take the swing. I wanted an excuse to punch him so bad it was like a pain in my gut.

But it was like he knew—like he could see how much I wanted to do it—because he suddenly leaned back in his seat, all the tension bleeding out of him.

'All right,' he said. 'Take her home, then. But you can tell Cat that I'll be back.' The asshole had the gall to grin at me. 'With a court order.'

I wanted to choke him then and there, but of course

I couldn't. Keep would kill me if I fucked up the situation we had with the cops, and I wasn't that stupid. Even one punch to his face was out of bounds.

A chill went down my spine.

Justin had never actually threatened to get custody of Annie before, and Cat had always said that was because he'd never wanted her in the first place. That the only reason he kept insisting on his parental rights was to hurt Cat. And I believed her. The guy had major control issues, and I knew because I had the same deal.

Except there was one difference between him and me. I'd never hurt a woman like he did and I'd never use a kid like he used Annie.

I gave him a grin back—the kind that promised his early death. 'Do it. If you think you can.'

He seemed to think this was the ace up his sleeve, or something, because his smile turned smug.

'Oh, I will—don't worry. Any judge in the country will grant me sole custody...especially against a single mom and her dangerous biker boyfriend.'

Only long years of control kept the grin on my face and my gun in my pocket. Otherwise I'd have put a bullet through his fucking head.

So he was going to use me against Cat.

You always knew this would happen.

Yeah, I always did. I always knew that somehow, someday, the shit was going to hit the fan.

Cat always hated the club—hated that I was a Knight—and, given her background, I couldn't blame her. But until now it hadn't really come between us because she didn't associate herself with club doings.

But now...

Jesus. How ironic that the most galling thing about this was the fact that I wasn't even her boyfriend—though every part of me wanted to be.

The rage started way down low in my gut, working its way through my veins. It would have to come out soon, but I had ways and means of doing that. Right now all I did was keep on smiling at the piece of shit sitting smug in his car. Imagining the death that was coming to him.

'You do that, Justin.' I made sure he heard the threat in my voice. 'And you'll get what's coming to you. No mistake. By the way, where were you going? You know it's illegal to break the custody agreement, right?'

He just laughed. 'It'll be legal soon enough. Hey, Annie. Are you ready to go see Mommy, honey?'

Annie, who'd been silent in the back, nodded. She wouldn't pick up the really adult vibes, but she'd know something was up. She was a perceptive kid.

'We're not going anywhere now?'

'Nope,' I said, before Justin could speak. 'Wanna go for a ride on my bike?'

'Yeah!'

I got Annie out myself, ignoring her father as he said his goodbyes. Then I grabbed her backpack and stowed it in the saddlebag on the bike, leaving Justin to go scrabbling around in the street for his keys.

Sitting her up in front of me, she grabbed onto my arms without me having to tell her. She'd been riding on the Harley almost since before she could talk, so she knew what to do.

I texted Cat to let her know I had Annie, then we roared out of there.

Fifteen minutes and we were at Cat's run-down apartment building. Yeah, it wasn't the greatest place to raise a kid, but she had good neighbours and the apartment itself was clean and tidy. She was a great mom and, really, that's all that counts for a kid. Annie had clean clothes, food, a bed at night and people who loved her. People who didn't beat the shit out of her. And that's plenty more than a lot of kids had.

Cat was waiting out front, her hands in the pockets of her jeans, trying to look casual, but I knew she wasn't. As I pulled up the bike she ran down the stairs, taking them two at a time to get to us.

'Hey, honey,' she said as she picked Annie up. 'How was Daddy's?' She didn't act panicked, but I could hear the sound of it in her voice anyway.

Annie didn't seem to notice, chattering on about what she'd done that afternoon.

Cat didn't say anything to me, but she didn't need to. The look she gave me out of those big green eyes of hers said it all.

I followed them up the stairs after I'd got Annie's stuff out from the saddlebag of the bike and into her apartment. Cat didn't bother to ask me any questions, too busy murmuring to Annie about how she needed to get into her pyjamas and brush her teeth because it was late.

I let her do all the kid shit first, going into the tiny, scrupulously clean kitchen and pulling open the fridge door. She usually kept a couple of cans of my favourite beer, and sure enough there was one on the shelf. I took it and went back out to the lounge, popping the tab as I sat down on the faded chintz couch that she kept covered with an Indian-patterned throw thing.

There was a low wooden coffee table in front of the couch and I swung my boots up on it like I always did, taking a swallow of my beer and sitting back.

I liked Cat's place. I had a room at the Knight's club-house, and that was cool, but I didn't have an apartment or anything. It was a choice I'd made a long time ago, but that didn't mean I didn't like coming around to Cat's and hanging out.

Cat kept the apartment homey, with all the decor shit she liked, despite the threadbare carpet and the dingy wallpaper. The most important thing, though, was that it had Cat in it.

That's why I liked it. That's why I kept coming there.

She'd been my friend since I was seven years old and with any luck she'll stay my friend for the rest of time.

As long as I didn't fuck it up.

I'd been good for years so far—no reason to think I wouldn't stay being good.

Cat finally appeared fifteen minutes later, walk-ing into the living area with her hands in the pockets of her jeans again. She always did that when she was nervous, as if she thought her hands were going to give her away or something.

Her black hair was in a loose ponytail at the nape of her neck, all glossy and shiny like a slick of oil on a hot day. But she looked pale. Tired. There were dark circles under her green eyes and lines of strain around her full, pouty mouth.

Yeah, even tired and stressed out, she was *so* fucking beautiful.

But then she always had been.

She didn't look at me as she came around one of the ratty armchairs opposite the couch and sat down on it. In fact it seemed as if she was avoiding looking at me completely.

For a second I wondered what the problem was. Then I remembered.

The last time she'd seen me I'd been standing in the hallway with my dick in Hannah's mouth.

Ah. Fuck.

'So what went down with Justin?' Cat asked.

She still wasn't looking at me, her attention on my boots resting on her table.

For some reason I couldn't figure out, I wanted to leave them there—which was stupid. She'd been through hell tonight with Annie and didn't need me being a tool about putting my feet on her furniture.

But I didn't move them.

'Up here, kitten.'

Her gaze flickered up to mine, then away again. 'Justin, Dane?'

Yeah, she *really* didn't want to look at me. And the Dane thing… Second time that night. Definitely had something to do with that moment in the hallway.

I took another sip of my beer. I'd ask her about it after we'd cleared up the shit that had happened with her ex. No need for her to get weird about a fucking blow job, for Christ's sake.

'Looked like he was trying to make a run for it

with Annie,' I said. 'When I got there he was putting her in his car.'

She was silent, looking fully at me this time, and I could see the panic in her eyes.

'Shit. I *knew* he was going to try and pull something like this—I just knew it.'

'Yeah, but that's not all.' This would be difficult for her, but she needed to know the truth. 'He's going to try for sole custody.'

She stilled. 'What? He's never wanted to before.'

'Well, he's serious now.' I held her gaze. 'He's going after you with the big guns, too. Single mom. Shitty apartment. Biker boyfriend.'

Her eyes widened, then flared with anger. 'No. Oh, *fuck*, no! He's *not* using you. The prick!'

That's what I loved about Cat. She always had my back. Always.

She shoved herself out of her chair, pacing angrily in front of the coffee table. 'Why now? He hasn't wanted this before. I don't get it. And anyway you're my friend—not my boyfriend.'

'Yeah, but that's how he's going to play it. Fuck, if I wanted my kid, I'd tell every lie I could to get them back.'

She stopped and stared at me. 'Not helping.'

'Hey, that's what he's doing. I'm just telling it like it is.'

'Well, don't.' She resumed pacing. 'This is crazy. He's doing it to hurt me. He doesn't really want Annie—he never did.'

'Why he's doing it doesn't matter. All that matters is how we stop him.'

She came to a halt again, her hands in fists at her sides. 'Yeah and how the hell are we going to do that? He's a lawyer. It'll be his word against mine.'

That was the problem. He was a fine, upstanding member of the community. A professional. No one knew he was also an abusive prick. No one except me and Cat.

The thing was, I'd already had to stand on the sidelines once to watch him take out his anger-management problems on someone I loved. I wasn't going to do it again. Still less when the person involved was a kid.

I needed to talk to Keep—see what he could do about the situation. He was friends with the police chief now, and that asshole was the chief's son. He'd be able to work something out. After all I was Keep's nephew, and he'd always told me that if I needed anything I only had to say the word.

I've never wanted to put anything on Keep—it wasn't his fault his brother was the biggest asshole ever to walk the earth. But this wasn't about me. It was about Cat and what *she* needed. And she needed something now.

'Don't worry. I'll deal with it.' I put as much authority as I could into my voice.

'What do you mean, you'll deal with it?' she demanded. 'How?'

'Doesn't matter how.'

'Bullshit.' Her whole posture was tense, almost vibrating. 'Don't give me that biker-secrecy crap—not when it involves Annie.'

I leaned forward, put my beer down on the table, then pushed myself out of the chair and came around the table to where she stood. Then I pulled her into my arms. She made an angry sound, putting her hands onto my chest and shoving, holding herself away. Her cheeks were flushed and she wouldn't look at me.

She was pissed and, hell, I understood. She was trying to protect Annie and she wanted to know what was going on. Except I wasn't going to tell her. Not until I'd worked it all out myself. Mainly because I knew she'd hate it.

Her mouth was a hard line, her body tense. It was difficult being close to her. Difficult having all that soft warmth against me. It made me feel guilty and it made me hard, both at the same time. Over the years I'd got better at hiding how I felt about her, but there were times when I couldn't quite do it—and tonight the interrupted blow job only made it worse.

Cat's familiar scent filled my head…a sweet, musky smell like jasmine and sandalwood mixed together. Fuck knew what it was, but it always made me feel good. Made me feel like I was home. Made me want to wrap her in my arms and hold her close, put my face between her breasts and inhale her.

A bad move.

Cat had never shown any sign that she wanted me and I'd never wanted to put our friendship at risk. It was too important to me and so was she.

So I told my goddamn dick to calm the fuck down and held her like I always did. Giving her comfort the way a friend would.

'I know you're scared,' I said. 'I know you're worried. But let me help you and Annie.'

Her palms were resting on my chest and I could feel

the heat of them settle right down through me, burning through my T-shirt and onto my skin. She was staring at them, and not at me, as if the backs of her hands were the most interesting things in the world.

'I don't want to involve the club,' she said quietly. 'Please, Smoke. You know how I feel about that.'

I did. But this wasn't just about her. This was about Annie, as well.

'Remember that the club hasn't done anything to you. And if they can help Annie, isn't that more important?'

'It's not... It's not about Dad.'

Sure it wasn't. Her father had been a biker and a nasty bastard. Like mine. Except *her* dad hadn't beaten her half to death every time he got drunk. No, he'd been more the absent type—away a lot on club business and not much interested in anything else. Especially not the poor little rich girl he'd got pregnant or the daughter he'd fathered.

Anyway, I called it like I saw it.

'That's a piece of shit, Cat. And you know it.'

Her body tensed and she looked up at me, her eyes sharp as green glass. 'This is about Annie, not Dad.'

'Yeah, it is.' My hands were on her hips and I found myself tightening my hold on her, as if I could make her see that her fears were all the product of her past with nothing but the strength of my grip alone. 'Which means if you want to make sure she's safe, you need to let me handle this.'

An expression I didn't recognise moved in her eyes. Anger and something else, too. Something unfamiliar.

Then her gaze dipped and—holy fucking shit—she was
staring at my mouth.

I went still. Completely and utterly still. She'd never
done that before, and there was only one reason in the
entire world she would.

Obviously picking up on my shock, she pushed at
me again. But I held on. No way was I going to let her
go—not now. Not when I'd caught her looking at me
the way I never in a million years thought she would.

'Smoke.' She pushed harder, her cheeks flushed, her
thick black lashes veiling her gaze.

'No.' I tightened my grip, suddenly desperate to
know what the hell was going on. 'We need to talk,
Cat.'

'What? No, we don't. Look, I'm tired and—'

'We need to talk about what you saw in the hallway tonight.'

CHAPTER THREE

Cat

I FROZE AS soon as he said the word *hallway*.

What a stupid bitch I was. I should never have looked. I should never have allowed him to get close. But he'd given me plenty of hugs before and it shouldn't have been a big deal.

Yet it was. There was something about the feel of his hands on my hips, the quiet strength in them, that I'd never noticed before. I'd never noticed how hot he was either. My hands on his chest felt scorched, like they'd been pressed against a furnace. He smelled delicious, too, his familiar aftershave reminding me of a forest—all dark and woody and spicy—along with the faintest tinge of leather from under his cut.

And when I looked up at him, angry and resistant to the idea of him going to the club for help with Annie, for some reason I couldn't hold his gaze. The darkness of his eyes seemed to draw me in, suck me down, wrap me up in soft velvet and keep me there. It disturbed me, so I looked at his mouth instead.

A big mistake. Because that wasn't any better. I

couldn't help noticing how beautifully shaped it was, how full the curve of his bottom lip was, and how if anyone had a kissable mouth, then surely it had to be Smoke...

Yeah, crazy. That's what I was. Certifiable. He was my friend—my best friend—and I didn't want to look at him that way. I didn't have many people in my life who'd stuck around, but he was one of them and I did *not* want to screw that up.

So I tried to dismiss my blush through sheer force of will, tried to ignore the heat that was stealing through me at the feel of his body against mine. Tried desperately not to notice that the chest beneath my palms was rock hard and so very, *very* hot...

'What hallway?' I said stupidly.

'You know what I'm talking about.'

'Oh, that.'

I tried to pull away, but he was having none of it. His hands moved to the back pockets of my jeans, and before I could do anything to stop him, he slid them down inside them, his fingers curving over my butt.

All the breath left my lungs in a wild rush and I looked up at him in shock.

His eyes were so dark—black as tar—and they glittered, making something inside me draw in tight like a hand closing into a fist.

'What are you *doing*?' My voice sounded breathless and frightened, which was annoying since I'd never been afraid of Smoke.

He ignored me. 'You saw me getting sucked off by Hannah.'

I blushed like a teenager but bluffed it out. 'Yeah, so what? It was disgusting.'

'Is that why you're acting so weird?'

I couldn't think. All I was aware of was how hot his hands felt inside the pockets of my jeans, with his palms pressing lightly, the heat of them soaking through the denim. But that wasn't the worst part. The worst part was the heat of him in front of me and how conscious I was of it. How conscious I was of *him*.

Beneath my palms his chest felt incredibly hard— a wall of firm muscle that probably wouldn't move no matter how hard I pushed. *If* I pushed. And his arms were around me strong and sure, like bands of iron.

He'd held me in those arms before. When Dad had gone away for that final time and never come back. That final job he'd had to do for the stupid club he'd been a part of. Not that he'd ever paid much attention to Mom and me, but a death was a death and my mom wasn't the hugging type. At least, she didn't hug me. So all I had was Smoke.

But back then I didn't notice the firmness of his chest or the heat of his body. Or how good he smelled. Back then all I felt was grief and rage.

Now, though, everything was different.

'I'm not acting weird,' I mumbled, staring at his chest.

God, I so did *not* want to have this conversation with him. Not when all this awareness was careening around inside me, and most definitely not while he had his hands in my back pockets and his arms around me.

'You are. Look at me.'

I don't know what it was in his voice. A note of

something...*hard*. Like it was an order. Normally I hated people telling me what to do, but right then I found myself doing it. Lifting my head and meeting his eyes.

They were black—like the extradark, extrastrong espresso I used to make him when he had a hangover. And they were just as hot, too. They made an electric shock go straight down my spine.

I shoved at him then, entirely instinctively, trying to get away from all the weird feelings...trying to get away from *him*. He let me go straight away and I had the strangest sense of disappointment as he did so, as if I'd been enjoying his hold.

You're crazy.

Yeah, I really was. I didn't have feelings for Smoke. He was the best friend I had in the world—like a damn brother. End of story.

He frowned. 'What the fuck, Cat?'

My cheeks were on fire and I really didn't want to look at him. But I made myself do it, folding my arms defensively over my chest. 'I need some space, okay?'

His dark gaze scanned my face and, damn him, he probably knew exactly why I was blushing. Jesus, how embarrassing was that?

Slowly he folded his arms, mirroring me, and I couldn't stop noticing the flex of his biceps as he did so, and the black ink of the stars cascading down his left upper arm flexing along with them.

I'd never been a fan of tattoos—not when all they ever spelled for me was bad news. But the stars on Smoke's arm suddenly seemed...fascinating, somehow. They drew my attention to the muscles there, to the tanned skin beneath the ink. Made me wonder what the rest of that skin looked like...

God, he was tall. And broad. I'd noticed that once, back when I was sixteen and crushing on him like crazy. Even at eighteen he'd been muscular and lean hipped, like a panther. Now, at thirty, he'd filled out, the cotton of his T-shirt stretching over his chest.

'Cat.' His voice had gone low and husky. 'Are you checking me out?'

You are. You're totally checking him out.

The blaze in my cheeks felt like a supernova. I should have looked him in the eye and brazened it out, but I couldn't make myself do it. Avoiding his gaze would tell him more or less the same thing of course, but it was way less confrontational. And I'd had too much confrontation tonight as it was.

'No, of course I'm not,' I snapped and turned on my heel, heading to the kitchen. 'I'm going to get a damn beer.'

Plus some space while I was at it.

In the kitchen, I pulled open the fridge and grabbed myself a can, popping the tab and taking a long, deep swallow to cool myself down.

I had no idea what the hell was going on with me. No idea why I was suddenly checking out my best friend like I hadn't had sex in years.

That's the problem. You haven't *had sex in years.*

I scowled at the cracked paint of the kitchen wall. That was unfortunately true. I hadn't. But men were such bastards and I'd had enough. I certainly had after Justin.

He'd started out so great—just the kind of guy I was

after. A lawyer earning good money, on the straight
and narrow. Definitely not a drug user or a criminal,
like the people my dad used to associate with. In fact
Justin was as far from that as it was possible to get—
which was why I'd fallen for him like the proverbial
ton of bricks.

It wasn't until I was pregnant and things weren't
going so well at his firm that the cracks in his good-
boy facade had started to show. He'd always had a
problem with anger, and when he got angry he lashed
out. At me.

The first time he hit me I was so shocked I didn't
know what to do. He cried and told me he was sorry,
that he'd never do it again. So I forgave him. It didn't
happen again until after Annie was born. Then he did
it again. And again. Three times I put up with it. The
fourth he nearly knocked me out.

So I left him.

Good boys were overrated… Bad boys were just
like my dad. And since there was nothing in between,
I took nothing. It was easier—better for me and better
for Annie. After all, between her and my two jobs—the
call centre during the day and Lucky's, the bar I worked
at some nights—I didn't have time for men anyway.

I didn't miss them. Sex with Justin had been pretty
average—certainly no better than what I could get with
my own imagination and a decent vibrator. At least I
was in charge of my own orgasms, which I found very
satisfying.

So why were you looking at Smoke?

That was the one question I couldn't answer, though

I wished I could. Because that was the very last thing I needed in my life right now.

'You gonna tell me what's going on?'

I turned sharply, my heart giving the stupidest jump at the sound of Smoke's voice.

He was standing in the kitchen doorway, one shoulder hitched up against the frame, his arms folded. His black eyes had narrowed. I'd never found that look threatening—not once. But I did now. Not because he was going to hurt me—I knew Smoke would never do that—but because he knew me. He knew that something was bothering me.

And if you're not careful he'll guess what that something is.

Shit. He would, too.

Trying for calm, I took a swig of my beer, the cold liquid putting out the strange fire burning in my veins. 'Nothing's going on,' I said. 'It's just been a hell of a night, what with Annie and—'

'And watching your best friend get blown?'

'Jesus, Smoke.' This time I managed to look him in the eye. 'How many times do you want to keep saying that?'

'I don't know. Until you stop acting weird?'

'I'm *not* acting weird. Okay, it was disconcerting, but I'm a big girl. I know what you guys get up to in the clubrooms. It's nothing I haven't seen before.'

But his narrow black stare didn't budge. Like he was seeing things in me that I didn't know were there. It was unsettling.

'And what about you checking me out?'

'I wasn't checking you out! You're my friend. You're

like my damn brother. Which means if I was looking at you like that, I'd be pretty damn sick. Don't you think?'

He didn't say a word. Just kept staring at me. And I could hear the echo of my voice bouncing off the walls, high and sharp and vehement. Too vehement.

I was incriminating myself with every word I spoke.

Man, could this night get any worse?

I turned away, running a hand through my hair. 'You know what? I'm exhausted and I need to go to bed. So let's talk about this later.'

For a second I didn't think he was going to say anything, that he was going to keep standing there staring at me all night. But then he said, 'Yeah, okay. You do look tired. But, Cat?'

I glanced at him. 'What?'

Something glittered in his black eyes that made my heart race fast and hard. 'We *will* talk about this later—get me?'

I swallowed and lifted a shoulder like I didn't give a shit. 'Sure.'

He sighed, his arms dropping to his sides, and pushed away from the doorframe. 'I'll handle that prick Justin, too, okay?'

'Yeah…' I let out a silent breath. 'Thanks for getting Annie, Smoke. I mean… Just thanks.'

They were paltry words for what he'd done, but I didn't have any other way to thank him. He'd know how much I meant them, though.

He smiled and, like always, it made me feel warm inside. Made me feel really good. Like the sun had come out to sit on my shoulder.

'Anytime, kitten. Anytime.'

CHAPTER FOUR

Smoke

'HEY, PREZ. YOU got a minute?' I stood aside as one of the club hang-arounds, a brunette called Bella, sidled out of Keep's office, tugging down her skirt and doing nothing to hide the satisfied look on her face.

Keep himself was sitting at his desk, his hands loosely linked behind his head, looking extremely fucking satisfied himself. I guess there's nothing like a lunchtime screw when there isn't much else going on.

He grinned, lifting his chin at the chair opposite the desk. 'Sure. Take a seat.'

I came in and sat down, leaning my elbows on my knees.

I didn't like to ask favours of people since I hated being in debt—another thing that made me different from my old man—but Keep was different. He was my uncle, Dad's younger brother, and the man who'd protected me when he could. He'd also been the one to introduce me to the Knights, becoming president not long after I patched in.

Being in debt to Keep was okay. He was a brother;

he was my president, and he had my back. He had everyone's back. That was why they called him Keep. Because he kept what was his and he didn't let it go.

He gave me a measuring look, letting the silence hang there for a bit. Then he said, 'So what's up? Something important? I can tell by the look on your face.'

It *was* important. This was Annie and Cat, and there weren't any other people on this whole fucking planet more important to me than they were.

But I had to be careful about how I was going to ask for this. Keep had a good relationship with the police chief, a relationship that was important, too—especially if you wanted to stay on the straight and narrow like Keep did. He made sure the club maintained a low profile with the law and stayed out of trouble.

Well, we weren't called the Knights in Shining Armor. We were the Knights of Ruin for a reason. But that reason didn't include drugs or whores or guns or any of that shit. We did the usual MC stuff for cash: a strip club, a couple of garages around town and a good bit of protection and hired muscle work. But we weren't in it for the money. We were in it because we wanted to ride and live free, our brothers by our side.

I was in it because the Knights were my family— certainly more of a family than my own had been— and I wanted it to stay that way. I didn't want to rock the boat.

Except this thing with Annie might just do a shit-load of rocking.

I had to try, though. For Cat's sake.

'Yeah, something's up.' I met Keep's gaze. 'It's got to do with Justin Grant.'

Keep's blue eyes narrowed. 'Campbell Grant's son?'

'Unfortunately.'

He sighed and unlinked his hands, sitting forward in his chair, folding his arms and leaning his elbows on the desk. 'Fuck's sake, Smoke. Not again.'

I fought a hot rush of irritation. Everyone knew I hated Grant's guts because of Cat, and that if I'd had my way I would have put him in the ground with no regrets if I could have got away with it. But I'd never actually put a move on him. So Keep getting pissed at me was annoying.

Still, I knew where Keep was coming from.

Yet this was Cat. And that was a whole other story.

So I swallowed my anger, kept my posture loose and held his gaze steadily. 'If it was just about Grant being a dick, I'd agree with you. But last night he didn't return Annie, and when I caught up with them I found him putting her into a car with a big suitcase.' I paused. 'He didn't look like he was planning on coming back, Keep.'

There was no expression at all on Keep's face. He was good at hiding his emotions.

'So? He's the kid's father.'

Keep knew all about Cat and Annie. He knew Cat was the only thing that kept me sane, the only bright spot in the entire damn world when things had got really dark. He knew what she meant to me and he knew why this was important.

The motherfucker was playing devil's advocate.

'And Cat is Annie's mother,' I said flatly. 'He doesn't have any right to take Annie away from her.'

Keep lifted a shoulder. 'Sounds like custody drama

to me. Let them sort it out themselves. Got nothing to do with us.'

'Grant's going to come back,' I went on, ignoring him. 'He's promised to get a court order giving him sole custody. And because he's a lawyer, and full of shit, he's going to tell them about Cat working nights and about how she's got a biker boyfriend, that it's dangerous for Annie to be around her.'

'Yeah, okay. I hear you. But, again, what's that got to do with us?' Keep's stare was sharp. 'I know Cat's important to you, but this isn't club business. I got a whole lot of things going on now, and I don't need any attention from the police. If the club gets involved with this...'

Frustration rose, but I swallowed it down, playing it cool. 'I know all that. But we have to do something. That prick hurt Cat. And I'll be damned if he does it again.'

Keep let out a breath. 'She's your friend—I get it. And the kid is cute. No doubt about it. But I'm saying no. We can't afford the heat it would bring down. Not now.'

Fuck. If it had been anyone else, I would have let it go. But it wasn't anyone else. It was Cat. And I hadn't been able to protect her from Justin last time, which meant I was *not* going to fail again.

'Keep,' I said clearly, levelly. 'I've never asked you for anything. Not one single fucking thing. Not even when that shit went down with Dad. But I'm asking you now. I need you to help Cat and Annie.'

Keep's blue eyes turned cold. He was an easygoing guy on the surface, but that only went so far. There was a reason he was club president, and it wasn't because he was a walkover.

'No.' His voice was very quiet. 'That's my final answer. I'm not saying it again.'

I knew that tone. It was his presidential do-not-fuck-with-me tone. No one argued with that—not if they liked their balls hanging where they were.

But I had a line, too. And Cat was it.

'If they were ours, you would, right?' A stupid question, since it should have gone without saying. I had to check, though.

'You know I would. But they're not.'

No, they weren't.

Yet.

I leaned back in my chair, an idea going around and around in my head. Because that motherfucker Justin was *not* going to hurt her again. Over my dead fucking body.

Luckily, there was another option.

Unluckily, Cat was going to hate it.

There was only one way to make Cat and Annie part of the Knights, and that was for me to take her as my old lady.

I couldn't deny that it was something I'd wanted for years—a secret fantasy that wouldn't ever make it into reality since Cat didn't feel that way about me. But, shit, we could fake it, couldn't we? Make it look like we were together at least enough for the rest of the MC to believe it and protect her, if and when Grant came gunning for her.

Are you sure she doesn't feel that way about you?

I blinked, the thought hitting me hard. Where the

hell had that come from? Admittedly her behaviour last night had been weird—not looking me in the eye and getting all strange and tense when I got near her. Then, when I'd brought up the topic of that blow job, she'd blushed. Like she was the one embarrassed about it.

Still, discussing your best friend's blow job would be pretty embarrassing for a chick.

So why did you put your hands in the pockets of her jeans?

I shifted uncomfortably in the chair.

Never in all the years we've been friends had I touched her like that. In fact I'd never made one single move on her, even though sometimes I wanted to so bad I was like a junkie in search of a fix. She was my friend. End of. Besides, I knew how she felt about MCs.

To say she wasn't the Knights' greatest fan was a severe understatement.

Anyway, I still didn't know what had made me slide my hands into the back pockets of her jeans, feel the heat of her against my palms, pull her close. She was trying to avoid me and I simply wanted to hold her there so we could talk about it.

Yeah, sure. You fucking liar.

I shifted again, my palms stinging from the memory. Fuck, she'd felt hot. Then she'd put her hands on my chest and it was like I'd been plugged into a goddamn wall socket. She'd touched me plenty of times before and it had never felt like that—mainly because I'd trained myself to ignore my reactions around her.

She'd been blushing, too. Had touching me *done* something for her?

'Jesus, Smoke,' Keep muttered. 'You got a problem

or something? You're shifting around like a two-year-old needing the potty.'

Mother fuck. If I wasn't careful Keep was going to notice something else, because my dick was starting to think interesting things about why Cat might have been blushing. And why she'd suddenly pushed me away as if I'd burned her.

Why she'd been so weird about not wanting to discuss that blow job.

Christ. Getting a hard-on in the absence of any naked chicks, while sitting talking your president, wasn't exactly a good look.

Shoving thoughts of her and how she'd felt in my arms away, I pushed myself out of my chair. 'Nope. No problem.'

'I'm sorry about Cat.' Keep looked it, too, but he had the club as a whole to consider and I understood that. 'We good?'

'All good, Prez.'

And we would be. Because I'd made my decision.

There was only one way to protect her and Annie from her dick ex and that was to make her mine.

Cat wasn't going to like it, but I'd talk her around. I'd convince her. This was all for Annie's sake, and nothing was more important than making sure she was safe.

CHAPTER FIVE

Cat

I WAS FINISHING up my shift at Lucky's when the door opened with a bang and Smoke strode in.

Carl, who owned Lucky's Bar, wasn't a fan of the Knights, and he didn't much like Smoke and the other brothers hanging around. He could make life difficult for me when he was in the mood, so Smoke tended to steer clear of Lucky's whenever I was working.

Though tonight it looked as if he had something important to say.

Dear God, if it was about that blow job again, I'd get security to haul his ass out of there myself.

'Hey, Cat.'

His deep, husky voice rolled over me as he approached the bar and I had no idea why I found myself staring at him like a complete idiot. Because there was no reason to stare—none at all. Not when he was dressed like he normally was, in black boots, worn black jeans and a faded black T-shirt, his cut over the top. Nothing special, nothing fancy.

Yet I couldn't take my eyes off him.

Looking at how the cotton of his T-shirt pulled over the hard muscles of his chest and biceps, how the waistband of his jeans sat low on his lean hips, how one corner of his mouth curved in a sexy half smile, how black his eyes were and how they drew me in, made me feel like I was drowning.

What was wrong with me? It was like he was projecting some kind of electric field, sensitising my skin, making it prickle with awareness and a heat that was totally unwelcome.

No. Just no. The weirdness of a couple of nights ago was fresh in my mind, and I'd been hoping that it would have all gone away and everything would be like it was.

Seemed I was destined for disappointment.

Smoke leaned his elbows on the bar and raised an eyebrow without saying anything.

I jerked my gaze away, busying myself with folding some of the cleaning cloths we kept behind the bar for drying glasses.

'What are you doing here?' The question came out quick and graceless, but I couldn't seem to moderate my tone.

If he took offence, or even noticed, he didn't show it.

'I got to talk to you.'

'Now? I'm in the middle of work.'

'It's important.'

I folded the cloth in half, lining up the edges and making sure they met. 'Can't it wait? You know Carl doesn't like you hanging around.'

'Yeah, but, like I said, this is important. It's about Annie and you.'

I couldn't avoid his gaze any longer—avoiding it

was already strange enough as it was. Bracing myself, I finally looked up and met his dark eyes.

There it was again, that electric shiver moving over my skin like static.

Crazy. He was here to talk about something important, to do with Annie and me, and all I could think about was my physical reaction to him.

I had to get a grip. I had to put this stupid…whatever it was…to one side and forget about it. I wasn't getting involved with a biker—not after the lesson my dad had taught my mom, let alone the fact that the biker in question was my best friend. So there wasn't any point fixating on this irrational attraction.

I was over men—possibly for good.

I had to let it go.

'Okay?' I leaned a hip against the bar. 'So what's the deal?'

'I've figured out a way to make sure Grant never comes near you or Annie.'

I blinked, my heart leaping inside my chest. 'Seriously?'

'I'm always serious, kitten.' He didn't smile, and there was an intense look on his face. 'Especially when it comes to you two and your safety.'

I let the *kitten* go, sagging against the bar in relief. 'How? What did you do?'

He still didn't smile, which maybe should have clued me in to the fact that what he was going to say next wasn't going to make my life any easier.

'You're not going to like it.'

The relief ebbed, my muscles tensing. 'What exactly am I not going to like?'

'It involves the Knights.'

Smoke was always like this when he was telling me stuff I didn't want to hear. Calm. Direct. Straight-up. Laying out the unpleasant facts so I knew exactly where I stood.

'It involves you and Annie being under their pro-tection.'

My first instinct was *no fucking way in hell*. I hated the MC and didn't want to have anything to do with them—and I *especially* didn't want any child of mine anywhere near them.

'I told you I didn't want to involve—'

'I know what you told me. But hear me out, okay?'

I bit down on my protest. I didn't want to hear him out, but if he'd gone to the trouble of figuring out a way to help Annie, then the least I could do was listen.

'Fine. So how are Annie and me going to be under their protection? We're not part of the club.'

He shifted on his feet, and if I hadn't known any bet-ter, I would have said he looked uncertain. Which was strange, because Smoke was *never* uncertain.

'Yeah,' he said. 'That's the hard part. To be under their protection you have to be a club member.'

'How? Unless they're suddenly recruiting women?' I put a little sarcasm into that last part, because obvi-ously no outlaw MC would allow women to be full members.

Smoke ignored that, gazing at me in a very focused, very intent way. It made that electric current stronger, lifting all the hairs along the back of my neck and my forearms, making me short of breath.

'There's one way,' he murmured. 'If you're my old

lady, you'll have the full protection of the club and so would Annie.'

Shock held me still. I had no idea what to say—no idea what to even think.

First there was the whole issue of the club. Then there was being his old lady... He couldn't be serious.

But he wasn't smiling. And the look in his eyes... Shit, I knew that look. He always had it when he meant to do something and he was going to do it whether I liked it or not. He'd always been a guy who liked his own way, and he got it enough that it made him unhappy when he didn't.

'You're not serious, right?' I tried to sound normal and not like a shaky little girl.

'Yeah, I'm serious.'

Of course he was. He was never anything but.

'You and me will be together as long as it takes for Grant to get off your back, but it won't be real or anything.' He stopped all of a sudden, as if he'd meant to say something else and held himself back at the last minute. 'We only have to make it look believable to the club.'

Make it look believable.

What the hell did *that* mean?

You know what it means, idiot.

Heat shot through me—a flare like a lighted match held against my skin. I tried like hell to ignore it. To concentrate on the facts instead.

'So,' I said carefully, busying myself with folding the cloths again. 'Let me get this straight. You think that if you make me your old lady, the club will protect me and Annie from Justin.'

'I don't think. I *know*.' He said it like the gospel truth, handed down from God himself.

'I thought your president didn't want to get on the wrong side of the police chief. If Justin comes after Annie and the club stops him…' I let the sentence hang.

'Checked it out with Keep this morning.' Smoke put his hands flat on the bar. 'He won't lift a finger if you're not part of the Knights. But if you're one of us, you'll have an army at your back. Club comes first, and the chief can go fuck himself.'

Club comes first.

Wasn't that the lesson I'd learned all through my childhood? That the club, the brothers were the most important things in my father's life.

My mother had learned that lesson, too, when she was still a silly socialite, falling for a badass biker with tats on his arms and a gleaming Harley. She'd thought he was going to give her the freedom from her wealthy family that she'd always craved. Instead he'd given her a one-way ticket to Junkieville.

He never married her—never made her his old lady. He got her pregnant, then left her in a shitty apartment trying to bring up his kid by herself because her family had cut her off. And the only reason she'd stayed was because he kept her in drugs.

Oh, yeah, and apparently she loved him, even though he used to hit her sometimes.

A real prince, my dad.

To this day I have no idea why he didn't make her his old lady. It was like he thought we weren't good enough to be part of his precious club—like it was far too special to share with us. Not that we *wanted* to be part of it… Or at least I didn't.

I hated him and, because of its influence on him, I hated that club.

I hated the Knights for their influence on Smoke, too. The day he told me he was going to sign up to be a prospect I didn't speak to him for two whole weeks. I didn't want him to join. I didn't want them to take him away from me.

We got over that years ago, but sometimes I still felt the betrayal of it.

Like now.

'Cat.' Carl's voice behind me was mean with annoyance. 'You've still got fifteen minutes. Get back to work.'

Smoke pushed himself sharply back from the bar.

'Don't—' I began.

But it was too late.

'She's finishing early tonight.'

Smoke's voice had that hard, flat quality it got whenever he was giving orders. Or stating facts. Or making decisions. Not that there was any difference between them.

'Excuse me?' Carl sounded pissed. 'Are *you* her fucking boss?'

'Smoke, don't.' The last thing I needed was trouble with Carl. It was shitty work, and the pay was terrible, but I needed it. Especially when my day job barely paid the bills.

But Smoke ignored me, digging his wallet out of the back pocket of his jeans and grabbing a couple of bills out of it. He tossed the bills down on the bar.

'Here. Her pay for the last fifteen minutes of her shift.' His black gaze shifted to me. 'Come on. We need to talk.'

I glanced at the money on the bar—I really did get paid shit—then turned to Carl.

'Carl, look,' I said. 'Smoke didn't—'

'I don't care what he did or didn't do. I told you I didn't want him hanging around here, and yet here he is.' Carl grimaced, then jerked his head towards the exit. 'Go on—get out of here.'

'But I—'

'And don't come back.'

Anger flared inside me. Wonderful. Not only did I have Justin making threats to take Annie away from me, and Smoke wanting to protect me by involving me in his goddamn MC, now I had to find myself another job.

Life was just getting better and better.

Swallowing the few choice words I wanted to level at both Carl *and* Smoke, I set my jaw, collected my purse and strode out from behind the bar. I headed towards the exit, not bothering to look behind me to see if Smoke was following.

Slamming open the door, I stepped out onto the street, then headed straight towards the bus stop.

'Cat—wait up.'

I didn't.

Frustrated rage burned in my gut. Rage at the world for the situation I was in, for all the decisions I'd made in good faith that had turned out to be really shitty ones that had not only put me at risk, but also my kid.

I thought Justin was one of the good guys. Clean-cut and earning good money—not some low-life ass-hole like my dad. I wasn't going to be like my mother, attaching myself to some man because I was desperate for drugs or love or whatever other crap people get needy over.

I was going to fall for a *good* man and we'd have a *good* life together. Have great kids and a nice place and a fulfilling career.

Instead all I got were black eyes, a shitty apartment and a hand-to-mouth existence.

There was only one good thing I'd got from Justin and that was Annie. Now she was under threat, and there wasn't a damn thing I could do about it. I hated being so helpless. It brought back all those crappy feelings I'd had when Justin first showed his true colours. Of powerlessness. Of worthlessness. Of weakness.

I'd promised myself never again, and yet somehow he still had the power to hurt me.

'Cat.' Warm fingers wound around my arm and held on, bringing me up short. *'Stop.'*

I halted, keeping my gaze on the bus stop ahead of me. 'Thanks for making me lose my job, Smoke,' I said. 'I'm sure I really don't need that money.'

'It was a shitty job anyway.' He sounded completely unrepentant. 'And I have money if you need it.'

Arrogant son of a bitch.

I turned to look at him, his handsome face shadowed by the streetlight behind him. The intense look in his eyes hadn't faded one iota, making me feel restless and shaky, wanting something I couldn't put a name to.

'The money isn't the point,' I said. 'You made me

lose my job, and I'm not feeling very happy about that right now.'

'Sure, you're pissed about the job, but tell it like it is, Cat. You don't like my idea.'

'About being your old lady? Of *course* I don't like it. I think it's stupid.'

Something crossed his face—I didn't know what it was. Maybe hurt or disappointment or a combination of both. And his mouth hardened. He didn't often get pissed with me, but I knew when he was. Like now.

'Yeah, well, maybe you should stop being so fucking one-eyed about the club.' There was a dangerous edge to his voice. 'Maybe you should stop thinking about your own issues for a change and start thinking about Annie's.'

Anger flared inside me, hot as a Fourth of July bonfire. I'd just lost my job because of him, and now he was telling me I wasn't thinking of *my kid*?

Everything I did was for her. *Everything.*

'Don't you dare tell me I'm not thinking of her just because you're pissed that I didn't like your idea.' I jerked my arm out of his hold, too angry with him to think about what I was saying. 'She's *my* kid—not yours. You're not her father. You don't get a say!'

CHAPTER SIX

Smoke

I FELT LIKE she'd kicked me straight in the balls. The pain was so bright, so raw. I acted on instinct, taking her by her forearms and spinning her around, pushing her up against the brick wall of the building next to us and holding her there.

'You'd really say that to *me*?' I couldn't keep the pain out of my voice. 'Fuck you, Cat. I knew that kid before she was born. I spent more time with her than Justin did. Hell, I'm more a father to her than he ever fucking was. So don't you *dare* tell me I don't get a say!'

Her eyes had gone very wide, the green in them darkening as she stared at me in shock. Like she saw a stranger standing there instead of me.

Like Justin maybe? Have you got more of your old man in you than you thought?

I went cold. No way. No fucking way.

Letting her go, I stepped back and turned away, trying to get a goddamn grip.

I knew Cat was angry—and yeah, putting that asshole boss of hers in his place and getting her fired hadn't been my best move. But Annie was a daughter to me in so many ways that it hurt to be told I had no right to help her.

So Cat had issues with the club. After what her old man had put her and her mom through, I couldn't blame her. But the Knights were different from the MC her dad had been in, and I sure as hell wasn't *him*.

You're just pissed she didn't fall gratefully into your arms when you told her your idea.

Couldn't deny it—there was a part of me that wanted that badly. That hoped she'd put her arms around me, tell me that being my old lady was what she'd been dreaming about all her life.

Yeah, I was fucking toast for her, and the fact that she hadn't done any of that only added to the pain.

'Smoke?'

Cat's voice was behind me—not so angry this time, more uncertain.

I didn't reply, not trusting myself not to say something stupid and make things worse.

There was a feather-light touch on my back, brief and over far too fast.

'I'm sorry. I shouldn't have said that. You *do* get a say. I'm just… You know I don't like the club and you know why. And this whole situation with Annie is scaring the shit out of me.'

Typical Cat. She blew up like a volcano when she was scared.

My normal thing would have been to turn around and give her a hug, tell her she didn't need to be afraid,

that all she needed to do was trust me. But she'd got
me where it hurt and I was still pissed.

You know what you want to do.

Yeah, I totally did. I wanted her to get down on her
knees and apologise the old-fashioned way. With my
dick in her mouth.

Another light pressure on my back and this time it
was staying there.

'Smoke? Please. I didn't mean it. You know I didn't.'

But that was the thing. I didn't know. Because she
was right. Annie wasn't my kid. Either Cat or that asshole Justin could take her away and there would be
nothing I could do about it.

The light pressure increased as her palm settled between my shoulder blades.

'I wish you were her father. You're a damn sight
better dad than Justin ever was.'

If I had been Annie's father, we wouldn't be standing here right now. I'd be at Cat's place and Cat would
be naked under me.

Something hardened in me at the thought, and for
once it wasn't my damn dick.

This was going to happen. Cat was going to be my
old lady, and I didn't care if she didn't want to be or
not. She was a grown woman and she could make her
own decisions, sure, but Annie was still a kid and she
needed protection. Which meant if Cat was going to
let her own issues get in the way of helping her kid, I
was going to call bullshit on them.

I turned around, the warmth of her hand lingering
between my shoulder blades, making me ache. But I
kept my expression hard.

She stared at me uncertainly, looking so fucking hot in the tight green Lucky's T-shirt she always wore to work. The one that clung to her tits and made me want to gather them in my hands, feel the weight of them against my palms, stroke her nipples through the fabric and watch them get hard.

Maybe you should do that. See what happens.

Fuck, that voice in my head was playing devil's advocate. I shouldn't listen to it.

'It's going to happen, Cat,' I said aloud. 'I'm not standing by and letting that prick get his hands on you or Annie—not again. Understand me?'

Her expression closed up, her pouty mouth flattening. 'I don't—'

'What?' I interrupted, folding my arms. 'You got a better idea?'

The look on her face became guarded, wary, and I knew why. She wasn't seeing me as a friend right now. She was seeing me as a hard-ass biker putting pressure on her.

Maybe that was for the best, though. Maybe she'd been seeing me as a friend for far too long.

'No,' she said quietly. 'I don't.'

'Then it's on. I'll take you as my old lady and if Justin comes after Annie again, he'll have the whole fucking club to deal with.'

Her throat moved as she swallowed, and I watched it, wanting my hand on it. Wanting to feel her pulse beneath my palm. Wanting to feel it get faster as I leaned in to take her mouth.

Christ, I was losing it. And there was a part of me that didn't give a shit. As if it had been waiting for this opportunity all this time—this chance to take her like I'd always wanted to. But I couldn't listen to that part of myself.

Cat had been burned—and burned very badly—and getting physical with her just because my dick was getting impatient would be a mistake.

She looked away, as if she knew exactly the kind of thoughts that had been sitting in my head, and there was a long silence.

Then she said, 'I'm not moving into that clubhouse with you and neither is Annie—okay?'

I let out a slow, silent breath. She was going for it. She was fucking *going* for it. But I didn't relax, holding her wary gaze with mine. I wanted to hear her say the word out loud.

'Was that a yes, kitten?'

Irritation flashed in her gaze. 'Christ, Smoke, I'm not going to—'

'Say it.' I hadn't meant it to sound like an order, but it came out as one all the same.

I saw something spark in those big green eyes—a reaction I was positive she hadn't meant me to see. A gleam of heat.

'Fuck. Okay.' Her voice was all irritation and impatience. 'I'll be your old lady. Satisfied?'

No, I wasn't satisfied. And I wouldn't be until she was mine in every way that counted. I always thought she didn't feel that way about me, but there had been a number of signs over the past couple of days that had made me wonder...

A thrill shot down my spine. The kind of thrill I hadn't felt for years.

'It'll do.' I made sure to let none of that show in my voice, because frightening her off now would be a real bad move.

'But it's not for real,' she insisted. 'We're just doing this to protect Annie. Once Justin gets the message and backs off everything goes back to normal.'

Sure it would go back to normal.

Like hell.

Because I had a feeling that once I had Cat where I wanted her, wearing my property patch, I wasn't going to be able to let her go.

'It may not be for real to us.' I held her gaze. 'But it'll have to look real to convince Keep and the others.'

'Oh. But I thought…' She trailed off, frowning.

'He told me he wouldn't protect you as things stand. So I asked him outright if he would if you were mine, and he said yes.'

I paused, wanting to make sure she understood exactly what I was going to ask from her.

'If Justin makes a move and the club has to respond, it's going to put us at risk with the police. And Keep won't want to do that if he thinks you're faking it. In fact if he realises that, he's going to be pissed.'

He wouldn't just be pissed; he'd be furious. And I'd seen him furious. If I hadn't done my old man in, Keep would have, and it wasn't anything I wanted directed at either me or Cat.

Her frown deepened. 'So we have to pretend it's real? Is that what you're saying?'

'Yeah. He'll remember the conversation I had with him and he'll be suspicious, no question. We'll have to convince him we're the real deal.'

Cat dropped her attention to the pavement, studying it like it was the most fascinating thing she'd ever seen. And…was she *blushing*?

She'd done that a couple of nights earlier, avoiding my gaze, staring at anything other than me. Then there had been her weirdness about discussing that blow job and her furious denial that she'd been checking me out.

The electric thrill intensified.

I knew when a woman wanted me.

I knew when a woman wanted me and didn't want me to know.

Cat definitely didn't want me to know.

Fucking finally. After all these years…

Triumph surged like gas down a fuel line, lighting me right up.

She wanted me. She really did.

I couldn't help myself. I reached out, took her chin in my hand and tipped her head back, forcing her gaze to mine. Her eyes were dark and shocked, the green lost in the night.

'Is that going to be a problem?' I asked roughly.

She'd gone very still. Even in the dim light of the street I could see the fire in her cheeks and the quick beat of her pulse at the base of her throat.

The space between us had got thick, like the air before a thunderstorm.

I could hear my own heartbeat, loud and heavy in my head.

'I don't know…' She stopped. 'I mean, I don't…' She stopped again and cleared her throat. 'What exactly are you saying, Smoke?'

Her skin was soft under my fingers and I wanted to

stroke her with my thumb, run it along the line of her lower lip, test how soft that felt, too.

'What do you think? We have to act like a real couple—know what I'm saying?'

She blinked, her attention dropping to my mouth. And staying there.

Holy fucking shit.

I was getting hard now, and my instinct was to push her against the brick wall and fuck us both into oblivion. But hard and fast up against a wall wasn't the way I wanted to do it—not with her and not after so many years.

No, I was going to take my time, make it last. Make her scream. Make her beg for me the way I would have begged for her if she'd only asked.

Maybe she could see that in my eyes, because she jerked her chin out of my grip, giving an abrupt, nervous-sounding laugh.

'That better not include sleeping with you, because you know that's not going to happen.' She was trying to make it sound like a joke and failing miserably.

For a second I debated asking her whether she was sure about that, but I kept my mouth shut. No point scaring her off before we'd even got started.

Still. I wasn't going to let this moment go—not yet.

'No,' I lied through my teeth. 'You're going to have to be comfortable with me touching you, though.'

She shifted on her feet, her Converses making scraping sounds on the pavement. Yeah, she was nervous, all right.

'Touching me how?'

I should have stopped right then. I should have let her go, turned around and taken her home.

But I didn't.

The devil had me in his grip and I wanted to keep pushing, to make her even more nervous. Because I'd been hanging out for her for years and now it was my turn to make her sweat.

I kept my posture loose and easy. Nothing threatening. Nothing that would scare her. But I held that green gaze of hers and let the hunger show.

'Come here and I'll show you.'

CHAPTER SEVEN

Cat

I STARED AT SMOKE, my heartbeat freakishly loud in my head.

Something was happening between us and it scared the shit out of me.

I knew as soon as I opened my big fat mouth and told him he didn't get a say about Annie that I'd crossed a line. That I'd hurt him and hurt him deeply.

I had no excuse except that I was frightened, and that when I got frightened I got angry.

Had *that* been the thing that had changed the atmosphere between us?

Or had it been the night I'd stormed into the clubhouse and seen Smoke getting head, with his hands in another woman's hair?

I didn't know. But maybe it didn't matter. Because right now it felt like I wasn't looking into my friend's eyes. It felt like I was looking into the eyes of a complete stranger.

And that stranger...

God, he was looking back at me like he wanted to eat me alive.

Like he looked at that woman in the hallway.
Shit.

Smoke made no move towards me. He simply stood there and put his hands in the pockets of his jeans, a relaxed kind of posture. But his gaze was black and there was fire in it—a heat I'd never imagined—not to mention challenge, too. Like he was daring me to do it.

I remembered that look. The first day I met him, after I'd watched him do tricks for a solid half-hour, he handed me his skateboard and dared me to try it. There had been many times after that when he'd pushed me to do something I didn't want to do or was scared of. Skateboarding. Riding his motorcycle. Drinking bourbon neat. Going to the school dance. Telling my mother she had to quit heroin or else I'd move out. Applying for law school. Leaving Justin...

Some of those things I'd ended up failing at, and some of them were among the best experiences of my life. But this challenge—this was different. This felt like it could threaten the very fabric of our friendship.

Seriously? You're acting like this is real and it's not. It's just pretend.

I drew in a shaky breath. Yeah, of course. Pretend. Which meant the way he was looking at me was pretend, too. He didn't really want me—just like I didn't really want him. Nothing would be threatened because we wouldn't actually be together. We'd just have to make it look like we were. And that was fine. I could do that.

Smoke wasn't wrong. No matter how much I didn't want to go anywhere near the Knights, this did seem to be our only option to protect Annie.

Plus, after what I said to him, I owed him.

'Okay.' I took a step away from the wall, getting closer to him. 'Show me, then.'

My voice sounded shaky and I couldn't seem to get my heart rate under control.

It was just Smoke. Only Smoke.

He stared down at me and I was suddenly aware of the height difference between us—something I'd only been vaguely aware of before. But it hit me now how much taller he was. How much broader. How much more powerful and muscular.

I wanted to make a joke about his workout regimen, yet I'd never felt less like laughing in my entire life.

'You'll have to come closer than that.'

His voice was quiet, with a dark, husky quality to it which was another thing I'd never noticed before.

I was looking at him like he was some stranger, but he wasn't. He was my friend.

I took another step towards him, trying to ignore my frantic heartbeat.

'That's better,' he said.

We were only inches apart now, and I could feel the heat of his body from where I stood. He was like the engine of his bike, running hot, and it was difficult to hold his gaze. The darkness of it was like a black lake I could fall into, drown in.

'So,' I said inanely, on edge and hyperaware, as if the slightest sound or sudden movement would cause me to jump sky-high. 'Are you going to?'

Smoke reached out and slid his arm around my waist, pulling me right up against his body. And everything I'd been going to say went straight out of my head.

I couldn't get enough air to breathe because he was hot. And hard. Everywhere. The arm around me was an iron band, holding me firmly where I was, and instinctively, I put up my hands and pressed my palms to the wall of his chest, trying to keep some distance between us.

But there was no distance to be had.

He was right there, up against every inch of me—my thighs, my hips, my stomach, my breasts. So fucking hot. So fucking hard. I could feel the flex and release of his muscles beneath my palms and I couldn't repress the shiver that went straight down my spine. The shiver of deep female appreciation for male strength. Insane when, after Justin, I knew what male strength could do to a woman.

I felt it, though. It made my mouth dry with want.

I was trembling and I couldn't stop. I felt like I was being slowly stripped down, taken apart like a gun or an engine, and all my pieces laid out so he could see how I was put together.

Don't be stupid. Pretend, remember?

Yeah. That's right. Pretend. Get a grip, Cat. Get a fucking grip.

I tilted my head back and looked up at him, because if this was a challenge, then I wanted to show him I could do it. I always wanted to show him I could do it.

The light behind him threw his face into shadow, but I could see his expression. It was taut, fierce, his gaze focusing on me with frightening intensity.

My heartbeat refused to slow down.

He lifted his other hand and, with careful deliberation, slid his fingers into my hair so they curved around my skull, cupping the back of my head in his palm. Then he curled his fingers up tight and I sucked in a startled breath as my hair was caught in his fist.

It didn't hurt, but I realised with a sudden crashing awareness that he was now holding me fast. That I couldn't pull away even if I wanted to.

And that he was going to kiss me.

'Smoke—' I began, to stop him…encourage him… I had no idea. I never got the chance.

His mouth was on mine before I knew what was happening.

I froze in shock, going rigid, my mind utterly blank.

Then heat erupted along the entire length of my body. *So* much heat. It was like one of those arc welders applied directly to my skin, lighting me up from the inside out.

Frightened for reasons I didn't understand, I pushed against his chest, wanting to get away, to put distance between us, between me and that all-consuming, terrifying heat.

But he didn't let me go. In fact the arm around my waist only tightened further, leaving me in no doubt about who was in charge of this. He was. In every way.

I shivered, feeling small and feminine, vulnerable and utterly at his mercy. Panic shifted inside me and something else—something that wasn't panic at all. Something that I very much feared was…excitement.

Then, before I could work out what the tangle of feelings were, slowly and deliberately Smoke continued to kiss me.

His lips were both hard and soft at the same time, brushing mine, a gentle tease. Then he ran his tongue along the seam of my lips, encouraging me to open and let him in.

I did and, oh, God, I tasted him. Raw, alcoholic, with a touch of sweetness like the kick of a really good bourbon. It made me tremble. Then his tongue slid into my mouth, exploring me, and I trembled even harder.

It had been so long since anyone had touched me like this, held me like this. So long since I'd been kissed. And now my best friend was kissing me and it felt like...

Jesus, it felt like a piece of a puzzle had clicked into place.

So wrong. This is your friend. This is pretend.

I tried to open my mouth to speak, to remind him or something—I didn't know. But he wouldn't let me do that either.

His fingers in my hair pulled tighter, urging my head further back, and his tongue pushed deeper into my mouth, the kiss turning hotter, wetter. More demanding. Taking all my words away and giving me heat and that sweet kick of bourbon instead, the raw, addictive taste of him.

My heartbeat was raging and I felt dizzy. Like I was drunk. On him. On this kiss. His heat was blinding and he was everywhere—his rock-hard chest against my aching breasts, his arms around me, holding me tight against him. His mouth was on mine, tasting me as I was tasting him. Kissing me as if he couldn't get enough. As if he wanted to eat me alive.

But, no. He couldn't want that. This was pretend, remember?

Yet my fingers curled into the warm cotton of his

T-shirt, gripping on for dear life, and it was hard to hold on to that thought. He knew what he was doing and it was so good.

I couldn't help myself. I began to respond. Blindly touching his tongue with mine, kissing him back, hungry for more of that terrifying heat. More of that kiss. More of *him*.

My nipples hardened against his chest and there was a heavy, pulsing ache between my legs. My skin felt tight, like I wanted to burst right out of it.

Smoke growled—a low animal sound that vibrated through me—then he slid one large warm hand over the curve of my butt, pulling me harder against him. I nearly gasped as I felt the hard ridge of his cock press against the zipper of my jeans, causing jolts of intense pleasure as the zipper hit my clit.

I groaned, shifting my hips against his, helplessly chasing that friction. I felt like I'd been starved and he was tempting me with all my favourite foods, holding them out to me, giving me a taste, making me *so* fucking hungry...

Then suddenly his arms around me were gone; that hot, demanding mouth vanished, and I was stumbling forward, off balance, breathing fast and hard like I'd run ten marathons in a row.

I blinked, somehow finding my feet, trying like hell to get my breathing under control.

Smoke had pulled back and was standing there with his arms folded. The expression on his face was unreadable. He was watching me with a detached kind of focus. As if that whole kiss had merely been an experiment he wanted to see the effects of.

He hadn't felt it like I had, obviously.

Something fell away inside me—something that I refused to call disappointment. Because there was nothing disappointing about him not feeling that kiss. In fact it was reassuring. Clearly the intensity of it had been all in my head—a product of going too long without sex and nothing to do with chemistry at all.

Anyway, it made sense that he didn't feel it. Because he'd been pretending, too.

Sure, and maybe his cock had been pretending, as well.

Yeah, but guys got hard at the drop of a hat, didn't they? It wasn't me. It was merely the presence of a female body—that was all.

I sucked in a steadying breath, hiding my hardened nipples behind my folded arms, mirroring his posture.

'So?' I couldn't keep the husky edge from my voice. Dammit. 'That convincing enough for you?'

'It'll do.' His voice, in contrast, sounded completely normal, the asshole.

My heart raced and the heavy, nagging ache between my legs just wouldn't let up. Perhaps if I didn't think about it, it would go away.

'Good. So, how do we do this? I mean, do you simply tell them I'm your old lady and that's it? What?'

He hadn't moved. He was standing there like a statue, all tall and dark and radiating menace, not to mention a fair amount of distance.

He hadn't forgiven me for what I'd said to him.

If you break this friendship, it'll be your own fault. Don't forget you pretty much break everything you touch...

Panic turned over in my gut before I managed to shove the poisonous thought away. No, shit. Wherever that had come from, it was wrong. Sure, there were things in my life that hadn't gone to plan—but that was life, wasn't it? Shitty, shitty life.

I had Annie and I had Smoke—my two constants. I wouldn't lose my daughter and I wouldn't break my friendship with Smoke. I just wouldn't.

'You going to do this, then?' he asked.

As if I had a choice.

'For Annie, yeah. I will.'

He gave a slow nod and I got the feeling that I'd agreed to something I didn't know anything about.

Panic gripped me again, but I forced it away. Being Smoke's pretend old lady… Really, how bad could it be?

A memory filtered through my consciousness of the night Annie had been taken, when I'd stormed through the Knights' clubhouse. All those men with all those women, having sex right out there in public, for everyone to see.

That was pretty bad.

'We…uh…we wouldn't have to do any…public stuff, would we?' I hated the quiver in my voice. 'Because, straight up, I'm *not* doing that.'

That distant look was still on Smoke's face, and it was like he was pulling away from me, even though he hadn't moved an inch. I wanted to reach out and grab his arm, pull him back.

'Don't worry.' Even his voice sounded remote. 'We wouldn't.'

'Okay, then.' I hesitated, then realised what I was doing.

I'd never hesitated in talking to Smoke before. Never, ever.

My throat closed. Things were different. Something had changed.

'Are we good?' I had to force myself to say it.

'Sure, kitten. We're good.'

But I didn't miss his own hesitation, and it slid like a sliver of glass under my skin. I opened my mouth to say something, but he'd already turned, jerking his head in the direction of the kerb, where I saw the gleam of chrome in the darkness. His Harley.

'Come on,' he said. 'I'll tell you the plan while I take you home.'

CHAPTER EIGHT

Smoke

'SERIOUSLY? THAT'S YOUR PLAN?'

Tiger was stretched out on the couch opposite me, a beer in one hand, a joint in the other, and a woman in his lap. She was taking puffs on his joint and looking bored, obviously waiting until we'd finished talking so she could get on with the more important job of sucking his cock.

Unfortunately for her, we hadn't finished talking.

'Yeah, that's the plan.' I leaned back in my chair, picking at a hole in the cheap vinyl on the arm of it and trying not to let Tiger's sarcasm get to me. 'Something wrong with it?'

We were in the Knights' clubhouse, over by the corner near the pool table, where it was quieter and no one would overhear us. I'd just told him how I was going to save both Annie and Cat, and he'd told me what a fucking stupid idea it was.

'Uh...who's going to believe Cat's your old lady?' Tiger shook his head. 'Everyone knows she's your friend.'

'And everyone thinks I'm fucking her already.' Which they did, since to them friendship between a man and a woman was apparently a goddamn unicorn. As in it didn't exist.

Tiger lifted his joint in salute. 'True.'

'So it's not exactly going to be a surprise.'

'Also true.' The woman sitting in his lap grabbed at his beer and he gave it to her. 'Though you taking an old lady might be.'

He wasn't wrong about that. I'd never wanted any permanent commitments and hadn't exactly kept it a big secret. Tiger was the same.

All I needed was my bike, my club, regular blow jobs and Cat. Sure, it would be great if Cat could provide the blow jobs, but you couldn't have everything.

That reminded me of the kiss a couple of nights ago and I shifted in my chair, trying not to think about it since every time I did I got harder than iron.

I'd been a prick to demand that of her, but I hadn't been sorry. Still wasn't. Because if nothing else ever happened between us, at least I'd have that kiss.

And, Christ, what a fucking kiss. I'd never had anything like it and I probably wouldn't have anything like it again.

She'd tasted exactly the way I'd dreamed, except better. Sweet, yet tart, too—like strawberries and really expensive dry champagne. Which was Cat all-up. It was also goddamn delicious and I wanted more.

Her body had felt soft and hot, and the moment the hard tips of her nipples had pressed against my chest, I'd wanted to eat her alive. Because that right there had been confirmation. She wanted me. She fucking *wanted* me.

Then she'd started to kiss me back and I'd nearly lost my mind.

I'd come *this* close to simply shoving her against the wall, pulling her jeans down and getting inside her as fast as I damn well could.

But I'd been good. I'd let her go, put her at a distance and made sure she knew it. Though if she'd tried to make like that kiss hadn't meant anything, like it was just some pretend shit between friends, I don't know what I would have done.

I'd never hurt Cat. But that didn't mean I was a good guy.

Anyway, I'd done what I'd intended. I'd put her off balance, shown her what there could be between us. And it was fucking incredible.

'Bro?' Tiger said, eyeing me. 'Have you *actually* been fucking her? 'Cause you've got that look on your face that—'

'No.' I cut him off. 'I'm not.'

At least not yet. And even if I was, it wasn't any of his business. It wasn't anyone's business except mine and Cat's.

'Sure, the brothers might be surprised I'm taking an old lady, but they'll just think we've finally acknowledged our feelings for each other or some such bullshit.'

'Yeah, I guess they will.' Tiger put his hand on the woman's thigh. 'What about if Justin goes after the kid? Think Keep'll definitely protect her?'

I scowled. 'He told me he would. He fucking better.'

'He's got shit going on with the police chief, though. He won't want to rock that particular boat.'

He wouldn't. Fucking politics. It was a necessary evil, though, especially with Keep trying to get us legit. But that came with its own problems. Justin fucking Grant being the main one—though hopefully Cat being mine would make him think twice about coming for Annie.

'So what are you going to do?' Tiger asked without waiting for me to respond. 'Move her in here? Can't see that happening, bro. She hates this place.'

'I know.'

I had my own plan about what I was going to do. Sure, I could make her move in here with me, but the clubhouse was no place for kids. Which left me with only one option.

'Thought I'd move in with her.'

I hadn't talked to Cat about it and I wasn't going to either. No point when she wasn't going to get a choice. If we wanted it to look real, I was going to have to live with her like a real couple would.

Tiger laughed. 'Oh, man, she's gonna *hate* that.'

He and Cat didn't get on. He thought she was up-tight and a control freak, and she thought he was a dick. Neither of them was wrong.

I shrugged. 'She'll have to suck it up.'

'Yeah, I'm sure she's going to have to do a lot of sucking.' He gave another laugh and drained the rest of his beer.

I said nothing to the stupid joke. Tiger had his demons, and being a tool was all part of his don't-give-a-fuck deal.

'So when are you going to break the happy news?' He slid his hand beneath the blonde's skirt and she shifted around, flushing.

'The party this weekend. I'm bringing her along.'

Cat wouldn't like that either, since I knew she hated club parties. Yet more stuff she was going to have to deal with.

The blonde nestled herself into the crook of Tiger's arm, her face pressed into his neck. It looked like things were only going to go downhill communicationwise, so I said, 'Catch you round, brother...' and got to my feet. 'I've got a few things to do before Saturday night.'

Like getting a property patch for my best friend.

'Can't wait for that.' Tiger grinned.

Then his gaze focused on someone behind me and his grin became wider.

'Good luck, man. Looks like you're gonna need it.'

I turned in time to see a curvy brunette coming across the room towards me, swinging her hips and giving me a sexy smile.

Fuck. It was Hannah. Blow Job Hannah.

She and I had an understanding. With her long dark hair and her delicate face it was easy to see—if you were looking—what I liked about her. She was my go-to girl when I couldn't get my goddamn best friend out of my head.

Probably I should have felt guilty about using her as a Cat stand-in, but I'd always figured it was better I do that than cut Cat out of my life completely. Yeah, I was a selfish fuck. I couldn't face the thought of doing that.

Cat was the one I turned to when Dad's fists had

been harder than the walls he'd thrown me into. She patched me up, listened to me as I raged, and she gave me no judgement that night I ended those fucking hits forever.

Not seeing her ever again was not an option.

'Hey, Smoke.' Hannah sidled up. 'Been meaning to catch up with you…see if you want to carry on where we left off, if you know what I mean.'

She gave her lips a surreptitious lick, to be sure I understood.

'I'm free now, if you are.'

Normally I would have been tempted—especially seeing as how it had been a week or so since that blow job and I'd been frustrated and on edge because of what was going on with Cat.

But that kiss had changed things, and the thought of letting off steam with Hannah didn't hold any attraction at all. Anyway, it seemed ridiculous to get Hannah to blow me when I could have the real thing in just a few short days.

If she lets you.

She'd let me. I'd make sure of it. And as for our friendship…it wouldn't be an issue—not when I wasn't planning on letting her go.

'Not now,' I said shortly, hoping she'd catch my drift.

She pouted and slid a hand over the front of my jeans, giving my dick a squeeze. 'Doesn't feel like "not now" to me.'

Because I'd been thinking of that fucking kiss, my dick was not uninterested in the thought of Hannah's mouth wrapped around it, the traitorous fuck.

'That's not for you.' I grabbed her hand and took it firmly away.

Her face fell and I thought I caught a look of genuine disappointment on it before she turned away, shrugging a shoulder.

'Your loss.'

Abruptly I felt like a tool. Some of the brothers didn't give a shit about club pussy. They didn't hurt the girls, but it wasn't like they cared either. The girls themselves knew what they were getting into when they hung around the clubhouse and slept with the brothers, but, hell, they had feelings like everyone else.

'Hannah,' I said, reaching out and grabbing her chin, turning her back to face me. 'It's not you, okay? I'm taking an old lady now, and that means I can't be doing that any more.'

And I wouldn't. Monogamy wasn't celebrated in the club, but I'd never been a fan of double standards. If Cat had to be faithful to me—and I sure as hell was going to expect that—then I'd do the same for her.

A rueful expression crossed her face. 'You're such a fucking problem. You're hot *and* a good guy, and there aren't many with that combination around here right now.'

I didn't know what to say, because she was wrong. I wasn't a good guy. Good guys didn't kill their fathers.

'I'm sorry, Hannah,' I said finally, and let her go.

Her eyes darkened. 'I'm sorry, too.'

Then she turned away before I had a chance to say anything more.

CHAPTER NINE

Cat

I'D JUST GOT Annie into the bath when my phone started buzzing with a call. I left her in the tub and stepped into the hallway, grabbing my phone from the pocket of my jeans and glancing down at the screen.

My heart sank right down into the bottom of my sneakers.

It was Justin.

Briefly I debated not answering it.

Tonight was the night of the party at the Knights' clubhouse—my debut with Smoke as a couple—and I had to bathe Annie and put her into bed before the sitter came, then get ready myself. I was in no mood to talk to my abusive ex.

Smoke had wanted us to go earlier in the evening, when there were apparently kids around, so Annie could go, too, but I didn't want that quite yet. I needed to check out the place first, before I brought her into it. He hadn't argued, had simply gone ahead and organised a sitter for her before I'd even broached the topic.

Now I wished I'd done what he said and gone early—then I wouldn't have to deal with this phone call.

Still, avoiding it would be cowardly, so I hit the answer button. 'What do you want?'

'Hey, don't be like that.'

Justin's smooth tones were warm and silky, like melted chocolate. To think I'd once loved his voice. What a lie it had been.

'I only want to talk.'

I gritted my teeth. 'What do you want to talk about?'

'Come on—don't play dumb. This is about Annie.'

'And?'

'What? Your boyfriend didn't tell you?'

'He's not my boyfriend,' I said reflexively. Then I realised what a mistake that was. Smoke *was* supposed to be my boyfriend. Crap.

'Yeah, like I ever believed that for a second.'

There was a bitterness I recognised in Justin's voice. He'd never liked my friendship with Smoke, and that had been the source of most of our arguments. Justin had wanted me to stop seeing him, but I'd refused. I wasn't cutting Smoke out of my life just because he couldn't handle the fact that my best friend was a guy.

'What do you want?'

I ran a hand through my hair, feeling exhausted. The past few days had been shitty. I'd been trying to find work to replace the shift at Lucky's, but hadn't managed to turn anything up, and rent was due at the end of the month—only a week away. I didn't have the money. Or at least I had the money for rent, but if we wanted to eat, then that might be problem.

'Like I said, this is about Annie. Thought I'd be a

gentleman and let you know personally that I'm going to be suing for full custody in the next couple of weeks.'

He sounded so pleased with himself I wanted to punch him.

'Unless you agree to give me full custody yourself and then we can save all the messy court drama.'

My heart clenched tight. 'Why the hell would I do that?'

'Oh, come on, Cat.'

His voice had softened, taking on the warm and tender note that had once managed to reach inside me and undo all my defences. The note that told me I was cared for. That I was loved.

'Being a single mom is hard. You're working two jobs… You're tired every night. How is that good for Annie? Having such a tired mom all the time? And that apartment is a dump—not to mention dangerous. Mine is big, and there's security, and—hey, you know how much she loves swimming, right? I've even got a pool.'

His voice poured over me, smooth and rich, lulling me.

'If she was here, you wouldn't have to worry so much. You wouldn't have to work so hard all the time. The pressure would be off.'

I closed my eyes, horrified to find that if I wasn't careful I was going to burst into exhausted, emotional tears.

He was right. Being a single mom *was* hard and I worried *so* much. There was no break, no respite. Sometimes I wished I could just have ten minutes when I didn't have to worry about Annie and whether I had enough time for her. Whether I had enough money to feed and clothe her. Whether I could actually be the mother I wanted to be for her.

'It wouldn't mean you'd never see her,' he went on, obviously knowing he'd hooked into my deepest fears. 'We'd work out a visitation schedule. Hell, you could even have her overnight a couple of times a week. Wouldn't that be better for you? You could actually spend time with her when you're not tired and worried and thinking about all the stuff you need to do.'

He knew me well. Knew what I was afraid of. Knew what I was desperate for. At first it had been so good to have someone know me like that. To love me the way I'd always wanted to be loved.

Then he'd shown me what a lie that was and how stupid I was to trust him. Just like he was lying to me now.

Never again.

I forced away the tears, swallowing back the lump in my throat. 'And if you get angry again, Justin?' I had to concentrate to make my voice sound strong and unaffected. 'What happens then? Will you hit Annie the way you hit me?'

There was a hard silence down the other end of the phone.

'That's not going to happen.' The warm note had vanished from his voice like it had never been there. 'I would never hit her.'

'The way you'd never hit me?'

'I've dealt with my anger issues,' he said calmly. 'Not that it would have ever happened if you'd done what I said and stopped screwing that friend of yours.'

Ah, *this* was the Justin I remembered. The asshole.

I said nothing—mainly because there was nothing to say. He wouldn't have listened anyway.

'Well? Last chance, Cat.'

'Why?' I asked suddenly. 'You never wanted her before. You never wanted her in the first place. Why do you want her so desperately now?'

'Because she's *my* damn daughter, and I want what's mine. That's why.' He sounded impatient now. 'Are you going to give me full custody? If not, I'll see you in court.'

My jaw was tight, my heart burning with anger. 'No. I'll never give you full custody of her. Never, ever.'

He gave a snort of disgust. 'Stupid move, honey. Guess we'll have to do this the hard way, then.'

The call was disconnected abruptly.

Fuck. I didn't even have the satisfaction of hanging up on him.

My fingers were white around my phone, but I couldn't afford to give in to the urge to throw it at the wall because I literally couldn't afford to get a new one if it broke. I had to make do with shoving it hard into my pocket and cursing viciously.

It was difficult to go into the bathroom and continue bathing Annie like nothing had happened, but I managed it, and luckily she was too young to know that there was anything wrong.

Fifteen minutes later, all dry and dressed in clean pyjamas, Annie was ready for a bedtime story when the doorbell rang.

For a second I froze, the horrible thought of Justin coming over to take Annie away from me right now popping into my head. Then I remembered. The party. It would probably be either the sitter or Smoke.

Leaving her with a picture book, I crept into the hallway and went to the door and looked through the peephole.

Smoke was in the hall outside, in his jeans and cut, and he was literally the best thing I'd seen all day.

I undid the chain and pulled the door open, grinning stupidly. 'You're early. I wasn't expecting you till later.'

He didn't smile back the way he normally would have, and his gaze was fierce on mine. 'Thought I'd come and drop my stuff off.'

'What stuff?' Then I noticed the big duffel bag he had slung over one shoulder. 'What's that for?'

'What do you think? I'm moving in.'

My mouth dropped open—to say what, I had no idea. Because at that moment Annie came charging down the hallway, screaming, 'Smoke!' at the top of her lungs.

The fierce look vanished and a heartbreakingly beautiful smile crossed his face as he stepped past me.

'Hi, kiddo,' he said, opening his arms as Annie flung herself into them.

I shut the door and leaned against it, stunned by his announcement and by the fact that watching the pair of them together made my heart ache like someone had hit it with a large baseball bat.

He hadn't smiled at me. He'd saved it for Annie and that was okay. It really was. But seeing them together after that phone call with Justin hurt for reasons I didn't want to examine.

You should never have said that he wasn't her father.

No. I shouldn't have. Not when what was happening right in front of me proved what a lie that was.

Smoke had picked her up and was carrying her down the hallway.

'Can I read you a bedtime story, or do you want Mommy to do it?'

'You!' Annie said excitedly, then patted his shoulder. 'What's that big bag?'

'That? It's a unicorn. It was too big to carry, so I put it in the bag.'

Annie giggled, delighted. 'It is not!'

'No, it's not. It's only boring stuff like clothes.'

'I *like* clothes.'

'They're not for you, kiddo. They're for me. I'm going to be staying for a while.'

I watched Annie's face light up at this as they both disappeared through the doorway into her bedroom, belated shock moving slowly through my system.

Staying for a while...

He hadn't mentioned moving in when he'd told me his plan on the way back from Lucky's that night. All he'd said was that he wanted me to go to the party.

Panic turned over inside me and I didn't know why.

Ignoring it, I went down the hallway and into my bedroom, deciding I might as well get ready. He'd be with Annie awhile. I would wait to talk to him about this moving-in business once she was asleep.

Pulling open my closet, I grimaced at the lack of decent things to wear hanging in it. What the hell did you wear to a biker party anyway? The one and only party I'd been to had been the one where I'd caught

Smoke getting that blow job, and none of the women at that party and been wearing anything at all.

God, I was *so* not going naked.

Pulling out a selection of things, I laid them on the bed, discarding my one and only little black dress as too dressy and the denim mini as too slutty. There was the plain black pencil skirt I wore to work at the call centre on occasion, but that seemed a little…boring.

This isn't a fashion show. You're not your mother.

I pulled a face, remembering my mom getting ready for the few parties Dad used to take her to. She'd always been so excited, thinking it meant something. Thinking that finally he was going to make her his old lady and everything would be different. She'd dress up in the few designer dresses she had left—the remains of her old, socialite life—and get herself looking beautiful.

But it never made any difference. And she always came home alone.

I always thought I'd never end up like her, and yet now here I was, a single mom, trying to find something to wear to a biker party. Even the fact that I was going as someone's old lady didn't change it—not when I wasn't a *real* old lady.

I was just like her. Struggling to make ends meet, to feed and clothe my kid. The only things I had going for me were that I wasn't an addict and I wasn't in love with a biker.

'Are you ready?'

I almost jumped at the sound of Smoke's deep voice coming from the doorway. He was leaning against the frame, his arms folded, the ink of his tats dark against his skin. That breathtaking smile he'd saved for my daughter was gone. The fiercely intense look was back again.

The same look he'd given me that night he'd kissed me.

I'd never felt shy around Smoke before, but I was now.

My mouth dry, I glanced down at the clothes on the bed. 'No, obviously, I'm not ready.'

I pushed aside the black dress, fiddling about with the black skinny jeans that were my favoured alternative.

'Annie must have gone down quickly.'

'She was tired. She said you were shouting at someone on the phone just before I arrived.'

Oh, shit. That kid had bat ears.

'Someone from work.'

I don't know why I didn't tell him about Justin. Maybe it was because Justin had made me feel so helpless and I didn't want Smoke to know how badly affected I was.

'Bullshit. Annie said you were talking about her.'

Busted.

I let out a breath, smoothing the fabric on the bed. 'It was Justin. He was trying to get me to give him sole custody voluntarily.'

I didn't even know Smoke had moved until I felt heat beside me and a powerful hand had my jaw in its grip, turning my face to his.

Black eyes pinned me. 'And you said what?'

'What do you think? Of course I said no.'

But he must have heard the catch in my voice because that fierce look suddenly softened. 'What else did he say, Cat?'

His thumb brushed absently along the line of my jaw, striking sparks along every nerve ending I had. I tried not to notice, tried not to shiver.

'He made like it would be a good thing.' My voice thickened. 'He told me it would be better for Annie if she didn't have a mom who was working all the time and who was so tired. Who had no time for her kid because she was always worrying. And he said how his apartment was safe, and he has a pool, and you know how much she likes swimming—'

I broke off, my eyes prickling, and tried to pull away again, not wanting Smoke to see how much Justin's words had slipped beneath my skin. How much they'd made me doubt myself.

But Smoke didn't let me go. 'There's no better place for Annie than with you,' he said with quiet emphasis. 'She doesn't need a fucking pool. All she needs is love, and you do that better than anyone.'

My heart swelled up tight in my chest. 'Sometimes I can't help thinking that maybe she'd be better off with him. He has money and—'

'Quiet,' Smoke interrupted, with so much authority I fell silent. 'That prick's got nothing Annie needs. If he was any kind of decent father, he would be in her life, but he's not. And if he was any kind of decent man, he wouldn't have fucking touched you in the first place. But he did. Which makes him and his opinions worth *shit.*'

I opened my mouth to tell him how much I'd needed

to hear that that, but he put his thumb across my lips and pressed down lightly, silencing me.

'Don't worry, kitten,' he went on softly. 'You don't need to worry—especially not about money. I'm here now, and I'll deal with it.'

I had issues with that, but for some reason my brain wouldn't work. I couldn't repress the helpless shiver that chased over my skin at his touch either.

A black flame leapt in his eyes, hot and dark, and for a second I had the mad urge to open my mouth and suck on his thumb. Bite it.

Maybe he saw that, too, because I swore I caught the flicker of a feral kind of smile on his beautiful mouth.

'Black pencil skirt. Green blouse. Black stilettos. Stockings.' His hand fell away, releasing me. 'Now, go get ready. The sitter will be here any minute.'

CHAPTER TEN

Smoke

THE PARTY WAS already underway by the time Cat and I got to the clubhouse. We were hosting The Demon's Share brothers—a smaller club from down south who were allies—and us Knights always liked to put on a good show.

The rides were parked outside—a massive line of them, chrome gleaming under the streetlights—and the prospects assigned to guard them were hanging out by the doorway, smoking and drinking and flirting with a bunch of girls who were trying to get in.

I helped Cat off my bike, unable to keep my eyes off her as she smoothed down the skirt that had got rucked up on the ride over.

She'd put on exactly what I told her to and she looked so fucking *hot*—exactly as I'd pictured her. The pencil skirt hugged her ass like a greedy pair of hands, and the soft green blouse was transparent enough to see the lacy black bra she wore underneath it. Plus, it was nearly the same colour as her eyes.

The effect was like a classy, sexy secretary. She'd

even done her hair in a loose bun that I wanted to pull the pins out of and run my fingers through.

All she was missing was my property patch on her back.

Well, I'd fix that once we were inside. My plan was to take her in, claim her in front of all the brothers so no one could be in any doubt, and when she came out again, she'd be my old lady.

My property.

A deep satisfaction sat in my gut, along with a desire so strong it was like a kick to the head.

Tonight I'd make her mine.

Finished with smoothing herself, she flicked a nervous glance at the doorway. Nervous was okay, though. Nervous was better than the weariness I'd seen in her face earlier, when she was standing by her bed looking at her clothes. Better than the terrible doubt when she'd told me what that asshole Justin had said to her.

He was a bastard for hooking into her doubts and using them against her, and I wanted to kill the guy with my bare hands. Hell, when he came for Annie with that custody order, maybe I'd even get the chance.

'It'll be okay,' I said to reassure her. 'It's not like your dad's club, remember?'

The Knights looked after their own way better than her old man's club had. And even if they didn't, *I* sure as hell did.

'Thanks, *Dane*,' she said tartly, pissed off that I'd picked up on her nervousness. 'I'll take that under advisement.'

I almost grinned. 'You want to be careful, Cat. I

might call you *kitten* in there, and then you'll be stuck with it for life. The brothers like a nickname.'

She rolled her eyes, but her mouth curved, and for a second, we were almost friends again. Then I remembered the way that mouth had tasted, and all the things I wanted to make it do, and I knew that it couldn't happen.

Because I didn't want friendship—not from her.

Friendship wasn't enough any more.

Reaching out, I grabbed her hand, lacing her fingers through mine. 'Ready?'

'As I'll ever be, I guess.'

We walked up to the entrance, ignoring the wide-eyed stares of the girls still trying to get in. The prospects gave me a chin jerk as we approached, stepping aside. As we went past them I could see them give Cat appreciative glances, no doubt noting the fact that she didn't have a property patch on her back.

I gave the little fucks my enforcer stare and they quickly looked away.

Damn straight.

There were a lot of people milling around—Knights and more than a few Demons. Some of them called my name, but I didn't stop, heading down the corridor that led out to the back of the building where the courtyard was.

That tended to be where the action was whenever there was a party, which meant Keep would be there. And it was him I wanted to see first of all. I needed him to know what I was going to do, because it was only polite to inform my president. Especially if he was going to give me shit about it.

Then I was planning to get the vest with the property patch on it and make Cat put it on in front of the whole club, so there would be no doubt about whose she was. So everyone would know she was fucking *mine*.

We went through the doors at the end of the hallway and outside into the courtyard, and sure enough a bonfire was blazing in the middle of the space.

There were plenty of people milling around, talking and drinking, some dancing to the music that was blaring from the outdoor speaker system. The smell of cigarettes and weed was in the air, combining with the scent of burning wood from the fire, reminding me of what I loved about the club so much.

It was home. It was friendship. It was having people at your back who you could trust with your life. It was being part of a family. It was everything I'd never had as a kid.

And now it would be Cat, too.

I led her through the crowds, spotting Keep's tall figure over by the fire. He was talking to Big Red, the VP, and Chase, the president of Demon's Share.

Some of the brothers were beginning to stare at us, nudging each other and grinning.

'Fuckin' told ya,' someone muttered as we went by.

I ignored all of them, catching Keep's eye as we approached, tightening my fingers around Cat's.

His brows rose, his gaze flicking to Cat, then back at me. 'What the fuck is this?'

I could feel Cat stiffen beside me, so I ran my thumb over the back of her hand in reassurance. Keep had met Cat a couple of times before but only in passing.

'It's exactly what you think it is,' I said.

Keep didn't take his eyes off me. 'Why don't you get Leanne to show Cat where to find a drink, Red? I need to talk to Smoke here for a second.'

Leanne was Red's old lady, and the fact that Keep had asked her to look after Cat was a sign he thought she was more than a casual fuck. But the look on his face was *not* friendly. Luckily it was directed at me, and I could handle it.

He might be my president, and my uncle, but he wasn't going to tell me who I could and couldn't have as my property. He mightn't like it, but in this case he was going to have to suck it up.

'Smoke—' Cat began, obviously not liking where this was going.

'It's okay.' I turned to meet her uncertain green eyes and cupped her cheek in my palm, blatantly taking advantage of our pretence to touch her. Her skin was so soft and so warm, and I allowed myself to enjoy the feel of it. 'I'll come find you in a second.'

I could tell she didn't want to go, but after a gesture from Red brought Leanne over, she allowed herself to be led off.

'Mind telling me why she's here?' Keep asked in the quiet voice he only used when someone was in deep shit.

Everyone else suddenly found other things to do, melting away into the rest of the crowd, leaving Keep and me alone.

I stared back, holding my ground. I knew he was going to be pissed, but I wasn't budging when it came to Cat and Annie's safety. I'd do anything I could to make sure the pair of them stayed where they belonged. *With me.*

'I think you know why she's here,' I said flatly. 'Going to make her my old lady.'

Keep's expression didn't change. He was a man who kept his feelings close to his vest. A family trait, that.

'This got something to do with what we talked about last week?'

No point in denying it. 'Yeah.'

His eyes had got cold. 'So you're willing to put at risk everything we worked for—everything *I* worked for—to save your friend?'

He said it casually, like it was no big deal. Generally that was a sign that it was a huge fucking deal.

I knew that. I knew what bringing Cat here would mean.

'It's not just her. It's the kid, Keep. It's Annie. She's six years old. You really want her to go back to her violent old man?'

It was a low blow that went deeper than just Annie and Cat, and Keep knew it.

I was talking about my dad. About how everyone had known he was handy with fists, that he knocked me and Mom around, and yet no one had done anything. Not until the day he hit Mom once too hard and she went into the hospital and never come out again.

It was only then that someone tried to do something. Me.

'Or is it not our business?' I stared hard at him. 'Not our fucking problem?'

He shifted, folded his arms, and I knew that I'd got to him.

'Jesus, Smoke. You're just playing pretend with her—I can see that. I've never believed she was anything more than your friend, no matter what the others said.'

I took a couple of steps until I was right in front of him, looking him right in the eye. It was a direct challenge, but sometimes that was the best way to handle things with Keep. The truth didn't hurt either.

'She's mine,' I said. 'She always has been, and she always will be.'

Keep's blue stare flickered. 'And if she puts the Knights at risk because of her fucking ex? Will you be saying the same thing then?'

'You can talk to the police chief. You can get him to call his motherfucking son off.'

'Yeah, and that'll damage the relationship we have with him—you know that.'

'We can handle it.' Hell, we'd handled every other challenge that had been thrown at us over the years. We could handle this, too. 'Unless, of course, you think we're not strong enough.'

Keep gave a short laugh. 'You're trouble, boy. I knew you would be.'

I didn't argue, and I didn't look away. 'I'm going to take her, Keep. Whether you like it or not.'

My uncle stared at me for a long, uncomfortable minute. 'For the record, I don't like it, and I'm not happy about it. And if this all goes to shit because of it, we'll all know where the blame lies. Understand?'

'Sure. I understand.'

He was silent, the look on his face unreadable. 'This is one favour you're going to owe me. Are we clear?'

I didn't like the sound of that, but what else could I do but agree? 'Yeah, crystal.'

Keep let out a breath. 'Okay, then, you claim her. But I'll need the pair of you to fuck off out of my sight for a couple of days.'

Like that was going to be a problem. If everything went the way I wanted it to, Cat and I wouldn't come up for air for at least a week.

But first things first.

There was a patch I needed to get.

CHAPTER ELEVEN

Cat

I DIDN'T MUCH like being shunted off with Leanne. It felt too much like being dismissed, leaving the men to talk about the important stuff while the women weren't to worry their pretty little heads, et cetera.

But Leanne was very up-front about that kind of behaviour.

'It's all bullshit,' she said as she handed me a beer from the cooler that sat under a nearby table. 'The brothers wave their dicks around like that all the time.' She smirked. 'Sometimes literally. Just ignore it. I do.'

'I'll keep that in mind.'

I sipped my beer, my attention on the two men by the bonfire.

Keep, the Knights' president, was about as tall as Smoke, but built on an even more massive frame. He had shoulders like a pro wrestler's and biceps that would have put Superman to shame. There was an air of contained violence about him, a menace that had me shivering inside. He was a good-looking guy, though. Black hair and blue eyes and a charisma that was almost palpable. I knew he was Smoke's uncle and I could kind of see the resemblance.

I didn't like that air of violence, though. It reminded me too much of people like Smoke's asshole of a father. Of Justin. Men who couldn't handle themselves and took to beating people up instead.

Smoke was standing right in front of him, looking him right in the eye, and I felt a sharp spike of trepidation. God, was he putting himself and his membership of the Knights on the line for me and Annie? It made me feel uncomfortable, made me want to protest. I knew what the Knights meant to him, and even though I didn't like them I respected the fact that they were important to him. I wouldn't want him leaving because of me.

Leanne had opened her mouth to say something when the VP, Big Red—black bearded and green eyed—came up behind her, putting his arms around her and bending to whisper something in her ear. She laughed and then shrieked as he started dragging her off towards the entrance of the clubhouse.

They disappeared inside and I was conscious of standing beside the table on my own, in a crowd full of leather-clad, tattooed bikers. There seemed to be a lot more than there was before, and the women around were of the short-skirt, tight-top kind.

By the fire, Smoke turned on his heel and strode off towards the clubhouse. Keep's gaze followed him.

God, I hoped nothing bad had gone down.

There was a high-pitched giggle not far from me as one of the girls was pulled into the arms of a biker, his hand pushing down under her top.

Great. So the sex games were already starting.

'Hey, pretty.'

There were hands on my hips, pulling me back against a wall of leather before I had a chance to protest.

'Looks like things are heating up. You need cooling down?'

The voice was unfamiliar. A hand slid up and cupped my breast.

'No. Fuck off.' I jerked myself away and turned around.

A massive guy with a greasy black beard stood behind me, glowering at me. He wasn't a Knight from the look of his cut. He was from The Demon's Share.

'That's no way to treat a brother, bitch,' he said belligerently. 'You ain't got no patch on your back, so how about you fucking show me some respect?'

This was bad. I took a shaky breath, trying not to panic. 'I'm Smoke's,' I said, with as much calm as I could. 'And he'll be fucking pissed you laid a hand on me.'

'Uh-huh. But, like I said, I don't see a patch on your back, which means—'

'Which means she's fucking Smoke's.'

Tiger's tall, muscled figure was suddenly between me and the bearded shithead.

'So how about you go find someone else to play with?

The other man grunted and with one last evil look at me turned and pushed his way into the crowd.

Relief left me feeling unsteady, so I leaned surreptitiously against the table, trying not to show it. 'Thanks, Tiger,' I muttered.

He turned, his weird golden eyes glinting in the firelight. 'What the fuck's Smoke doing leaving you here alone?'

'I had Leanne with me, but Big Red took her away. Smoke just went into the clubhouse.'

'Huh. Fucking idiot.' Tiger raised the beer he was holding and took a long swallow, his gaze never leaving mine. It was guarded, suspicious. 'I'd better stay with you, then. Make sure no other fucker tries to take a shot at you.'

I wanted to tell him he didn't need to, that I could take care of myself, but clearly that would be playing the 'stupid' card one too many times. So I said nothing, turning away and gazing at the gathered crowd of bikers as they whooped and hollered around the fire.

There were a couple of live-sex shows happening already and I could feel my face flaming.

I looked away, my heart hammering, wishing I was anywhere but here.

Tiger said nothing, guarding me silently, warning anyone who came near with a hard stare.

It was uncomfortable and awkward, and I was on the point of saying I'd go inside and find Smoke myself when an arm snaked around my waist, drawing me up against hard muscle and heat. But this time it was familiar and I leaned into it with relief before I could stop myself.

'You okay, kitten?'

Smoke's deep voice was in my ear.

'Yes.'

I wanted to turn and lay my head on his chest, relax for a second. But I didn't.

'I'm fine.'

'You shouldn't have left her alone, man.' Tiger was scowling. 'Already had Bear trying to stake a claim.'

Smoke's arm tightened around me and I was acutely conscious of the feel of him against my back. Heat and strength and the dark, earthy scent of a forest.

'Leanne was supposed to be looking after her.'

'Red decided he had other plans for Leanne,' Tiger muttered.

'I'm fine,' I repeated, annoyed at being talked about like I wasn't there and irritated by the relief I felt at Smoke's return. 'Tiger looked out for me.'

Surprise flashed in Tiger's eyes, as if he wasn't expecting that. Okay, so I didn't much like the guy, but I appreciated him being there.

'Thanks, bro,' Smoke said. 'I owe you.'

'Yeah, well, you'd better hurry this show along.' Tiger jerked his head towards the fire. 'I got better things to do than guard women.'

Smoke released me, then took my hand. 'Come on. Time we introduced you to the club.'

My gut twisted. I didn't know what I expected, but clearly whatever it was that Smoke was going to do he was going to do it in front of everyone.

I tried to calm myself down as he led me over to the bonfire. People were turning to look at us and I felt self-conscious in my pencil skirt and stiletto heels. No other woman was wearing clothes like that and I felt overdressed. As we got closer to the fire, I began to feel hot and panicky.

'Hey, assholes!'

Keep's deep voice cut through the noise like a sharp knife through leather. He was standing on the other side of the fire and had obviously seen us coming.

'Shut the fuck up for a second! Smoke's got something to say.'

Surprisingly, everyone quieted, turning to look at where Smoke and I stood. His fingers, laced through mine, were warm, his grip firm, and I had a strange urge to pull away and start running. Get away.

'To all those fuckers who've taken bets on whether Cat and I are together!' Smoke shouted, his voice husky, gritty, with a thread of what sounded like triumph winding through it. 'It's time to either collect what you're owed or pay up.'

He lifted his other hand and I saw he was holding something in it. A black leather vest, like the cut he wore. On the back was a patch that read Property of Smoke, Knights of Ruin MC.

People cheered. Some of them shouted encouragement and punched their fists into the sky. Others called out cheerful yet filthy curses.

The firelight leapt across Smoke's face as he looked at me, the flickering shadows making him a stranger. His eyes were as dark as the night sky above our heads and he was smiling. But it wasn't the amused, friendly smiles I was used to. This was different. It was hungry...feral. A predator's smile.

He held up the vest between his hands and it was obvious what he wanted me to do.

People were shouting and cheering as I walked over to him, the ground feeling unsteady under my feet. My heartbeat was loud in my head, and despite the beer I'd had, my mouth was dry.

This was insane. It was pretend. Why the hell was I feeling so weird about it?

I turned when I got to Smoke, giving him my back while I held my arms out. He put the vest on me, the leather hot and heavy against my spine.

The brothers were shouting and cheering, raising their beer bottles or whatever else they were drinking into the sky.

I couldn't get a breath. The whole situation was freaking me out. This was what Mom had wanted—what she'd been desperate for Dad to give her—and now I had it. Now I was part of a club, even though it was the last thing in the world I wanted.

Smoke's hands settled on my shoulders and he turned me around. The stranger's smile had gone. Now he simply looked intense, the way he'd looked right before he'd kissed me outside Lucky's.

My pulse began to go crazy as he lifted a hand, sliding his fingers around the back of my head, drawing me close. I wanted to push at him, keep the distance between us, because I wasn't ready for this. But his mouth was on mine before I had a chance to do anything about it.

It was another hot, possessive kiss that had my toes curling in my stilettos. And he wasn't slow this time, or coaxing. His tongue pushed deep into my mouth, demanding and hungry, and all I could do was let him take whatever he wanted.

People were shouting all around us and then the kiss was over. Smoke was lifting his head. His grin was pure triumph, pure satisfaction—almost the same as the grin that had lit his face the day he'd first brought his Harley home.

The possessive hand at the back of my head dropped to my waist, curling around me as he brought me close to his side.

I swallowed and muttered, 'Now what?'

People were starting to approach us, guys slapping Smoke on the back and congratulating him, calling him a sneaky motherfucker and then grinning at me.

'Now we enjoy the party,' he said, his arm like an iron bar around me.

'Can't I just go home?'

'No.' There was no arguing with that tone. 'You want to make this look real? We have to make it look real.' He glanced down at me, his black eyes glittering in the firelight. 'Unless you want to go to my bedroom here?'

My stomach lurched at the same time as an electric thrill shot through me. He was joking, of course. He had to be, didn't he?

I looked away, back at the crowds. 'Uh…no, I'm fine.'

The music thumped and the party started to get more raucous, as if Smoke's announcement had been some kind of signal to finally go wild.

Tiger had joined a group by the fire, all gathered around a short, curvy brunette in a tiny skirt and tank top who was grinding away to the music. As I watched, the brunette turned to Tiger and put her arms around his neck, her hips still grinding, giving him what was basically a vertical lap dance.

She looked familiar to me for some reason.

Tiger bent his head, whispering something in her ear, and she tipped her head back, laughing. Then she dropped to her knees in front of him and reached for his zipper.

Okay, *now* I recognised her. It was the woman I'd seen giving Smoke a blow job in the hallway.

Beside me Smoke was easy, relaxed, and when I flicked a glance at him I saw he was watching the show the woman and Tiger were putting on. I found myself studying him for signs that he minded what was happening in front of us, but there was no jealousy in his face whatsoever.

'It was just a blow job, Cat,' he said, without looking at me, like he knew exactly what I was thinking. 'It didn't mean anything.'

'I wasn't… I mean, I didn't…' I couldn't finish.

He glanced down at me. 'Are you jealous?'

I could feel my cheeks heat. 'No, don't be stupid.'

I turned back to the show by the fire. I didn't want to watch what was going on in front of us—I really didn't. Yet something in me wouldn't let me look away as the woman began to give Tiger a blow job right in front of everyone.

Smoke's hand moved, sliding up to cup my breast.

I went still, the breath catching in my throat.

My blouse was very thin, and his hand felt like one of the coals from the fire, burning right through the material. Then his thumb brushed over my nipple. Electricity shot through me and I nearly gasped aloud. He began to circle my painfully hard nipple through my blouse slowly, lightly, and I shuddered before I could stop myself.

'What are you doing?' I asked thickly.

He didn't turn his head, his attention still on the show that was being performed in front of us. 'Making it look real.'

My mouth was dry and I couldn't hear anything else through the sound of my heartbeat. There was a deep, aching pulse between my thighs, an intense pressure.

Tiger drained his beer and tossed the bottle away, so he could put both hands in the woman's hair, moving his hips faster.

Don't, I wanted to say to Smoke. *Please don't.*

I didn't know why I didn't. Because this was wrong—this shouldn't be happening. He shouldn't be touching me and I shouldn't be getting worked up about it.

But he was. His thumb was moving in slow, aching circles around my nipple, making me tremble, making it hard to breathe.

This wasn't making it look real. No one could see his hand, so what the hell was he doing?

A blind, unreasoning panic squeezed my chest tight, and before I knew what I was doing, I'd jerked away from him, turning and shouldering my way through the crowd, heading towards the clubhouse. Someone called my name but I ignored them.

I had no idea where I was going or why. I only knew I had to get away from what was happening in front of me, away from the woman and Tiger, and most of all away from Smoke. From the intense, hungry feeling that had wrapped its hands around my throat and refused to let go.

There were crowds inside the corridors of the clubhouse, but I didn't meet anyone's eyes, walking blindly, not looking where I was going. I didn't even have a direction. I only wanted to get away, find somewhere I could be alone and figure out what was happening to me.

I didn't realise I'd gone through the main set of clubrooms and into the back of the clubhouse, where all the bedrooms and other offices were, until the dim lighting and the lack of people brought me to a stop. There were lots of doors in the hallway and the sound of people talking behind them—other sounds, too, of pleasure.

The place was familiar. And I knew why.

'There's a reason you came here,' a voice said from behind me, deep and dark and full of rough heat. 'Isn't there, Cat?'

Smoke. He'd followed me.

I sucked in a ragged breath, my legs trembling. No, I had no idea why I'd come here—to the place where I'd found him getting a blow job from that woman. I should have gone out to the front, called a taxi and gone home.

But I hadn't.

His footsteps sounded behind me and I tensed, but he walked past me, going down the hall a little way. Then he stopped and turned, leaning back against the wall, looking straight at me. His hands were in his pockets. There was nothing threatening in his stance. Yet I felt like he'd pinned me where I stood all the same.

He'd brought the heat of the bonfire inside with him and the flames were flickering in his eyes.

'Come here,' he ordered softly.

I couldn't tell myself I didn't know what was happening between us any more. I couldn't tell myself this was only pretend. I couldn't tell myself I didn't want it more than I wanted my next breath either.

I'd run from him, but I hadn't run in the direction I should have. I'd run here.

He was right—there was a reason for that.

My feet were moving before I even knew what I was doing. I was walking towards him as if he had control of me, as if he was reeling me in like a fish on the end of a line. I stopped in front of him, my breath coming hard and fast in time with my hammering pulse.

He looked calm and relaxed, leaning back against the wall. Except for his eyes. They burned so bright.

'On your knees.'

Again the order was soft, yet there was no denying the authority of it. I found myself doing exactly what he said, dropping to my knees in front of him.

It seemed like years since the night I'd come here and found him getting blown by that woman. When my mind, the traitor, had wondered what it would be like to be that woman.

Now I was going to find out.

The thought made me dizzy.

He lowered one hand and slid his fingers along my jaw. I shivered.

'You know what to do, kitten.'

I swallowed and reached to undo the top button of his jeans. My hands were shaking, but somehow I managed it. He put his own hand over mine, directing my fingers, helping me draw the zipper down.

Oh, Jesus. I was going to do this right here, in the hallway, where anyone could find us. Just like I'd found him a week ago. Maybe I was drunk... Maybe I was stoned. Maybe I was insane.

Maybe this is just what you've always wanted...

His fly was undone now, and I could see his cock pressing against the black cotton of his boxers. He was hard.

I felt weirdly disconnected from myself as he guided my hand inside his jeans, using his free hand to pull down the cotton. Then my fingers were sliding over his cock, lifting him out, and he was long and thick and hard. God, *so* hard.

Someone was panting. It was me.

I took him in my fist. His skin was hot and smooth and it felt like velvet. I couldn't remember the last time I'd wanted to taste something so badly in all my life. He guided my fingers up the length of him, and half of me was already a little insane with desire. The other half was horrified at what I was doing. His hand tightened around mine, making me squeeze him, but it was my thumb that rubbed over the slick head. The feel of him was so good.

Dimly something screamed at me that this was *Smoke*, my best friend, and that sucking your best friend's dick was pretty much guaranteed to ruin a perfectly good friendship. But I couldn't seem to think about why that was.

'Look at me.' His voice had deepened, become thick and hoarse.

I obeyed, letting the darkness and the flames in his eyes wash over me, consume me.

'Suck me, Cat,' he ordered.

So I leaned in, inhaling the musky, woody scent that was all Smoke, and I opened my mouth, touched my tongue to the head of his cock, licking at him delicately. The salty flavour of him burst on my tongue and I heard the sudden harsh intake of his breath.

'No. Put my cock in your mouth.' There was a desperate edge to his words now. 'Fucking *do* it, kitten.

I didn't hesitate, responding to him on the most basic level, taking him in as deep as I could, the size of him stretching my mouth wide, letting him nudge the back of my throat.

He groaned. The sound was a caress, like he'd run his hand right the way down my naked body. It was the most unbelievably erotic thing I'd ever heard and I wanted more of it.

I gripped his cock harder, squeezing as I sucked him, using the pressure, using my tongue, taking him even deeper.

'Cat...'

The sound of my name was threaded through with hunger. He took his hands out of his pockets and pushed his fingers into my hair, holding on so tight that prickles of pain erupted all over my scalp. Hairpins fell onto the floor as the weight of my hair fell out of its loose bun and slowly down my back. I didn't care.

He was holding me the way he'd been holding that woman, directing me the way he'd directed her. And the look in his eyes was the same—intense and so hungry I nearly caught fire.

'You know…who I was…thinking about…when you saw me with her?'

He knew what I was thinking about. Of course he did.

'You, kitten. I was thinking about…you…'

Shock coursed through me.

Me. He'd been thinking about *me*.

That meant something—something I wasn't prepared to face just yet. So I ignored it. I concentrated instead on what I was doing: sucking him deep, pumping him with my fist, turning him inside out the way he'd been doing to me for the past week. Watching him as he groaned again, his head tipping back, exposing the strong muscles of his throat.

'Oh, fuck… Cat…'

The harsh edge in his voice was the sexiest thing I'd ever heard in my life. I could feel his hands in my hair trembling.

I was doing this to him. This strong, immovable man. *I* was making him shake. *I* was making him desperate.

I couldn't take my eyes off him. Lines of agonised pleasure were carved into his familiar, beautiful face, and the sounds that were coming from him—harsh and deep, ragged gasps of breath—made the ache between my thighs even worse.

I didn't want this to end. Because in that moment I felt more powerful than I ever had in my entire life.

I thought being on your knees meant you were weak, that you were beaten, with your eyes swelling shut and the sick, bitter taste of defeat in your mouth.

Not here. Not now. Not with Smoke.

No, Smoke made me feel like there was more to my power than I'd ever dreamed possible. But that was what he always did. He made me feel powerful even when I'd thought I wasn't.

His hands were tightening on my head and he began to direct my movements, flexing his hips, thrusting faster, harder, and I let him do it—let him take control of me.

'Fucking look at me, Cat,' he whispered roughly as I let my lashes fall shut. 'I want your eyes up here.'

So I looked at him, meeting the ferocious blackness in his gaze, holding it.

This is going to change everything. Nothing will be the same again.

I ignored that unwelcome thought and lost myself in my best friend's dark eyes, watching as the climax hit him, as his head was thrown back as he called my name, raw and harsh, his fingers in my hair a sweet agony. As he came down the back of my throat and I swallowed everything he gave me.

There was silence afterwards, broken only by the ragged sounds of his breathing and the thunder of my own heartbeat. I didn't want to think about anything—not what was going to happen later, or what it meant for our friendship. What it would change and what it would break.

Because something always got broken when lines were crossed. Always.

His hold in my hair eased as he withdrew from my mouth, and I rested my cheek against the hot skin of his taut stomach and closed my eyes, feeling the flex and release of hard muscle in time with his breathing.

I was aching, the pulse between my thighs heavy and insistent, but I didn't want to move. I wanted to stay here, in this peaceful moment, where it was just him and me and silence. Where we didn't have to talk or angst about the choices we'd made… Where the only thing that mattered was the feel of his fingers in my hair, gently massaging my scalp.

But of course it didn't last.

He was still semihard and getting harder with every second. Then the gentle hands in my hair weren't so gentle any more as he pulled me to my feet.

I looked up at him, abruptly panicking about what this would mean for our friendship, opening my mouth to tell him that we had to put this behind us, that we had to pretend it hadn't happened. Yet before I could say anything he bent his head and his lips were on mine, the kiss forcing my head back, forcing my mouth to open for him.

The demand in his kiss made me tremble—because there was no resisting him, no holding out or holding back. He took everything. His tongue was pushing inside, sliding along mine, exploring me, and he must have tasted himself because he growled all of a sudden, his fingers tightening around my upper arms.

Then we were moving as he walked me backwards down a short, dark, dead-end corridor. There was one door to the left, a blank wall to the right, and he pushed me into the corner where the blank wall met the end of the corridor. His hands were pressed to the wall on either side of my head, his big, lean body caging me there while he kissed me, deep and wet, with total and absolute demand.

The scent of him—so familiar and yet now so heavy with the musk of male arousal—was the most erotic thing in the entire goddamn universe. And the heat of him, so agonisingly close to me, was making me crazy.

Yet I was shaking. Because some part of me knew what was going to happen next and I was terrified. It would be a step we couldn't come back from. I knew that deep in my soul.

Like that blow job hasn't changed things already?

Of course it had. But this…this was different. It was one thing to turn him inside out, make him come. It was quite another to give him the same power over me.

His hands dropped from the wall to grip the fabric of my skirt, pulling it up higher and higher. My breathing was fast and I felt dizzy, as if I didn't have enough air. I reached for his hands to push them away, but he was too strong, too insistent. My skirt was around my waist before I could stop him, and then he lifted me up against the wall, pinning me there with his body.

His strength was effortless, and the hard flex of his muscles as he held me tapped into a very feminine part of me, making me shiver with delight. It was insane that I should like this—his control, his dominance— but I couldn't help it. I *did* like it.

He shifted, pushing his lean hips insistently between my thighs, and because his jeans were open I could feel his cock, hard and hot, pressing against the soaking-wet fabric of my panties. The sensation was a lightning burst in my head…a shock of sensation overloading every nerve ending I had.

My mouth opened beneath his as I gasped, my

hips rocking, pushing against him, and he muttered a vicious-sounding curse against my lips.

His fingers curled into the waistband of my panties, jerking hard, tearing through the lace. Then they were gone and his fingers were between my thighs, sliding through the slick folds of my pussy, finding my clit and circling in hard, tight circles.

I stiffened, unable to stop a desperate, choked sound escaping my throat. His touch was electric, the pleasure white-hot—unlike anything I'd ever felt before.

The sheer intensity of it hooked into the panic that was simmering below the surface, frightening me. My hands were on his chest, wanting to push him away, to stop this, but he eased one finger into me, then another, spread them apart, stretching me.

'Smoke… Oh, God…' I couldn't stop the words pouring out of my mouth. 'Jesus… Please… Smoke, I can't… I don't…'

His mouth was on mine again, kissing me hungrily, and his fingers were sliding deeper into my pussy. I shuddered, the hot wall of muscle beneath my palms searing me like the element on a stove. I was going to catch fire. I was going to burn alive right here in his arms.

His mouth moved to my jaw, down my throat, his teeth closed around the cords of my neck. 'You're so fucking wet.'

His voice was dark as midnight, husky and rough.

'So fucking tight. I knew you would be. I just knew it.'

He drew his hand back, sliding his fingers out, then

back in, again and again, fucking me slowly, making me pant and gasp and writhe in his arms.

'You want my cock, kitten? Tell me you want it.' His voice got impossibly deeper. '*Beg* me for it.'

I couldn't breathe. It was like everything in me was drawn so tight the slightest breath would shatter me into a thousand pieces. Yet I wanted to move. I wanted to end this desperate ache, this need that was eating me alive.

I knew he was going to do it—fuck me right here in this hallway, where anyone could see us. And I didn't care. I just wanted this hunger to be gone.

'I w-want your cock,' I stuttered hoarsely. 'I want it right now.'

'Where do you want it?'

His fingers curled inside me, his thumb moving in a slow, slick circle over my clit.

I groaned. 'I want it in my pussy. Please, Smoke. *Please…*'

He shifted again, his fingers sliding out of me, making me tremble at the loss. While he held me against the wall he reached behind him to his wallet, deftly extracting a condom packet one-handed, before letting the wallet fall carelessly to the floor. He ripped the packet open with his teeth, discarding the wrapper and rolling the latex down. Then he gripped my thighs hard and positioned himself.

I could feel the head of his cock press against the entrance of my pussy, and I shook so hard it felt like I was going to come apart right there and then.

'Cat.'

My name was a harsh order.

'Fucking *look* at me.'

I did, but the expression on his face was so intense I could hardly stand it. Hunger and desperation and also anger. An anger I didn't understand.

His hips flexed and he was pushing into me, my slick flesh was parting before him, stretching around him, and the feel of him tipped me off the ledge I was only barely clinging to. The orgasm crashed over me, a massive shudder shaking my body as I cried out, lights bursting behind my eyes.

He didn't even pause, sliding deep inside me, holding me fast with my legs wrapped around his lean waist, the unbelievable heat of his body between my thighs.

I groaned at the sensation of him inside me, because he was big and it had been a long time since I'd had sex. Not to mention the fact that the aftershocks of my orgasm were like tiny bolts of electricity arcing from nerve ending to nerve ending, sensitising every part of me.

Then he was drawing his hips back, driving into me deep and fast and wild. Each thrust slammed me hard into the corner. I arched in his arms, shocked as that tight, impossible ache began to build again, the sharp need coiling tighter with each slide of his cock inside me. I gripped his T-shirt, my fingers fisting in the cotton, panting and then groaning again as he tilted my hips and changed the angle of his thrusts, so the base of his cock was grinding against my clit.

My head fell back against the wall, pleasure rising higher and higher, and the sounds of his ragged breathing and his sharp, hard grunts as he fucked me filled the space between us.

I'd never imagined it would be like this. Not with him. I'd never imaged this with him at all. And the worst part was knowing that it wasn't something we could pretend hadn't happened. We couldn't ignore it.

It was fierce, incendiary. It was going to change everything.

I said his name a thousand times, over and over, my voice so hoarse it didn't sound like mine. Then, when I didn't think I could bear it any more, he jerked my hand away from its death grip on his T-shirt and forced it down between my legs.

I tried to resist, for what reason I didn't know, but he was too strong, forcing my fingers to where we were joined, to feel my own wet pussy stretched around the thick, hard length of his cock. To feel the slick glide of him as he pulled out, the give of my flesh as he pushed back in.

'Feel me, kitten. This is *me*, inside *you*.' He held my fingers there, flexing his hips with each word to prove his point. 'This is me *fucking* you.'

I groaned, trembling so hard I thought I would break, the dirty words as much of a turn-on as the feel of his cock sliding into me.

My best friend. Fucking me in the hallway, where anyone could see us.

He moved his hand, urging my fingers higher, to my clit.

'Touch yourself,' he ordered harshly. 'I want you coming all over my cock in five seconds.'

I obeyed without thought, my fingers stroking my

clit over and over as he fucked me hard against the wall until I was desperate and shaking and raw. And it didn't even take five seconds. In three I screamed his name into the silence of the hallway, my eyes shut tight as the sensation swept over me, annihilating me completely.

Dimly I felt him move harder and faster, his rhythm wild and out of control, and then he bent his head, turning his face into my neck. And he bit me hard as orgasm took him, too.

CHAPTER TWELVE

Smoke

I DIDN'T WANT to move. I wanted to stay there, my head turned in to her neck, inhaling the musky scent of aroused Cat and sex, with my dick buried so deep inside her I felt like I was part of her. She was panting, her body shaking, her legs wrapped tight around my waist, and I simply held her there, losing myself in the smell and feel of her.

I'd fantasised about her for years, and yet all those fantasies hadn't even come close to the reality. To the pressure of her mouth as she'd sucked me. To the tight, wet heat of her pussy around my cock. To the salty taste of her skin as I'd bitten her neck. So fucking good. So fucking intense.

I couldn't remember the last time I'd come so hard, and even now, two orgasms later, I was already getting hard for her again. But I didn't want to do anything more here in the clubhouse. I wanted to get her back to a bed, where I could take my time, undress her, taste every inch of her delicious body before sinking into her again. Fucking her slow, fucking her fast. Driving us both insane.

This was going to happen again, and soon, and I wasn't going to take no for answer. Not now that I'd felt how wet she'd been or heard her scream my name in my ear as she'd come.

Her hands pushed at my chest and, reluctantly, I slid out of her, letting her down onto the floor. She was shaky on her feet and had to keep her hands braced on my chest, which was fucking satisfying.

It was *all* so fucking satisfying.

For so many years she hadn't even noticed the fact that I was a man, and yet tonight, when she'd come to a stop in the hallway and turned to face me, I'd known that she'd noticed. That she'd run from what was happening around the bonfire was *because* she'd noticed. Which had made my decision real simple.

She'd gone down on her knees when I'd asked her to. Begged for my cock when I'd ordered her to. And then she'd come, screaming, exactly when I'd told her to.

She'd wanted it, whether she liked it or not. She'd wanted it. She'd wanted *me*.

Her head was bent, her dark hair hiding her face, but I didn't make her look at me—not yet. Instead I dealt with the condom in a nearby wastebasket and tucked myself back into my jeans. Then I pulled down her skirt, smoothing it over her thighs, covering her up.

She tried batting away my hands, but I ignored that bullshit. She was mine now, and if I wanted to take care of her I was going to take care of her—no goddamn arguments.

'Smoke…'

My name sounded all husky and raw.

'Can we just—'

'No,' I interrupted. 'Don't say another fucking word, Cat.'

Sliding a finger beneath her chin, I tipped her head up so she had to look at me. Her cheeks were deeply flushed, her green eyes dark, tendrils of black hair sticking to her forehead and neck. She looked shell-shocked, and I was asshole enough to get a kick out of it.

'I'm taking you back home. Now.'

Her mouth opened, but I put a finger on her soft lips, silencing her.

'What did I say about another fucking word?'

A muscle flexed in her jaw but she remained silent. Good girl.

I made sure our clothing was all good, then I took her hand and held it tight, turning and heading back down the corridor towards the club's exit.

Christ, I couldn't stop thinking about it. About her mouth and the feel of her body against mine. The little movements she'd made and her soft, desperate sounds of pleasure. I glanced down at her as we walked, watching the ebb and flow of colour in her cheeks, and I knew she was thinking the same thing.

But she didn't look back at me, which told me everything I needed to know about her feelings: she regretted it and it was obvious.

My chest tightened but I ignored it. If she thought we were going back to nothing but friendship, she was shit out of luck. She was *mine*. She was *my* property and I was going to have her every way I could.

Nothing about this was going to be pretend—not any more.

A couple of people asked where we were going, but I ignored them, too.

Outside, I put her on my bike and we left the club, riding through the dark city streets. Her arms around my waist were a special kind of torture, as was the feel of her heat against my back, and by the time we rolled up outside her apartment I was hard enough to hammer nails.

But I'd decided I was going to give her space tonight. Just one night to let what had happened between us sink in. Because tomorrow I had plans. And they sure as shit didn't include keeping my distance.

The babysitter—a friend of Red's old lady—was surprised to see us and no wonder. We were probably way earlier than she was expecting. But I paid her for the whole night, and apparently Annie had been good, so everyone was happy.

Cat disappeared into Annie's room as I paid the babysitter and didn't come out after the woman had left. Probably didn't want to face me after what had happened in the hallway and, hell, I couldn't blame her. She hadn't been expecting it. Unluckily for her, I didn't have any problem with dealing with the fallout.

Closing the door after the babysitter, I went down the narrow hallway to Annie's bedroom and stood in the doorway. Sure enough, Cat was sitting on Annie's bed, stroking her hair. The nightlight threw shadows everywhere, its shade with cut-outs scattering stars onto the ceiling, and the only sound was Annie's gentle, deep breathing.

It was a peaceful picture. A beautiful one. It made the tightness in my chest get even tighter—because this was mine. This was my family. One I never thought I'd ever have, never thought I'd even want.

After the shit had gone down with my father—after he'd made my mother's life and mine a living hell—I'd decided I didn't want a wife. Didn't want kids. Didn't want a family. But it had been Cat who'd showed me that a family didn't have to be about fists and shouting. That it could be about respect, about love.

Until you took him out.

Yeah, there was that. My soul wasn't clean and I knew it. Yet somehow, clean soul or not, I had a family right here. A woman I would have moved heaven and earth for and a kid who wasn't mine and yet I'd lay down my life for her.

I wasn't going to give this up for anything. And if anyone tried to take Annie and Cat away from me, they'd have to prise them from my cold, dead hands.

Maybe she sensed me standing there, because Cat turned her head and her eyes met mine. I said nothing, just leaned against the doorframe, my hands in my pockets. Letting her know that I wasn't going anywhere in a hurry and that she couldn't escape me.

She flushed and turned away, leaning over to give Annie a kiss before rising to her feet. Giving her daughter one last look, she came towards me, and I could tell she was gathering her courage because her chin came up and her green eyes didn't flicker away from mine.

She said nothing as she went past me and didn't stop, heading out into the hall, so I followed on behind, watching the sway of her butt in that tight-fitting pencil skirt. Fuck, what had I been thinking about keeping my distance tonight? I wanted to bend her over the nearest hard surface, shove that goddamn skirt out of my way and bury myself so deep in her pussy she'd feel me for days.

But I knew Cat. I knew she was going to need at least a night to get her head around this. A night for her body to understand what it needed.

Me.

In the lounge she turned to face me, folding her arms, all defensive, but I didn't stop. There weren't going to be any damn lectures about how we needed to forget all about this, put it behind us, make like it didn't happen. No—fuck that. She was my property now, and that meant I got to call the shots.

'Smoke—' she began.

But I walked straight up to her, grabbing her hips and pulling her in nice and tight, feeling the heat of her perfect little pussy against my aching dick.

'No,' I said. 'Don't speak. Don't say a fucking word.'

Her jaw tensed and her mouth settled into a hard line. But she didn't talk.

'Here's what's going to happen,' I went on, pressing my fingers against her hips, feeling her warmth and softness, letting myself enjoy it. 'I'll leave you to sleep alone tonight and I'll take the couch. But tomorrow you're taking the day off, and after Annie's gone to school, you and me are going to have a little talk.'

She didn't try to pull away, but neither did she soften against me. Her whole body was tense. She was holding herself rigid.

'And I guess when you say "little talk" you mean…?'

'Fucking, Cat.' No point in mincing words or pretending otherwise. 'You and I will be fucking.'

Her cheeks flamed. 'Well, I guess that's clear.' Her voice was heavy with sarcasm. 'Nothing like reducing it to the level of a porno.'

'I don't recall you having a problem with it when I had you screaming in my ear in the damn hallway.'

She flushed even deeper, biting her lip and looking away.

I knew what was going on. She was doing what she always did when she was scared, which was to get snarky and defensive. Sadly, I wasn't going to be putting up with that bullshit.

'I'm not going to let you push me away.' I moved my thumbs back and forth over her hips, stroking her, keeping up that physical contact. 'Not any more. This is how it's going to be—starting tomorrow. You and me. Together.'

A lock of silky black hair fell over her face, hiding her expression as she looked down at her feet. 'I thought… I thought all this was supposed to be pretend.'

'It was *supposed* to be.' I didn't want to hide the truth from her—not now that we'd crossed the line. 'Then I changed my mind.'

'Why?' She still wouldn't look at me. 'Since when did things change?'

I looked down at the light glossing her black hair, at her lashes dark against her cheeks like splashes of black ink. Christ, I was turning into a fucking poet.

'They never changed. Not for me. I've always wanted you, kitten. *Always*.'

Her head came up sharply, her eyes wide, the look in them shocked as hell. 'What? But...' She blinked, the shock giving way to confusion. 'Really? You never said anything... I mean, I never got the impression that...' She stopped. 'Seriously, Smoke?'

But I was done for the night, and I suspected so was she. We could have all this out in the morning, when the shock had worn off.

'Tomorrow,' I said shortly. 'We'll talk about this tomorrow.'

A spark of green temper flared in her gaze. 'In between all the fucking, you mean?'

She was *such* brat... Jesus Christ.

I lifted my hand, took her little chin in between my thumb and forefinger, holding her still. 'Maybe.' I kept my voice quiet. 'But only if you're a very good girl and do exactly as you're told.'

She snorted, like she was still my friend and we were kidding around with each other. But it was time she stopped thinking that shit, so I bent my head and kissed her hard, pushing my tongue into her hot mouth, silencing her.

A tremble shook her and she made a soft, desperate noise. Then she tipped her head back further, letting me kiss her deeper, her tongue meeting mine and sliding along it. It was a taste and a tease and a taunt all in one. Her hands were pressed against my chest, there was the scent of musk and Cat filling my senses, and suddenly I didn't want to wait till morning. I wanted her again—right the fuck *now*.

But she'd been leading me around by my dick for years and I was sick of it. It didn't matter that she hadn't known I wanted her. I didn't give a fuck how unfair or otherwise that was. *I* was the one in charge from now on and that was how it would stay.

I lifted my head, ignoring her soft moan of protest, and with my stupid fucking cock aching like it hadn't been inside her only an hour ago, I stepped back and away from her. 'Time for bed, kitten.'

An expression I couldn't read flashed over her face, then it was gone. She lifted a shoulder like she didn't give a shit—which made her a damn liar, considering her cheeks were flushed and her mouth looked full and swollen.

'I'll get you a pillow and a blanket,' she muttered, and turned away, heading out of the lounge.

A minute or two later she was back, a pillow in one hand, a blanket in the other, and going over to the couch, making a production of putting the pillow down and laying the blanket out flat.

Once she'd finished she made an awkward gesture towards the couch. 'There. It's done.'

A silence fell and I let it hang, because I was being a prick and enjoying the way the tension between us made her blush even more. Another sign that our friendship really was dead and gone.

Maybe I should have felt regret about that, but I didn't. Our friendship had been built on lies anyway—or at least for me it had been. The lie that I didn't want to make her mine in every way that counted.

Yeah, I was risking everything on this. But, then again, how much of a risk could it truly be? I wasn't going to let her go. Not now. Not ever.

Pushing my hands into my pockets, I met her gaze. 'Goodnight, Cat.'

She held it. 'Goodnight, Dane.'

Then she turned around and walked out.

CHAPTER THIRTEEN

Cat

I DIDN'T SLEEP all night. I was exhausted, yet my body was buzzing and my mind wouldn't stop replaying what had happened with Smoke over and over.

I shut my eyes, willing the images away, but they wouldn't go.

My body ached, my pussy was throbbing, my nipples were in hard, tight points. Pressing against the tank top I'd pulled on to sleep in.

'Fucking, Cat. You and I will be fucking.'

I turned my head into the pillow, trying and failing to find a cool spot, my skin feeling like it was on fire.

Crazy. I'd gone all these years without being attracted to Smoke, yet now I couldn't sleep because I couldn't stop thinking about tomorrow, about what we were going to do together.

It terrified me.

Shit, if the sex had been bad, we might have been able to put it behind us, carried on as normal. But the sex hadn't been bad. It had been…incredible. And there was no way we could put that behind us—no way in hell.

It was going to change things and they would never be the same again.

I squeezed my eyes shut tighter. No, I wasn't going to fucking cry about it. *I wasn't.*

'I've always wanted you, kitten.'

Oh, God, that look in his dark gaze. The one that went straight through me, that pinned me to the ground with a truth so sharp and so obvious I was amazed I hadn't seen it before.

Or maybe I simply hadn't wanted to look.

He'd wanted me all that time and it made me so shit-scared I could hardly breathe. He had to stay a friend—I *needed* him to stay a friend. Because anything more—like love—that was bullshit. It was *all* bullshit. Love was a lie, and in the end it always, *always* let you down.

Love had deserted my mom in the end, and in the end it had made her desert me.

And love always hurt—like Justin hurt me.

Relationships sucked and I didn't want one. But friendship—that was strong. That was true.

Friends never let you down—like Smoke had never let me down—and that was what I wanted. What I needed.

Except Smoke clearly had other ideas.

I was fucked. Literally.

I flung an arm across my hot face, trying to settle, but the memory of how I'd knelt before him and taken his dick into my mouth grabbed me, and this time I let myself fall into it, feeling the power of it…

Somewhere in the middle I must have fallen asleep, because the next thing I knew I felt something hot lying across my face. In fact I felt hot all over.

I opened my eyes to find the sun streaming through a crack in the curtains and fully over my bed, in a way it never did when I woke at 6:00 a.m.

I groaned and turned to look at the clock.

Holy shit—it was *nine*. What about Annie? What about school? I'd never slept in like this before. Never.

Cursing, I hauled myself out of bed and flung open the door, stumbling down the hallway to Annie's bedroom only to find it empty. Oh, God, where was she?

I went back along the hall and into the lounge, trying not to feel frantic about the heavy silence that lay over the apartment. The living area was empty, too; the blanket Smoke had slept in was folded neatly on the end of the couch.

On the coffee table was a piece of paper with some writing on it.

I snatched it up.

Took Annie to school and you've called in sick.
Back soon. Be ready.

Jesus, the bastard really was handling all this, wasn't he?

A shiver snaked down my spine and it wasn't fear. In fact it felt horribly like anticipation.

Irritated, I scrunched the paper up into a ball. Because there was no way. It wasn't happening. I didn't want some guy swanning in and taking over my life the way Justin had. Telling me what to do and expecting me to be grateful. Even if he was my best friend.

What was going to happen was me sitting down with Smoke and telling him the truth. That I couldn't be more than friends with him. He knew my background...knew why my friendship with him was so important. He'd understand, surely? He *had* to.

Sighing, I dropped the balled-up paper and headed to the bathroom for a quick cold shower. Then I wandered back into the bedroom, wrapped in a towel, pulling open drawers and trying to decide what to wear.

It took me a moment to realise what I was doing.

I *never* stood in front of my drawers debating over clothes. I simply pulled on what was appropriate for work or what was comfortable for home. That was the extent of it.

Yet here I was, looking at the contents of my drawers with my head full of Smoke. Wondering what to wear that he'd like. Wondering what would make me look sexy.

Feeling like an idiot, I dropped the towel and reached for my usual jeans and T-shirt, pulling them on and resolutely not looking in the mirror.

Turning to the door to head out in search of coffee, I nearly had a heart attack when I found Smoke's black eyes staring back at me, the length of his hard, muscular body filling the doorframe.

I blushed the moment I met his gaze, a wave of heat rolling through me as every single one of last night's memories descended on me like a ton of bricks.

'F-fuck, you gave me a fright,' I stuttered. 'I didn't hear you come in.'

He lifted a shoulder. 'Yeah, sorry about that.'

Resisting the urge to tug at my hair or my T-shirt, I stuck my hands in my back pockets. 'Um...thanks for taking Annie to school. I guess I kind of slept in.'

He didn't move, staring at me with such intensity it was like an X-ray, memorising me right down to my bones.

'No worries. You seemed like you needed it.'

An awkward silence fell, which he made no move to break—the asshole.

'I...I need to talk to you,' I said, not knowing how to begin and irritated that he wasn't giving me any help.

He didn't look surprised by this. 'Sure.' He turned. 'Come out to the living room.'

Pausing to grab a hair tie and put my damp hair in a ponytail, I followed him down the hallway, coming out to find him sitting in the middle of the couch with his arms along the back of it and his legs stretched out in front of him.

He was in his usual T-shirt and jeans, both black, his cut on over the top, and I could feel my heart literally slow and come to a dead stop because of the way he was sitting: his long, lean body all stretched out, so fucking arrogant. So fucking *hot*.

His T-shirt was pulled tight over his chest, highlighting the width and shape of the perfect musculature beneath. Tight over his shoulders, too, with the cotton moulding to the broad, powerful shape of them. He was strong enough he'd been able to lift me against the wall the night before like I weighed nothing...

My throat constricted, my breathing shallow.

I couldn't stop staring at his body, at the lean hips

and muscular thighs. I remembered what he'd felt like against me, how hot his skin had been…

Asshole. It was like he'd turned something on inside me and now I couldn't turn it off.

He stared back, black eyes burning with the same dark flame I'd seen in them in that hallway as I'd knelt at his feet.

'Strip,' he said flatly.

I blinked. 'W-what did you say?'

'Take off your clothes. *Now.*'

A helpless shiver broke over me. 'I thought we were going to talk.'

'We are. You can talk and I'll listen. But I want you naked.'

'But…but I—'

'That's how it's going to be from now on, kitten. We compromise. I get what I want and so do you.' His sensual mouth hardened. 'Now, take your fucking clothes off, or I'll take them off for you.'

Anger flared in my gut—reflexive, bonfire bright. Where the *hell* did he get off, ordering me around in my own home?

Yet there was another part of me—a part I'd only discovered the night before—that liked the freedom of doing nothing but obeying him. That was tired of having do everything all the time. Tired of having to shoulder the responsibility of bringing up a child on my own. That wanted someone else to make the decisions and take charge. Just for a little while.

It felt weak to give in to it. Like I was making myself vulnerable. And I knew what happened when I made myself vulnerable. Fists. Pain. My pride in tatters on the floor. I couldn't do it. Once had been enough last night.

But don't forget this is Smoke. He would never hurt you. And didn't you feel powerful last night?

I swallowed. It was still difficult for me to understand how that worked. How I could be on my knees and yet feel strong? But there was no doubting that was how I'd felt the night before. I could do it again, couldn't I?

Of course you can. You want to. Don't deny it.

Yeah, I did want to. A deep part of me wanted more of that—his hands and his mouth and his cock—no matter how wrong it was. No matter how scared it made me feel. The switch was firmly turned to On, and it looked like nothing was going to flip it back.

'Don't be a chickenshit, Cat.'

His low voice was a rumble I felt in my chest, taunting me the way he always used to when I baulked at doing something I was scared of.

He would never force me. He would never hurt me. He was a totally different man from Justin. A totally different man from my father.

Yet I was still scared.

I didn't want anything to change between us.

But then, of course it already had.

'What if I don't want this?' I asked. 'What if I want to talk without anything else?'

'Then I'm walking out of here,' he said without hesitation.

'Does that mean you'd walk out on Annie, too?'

Something even darker flickered in his eyes. 'Don't

you fucking *dare* use Annie like that. You know I'd rather die than let anything happen to that kid.'

Shame crept over my skin, a creeping, prickling heat, and before I could stop myself the words just came out of me. 'I'm scared, Smoke.'

He didn't move, and the look on his face didn't soften. But the darkness in his eyes lessened slightly. 'I know you are. But I won't hurt you, kitten. You know I'd rather die than do that.'

I don't know what it was—maybe it was merely the reassuring sound of his voice, the normality of it. The voice of my friend. But the fear inside me ebbed…the tension eased.

And before I was even conscious of having made a decision my hands reached for the hem of my T-shirt and I was pulling it up and over my head and unclipping my bra and letting it fall. It had been a long time since I'd undressed in front of a guy, so I kept my attention on my hands as I undid the button on my jeans and slid down the zipper. Then I pushed down the denim, taking my panties with it.

It felt weird, undressing for my best friend. And when I stepped out of my jeans I found I still didn't want to look at him. My heartbeat was so fast, so loud, my skin felt raw and exposed. I wanted to cover myself, but kept my hands at my sides.

I wasn't a fucking coward. I wasn't.

Raising my head, I forced myself to look at him.

The expression on his face shook me all the way down to my soul.

It was so intense. So hungry. As if he'd never seen a naked woman in all his life.

A feeling swept through me—the same one I'd felt the night before. A feeling of power, of strength.

He wanted me. He was desperate for me.

I straightened, threw my shoulders back, and his gaze dropped to my breasts, then down further. A stain of red appeared on his high cheekbones.

'Come here,' he ordered, his voice thickened and rough.

I hated being told what to do, and yet I found myself going to him all the same. Like there was a collar around my neck and he held the leash, drawing me closer and closer.

I watched his face as I got nearer, watched him watch me, my heartbeat racing. My nipples had hardened and I could feel slickness between my legs, the heavy ache of desire making my breathing short and fast.

There was a part of me that didn't want him to see me so obviously turned on by him, but after last night that ship had sailed. I couldn't hide it. And he certainly didn't bother, making no effort to conceal the long, thick outline of his cock pressing against his zipper.

Breathless, I stopped in front of his outstretched legs, looking down at him. 'So?' I said awkwardly. 'Here I am.'

He didn't move and only patted his lap. 'Facing me, kitten.'

He definitely wasn't going to make this easy for me, was he? Facing him meant kneeling astride him and looking into his eyes…meant being vulnerable to him. And he knew it.

That challenge glittered in his black gaze—the one

I couldn't refuse. So I moved towards him, climbing into his lap and spreading my thighs so I could straddle him. He made no move to help me, his attention dropping to my swaying breasts as I gingerly settled myself astride him.

My cheeks flamed. I wasn't used to this—to being naked in front of him while he was fully dressed, to him watching me so intently. Then I noticed that the lines of his gorgeous face were pulled taut and his mouth set hard. His body beneath mine was rock hard, as if every muscle was clenched tight.

He was holding himself back.

The realisation made my embarrassment fade, leaving me aware of how rough the denim of his jeans felt against the insides of my thighs, of how hot he was, like lying right next to a roaring fire.

He didn't take his eyes off me, staring unspeaking as he lifted his hands and settled them lightly on my hips. I trembled, his touch setting off electric shocks that spider webbed all over my skin, catching me in a fine net of heat I couldn't escape from.

I tried to take a breath, but it sounded more like a gasp, and I realised with a start, as his fingers tightened on my bare flesh, that he was pushing me down onto him with slow, irresistible pressure.

Unable to do anything else, I let him push until I was sitting properly on him. Until the soft, vulnerable flesh of my pussy was pressed against the denim of his jeans and the rigid outline of his cock underneath it. Just that bit of friction caused the net of heat to tighten, pulling against my skin, making me tremble even harder.

'You wanted to talk?' His voice was soft and rough. 'Then let's talk.'

Strange to sit naked on him like this and look into his inky eyes. I couldn't get rid of the almost over-whelming urge to move on him. To rub myself against the hard outline of his dick. Pull up his T-shirt, touch his smooth, hot skin. I wanted to kiss him, drive him crazy, make him feel the same terrifying desperation he made me feel.

But I didn't. My voice had got stuck in my throat and I couldn't speak. Dumb. I'd never been a woman who let herself get overwhelmed by a man—not even when I'd been in love with Justin—and yet apparently all I needed was to be sitting naked in Smoke's lap and I couldn't say a word.

'You don't trust me, do you?'

I could hear the accusation in his voice, could hear the hurt, too. It made me hurt in response. Jesus, all I seemed to be able to do lately was hurt him.

'No,' I said thickly. 'It's not that.'

'Yeah, it is.'

His thumbs moved on my hips, stroking me, send-ing flames over my skin.

'If you trusted me this wouldn't be scary.'

I met his searing black eyes. The intense heat in them nearly stole my breath. 'I do trust you. It's just...' I stopped, trying to get my thoughts together. 'It's scary because you're my closest friend. You're all I have. And I don't want to fuck that up. I don't...'

My voice shook, but I knew I was going to have to say it. I had to make myself.

'I don't want to lose you.'

His jaw was tight, his mouth hard, and the look he gave me was unrelenting.

'Yeah, and that's what I mean by not trusting me. Do you seriously think I would ever leave you? I've been your friend for over twenty fucking years, Cat. Nothing's ever going to make me go.'

It felt like he'd taken my heart in those big, warm, strong hands of his and was slowly squeezing it.

'Sex changes things. Sex makes things—'

'Don't confuse this with what happened between your parents, or between you and that asshole Justin. This is different and you know it. Fuck, *I'm* different.'

Of course he was different. Rationally, I knew that. But emotionally I was so fucked up I couldn't shake the sense that I was getting in too deep, that if I let him he'd overwhelm me. That I'd somehow end up being powerless and alone.

'I know, but...' I struggled to articulate it. 'This chemistry between us... It's kind of insane. And it scares me. I hate feeling out of control, and last night... what we did...' I stopped, not wanting to say anything more.

Something intent and angry glittered in his eyes. 'Have I ever once given you a reason not to trust me?'

'I...'

'*Have* I, Cat?'

My throat tightened, because no, he hadn't. 'It's not you, Smoke. It's me.'

His mouth hardened. 'Say it.'

'No,' I croaked. 'You've never given me a reason not to trust you.'

'No, I fucking haven't.'

Unexpectedly, he shifted beneath me, giving a subtle roll of his hips that made the denim of his jeans rub against my pussy and the hard outline of his dick push against my clit, making me shudder helplessly.

'This chemistry *is* insane and I want it. What we did last night—I want that, too. Every goddamn night. And you know what else? If you trusted me, you wouldn't worry about being a little out of control.'

The net of heat pulled even tighter over my skin, trapping me. 'S-Smoke…'

'Over twenty years and you still don't trust me.'

His hold on my hips firmed and he exerted pressure, holding me down on his lap.

'That means I'm going to have to teach you a lesson.'

He rolled his hips again, grinding slowly, making me ride the hard ridge of his dick, pressing it against my clit. I groaned as the unbearable pleasure began to ripple outwards and my face got hot. Everything got hot.

'I want you out of control, kitten,' he murmured, his breath feathering against my ear. 'I want you screaming. I want you to lose it so that you understand I'll always be there to hold you when you fall.'

His hips moved again, sending another electric jolt through me.

'I'll always be there to keep you safe.'

I gasped, desperate to pull away from the overwhelming sensation, but he held me down and all I could do was sit there as his hips rolled again, rubbing the rough denim against my achingly sensitive flesh, the ridge of his cock hitting my clit. Over and over.

Shaking, I lifted my palms and pressed them flat
to his chest, tipping my head against his shoulder. But
one of his hands tangled in my hair, pulling my head
back instead, and his mouth covered mine in a hot, wet,
open-mouthed kiss. The other slid over my hip to stroke
the curve of my butt, his fingers trailing around and
down to the inside of my thigh, his fingertips lightly
brushing the slick folds of my pussy.

I groaned, feeling his fingers teasing as he ground
against my aching clit, as he kissed me, slick and hot,
nipping and biting, exploring my mouth with a single-
minded mastery I had no hope of resisting.

Then those teasing fingers moved higher, to the
crease of my ass, slipping between. I froze, every muscle clenching hard with shock, as he pressed one fingertip against the tight ring of muscle. But he didn't
stop, pushing and pushing, his finger sliding relentlessly inside me.

I shuddered, gasping into his mouth as an intense,
dirty kind of heat swept over me, making me sweat.
He kept moving his hips, rubbing his dick against my
swollen, wet flesh, and the pleasure become sharp,
like the point of a knife. His finger pressed deeper…
The roll of his hips was faster. He bit my lower lip—
enough that the hurt was a bright spot of pain—and
that made the pleasure even sharper.

My thighs were trembling and I had to close my
eyes, pushing against his chest, trying to pull away
from the finger in my ass, only to press my clit harder
against the rigid line of his cock. Stars burst behind
my lids—pinpricks of light in the darkness.

He tasted like coffee and smelled like sex, and a

thick velvet blackness was wrapping itself around me. Making me move against him, with him, chasing the friction, chasing the climax I knew was just out of reach.

'You want to come. Don't you?' he whispered against my mouth, and the finger in my ass was moving slowly, lazily, as he ground his hard cock against my clit until I sobbed. 'You want to come so bad.'

My body was shaking like I had a fever, unbelievable pleasure roaring in my head. The hard points of my nipples were grazing his chest and that was almost too much to bear. I felt like I was drowning in sensation and helpless to stop it.

'Yes, please… Smoke…' My voice was so hoarse. 'I want it… I need it…'

'What do you want?' His finger pushed deeper, tearing a groan from my throat. 'Say it.'

'I want to…c-come.'

His hips moved in a slow circle and my fingers curled into the fabric of his T-shirt as pleasure began to tear me apart.

'Do you trust me?'

'Yes… Oh, God…' Another agonising roll, even slower this time, the friction relentless, insane. 'I…t-trust you.'

His finger pulled out, then pushed back in, making me want to scream. 'Prove it to me.' His voice was rough, guttural. 'Give me control, kitten.'

The last shreds of a resistance I hadn't known was still there were torn away.

'Yes!' My voice was ragged and cracked. 'Take it. It's yours.'

He didn't wait. His hips pushed up at the same time as he pressed me down, and everything was squeezing me into a small, tight, hard ball. The pressure of his dick against my clit, the push of his finger in my ass, his hand on my hip, squeezing me so hard. And then, like a fist uncurling, it was released, the orgasm detonating inside me, making me push my head against his chest and scream.

Breaking me into pieces and leaving me shattered in his lap.

CHAPTER FOURTEEN

Smoke

I WAS SO hard I was in agony, but I didn't fucking care. The pain was worth it for the pleasure of holding a naked Cat in my arms as she came, screaming against my chest. I didn't let go, holding her as she shuddered, riding out the climax.

As her tremors faded I stroked her back, loving the feel of her satiny damp skin under my palm. She'd gone heavy and still, resting her forehead on my chest, her breathing ragged and loud in the silence of the room.

I bent to nuzzle her hair, the sweet smell of her shampoo almost drowned by the salt and musk of feminine arousal. I nearly growled, wanting that scent all over me—on my skin, in my mouth, every-fucking-where. I wanted to eat her alive, taste every inch of her, explore every part of her with my tongue and my fingers and my cock.

For too many years that had been an empty, hollow dream.

Not any more.

Now she was mine.

Now I could indulge every fantasy I'd ever had and that reality—after years and goddamn years of trying to resist—was almost overwhelming.

But we had the whole day. There was no rush, no hurry. Even so, I was a greedy bastard, and there was no way I was going to waste time doing nothing when I could be doing something.

And right now that 'something' was getting inside of Cat.

I eased her off my lap, handling her with care. 'I'll be two seconds,' I murmured. 'Stay right here. Don't fucking move.'

I didn't wait for a reply, getting up and going down the hallway and into her small bathroom.

I soaked a washcloth in hot water, then went back to the living room. She'd curled herself up at one end of the couch, her face turned away, her cheek pressing against her arm. She was hugging herself as if she was cold, and that made my chest get tight.

I knew I'd been hard on her—knew that I'd pushed her. Maybe I'd pushed too hard.

Yeah, but that's what you do, isn't it? You always push too fucking hard.

Ignoring the voice in my head, I moved over to the couch, sitting down and then pulling Cat back into my lap. There was only a moment's tension before she relaxed, resting her cheek against my chest.

Gently, I coaxed her legs apart, checking the vulnerable flesh between them. As I'd thought, her little pussy had been rubbed raw against the denim of my jeans, and her skin was an angry red.

Fuck. I shouldn't have held her down so hard. Pissed

with myself, I stroked the washcloth lightly between her thighs, hoping the heat would help. Her head fell back against my arm, and there was a flash of green as she looked up at me from beneath her silky black lashes.

I met her gaze, the tightness in my chest easing. Something glowed in the depths of her eyes and it wasn't devastation, or fear, or any of the other things I realised I'd been half expecting. It was something warmer, fiercer.

'You bastard...' she murmured. 'I think you've broken me.'

But she wasn't broken—I could see that. I'd pushed her—and pushed her hard—but she was strong. Christ, she was probably stronger than I was when it came down to it. Women always were. Certainly my mother had been.

'Liar.' I moved the washcloth gently, watching her shiver in response. 'Broken is the last thing you are.'

Her mouth was swollen from the kisses I'd given her, and now it curved in a smile. I bent, brushing my lips over hers, the tip of my tongue dipping in to taste her purely because I could. Because I wanted to.

She didn't resist, opening her mouth beneath mine as if she'd been waiting for the moment.

So good. Fuck, she went straight to my head—sweet and hot like the best bourbon money could buy.

I could control myself. I wasn't a teenage boy. Yet one kiss from Cat and I almost came in my jeans.

Carefully I pushed her out of my lap, dropping the cloth, my hands shaking as I got to my feet and started ripping off my clothes. So much for not being in a rush.

On the coffee table was a plastic bag with the box of condoms I'd got from the drugstore and I reached for it, unable to get the damn thing open fast enough.

Cat watched me from the couch, her eyes wide, staring as I ripped open a packet and got out the condom, rolling the latex down over my painfully hard dick. Her eyes widened even further as I came over to the couch, her gaze roaming over me like she'd never seen me before in all her life.

There was heat in the green depths of her eyes and it made me feel like a fucking god. Women liked me, but Cat's appreciative stare was like gas down a fuel line, sending my heartbeat into overdrive.

I turned her over onto her back and spread her legs wide before kneeling between them. She gave a shiver as I ran my fingers over her inner thighs, stroking her, green lightning in her gaze.

'You okay?' I let my fingers trail further, through the silky black curls of her pussy, brushing her soft, wet flesh. 'Sore?'

The breath hissed in her throat, and a red flush stained her cheekbones. 'A little.'

I was too far gone to stop, so I said, 'Let me know if it's too much.'

I reached down, spreading her with my fingers and easing the head of my cock into position. Then I leaned over her, putting one hand beside her head, looking down into her flushed face.

'Watch me, kitten. Don't take your eyes off me.'

I pushed into her, long and deep and slow, and the hot, wet grip of her slit closed around me, holding me so tightly I could hardly breathe.

So good. So goddamn good.

She moaned, her lashes fluttering, her back arching. The sight was fucking erotic. Cat, naked, beneath me at last…at last. Her nipples were tight and hard. Sweat gleamed in the hollow of her throat. I looked further down to where my cock had disappeared inside her, saw the wet pink flesh of her pussy spread apart.

'Fuck, *yes.*' I pushed her knees up and out, opening her wider so I could watch myself sink even deeper. 'Take me, kitten. Take it all.'

She groaned again and I slid one hand beneath her hips, lifting her, tilting her so I could get as deep inside her as I could.

'S-Smoke… I can't… I don't think…'

'Yes, you can.' I drew my hips back, watching the wet gleam of her pussy around my aching dick. 'You fucking can.'

Then I thrust in slowly, making us both groan as pleasure rippled outwards.

The urgency had faded now I was inside her and I wanted to take my time. Savour it. Savour *her.* Give her all the pleasure she deserved…make her scream my name over and over again.

Her fingers closed around my biceps, digging in the more deeply I settled inside her, and her head went back, exposing the arch of her throat. Sweat glittered on her skin, and her breathing shuddered in the space between us.

She was so fucking beautiful.

'This is the way it should have been, Cat.' My voice got hoarse as I drew my hips back in a long, lazy glide. 'And this is the way it's going to be from now on.'

I thrust in with the same lazy movement.

A ragged gasp escaped her. I felt her nails against my skin. 'I'm not sure… I can…handle this…'

I thrust again, taking my time, enjoying the sound of her ragged breath and the sight of the agonised pleasure on her face.

'You can handle anything, kitten.' Another deep thrust, teasing us both as her flesh gripped mine. 'You're so fucking strong.'

'I don't know…' She began to pant, her hips lifting. 'You might be…too much for me… Oh, God…'

Too much? No fucking way. This woman had had a child on her own. Had faced down that prick of an abusive ex. Had created a life for herself out of nothing. She could handle me—oh, yes, she damn well could.

It made me want to prove to her exactly how much she could take.

I paused and slid a hand beneath one of her knees, lifting it up and over my shoulder while keeping the other held wide, making her even more open to me. Then I leaned forward, pushing as deep as I could get.

'Oh…*fuck*…'

Cat's eyes squeezed shut. Her hands clenched on my shoulders, her nails scratching again, but that was all good. I wanted her marks on me. I wanted the scratches, the signs of the pleasure I'd given her. The pleasure that *only* I had given her.

I moved faster, pushing her against the arm of the couch with each thrust into that slick, perfect little pussy of hers.

'See what you can take? You can take everything I throw at you.'

It was starting to get to me now. The intensity of the sensation. The heat of her bare skin all silky and smooth against mine. The musky, salty scent of sex and Cat. Pleasure was uncoiling up my spine, roaring in my head like the sound of my Harley's pipes, and I wanted to go faster, to drive so deep and hard I lost myself.

She was mine. She was *all* mine.

'S-Smoke...' She twisted beneath me, her hips moving faster, rubbing herself against me. 'Oh... Jesus... Please...'

I upped the pace, loving the feel of her pussy clamping around my cock as I drove inside her, feeling the pressure of her leg over my shoulder and the slight pain of her nails in my back.

Her face was deeply flushed, her bottom lip between her teeth, and her eyes were tightly shut—black lashes against red cheeks, tears caught there, glittering like tiny diamonds. She was perfect...fucking perfect.

Except I wanted her to look at me.

I paused and reached down, gripping her chin in my hand. 'Eyes on me.'

Her lashes lifted. The green of her irises was now lost to the black of her pupils and it made me want to growl in satisfaction, because there was nothing but pleasure deep in that beautiful gaze of hers. No fear—not this time. And no looking away.

'You're mine.' My voice was guttural, unrecognisable, and I couldn't stop myself from repeating it. So we both knew exactly what was going on here. 'You're fucking *mine*.'

Then I bent and covered her beautiful mouth, pushing my tongue inside as I pushed my dick deep into her hot little pussy.

She shuddered, a moan vibrating in her chest. Then she began to kiss me back as hard as I was kissing her, her tongue sliding against mine, her body twisting, thrusting up to take me even as I was taking her.

I didn't want it to be slow any more. I wanted her harder, faster. Wanted the sound of her cries and the smack of my flesh against hers.

I wanted to fuck her into the middle of next week.

It became something like a fight—me trying to hold her down so I could fuck her hard while she thrust her hips up, trying to rub her clit against the base of my cock, kissing me hungrily, frantically.

Her nails scratched down my back and I swear she drew blood.

She drove me fucking crazy.

It got hotter, more desperate. I cupped the back of her head to protect her as I slammed her against the arm of the couch, her tits bouncing with each thrust, her cries loud in my ear. Then I turned my mouth into her neck, biting down on the delicate tendons at the side as she clenched hard around my cock.

Her skin tasted salty and sweet. I swear I thought I'd died and gone to heaven.

Another deep thrust. And another. And another.

Pleasure was like a fucking nightclub at the back of my head—a drumbeat that wouldn't let up. I tried to hold on, take it slow, make it controlled, but she was becoming frantic, clawing at me, sobbing and desperate.

I'd never experienced anything hotter in all my goddamn miserable life.

Yeah, cause you don't deserve it.

But no, I wasn't having any of that bullshit. Of course I deserved it. After all the bad shit I'd done in my life having Cat finally beneath me was something I'd never looked for, but now the moment was here I'd be damned if I let it slip through my fingers.

So I kept on moving, kept driving us both to the edge of insanity. And then, when she was sobbing my name, tears streaking her cheeks, our bodies slippery with sweat, I slid my hand between us, down to her small, swollen clit. I brushed my fingers over it. Once. Twice. Then I thrust hard, burying myself as deeply inside her as I could get.

Cat screamed my name, her pussy clamping down hard on my cock, her nails digging into my skin and her back arching like she'd been given an electric shock. Then she began to sob, her whole body shuddering as orgasm took over.

I held her tight, turning her face into my neck as I gave a couple more hard thrusts, my orgasm shooting up my spine and exploding out through the top of my head—the purest fucking pleasure I'd ever known.

And afterwards such complete… Jesus, I didn't have a word for it. Maybe it was peace. The kind of peace I'd felt in the moments after Dad took his last breath, when a weight had just lifted right off me. A weight I hadn't realised was there.

Fucked up to think *that* right now, but that's what I was. Fucked up.

I bent my head and buried my face in Cat's hair,

inhaling the sweet scent of shampoo, of salt and musk and sex. Of home.

I was never going to let her go.

Never. Ever. *Ever.*

CHAPTER FIFTEEN

Cat

IT WAS THE second time that morning I'd come apart in Smoke's arms. The second time I'd screamed his name. The second time I'd been annihilated by pleasure.

The first time I'd been scared of what was happening between us.

Now I didn't give a fuck.

It was like he'd taken all the fear, all the doubt, all the uncertainty away, leaving me with just sensation. But then that was what Smoke did, wasn't it? He made everything okay—he always had.

It seemed ridiculous to me, now that I was lying wrapped tight in his arms, his face pressed into my hair, that I'd been so scared before—that I'd had so much difficulty trusting him. Because I should have. Of course I should have. I mean, I trusted him with my child. What was my heart in comparison?

Your heart?

Figure of speech. I loved Smoke. He was my best friend in the world, the person I counted on most. Of course I loved him. But I'd never been 'in love' with him. That had been a step I'd never wanted to take, a place I'd never wanted to go—not with him. Love was shit and I didn't want to stain our friendship with it.

Things are going to change now, though, aren't they? You've kind of taken a step in that direction.

Yeah, there was no denying it. Things *had* changed—and it wasn't even just the sex. He wanted us to be together the way an old lady was together with her old man—virtually married—and if I wanted Annie to stay safe, I wasn't going to get a choice about it.

So? He's a man who'll never hurt you, who'll do anything for you, who'll protect you and Annie, and give you astounding orgasms. What more could you want?

Good point. Something in me wanted that more than anything I'd ever wanted anything in my entire life, and yet something else kept resisting. I didn't know what it was—my daddy issues, my ex issues, or something else again—but I could feel it holding me back.

I didn't want to get hurt again—that was the main thing—and if I gave Smoke everything, the power he'd have over me...

His big, lean body shifted, the feel of his bare skin moving over mine, making my mouth go dry and scattering every thought in my head. He lifted his head, those dark eyes staring down at me. He was pressed against every inch of me, his still-semihard cock resting against the inside of my thigh. The heat of him was incredible, and the musky scent of aroused male filled the space around us.

I wanted to arch against him, rub myself all over him, trace his ink, run my hands over those powerful shoulders, feel all the hard-cut muscle of his pecs and then down to the corrugated lines of his abs. Explore every inch of his smooth, hot skin.

I'd never felt that way about a man. *Ever.* Not even with Justin. Perhaps that should be a warning, and maybe a day or two ago I would have listened to it. But now…now I ignored it, looked up into his black eyes and lost myself.

'You,' he said, his voice all rough and sexy, 'are fucking incredible.'

You're fucking mine.

The possessive note in those words should have had me running for the hills—especially after Justin—but when Smoke said them it was different. It made me feel wanted, desired. It made me feel cared for. As if for the first time I wasn't merely my father's unwanted daughter or my mother's little mistake. I wasn't Justin's punching bag. I wasn't even Annie's mom.

I was Smoke's old lady. I was Cat.

I touched his face, sliding a finger down his straight nose and across one high cheekbone. Trailing it down to his jaw and along the rough stubble of his morning beard, prickling against my fingertip, I reached his mouth, traced his lower lip. It felt firm and yet soft— the only soft thing there was about him.

'So are you.'

It didn't encompass what I felt, but it was true all the same. He was. Absolutely fucking incredible.

He smiled, his mouth curving under my fingertip, and the sight of it made my heart stretch out inside my chest and shivers chase all over me. Hungry, sexy, dangerous.

My best friend. My lover.

Gently, he took my fingertip between his strong white teeth, nipping me, sending an intense jolt of sensation straight to my core.

'It's not over yet. We have the entire fucking morning. And I intend to use all of it.'

Even now, even like this, when there was nothing between us but skin, I blushed. 'Don't you have other stuff to do?'

'Nope. Like I said, I'm planning on doing nothing but fucking you.'

I blushed even harder—which was ridiculous. I'd heard him say worse stuff. Then again, it was never usually me he was talking about when he referred to fucking.

'Well, we've done that now, so—'

'What?' he demanded, his brows rising almost up to his hairline. 'We've "done that"? I don't fucking think so. I've got a lot of fantasies where you're concerned, Cat, and they don't include one vanilla missionary on the couch.'

I swallowed, feeling self-conscious and out of my depth. My sex life so far had been nothing to write home about, but it had been okay. I'd never had a lover like Smoke before—a man who took what he wanted. Who was raw, uninhibited and completely unselfconscious about anything. I was not any of that.

One corner of his mouth turned up, as if he'd read my mind. 'What? Still scared?'

'No, of course not,' I replied hotly, and he laughed at my rise to his obvious bait. I hit him lightly on one muscular shoulder. 'Don't be such an asshole. This is new for me. I need a bit of time to come to terms with it. I mean, you only just told me you've apparently wanted me for years.'

The wicked look on his beautiful face made my heart turn over in my chest.

'You don't need time,' he said.

And before I could say another word, he'd flipped me over onto my front, with him hot and hard and heavy pressed to my back.

'All you need is more of my fucking cock.'

I took a startled breath as his hand came down on the back of my neck, gently but firmly urging my head down onto the couch cushions, turning my face towards the door.

'You always have an answer, don't you?' My voice was starting to get husky… My heartbeat was speeding up.

'That's because I'm always right.'

He kept his hand there as his arm slid under me, pulling me up onto my knees, my butt in the air.

'I mean it, Smoke. I need time and—'

I broke off as he pushed his knees between mine, making me widen my stance, and the heavy heat of that cock pushing between my thighs and sliding along the slick flesh of my pussy made my legs tremble.

'Is this too much for you, kitten?'

He flexed his hips, his dick stroking the tender skin between my legs, its rounded head hitting my clit and drawing a groan from me. At the same time he kept that hand on the back of my neck, in a not so subtle domination.

'Tell me and I'll stop.'

Relentless pleasure was beginning to build again with every push of his hips, with every slide of his cock through the wet folds of my pussy.

But it wasn't pleasure I was afraid of. It was the loss of my control...the way I could feel my heart slipping from my fingers and falling straight into his waiting palms.

It had always been there, this possibility. Just waiting for me to notice. I deliberately hadn't noticed. I'd looked away.

I didn't want to fall for him—and not because of the club. That was a smokescreen and I knew it—we both did. I didn't want to fall for him because of what I could lose. And it wasn't about the loss of our friendship.

It was about the loss of him.

I couldn't lose Smoke. I just couldn't.

Because you're in love with him already.

I shut my eyes tight. I couldn't think of that. I didn't want to think of that. Better to concentrate on physical sensations. The slick, slow drag of his dick through my folds. The scent of sex and sweat, of his need and mine. The fabric of the sofa cushion beneath my cheek.

Yeah, so much better to think about that.

'Well?'

The word was rough, hard edged. He pulled back and I felt the head of his cock press against my ass.

'What about this? Is this too much?'

I shuddered, my breathing catching.

He pressed a little harder, his free hand sliding around and across my stomach, down between my thighs, finding my clit and stroking me.

Pleasure stretched out, lazy and hot, and I panted, watching the darkness behind my lids fissuring, cracking.

'Cat?' A flick of his fingers against my aching clit. 'Answer me.'

I heaved in a breath. 'I...I...don't know...'

Another push and my flesh was parting, momentarily painful, making me shiver and groan, my muscles tightening in response. I didn't think I would ever want that, but it seemed like there were a lot of things I'd thought I wouldn't want, only to find I needed them more than my next breath.

Perhaps he knew, because a deep, husky laugh broke from him—the utter bastard. 'Thought as much. Don't worry. There'll be plenty of time for that later. Right now I haven't got much patience when it comes to getting inside you.'

He pulled away again, and this time a hint of anger and not a little bit of shame coiled through my relief. Jesus, backing away from this because I was scared meant I was being the goddamn chickenshit he'd accused me of being earlier.

And I wasn't. I *so* wasn't.

'I'm *not* scared.'

I wanted to prove it to him, backing up against him, pushing insistently, or at least as much as I could with his hand on my neck.

That hand firmed, stilling me. 'Stop,' he ordered quietly, and I did, unable to resist the gentle command in his voice. The pressure eased. 'You don't have to prove anything to me, Cat.'

'Don't I? Didn't you call me chickenshit before?'

He muttered something under his breath that sounded like a curse. 'I shouldn't have. I was a tool.'

His free hand moved to my back, stroking down my spine in soothing motion.

'I'm not fucking you in the ass right now anyway. I've got some lube, but you'll need preparation—and, like I said, I haven't got the patience right now. I'm not into pain—least of all yours.'

A blush worked its way up my throat to my cheeks. Not knowing what else to say and feeling ridiculous, I tried to sit up. But his hand was heavy on my neck again, keeping me where I was.

'Doesn't mean I'm not going to fuck you, though,' he murmured. 'So stay exactly like that. Don't move.'

The hand on my neck and the heat at my back disappeared as he got off the couch. I could have got up, too, if I'd wanted to. But he'd told me to stay there so I did, with my head on the couch cushions and my butt in the air, watching him as he went to get another condom from the box. All lithe, easy grace and fluid muscle, the Knights tattoo spread out on his back flexing as he tore open the packet and rolled the latex down.

The pulse of desire was back between my legs... hungry and empty.

Smoke turned and came back, kneeling behind me again, leaning over me, his hands coming down on either side of my head. The heat of his body was there once more, pressing against me... God, I loved the feel of him.

I shivered as I felt him shift, his right hand lifting from beside my head to touch my shoulder and then sliding down the curve of my spine. A long, gentle stroke to the small of my back and then up again. I arched into his hand like the kitten he called me, a ripple of pleasure making me lift my hips, press my butt insistently against him, wanting him.

He didn't seem to take the hint, just stroking me easy and slow. Then I felt the warmth of his breath on the small of my back.

I tensed. What the hell was he doing *now*?

His hands curved over my butt in a gentle caress, moving lower between my thighs, easing my legs wide apart. And then, shockingly, his tongue pushed into me from behind—a hard, deep thrust.

I gasped, my fingers sinking deep into the couch cushions as a bolt of the most intense pleasure shot up my spine, exploding in my head. Instinctively I tried to move, but his hands gripped the backs of my thighs, holding me in place as he gave me another long lick, his tongue sliding inside me.

I groaned and shut my eyes as he did it again and again, tearing gasps from my throat, making my legs shake, making me want to lift my hips to give him better access. But he held me so tight I couldn't move. All I could do was stay on my hands and knees, sobbing with pleasure while he ate me from behind, begging him to end it.

But he didn't. Only when I was incoherent with pleasure did he stop, leaving me wet and throbbing and empty.

Straightening up to cover me again, he pushed his weight against my back, the heat of his groin against my butt.

Then he thrust his cock deep inside me. *Hard.*

I came instantly, screaming into the cushions, my pussy clenching hard around him as he slid in and out, slow and easy and deep. And he kept going as if he had all the time in the world, his fingers slipping around and underneath me to find my swollen, aching clit. Toying with me until I was shaking and gasping all over again.

I don't know how many times I came before he moved harder, faster, taking for himself what he'd given me. But there was one thing I was certain of.

He'd wrecked me.

He'd ruined me.

And I would never be the same again.

CHAPTER SIXTEEN

Smoke

As soon as I finished up the meeting I'd had with Keep—some shit to do with problems with The Demon's Share—I walked straight out of the clubhouse and headed for my Harley, impatience gnawing a hole in my gut.

It was near 5:00 p.m., and if that meeting meant I couldn't get to the jeweller before the store closed I was going to be pissed.

I had something important to pick up. Something I wanted to give to Cat.

It had been nearly two weeks since we'd got together, and living with her had only cemented the certainty deep inside me.

She was mine—every part of her. Her long glossy dark hair and her big green eyes. Her hot little pussy and her delicious tits. The way she kissed me when she came home from her day job and the way she snuggled up to me on the sofa as we watched TV. The way she unconsciously touched me and let her hand linger, trailing over my chest or my abs or my shoulders, as if she couldn't keep her hands off me.

She'd told me that morning after the club party that I'd ruined her. Well, she'd ruined me back.

Before, I buried my craving for her in other women, because I knew she'd never want me the way I wanted her. And I'd been okay with that. I'd handled it the only way I could.

But now I *had* her. Now I knew how she tasted when I kissed her mouth, when I pushed my tongue into her pussy. Now I knew how it felt to be balls-deep inside her, to have her legs wound around my waist and screaming my name in my ear.

Now I knew how good it was to have her curl up in my arms and put her head on my chest and fall asleep, as if she was safe, as if she trusted me completely…

Yeah, she'd ruined me.

There would be no one else for me.

That morning we'd had an argument about me handling her bills, paying her rent for the month, and then I'd made the mistake of mentioning that maybe we should find a new place to live. She'd been pissy, reminding me that this arrangement wasn't supposed to be permanent and that she wasn't going anywhere until the threat to Annie from Justin had been sorted out.

Except the 'arrangement' *was* permanent for me. This was real and it always had been.

I wanted to tell her there and then what I was planning—I'd been waiting because I wanted to give her some time to get used to having me around—but she'd cut me off because she had to go to work, telling me we'd talk about it tonight.

She was still scared. I could see it in her eyes. She was still doubting me—doubting us. So I decided to pay extra to get the ring I'd had made for her finished that day. It would be proof of my commitment to her— my promise that I'd never leave her. That she was stuck with me for good.

What if she doesn't want to be stuck with you?

I revved the Harley, the thought making me growl like the bike.

Too bad. She was mine, and I wasn't letting her go.

Picking up the ring from the jeweller didn't take long, and then I was on my way back to Cat's apartment. She was already home. I could hear her in the kitchen on the phone as I walked in, talking to the sitter who looked after Annie after school on the days I wasn't able to.

My pulse started doing crazy shit. The ring was burning a hole in the pocket of my jeans, what-ifs were spinning in my head, and I found myself pacing around the room trying to calm myself the fuck down.

The territorial biker in me was never going to let her go, regardless of what she wanted, but there was another part of me—the friend—that wanted her to want that, too. That wanted her to put on my ring and tell me that she'd stay with me forever.

'Hey.'

I looked up at the sound of her voice to find her standing in the doorway, wearing that little black pencil skirt and the green blouse, black heels on her feet. My favourite outfit. Her gaze was wary—clearly she still remembered our argument from that morning.

Raising a hand, she pulled the hair tie from her

ponytail, releasing her silky black hair down around her shoulders.

My fingers itched to bury themselves in it, to take it in my fist and pull her head back, kiss her throat, bite her. Leave a mark on her smooth skin. I fucking *loved* having my marks on her, showing the civilian world that she was taken, that she was mine.

But first things first.

I stopped pacing, thrust my hands in my pockets, curling my fingers around the ring box.

'Hey,' I said.

She sighed and came over to me, sliding her arms around my neck, rising up on her toes to kiss me. Christ, the way she did that, coming to me without hesitation... It gave me a thrill every time.

My heartbeat was revving like the engine on my bike by the time she pulled away, and when a crease settled between her black brows I knew she'd sensed my unsettled mood.

'What's up?' she asked softly. 'Is it about this morning?'

My mouth had gone dry and my pulse was out of control—which was insane. There was no reason to be such a pussy about this.

'There's something I need to say to you.' The words came out rougher than I wanted them to.

Cat blinked, then lowered her lashes—but not before I caught the spark of fear in her eyes.

'That sounds serious.' She took a step back and folded her arms.

Shit. She was doing what she always did when she

was afraid. Retreating from me. Protecting herself.
Which was *so* not happening.

I took my hands out of my pockets and pulled her
back into my arms, keeping her little soft, warm body
pressed to mine.

Her gaze widened. 'What's going on?'

Keeping one arm around her waist, I reached into
my pocket and grabbed the ring box, then held it out.
'This is for you.'

She glanced at the box, then back up at me, shock
rippling over her features. 'Smoke, I—'

'Let me say something first. You told me this morning that you didn't want to think about getting a new
place because this isn't supposed to be permanent.' I
looked deep into those beautiful green eyes. 'Cat, this
is permanent for me. When Justin finally gets what's
coming to him, I'm not walking away from either you
or Annie—get me? When I said I'd never leave you I
meant it.'

She stared at me, not saying a word.

Not exactly the response I'd hoped for, but I made
myself be patient. I'd had years to think about what I
truly wanted from her, while all this—being with me—
was still very new for her.

'We're not going back to the way it was before, kitten,' I went on, making sure she was absolutely clear
on where I stood. 'Because I don't want to be your
friend. I want to be more than that. I want to be your
everything.'

Colour flooded her face, and I could feel her stiffen.

I didn't let her pull away, keeping my arm around
her waist. 'Open the box.'

She hesitated, her reluctance obvious. I tried not to let it get to me. This would be a big step for her—especially given the shit she'd had to put up with in her last relationship. But I wasn't Justin and I'd told her that already. Surely she knew that?

She picked up the box from my palm and opened it. The ring I'd bought her gleamed on black velvet. It was silver; a delicate, stylised cat face, with pointed ears projecting out from the band and two genuine emeralds where the eyes should be. It had cost shitloads but I didn't care. She was worth every cent.

At least her reaction was what I wanted. Her mouth opened, and a surprised sound escaped from her. I could see that she didn't want to take the ring from its box and yet her hand reached for it anyway, as if she couldn't help herself.

I grabbed the ring before she could, though, because this was something I wanted to do. Gently I took her left hand and slid it onto her finger.

The fit was perfect, like I'd known it would be, and the emeralds glittered in the fading light coming through the windows.

'Smoke…'

Her voice was hoarse and she didn't look at me, her attention all on her hand.

'I don't understand. What does this mean?'

'What do you think?' I gripped her chin, turning her face towards mine. 'You're already my old lady, but the civilian world needs more than that. I want to make you and me legal. And I want to adopt Annie, be her dad for real.'

Emotions flickered across her face, too fast for me to read. But I got at least one loud and clear: *fear*.

She tried to pull away, but I wasn't having it. I'd told her she wasn't going to get any distance from me and I'd meant it.

'What are you afraid of?' I demanded, searching her expressive face. 'I thought you trusted me.'

Her hand pushed at me. 'Let me go.'

'No.' I gripped onto her jaw so she couldn't pull away, trying to ignore the hollow feeling in my gut. 'You've been happy being mine for the past two weeks—I know you have. So why is making this permanent a problem?'

'Smoke.' She pushed again.

I didn't move. 'You think I don't know you're scared? You think I can't see it in your eyes?'

Her hand pressed harder against my chest.

'You don't understand. Two weeks ago you were just my friend, and now suddenly you're putting a ring on my finger and telling me you want to make it legal. You're in my bed and in my life, and… Jesus, it's all happening so fast. *Too* fast. I can't…think.' Her eyes darkened. 'I need some time. I need some space, okay?'

A part of me understood that for her all this *was* fast. But that didn't stop the gut punch of disappointment.

I wanted to argue that over twenty years of friendship didn't make this 'fast', then crush her mouth beneath mine, take away her fear, give her pleasure instead. Make her see that all she needed was me.

Instead I let her go, taking a step back, giving her the space she wanted.

She sucked in a breath, straightening her back and

lifting her chin. Then she slid the ring off her finger and put it back in the box, closing the lid and setting it on the coffee table.

The hollowness in my gut got wider, deeper. It felt like she'd reached inside my chest, put her fingers around my heart and squeezed it tight.

'You don't like it?' I couldn't keep the demand out of my voice, disappointment making it sound harsh.

Cat had folded her arms again, as if she was protecting herself against me, and her gaze was full of a hurt I didn't understand.

'I don't like it,' she said thickly. 'I *love* it. The ring is beautiful and that's the problem. This is everything I ever wanted, and yes, that's…scary. Because I've wanted stuff before and it all went horribly wrong.'

The pressure around my heart eased. Okay, so she *did* want this after all. She wanted *me*.

'The past doesn't mean shit.' I tried to resist the urge to grab her again. 'And nothing's going to go wrong— not if I have anything to do with it.'

She glanced away, running a hand through her hair. 'You don't know that. Every single relationship I've ever had has gone bad. Every single one. And every time that happens, I lose.'

Her gaze came back to mine and this time she didn't hide her fear. It was there in her eyes.

'I'm tired of losing, Smoke. I'm tired of being left with nothing. My friendship with you is the only thing I have that hasn't gone wrong.'

I wanted to go to her and take her hand in mine, be the caring friend I used to be. But disappointment and frustration were eating away at me like battery acid.

It felt like everything I'd always dreamed of was just within reach, and yet she kept pulling it away.

'I won't stop being your friend just because we're sleeping together.' I couldn't keep the harsh note out of my words. 'It won't change what we have now.'

She didn't look away this time. 'It's not change I'm scared of. I'm scared of getting in too deep. I need to have something left if this doesn't work out.'

'Why the fuck do you think this won't work out?'

My temper began to slip out of my grip, no matter how hard to I tried to keep hold of it, and frustration was gouging a ragged hole inside me.

'I've been your friend for over twenty goddamn years, Cat, and I'm still your friend now. That's never going to change. I don't know how many times I have to say it. I don't know what else to give you. I don't know what you want from me.'

Her mouth tightened, her green eyes dark. 'I don't know either.'

I couldn't stand still any more—couldn't have this distance between us. A distance that felt like it was getting wider with every passing second.

She put up her hand again as I moved but I ignored it, grabbing her hips and pulling her hard against me, pressing my rapidly hardening dick to the heat between her thighs.

'So fucking think about it, then. What do you need? Do you need to hear the *I love you* shit? Is that what you want?'

A green flame leapt in her gaze and her temper answered mine. 'So *I love you* is shit? Is that what you're saying?' She shoved at me. 'Fuck you.'

I knew I was making things worse, but I couldn't seem to stop. All I could feel was that distance opening up and I didn't know how to close it.

'But is that what you *want*?'

I slid my hands over the curve of her butt, digging my fingers into her softness through her skirt, flexing my hips so my cock pressed harder against her groin.

'You want me to tell you I love you?'

Her mouth compressed, as if she didn't want to say it. But I knew anyway. That was exactly what she wanted.

Love. What the fuck did it even mean? Not a god-damn thing. Love was a woman dying in a hospital bed from the injuries her husband had given her. Love was a backhand across the face and a cigarette ground out against bare skin. It was years of pain, years of abuse.

'Love *is* shit, Cat,' I went on roughly. 'And you of all people should know that. But this…?' I flexed my hips again, grinding against her, making her gasp. 'This is fucking *real*. This means something. Everything I give you, everything I do for you, means something. But, Christ, if you want the words so you can feel safe, I'll give them to you. And if you want to walk up the aisle in a fucking white dress, with bridesmaids and all that other crap, then you can. And if you want to stay in this shitty apartment then, sure, we'll stay in this shitty apartment. Anything and everything, kitten. Just say the word.'

The flush in her cheeks deepened, the flame in her eyes getting hotter. Her fingers had curled in the cotton of my T-shirt and the tension had gone from her muscles. She was moving with me now, her body softening against mine, because even if her mind was having problems accepting me that greedy pussy of hers had no such issues.

'What if I want to go back to being friends?' Her voice had got husky. 'What about that?'

'No.' I pulled her up on her toes, the length of my aching dick pushing against her clit, making her inhale sharply. 'No fucking way.'

Her gaze had gone even darker, the way it did when she wanted me badly.

'Then...you h-have to give me time.'

Jesus. Even when she was turned on and ready to fuck she wouldn't give one goddamn inch. I loved that about her, but it was driving me crazy right now. All I wanted was for her to say yes. To be mine, to choose me. Was that really too much to ask?

I knew how to convince her, though. Use our chemistry. Pull up her skirt and play with her pussy until she was sobbing and ready to give me anything I wanted. But I'd been hoping she'd say yes without that.

The battery-acid feeling was fire in my gut, with anger and disappointment and frustration all joining the party. Making me want to punch something. Or preferably fuck something.

Fine, if this was the way she wanted to play it, I'd play.

And I'd fucking win.

I was already hauling her skirt up, my hands sliding over the silky skin at the backs of her thighs, when my phone started buzzing in my back pocket. I knew the ringtone. It was Keep—which meant I couldn't ignore it.

Cursing, I let Cat go, but kept my gazed locked

with hers as I dragged my phone out and answered it. I wanted her to know that this shit wasn't done—not by any stretch.

'What?'

I made no effort to be polite, because what was happening between me and Cat was important, and I'd already had one meeting with Keep today.

'I need you to come to the clubhouse for a chat,' Keep said shortly. 'Got a complaint from the cops about you.'

I scowled. That didn't make any sense. I stayed out of the cops' way and they stayed out of mine.

'What the fuck? I don't know what—'

'Just get here, Smoke,' Keep interrupted and disconnected the call.

Anger and thwarted lust simmered inside me. I could still feel Cat's heat against me, and the last thing I wanted to do was go back to the clubhouse and have a 'chat' with my president. But ignoring an order from Keep wasn't a good move, so I stuffed my phone back in my pocket.

'I got to go.'

Cat was already smoothing her skirt down, her hands shaking as she did so. It made a part of me savagely glad that even after two weeks of being in her bed I still had the power to affect her like that.

'Oh?' she said huskily. 'What's happening?'

'Club shit.'

I took a step towards her, hooked an arm around her neck and brought her in for a deep, hard kiss.

I lifted my head. 'This isn't over, kitten.'

Then I left.

CHAPTER SEVENTEEN

Cat

AFTER SMOKE HAD GONE, I sat down on the couch, my legs too shaky to hold me up. My heart rate was going through the roof and the heat of Smoke's hands lingered on my thighs. I could still feel the pressure of his cock against my throbbing clit and see the searing intensity in his dark eyes…

I took a breath, glancing at the little box on the table. The ring was perfect. Beautiful. I loved it. No one had ever got me anything so special and so completely *me* before. I wanted to put it on my finger and never take it off.

But I couldn't.

The past two weeks with Smoke had been amazing. He'd always been such a huge part of my life that I'd expected nothing to change. Yet somehow everything had changed.

He helped with Annie, talked with me, laughed with me, supported me the same as he always did.

But when night fell he didn't leave.

Instead he took me to bed. Made me scream into my

pillow as he systematically explored and then destroyed every single one of my inhibitions—until there was no part of me that remained untouched by his mouth, his fingers, his cock. There was nothing I wouldn't let him do. He overloaded me with pleasure until I forgot why I'd ever been afraid in the first place.

Then there were those moments out of bed, when he'd put his hand on my back or thread his fingers through mine. When we'd be watching TV and his arm would come around me and I'd rest my head on his chest. Little touches, small reassurances.

I loved those. I hadn't realised how starved I'd been of them. Every time he touched me I wanted to arch into his hand and purr like the kitten he kept calling me.

Far from hurting our friendship, our physical relationship had only deepened it, made it richer. Made it into something really, really good.

And yet...

I stared at the ring box. I don't know why what he'd said, what he wanted from me, scared me so much. I should trust him, and I did, but the thought of putting on that ring made our relationship feel permanent in a way that wearing his property patch didn't.

Of course that was what he wanted, but the horror of my parents' relationship and then falling for Justin and having him hurt me so badly had hardened something inside me. I wanted to protect myself at all costs—protect my heart from the pain when everything went wrong, because it always did.

I wanted to protect myself from falling in love again, making myself vulnerable to someone who could hurt me. And Smoke *could* hurt me. He had the power to rip me apart without even lifting a finger, and that made him far more terrifying than Justin in every way.

Did I really want to give him that kind of power? Especially when he already had so much?

You're not exactly powerless yourself.

Well, that was true. I'd seen the disappointment in his eyes when I took the ring off and put it back in the box. He'd wanted me to say yes—that was obvious. And I couldn't deny that a part of me was perversely glad that somehow I'd managed to cause him pain, because I felt like he held my heart in the palm of his hand while he kept his own safely locked away.

'Love is shit, *Cat.*'

He would think that. Love for him meant everything bad, same as it did for me. But was he right? Were those words I wanted to hear make everything better? Would they make me feel safe? *I love you.* I didn't know. I *did* know that I didn't want him to say them to me just because it was what I wanted to hear. I wanted him to say them to me because that was what *he* felt.

Did he *actually* love me? Or was I simply a possession to him? Was I simply his property, like his bike or his cut? He did all these things for me—but was that because he'd do the same for anyone he considered his, or was it because of who I was to him?

How can it be you? You're not that special, remember?

The thought was hateful, so I pushed it away and got to my feet. I couldn't think about this right now—not when I had to go and collect Annie from the sitter.

I was in the hallway, ready to leave, when a knock came on the door.

Too busy thinking about Smoke, and what I was going to say to him when he came back, I didn't check the peephole, simply pulled the door open.

'Hi, Cat,' said Justin.

Everything inside me froze. My ex was standing there in his expensive suit, his slightly overlong brown hair expertly styled, looking handsome and success-ful, with his I'm-a-hell-of-a-nice-guy smile plastered on his face.

Taking advantage of my shock, he pushed his way inside, shutting the door firmly behind him. I took a couple of steps back before I could stop myself, my body instinctively remembering the shock and the pain of his blows and wanting to avoid them. Then I halted, furious with myself for backing away.

'What the hell are you doing here?' I tried to keep my voice steady. 'I didn't invite you in. Get the hell out!'

'Nope.' Justin shook his head, still smiling. 'I want to talk to you first.'

'Yeah, well, I don't want to talk to *you*. Get the fuck out of my apartment.'

He raised his hands in a calming gesture. 'Five min-utes, Cat. Give me five minutes.'

I didn't want to, but short of shoving him out through the door—and I didn't want to get that close to him—it didn't look like I was going to get much choice.

Folding my arms, I lifted my chin. 'Five. Then you're gone.'

He let out a breath, as if relieved, and ran a hand

through his hair, that smarmy grin he thought was so charming curving his mouth.

'Okay, look… I've been thinking about Annie, and custody, and all that stuff. And how you're kind of trapped here in this…' He looked around, his lip curling. 'Well, it's not exactly the best place for a kid, huh? Anyway, I wondered if you'd consider maybe getting back together again.'

All the air in my lungs abruptly vanished, making it difficult to breathe.

'You're joking,' I managed. 'Please tell me you're joking.'

Justin's grin faded, a glint of heat entering his blue eyes. 'No. The truth is I miss you, Cat. And I want you back.'

He could *not* be serious. He couldn't.

'Are you insane?' I didn't bother to hide my shock. 'Why the hell would you think I'd *ever* want to come back to you? After what you did to me?'

His gaze flickered. 'I'm different now. I promise. And anyway it's better for Annie that we're a family. She needs a father.'

'She already has a father.'

The words came out before I could stop them. Because, of course, she did. She had Smoke. And he was a better father to her than Justin had ever been.

A mistake to say it out loud, though.

All the charm slid right off Justin's face like a switch had been thrown. The heat faded from his eyes, to be replaced by a hard, cold glitter. 'That biker asshole is *not* her father. *I* am. And if you care anything for her you'll know that her place and yours is with *me.*'

'Sure—with a man who can't control his own anger.' I didn't hold back the sarcasm. 'Who'd rather hit me than talk to me. Yeah, she'll be safer with you, all right.'

Justin's features rearranged themselves, the charm oozing back again. 'Oh, come on. You're really going to keep holding that against me? I loved you, Cat. I still do. Doesn't that count for anything?'

I stared at him—at Justin with his smarmy smile and his handsome face. Who'd told me he loved me countless times. And it hit me hard—like a brick to the side of the head—that, yes, he'd given me those words and I'd lapped them up, desperate for love and acceptance from someone.

But although the words had been what I wanted to hear, his actions had told a different story. When we were together he'd criticise me constantly, undermining me, making me feel that I wasn't good enough for him, that I had to work to be worthy of him.

He hit me.

He hurt me.

He made me feel small and weak.

But Smoke didn't do any of those things. No, he hadn't given me the words I'd been wanting to hear, but everything he did was for *me*. He built me up...made me feel beautiful. Made me feel strong. He was constantly pushing me, challenging me, making me step up because he knew I could take it. And he wanted the best for me. He wanted more for me.

Because he cared.

I could feel the truth of it sliding down inside me, imprinting itself into my blood, my bones. Into my soul.

He loved me. He might not have said it, but every day he showed me in the way he touched me, looked at me. In the way he cared for Annie. In every way there was.

And just like that my fear vanished.

I dropped my arms to my sides and took a few steps forward, getting right up in Justin's handsome, smarmy-ass face.

'No,' I said calmly. 'It counts for exactly zero. Because you don't love me, Justin. You never did. If you had, the last thing you would have done is treat me like shit, the way you did.'

He snorted, drawing himself up as if to emphasise his height, trying to make me feel small and weak.

'You're still pissed about a couple of slaps across the face? Come *on*. They didn't hurt that much.'

I don't know what came over me then—a tidal wave of rage, a firestorm burning away my fear and my vulnerability, burning away my weakness. I lifted my hand, drew it back and punched him in the face. *Hard*.

He reeled back in shock, blood pouring from his nose, and even though my knuckles were throbbing, it was the most satisfying sight in the entire world.

'What the fuck?' His hand went to his nose, his face going red.

'What are you getting so pissy about?' I asked. Rage was making me shake. 'It was just a little punch in the face. It didn't hurt that much.'

'You're fucking *crazy*!'

I took another step towards him, and it was even more satisfying to see him take a step back. 'You know the difference between you and Smoke, Justin? *Every-*

thing. Every fucking thing. He's a better friend, a better lover, a better father. And he's sure as hell a better man than *you'll* ever be.'

Justin's face twisted and he reached out to grab me, yanking hard on my hair as he pulled me close. 'You crazy bitch. I'll teach you a fucking lesson about who's the better man.'

I wasn't afraid of him when his hands turned painful, ripping at my blouse, jerking up my skirt. Instead I was made of rage. I could feel it turning hot, burning bright, and I gathered myself, ready to explode.

Then suddenly Justin's hands were gone from me and the hallway was full of a harsher, deeper voice roaring, 'Touch her again and I'll fucking *kill* you!'

Smoke was there, and he'd grabbed the back of Justin's suit, hurling him into the wall so violently Justin bounced off it. Then Smoke closed in again, punching Justin in the face. Once. Twice. Justin fell to the floor, groaning, but Smoke hadn't finished. He kicked him in the ribs—a hard, driving blow. And again. And again.

My anger had begun to seep away, fear taking its place.

Smoke's face was a mask of rage and I knew without a doubt that if I didn't stop him he'd kill Justin—or put in him in the hospital at the very least.

I flung myself at Smoke's back, pulling on the leather of his cut. 'Stop it, Smoke! He's not worth the effort—he's not!'

But Smoke didn't listen. His boot was connecting with Justin's ribs again and again.

Trembling, I slid my arms around his lean, rock-hard body and laid my head against his back, letting him know that I was there.

'Stop,' I said hoarsely. 'Please, Smoke. *Stop.*'

I could feel the heave of his chest and the shake in his muscles, the intensity of his rage. It was like the rage that burned in me. But there were better ways of letting it out than battering a man to death.

Hell, I shouldn't have hit him myself—but then I owed him one.

I held on tight to Smoke and eventually he stopped, standing over Justin's groaning body, his breathing fast and harsh in the enclosed space of the hallway.

I thought that maybe it was too late, that we'd have to call an ambulance, but eventually Justin moaned and rolled over, climbing slowly and painfully to his feet. His face was a mask of blood, his hand curled protectively over his ribs.

'You're fucking *dead*,' he said viciously to Smoke, his voice thick and mangled. 'No court in the state will give custody of Annie to her now. Especially not when I have you up on assault charges.'

He spat blood on the floor.

'Have fun in jail, *prick.*'

Then he turned and limped out through the door.

CHAPTER EIGHTEEN

Smoke

I WAS SO angry I couldn't see straight. People talk about a red rage and that was exactly what came down over my vision when I opened the front door to find fucking Justin tearing at Cat's clothing and pulling her hair.

There'd only been one other time I'd lost control of my temper so completely, and that was when I found Dad kicking Mom, over and over.

I'd shot him then, fucking up my life completely. Just like I'd fucked it up now.

I could feel the inescapable truth of it coiling and twisting inside me, and rage burned like rocket fuel in my bloodstream.

I should never have touched Justin, should never have punched him, but all I'd seen was his hands on my kitten, hurting her the way he always hurt her, and all I'd been able to think was that he had to pay.

She held me now, her arms around my waist, the warmth of her body against my spine, and that was what pushed back the red haze.

Too late, though. *Too fucking late.*

Justin had me now. He'd press charges, and since Keep wouldn't want his good relationship with the cops put at risk I'd have to take some jail time. Especially since I'd disobeyed Keep's direct order and laid a hand on the police chief's son.

That would leave Cat and Annie unprotected, since there was nothing Keep could do legally to stop Justin from claiming Annie. Illegally he could, but I was betting he wouldn't want to deepen the shit with the cops that I'd already dumped him in.

Fuck.

I'd lost it for the club and I'd lost it for Cat, too.

I should have known that call from Keep was bullshit. As soon as I got back to the clubhouse he mentioned that the police chief had called through some complaint from a cop about me and he wanted me to explain. Easy enough. I hadn't even been in the city at the time, and Keep knew that because he was the one who sent me out of it in the first place. I realised in that moment that someone was screwing with me and it could only be one person. *Justin.* He'd made his father put through that call to get me away from Cat.

I'd headed straight back to her place immediately, riding like a fucking maniac, only to find that asshole with his hands all over what was mine. So I'd hit him and hit him, and now I was completely fucked.

And what made everything worse was that I knew there was only one way to fix this. Only one way to give Cat any chance at all of keeping Annie. Because she wasn't going to lose her—not because of me.

'Smoke?'

Cat's voice was soft, her fingers spreading out over my stomach, making my dick twitch.

'Are you okay?'

Jesus fucking Christ. I'd ruined her life and all she wanted to know was whether I was okay.

Abruptly I couldn't bear her touch—not when I knew what I had to do and how badly it would hurt her. So I pulled her arms from around me, making sure I was gentle and not the raging, violent animal I was inside, and stepped away.

'Smoke?'

I didn't want to look at her. All it would take for me to lose my nerve would be one glimpse of those big green eyes, so I kept my back to her and turned in the direction of the bedroom, moving towards it.

'Smoke.' She sounded sharper now. 'What's wrong?'

I stopped, but didn't turn. 'I screwed up.' My voice sounded like I'd just come back from a three-day drunken orgy. 'I screwed up totally. I'm sorry.'

'You mean the assault charges? You were protecting me. I'm a witness. I'll tell them that he was going to—'

'It doesn't matter what you say.'

I stared hard at the bedroom door, my knuckles throbbing from where I'd punched that cocksucker in the face.

'It doesn't matter what he did. No one's going to give you custody of Annie while you have a violent biker for a boyfriend.'

My chest hurt—a deep ache, like I'd been stabbed with a rusty knife.

'No.'

She said it like the word was all she needed to make it

true and her hand was there again, settling between my shoulder blades, warm as the sun on a summer's day ride.

'We have the club. That's why I became your old lady to start with, right? They'll help us.'

'Yeah, I've fucked it up with the club, too.'

I could feel blood on my knuckles, could feel it drip down over my skin. A reminder of my past...of who I was. The ache in my chest deepened.

'Keep was real clear that I couldn't touch Justin because we had to stay sweet with the police. He won't be happy if that asshole presses charges and it makes it difficult for him.'

'But once you explain—'

'Explanations won't matter. All I can do is take responsibility for it and accept the consequences.'

Cat's hand was gone from my back and suddenly she was standing in front of me, her dark brows drawn down, her eyes full of worry. Then I noticed the tears in her blouse and the red marks on her skin from where that bastard had touched her. All the rage came flooding back.

'He hurt you.' My voice was guttural, making me sound like the fucking rabid animal I was.

'No, he didn't. I hurt *him*, in actual fact.'

'Your shirt...'

I reached out to touch the delicate material, fighting to keep myself together with the pressure of my fury crushing all the sense out of me. I wanted to put my hands on her, cover the marks Justin had left on her with my own. Reclaim her as mine as thoroughly and completely as possible.

Cat's attention dipped to my hand and she let out a soft breath. 'Oh. You're bleeding.' She reached for me.

No. Jesus. I couldn't have her touching me. Not now. I lowered my hand and stepped back.

Her eyes widened. 'Smoke?'

It felt like that rusty knife was cutting a hole in my chest, peeling back my skin, pulling my ribs apart. I had to do this and do it fast.

'I can't stay.' Pain bled into my voice, no matter how hard I tried to stop it. 'I can't be with you any more. Not if you want to keep Annie.'

She blinked. 'What do you mean, you can't be with me any more?'

'I mean if the courts see you with me you're screwed. You're going to lose Annie. And the club won't save you—not now I've fucked with Justin. Keep needs his relationship with the cops and he won't want to put that at risk if Justin has me up on assault charges. I'll have to take the rap for it. I'll have to go down.'

'You mean jail? No, don't be stupid. You're not going anywhere—let alone to prison. There are plenty of other ways we can—'

'There are *no* other ways.' I cut her off harshly. 'You'll never get to keep Annie if I don't go.'

'But when you say you'll go, how long are you talking about? Just until this is over, right?'

That knife in my chest had turned into an animal, clawing at my guts, tearing me to shreds inside. I'd nearly killed a man in her hallway—would have killed him if she hadn't been there to stop me—and I was dripping blood all over her carpet.

Now she might lose her daughter because of me.

Now she might lose *everything* because of me.

She'd been right not to wear my ring. Right to take

it off and put it back in that box. Right not to give me what I wanted. Right to be afraid.

I was dangerous. I hurt people. I killed people. And one of these days, no matter how hard I'd try not to, I'd hurt her. Shit, I already had. I changed our friendship, forced her to be my old lady. She hadn't wanted any of that and yet I'd insisted.

What kind of man did that to a friend?

You know the answer to that, motherfucker.

'No, Cat.' I had make myself say the words. 'When I say I have to go, I mean I have to leave you. For good.'

She paled. 'What?'

'I can't be with you any more. It's better for you and it's better for Annie if I'm not in your lives. I'll take a jail term for the club if I have to, but I'm not having you or Annie connected to that. Not if it means you losing her.'

Her mouth had dropped open and she was staring at me like I'd turned into a stranger. 'You can't mean that.'

I held her gaze, letting her see the truth. 'I mean every fucking word.'

Green sparks of anger leapt in her eyes. 'No,' she repeated. 'You're not going to jail just because you were protecting me. And you're not leaving me. Just *no*.'

Of course she was being stubborn. Of course she was going to make this even harder than it was already.

'You didn't want this anyway, remember?' I couldn't help pointing that out. 'You wanted some time to think about it.'

Those green sparks leapt higher, her chin lifting in challenge. 'I know what I said. But what if I was wrong? What if I *do* want it after all?'

Oh, Jesus Christ. Please don't say she'd changed her mind. I couldn't deal with that—I just couldn't.

'Well, it's too late now,' I said harshly. 'This is the way it has to be.'

Not waiting for her to respond, I sidestepped her and headed into the bedroom.

I didn't want to have this discussion. Not with her standing there with that look in her eyes. Anger and, beneath it, pain. Not when everything I said would only make her angrier, cause her more hurt.

It was better I just go. Make the moment quick, like ripping off a Band-Aid.

In the bedroom I grabbed my duffel bag, then went to the dresser where Cat had cleared out a couple of drawers for me, taking out my clothes and stuffing them in the bag.

'You bastard.'

Cat's voice came from behind me, low and shaking.

'You don't get to do this. You don't get to change our friendship, make me want you, tell me you'll never leave me and then walk away.'

Each word hit like a bullet, opening up a thousand holes inside me, their edges jagged and ripped, my entire fucking soul pouring out through them like blood from a fatal wound.

'It's better this way.'

I kept my teeth clenched against the agony, balling up a T-shirt and shoving it into the bag.

'Better for who? For me and Annie? Or for you?'

The raw note in her voice hooked into the anger that was already boiling away inside me, making it sizzle like water on a hot exhaust pipe.

I turned around sharply.

She was behind me, her expression furious, her green eyes bright with hurt.

'You really want a man like me?' I demanded, unable to shut the fuck up. 'I'd have killed that fucker if you hadn't been here. I'd have beaten him to death for touching you.'

I took a step towards her, wanting to intimidate her so she'd back off.

'Is that the kind of man you want in your life? The kind of man you want around your daughter?'

Strangely, the look in her eyes softened, as if she could see something in me that I couldn't.

'This isn't about Annie and me, though, is it?'

I stiffened as she took a step forward, apparently not giving a shit that I was enraged and in pain and ready to smash something into oblivion.

She lifted a hand to touch my face. 'This is about you losing it with Justin. About your dad.'

Her gaze was sharp, opening me up, and I grabbed her wrist to stop her from touching me before I could think better of it.

'No.' I tried to ignore the warmth of her skin and the race of her pulse beneath my fingers. 'That shit's got nothing to do with this.'

I was lying, though, and we both knew it.

I'd killed my Dad and that ghost wouldn't *ever* fucking die.

Cat didn't move. 'You know what I thought back then, and that hasn't changed. You shot your dad because you were trying to protect your mom. And you beat the hell out of Justin because you were trying to protect me. You're a protector. *That's* the kind of man you are, Smoke. That's the kind of man you've always been. I thought you knew that.' She took another step closer. 'Being near Annie and me hasn't bothered you before. So what's changed? Is it Justin? Is it me?'

She was so close I could smell her familiar scent. It was getting me hard. The tear in her blouse didn't help either, revealing the curves of her delicious tits.

Fuck, I wanted her so badly.

My grip tightened on her wrist and I felt her pulse begin to accelerate.

What had changed? *I* had. And she was the one who'd changed me. Being a friend was easy—there was a distance in that. But being more than a friend was different, and I hadn't realised 'til now what that meant.

Justin had not only shown me the truth of what I felt for her, he'd also shown me the truth of what I was inside. I was violent. Possessive. Territorial. I wanted to make Cat mine in every way, and the thought of her even touching another man filled me with murderous rage.

She didn't deserve that. Annie didn't deserve it either. Cat needed a man who wasn't controlling or jealous or demanding. And Annie needed a father figure who wouldn't lose his temper and beat to death some asshole simply for touching his woman.

'It doesn't matter what's changed.' I stared down into her beautiful eyes. 'Fact remains that me leaving is better for Annie, and that's who you should be thinking about right now.'

An intense expression flickered across her face. 'That's not true. You leaving is *not* better.'

She put her free hand on my chest, the warmth of

her touch seeping through my T-shirt, making me *so* fucking aware of exactly how far away she was from me and how much I wanted to close that distance. Making the pain that was ripping me apart even worse.

'And what's good for us is you staying here. Because you're good for *me*, and what's good for me is good for Annie—can't you see that?'

I wanted to see it. I really did. But I couldn't. Not when I'd never been good for anyone in my entire fucking life.

Unable to resist the urge to touch her, I let go her wrist and took her face between my hands, cupping her jaw. 'I've made my decision. I'm sorry, kitten. This is how it is.'

Her mouth tightened, fury glowing in her eyes. 'No,' she said. '*No.*'

And before I could avoid her she rose up onto her toes and pressed her lips to mine. Kissing me.

I struggled not to respond. Every muscle in my body was tight with the need to grab her, push her down on the floor. Bury my aching cock in her tight little pussy, make all the pain and the rage disappear.

But that would only make things worse.

And yet Cat was obviously hell-bent on making this as hard for me as possible, because when I didn't respond she pushed her tongue into my mouth, tasting me, kissing me as demandingly and as desperately as I'd ever kissed her.

It was the hottest fucking thing I'd ever experienced.

She'd never been aggressive like this with me before, never been this hungry. Like she was suffocating and the only way to breathe was to put her mouth on mine.

My dick was like iron in my jeans, and I knew if I

didn't put a stop to this now I wouldn't be able to. And then walking away from her would be next to impossible.

So I buried one hand in her hair and fisted it, trying to pull her head back. She resisted, making me pull harder, which had to hurt her, yet she didn't make a sound when I finally managed to yank her away. Her eyes were huge and dark and full of rage, and I felt like my chest was made of nothing but broken glass.

'You can't leave,' she said furiously, before I could get in a word. 'I won't let you.'

Her hands reached down as she spoke, sliding over the front of my jeans, cupping my aching dick through the denim.

'I've changed my life for you and you don't get to walk away like that doesn't mean a goddamn thing.'

'Don't.'

I twisted her hair in my grip, some part of me wanting to hurt her for making this so difficult. For making this as painful as it was possible to get.

'Let me go, Cat. Just fucking let me go.'

Tears started in her eyes, but she ignored me, squeezing me instead.

And something in my head exploded.

I was angry, hard, and hurting like a bastard. Violence was humming in my blood. And she was so close, touching me, messing with my head, and all I could think about was showing her how wrong she was.

Showing her that it would be better for all of us if I wasn't in her life.

If she really wanted to know what kind of man I was, she was going to find out.

Right now.

CHAPTER NINETEEN

Cat

HIS HAND IN my hair hurt, but that was nothing compared to the pain in my heart.

I looked up into Smoke's beautiful face and saw my own agony reflected in his gaze along with the rage I'd seen as he'd launched himself at Justin.

That rage was mine, too, because I knew what had changed. Why he'd wanted this relationship to be permanent only to change his mind a couple of hours later.

Beating Justin up had brought back old memories. Memories of his father's death and his own role in that. And sure, that was hard. It wouldn't ever go away. But surely he knew what happened all those years ago didn't define him? That it didn't change my feelings about him?

He couldn't leave me. He couldn't alter our friendship forever, tell me I was his, promise me he'd always be there, only to walk away.

He couldn't make me fall in love with him, give me everything I'd ever wanted, only to take it all away.

I knew what he was going to do because I knew him. I could read it in those searing dark eyes as he bent me back over his arm, winding my hair around his wrist, making my scalp prickle with pain.

'You're going to try and distance me, aren't you?' The words were shaky and rough as he lifted his hand to the front of my blouse. 'You're going to try and show me exactly how bad you are for me. How much you could hurt me.'

He said nothing, his mouth closing on my throat, his teeth grazing my skin.

I trembled. Then trembled harder as he simply tore my blouse straight down the middle, the fabric sagging open.

'You're forgetting something,' I went on, my voice getting ragged as he nipped at my throat. 'I know you, Dane Kingsolver. I've known you since you were seven years old. And you've never once, not in twenty-odd years, ever been bad for me.'

Again he didn't reply, grabbing the delicate lace of my bra and jerking hard.

My bra ripped apart, and then his big, hot palm was cupping my bare breast, squeezing it, shaping it, his thumb flicking over my rapidly hardening nipple. I gasped, pleasure arrowing through me, getting sharper as he bit the side of my neck. Then he pinched my nipple—hard.

The pain made my eyes water, yet at the same sent a jolt of excitement right through me. A throb had started up between my thighs and when he pinched me again, twisting my nipple in his fingers, I felt that same jolt deep in my pussy, too.

He pulled my hair harder, arching my back and pressing my body to the furnace of his, lifting my breasts so he could bring his teeth there, too, licking the aching tips. I squirmed against him as his hot mouth closed around my nipple, sucking rhythmically, nipping at it, biting at it.

My breathing had become ragged and I was shaking, and then he yanked my skirt up, his fingers sliding into the lace of my panties, grabbing a handful of the material and tearing them away as easily as if they were tissue paper. Once they were gone his fingers pushed between my thighs, sliding over the bare, slick flesh of my pussy, massaging my clit roughly.

Pleasure cut me like a knife.

'Smoke… Oh, God…' My voice was as ripped and torn as my clothes.

His scorching dark gaze was on mine as he slid one finger into me, keeping his thumb pressed hard to my clit, staring at me as another finger joined the first, pushing deep. Then he separated both fingers, stretching me, making me groan and tremble and burn. Crushing me with pleasure.

I knew what he was doing. He hadn't wanted me to fight him so he'd taken control, the way he always did. But I couldn't let him do that—not today. He was trying to leave me and I'd be damned if I let him go. I couldn't stop him physically—not when he was so much stronger than me—but, as I'd learned over the past couple of weeks, I wasn't exactly powerless.

I knew what his weakness was.

Me.

I looked up into his face as his fingers worked in a short, hard rhythm that made my hips lift and jerk, building the pleasure relentlessly.

He wasn't untouched by what he was doing. I could see the black flame in his eyes, the darkness burning, searing. The lines of his face were taut and hungry, something like a snarl twisting his beautiful mouth.

I stared into that heated darkness, let myself melt into him.

Maybe he knew what I was trying to do, because he pulled his fingers from my body and brought them to my mouth, shoving them between my lips, a feral look on his face.

'Lick them,' he ordered. 'Taste how wet you get for a fucking killer.'

I obeyed, keeping my gaze on his as I licked his fingers, tasting my own musk and the saltiness of his skin. Tasting *us*. Together.

There was strength in resistance, but sometimes true power lay in surrender.

'I love you,' I whispered, falling into his midnight eyes. 'I love you so much.'

Anguish flooded his face and suddenly I wasn't bent over his arm any more but turned to face the wall, shoved up against it, his hot, hard body coming up behind me, pinning me there. I turned my face to one side, the texture of the wallpaper pressing into my cheek and against the stiff points of my nipples, making my breathing wild and my heartbeat stampede in my head.

He put his arm against the back of my neck, keeping me jammed to the wall. His short, ragged breath was in my ear.

'Those words mean nothing.'

There was a whole world of pain in his voice.

'Don't ever fucking say them.'

'But they mean something to me,' I gasped out. 'I don't want you to leave. I love you and I—'

His palm covered my mouth, stopping me from finishing.

I didn't struggle. I let him keep his hand there. Because not being able to say the words didn't change the intense rush of feeling in my heart.

But I shuddered as I felt him nudge my feet apart, knowing what was coming next. Wanting it. Craving it more than my next breath.

I heard his zipper being pulled down and then his lean, powerful body covered mine, worn denim and warm cotton against my bare back, his free hand reaching around to spread me open, the long, hard length of his cock pushing inside me.

We hadn't bothered with condoms since I'd gone on the pill, and I shivered at the feel of his hot skin against my slick flesh, at the exquisite stretch and burn as he slid deeper, filling me. Impaling me.

I whimpered against his palm, the pleasure of him inside me making me arch against him, wanting more, wanting him deeper still.

'Fuck… *Cat*…' His whisper was desperate, and I felt him turn his face into my neck, the hand over my mouth sliding down to grip my throat in a possessive hold.

His free hand reached for the back of my knee, lifting my leg up, spreading me wider for him. Then he pressed his palm to the wall with my knee hooked over his wrist, opening me up, his cock pushing so deep I shook.

He began to fuck me hard, each thrust powerful, crushing me between the wallpapered surface at my front and the furnace heat of his body at my back.

I should have tried to protect my cheek from the rough scrape of the wallpaper. But I didn't. I simply relaxed against him and let him do what he wanted, gave myself to the grip of his hand on my throat and the feel of his cock slamming in and out. His breath was hot against the back of my neck as he slid the hand on the wall up, lifting my leg higher, spreading me even wider. Then he adjusted his stance, thrusting up hard enough to lift me onto my toes, tilting my hips and making my back bow, penetrating me even deeper.

A choked sound escaped me as his rhythm picked up speed. The hand on my throat tightened, making me short of breath and light-headed.

But I wasn't afraid. I would never be afraid of him.

'There's nothing you can do to push me away,' I whispered. 'There's nothing you can do that I won't want. There's no part of me that isn't yours. And even if you leave me I'll still be here for you. I'll always be here for you.'

'Don't say that.'

The raw anguish in his voice made my heart clench tight.

'Don't say that. *Please.*'

He thrust harder, faster, moving the hand around my throat down between my legs, his wicked fingers finding my clit, stroking me firmly, making the words mixed up in my head and my thighs shake. Making me pant like a dog as the orgasm rushed towards me and then crashed over my head, screaming Smoke's name as I came.

His thrusts became wild, and then he slammed into me one last time, his teeth sinking into my shoulder as he came, too, the raw sound he made loud in my ear.

I was too dazed to move for long moments after that, content to stand there with the heat of his rock-hard body at my back and the warmth of his breath against my nape.

But then I remembered what he'd been going to do and I squirmed, making him drop the hand with my leg hooked over it so I could stand. I turned, pushing at him because he was leaning heavily against me, wanting to see his face. Wanting to kiss him. Wanting to hold on to him before he tried to leave again.

His dark eyes met mine and for one long, aching second I thought I'd won. Then he looked away and I knew I hadn't won after all. I'd lost.

Despair opened up inside me and I reached for him. But he'd already pushed himself away, stumbling back as he adjusted his clothing. His face was a mask, un-yielding as stone.

But I wasn't stone. I was nothing but exposed nerve endings.

'Don't go.'

I couldn't hide my desperation. If I'd had the strength, I would have tried to grab hold of him, but the wall was the only thing holding me up.

'I'm sorry,' he said emotionlessly, turning away and reaching for his bag.

'You said you'd never leave me.' The pain was sharp in my voice, but I didn't care. 'You said you'd always be there for me.'

'Yeah.'

He headed towards the door and didn't stop.

'I lied.'

Then he was gone.

CHAPTER TWENTY

Smoke

I RODE BACK to the clubhouse on autopilot, parking my bike and ignoring whatever the prospect at the door said to me as I strode inside.

I was vaguely surprised that I wasn't trailing blood everywhere, because it sure felt like I was bleeding to death. Like my heart had been ripped from my chest and all that was left was a bloody hole.

My head was full of Cat, full of the wet grip of her pussy around my cock, the soft give of her body as I shoved her against the wall. Full of the rapid beat of her pulse as I put my hand on her throat.

Full of her voice telling me she loved me. That she'd never leave me.

I'd been shot once or twice before, and that was nothing compared to the agony I was feeling now. Walking out through that door had been like ripping myself in two.

But what else could I do?

She hadn't listened to me—hadn't done anything but relax into me as I'd torn her clothing and nearly choked her. As I fucked her hard and deep against the wall. I wanted her angry, wanted her fighting me, but she wasn't and didn't.

She just…gave me everything.

And you flung it back in her face.

Ignoring the sound of my stupid damn conscience, I headed straight for Keep's office for the third time that day. Brothers nodded to me, saying, 'hey', but I ignored them, too. I didn't have the time or the patience for meaningless fucking chitchat.

'Jesus Christ,' Keep said as I entered the office without knocking, coming to stand in front of his desk. 'What the fuck is it *this* time?'

I put my hands in my pockets and came straight out with it. 'I beat up Justin Grant. Smashed his pussy-ass face in. So now he's going to press charges. I just want you to know that I'll take full responsibility and that—'

'Shut the fuck up,' Keep snapped, glaring at me. 'Again. From the top.'

I gritted my teeth, violence simmering inside me, itching to get out.

'That bullshit call from the chief? It originated from Justin. He wanted me out of the house, so he could get to Cat. That's what I found when I got back home. Him with his hands all over her.' My rage boiled over. 'So I taught him a fucking lesson about not touching what's mine.'

Keep sat slowly back in his chair, his gaze sharp. 'You couldn't have kept better control of yourself?'

My jaw ached, every muscle in my body tight. 'Funnily enough, when he was tearing her clothes and hurting her, controlling myself wasn't uppermost in my fucking mind.'

Keep said nothing, continuing to stare at me.

'Like I said,' I went on, since it didn't look like he was going to break the silence, 'the asshole's going to press charges and he'll sure as hell make sure Cat won't get custody of Annie. So I'm here to tell you she's not my old lady any more and to that I'll plead guilty. I'll do the time.'

Keep scowled. 'What do you mean she's not your old lady any more?'

'I can't stay with her. Being with me is only going to hurt her.'

There was a dull throbbing in my chest—a low-level pain that wasn't ever going to go away.

'I only made her mine because I wanted the club to protect her anyway.'

Keep snorted. 'What a fucking load of bullshit. You made her your old lady because you're in love with her—everyone knows that.'

That word. Christ, why did everyone keep saying that word?

'It's not like that. It was fake. It was supposed to protect her and—'

'Yeah, and that's bullshit, too. You've been in love with that girl for as long as I've known you, and that's a fuck of a long time. And she loves you, too. Jesus, the way she looked at you at the party that night, it was written all over her face.'

I said nothing, every part of me tense with denial.

My uncle shook his head slowly. 'You fucking idiot.

Why did you leave her? And don't give me that shit about protecting her.'

'I had to.' I could feel a muscle jumping in the side of my jaw. 'I nearly beat to death the father of her child. What kind of role model does that make me for Annie? Fuck's sake, Keep. Cat already ditched one violent asshole—she doesn't need another.'

Again, Keep stayed silent. Then, after a while, he said, 'You're a lot of things, Smoke. But I didn't think being a little bitch was one of them.'

My hands clenched into fists in the pockets of jeans, rage surging through me. 'Sorry, Keep, but you say that again and, president or not, I'll smash your goddamn face in.'

The bastard just laughed.

'Oh, come on. Admit it. You're not leaving Cat to protect her. You're leaving her to protect your own worthless hide.'

The ground felt suddenly uneven under my feet, my gut lurching.

It's true. You know it's true.

No, it couldn't be. I wasn't that much of a fucking coward, was I?

Keep cocked his head. 'What are you so afraid of? What do you think she's going to do? Leave you? She's been your friend for years. She knows all your skeletons and yet she's still here.'

'How can I be with her?'

I hadn't meant to say it, but it came out all the same, raw as a gunshot wound.

'I killed your fucking brother and I nearly killed

Grant. I'm no good, Keep. You know it. I know it. Cat needs to know it, too.'

'And you're full of it. David earned his death and I don't blame you for it—you know that. All I know about Cat is that you've been a good friend to her for over twenty years. You love her, and you love her kid, too, and I know you'd die to protect the both of them. What more needs to be said?'

He paused.

'Whether she wants to be with you or not is her decision, and if she wants you—well, shit… Who are you to tell her she's wrong? And don't give me that crap about not loving her. Giving her up is killing you. I can see it in your face.'

My jaw ached—everything fucking ached.

'I don't deserve her.' My voice didn't even sound like mine. 'She's…everything I'm not.'

Keep sat forward and leaned his elbows on his desk. 'Of course you don't deserve her. That's why you're gonna spend every goddamn minute of your life making sure you do.'

I stared at him. My uncle, my president. The man who'd been more of a father to me than my own dad ever had been.

'It's not just Cat.' The words were as rusty as old nails. 'I screwed up with the club, too.'

Keep's blue eyes were very direct. 'What the fuck kind of club do you think I run? Think I'd let a piece of shit like Justin Grant take a good brother down?' One corner of his mouth tilted up. 'I've got your back, Smoke. You should know that.'

The raw, aching wound in my chest throbbed. 'What I did is going to make—'

'Leave me to deal with the club. You go deal with your woman. And for fuck's sake do it quickly—because I can only imagine what your drama's doing to her right now.'

I couldn't move—just stood there frozen.

Of *course* the club had my back, and so did Keep. How had I forgotten that?

Like you forgot Cat had your back, too. She always did.

A hot, painful feeling shifted inside me. Shame. Remorse. For the way I'd walked out on her. For forgetting everything she'd done for me. For forgetting twenty-three fucking years of friendship.

Twenty-three fucking years of love.

Keep was right. I *did* love her. I loved her with everything in me. And I'd been as big a pussy as Justin to leave her the way I did. Because I was scared of how much I wanted her. Of how much she meant to me. Horribly afraid I wasn't worthy of her and never would be.

Except there was no reason for me to be such a goddamn coward. Cat had never rejected me—not once. Not even in the terrible aftermath of Dad's death. Every single time she'd been there for me when I needed her. Without judgement. Without criticism.

She loved me.

'Even if you leave me, I'll still be here for you. I'll always be here for you...'

Her voice echoed in my head and the pain was more than I could bear.

'Thanks, Keep,' I said hoarsely. 'I got to go.'

Keep sighed. 'About fucking time.'

CHAPTER TWENTY-ONE

Cat

I PICKED ANNIE up from the sitter and brought her home, gave her dinner and a bath, tucked her into bed, trying to act like nothing was wrong. Like I didn't have an empty hole in the centre of my chest where Smoke had ripped out my heart and flung it onto the floor, grinding it into nothing under his heel.

I didn't know how I was going to manage without him in my life. He'd been my friend for so long that I couldn't imagine him not being there. And the past couple of weeks, when he'd been more than just a friend... God, thinking about *them* only made the loss more painful.

I loved him, but for some reason that wasn't enough, and now he'd gone.

Once again I'd lost everything.

It hurt so much.

I knew eventually I'd pull myself up and start again, like I always did. Find my feet and get my life back together again. Figure out what I was going to do about

Justin—all that shit. But right now it felt like it was all too much.

Right now all I wanted to do was cry.

I sat on the couch with a pillow in the time-honoured fashion, curling around my pain. And then I saw the ring box sitting on the coffee table, and that sank the knife even deeper into what remained of my heart.

It was all I had left of him, that ring. He'd taken everything else.

I reached for the box, opened it and looked down at the little cat face with its glowing green eyes. It was perfect. *So* perfect.

A tear slid down my nose, splashing on top of the silver band, making the eyes sparkle.

Had my taking it off pushed him over the edge? Was that why he'd walked away? Perhaps if I'd left it on, everything would have been different and I wouldn't be sitting here, sobbing on my couch with my heart in pieces.

The sound of the front door's handle turning came suddenly from out in the hallway and my whole body went cold. No one but me had a key, and unless Justin had somehow managed to—

The living room door slammed open, bouncing on its hinges. Smoke stood in the doorway.

And I found there must be something left of my heart after all, because it was racing and throbbing and hurting. And my body wasn't cold any more, but burning hot.

Smoke's dark gaze found mine, and the look on his face was searing in its intensity.

I opened my mouth to say something, though I had no idea what.

I never got the chance. Because Smoke strode over to where I sat and before I even understood what he intended to do he swept me up into his arms, and his mouth was coming down on mine.

It was a hungry, desperate, demanding kiss. It was hot and it was raw, and when I tried to pull away, he gripped me hard, holding me still. Kissing me and kissing me and kissing me, as if he was afraid to stop.

All I could do was let him devour me, with my hands pinned to the hard wall of his chest, feeling the frantic beating of his heart against my palms matching my own.

It felt like forever before he finally lifted his head, staring down at me with those familiar dark eyes. Full of heat. Full of desire.

'I was such a fucking coward, Cat,' he said hoarsely. 'I should never have walked out on you. I'm sorry. I'm sorry for hurting you. I'm sorry for not listening to you. I'm sorry for turning my back on you.'

He lifted his hands, cupping my face, his thumbs stroking lightly along the side of my jaw, making me shiver. Making me tremble.

'But most of all I'm sorry for being such a little bitch and not telling you how I feel.'

I couldn't speak. My throat was too tight—every part of my body was too tight. I didn't want to move in case this was a dream and he'd vanish, leaving me being held by nothing but empty air.

'I thought I was protecting you,' he went on, his voice dark and ragged. 'But I wasn't, kitten. The only person I was protecting was myself. Keep put me straight about a few things and that was one of them.'

'Why?' I finally managed to ask shakily. 'What did you need to protect yourself from?'

'What do you think?'

He looked down at me as if I was the only thing worth looking at in the entire universe.

'I was protecting myself from *you*.'

I stared at him in shock. 'Me?'

'There's no one on this entire planet who has more power to hurt me than you do. You could fucking destroy me with a snap of your fingers.'

His thumbs moved over my skin, a gentle back-and-forth movement, raising goosebumps everywhere.

'I've loved you for so long. So fucking long. And then Justin made me lose it, and... Well, I guess I was looking for an excuse to run the hell away. I'm not worthy of you, kitten. You're the most perfect woman I've ever met and I'm just a violent biker with a temper and a really shitty past.'

I swallowed, trying to get past the lump in my throat. 'So why did you come back?'

'Because you were always there for me. Because you never let me down. You had my back, Cat. You always had my back. And I thought that if you'd stuck around for twenty-three years, it must be because I wasn't such a lost cause after all.'

That beautiful mouth turned up into one of his rare, heart-stopping smiles.

'Plus, Keep said he was going to kick my ass if I didn't come straight back here and make it right with you.'

I took a shaking breath. 'Wait... You said you love me.'

'I did. I do. And no, before you say it, it's not because you want to hear the words. It's because that's what I feel every time I look at you.' His smile deepened. 'Turns out love *does* mean something after all.'

It was only then that I had the courage to lift my hands from his chest and touch his face, run my fingers over the rough stubble along his jaw, check that he was real and this wasn't a dream.

'You know you don't have to deserve me, don't you? You only need to keep doing what you've always been doing. Being my friend.'

Something in his eyes flared hot. 'Oh, kitten. I'm sorry, but I don't want to be your friend any more.'

'Then don't be,' I murmured and slid my arms around his neck. 'Be my husband instead.'

Much, much later, as we lay naked on the floor of the living room together, our skin streaked with sweat and our bodies sated, Smoke opened the ring box and took out the ring. Then he held my hand in his and looked into my eyes.

When he slipped the ring onto my finger, he didn't ask me to marry him. Instead, he asked, 'Will you love me, Cat?'

I didn't need to answer. He knew what I was going to say. But I answered him all the same.

'Always, Dane. With all my heart.'

EPILOGUE

Smoke

I DON'T KNOW how Keep did it in the end, but he got Justin to drop the charges. The prick also dropped his custody suit, leaving me free to adopt Annie. Which I did the first moment I could.

It turned out Cat *did* want to walk up the aisle in a white dress—*and* with a goddamn bridesmaid. I could hardly refuse, especially since I'd promised her she could. We even had a flower girl—a job Annie took very seriously.

I'm not a big fan of weddings, but I have to say that mine was the best ever. I even got a bit fucking misty when Cat came down the aisle towards me in her wedding dress, her big green eyes staring at me from behind her veil.

So damn beautiful.

She made my heart ache.

She taught me that *love* isn't just a meaningless word. That it's deeper and richer and more powerful than I ever imagined.

She was my friend, my lover, and now she was my wife I didn't think life could have got any more perfect.

But it did.

It sure as hell did.

* * * * *

LET'S TALK
Romance

For exclusive extracts, competitions
and special offers, find us online:

f facebook.com/millsandboon

@ @millsandboonuk

🐦 @millsandboon

Or get in touch on 0844 844 1351*

For all the latest titles coming soon, visit
millsandboon.co.uk/nextmonth